"If yo
the-to
rip-roa

"Koch still pulls the neat trick of quietly weaving in plot threads that go unrecognized until they start tying together—or snapping. This is a hyperspeed-paced addition to a series that shows no signs of slowing down."
—*Publishers Weekly*

"Aliens, danger, and romance make this a fast-paced, wittily-written sf romantic comedy." —*Library Journal*

"Gini Koch's Kitty Katt series is a great example of the lighter side of science fiction. Told with clever wit and non-stop pacing . . . it blends diplomacy, action and sense of humor into a memorable reading experience." —*Kirkus*

"The action is nonstop, the snark flies fast and furious. . . . Another fantastic addition to an imaginative series!"
—Night Owl Sci-Fi (top pick)

"Gini Koch has another winner, plenty of action combined with just the right touch of humor and a kick-ass storyline. What's not to like?" —Fresh Fiction

"This delightful romp has many interesting twists and turns as it glances at racism, politics, and religion en route . . . will have fanciers of cinematic sf parodies referencing *Men in Black*, *Ghost Busters*, and *X-Men*."
—*Booklist* (starred review)

"Gini Koch mixes up the sometimes staid niche of science fiction romance by adding nonstop humor, blockbuster action, and moments worthy of a soap opera."
—Dirty Sexy Books

DAW Books Presents GINI KOCH's
Alien Novels:

TOUCHED BY AN ALIEN
ALIEN TANGO
ALIEN IN THE FAMILY
ALIEN PROLIFERATION
ALIEN DIPLOMACY
ALIEN VS. ALIEN
ALIEN IN THE HOUSE
ALIEN RESEARCH
(coming in December 2013)

ALIEN
IN THE HOUSE

GINI KOCH

DAW BOOKS, INC.
DONALD A. WOLLHEIM, FOUNDER
375 Hudson Street, New York, NY 10014

**ELIZABETH R. WOLLHEIM
SHEILA E. GILBERT
PUBLISHERS**
www.dawbooks.com

First Printing, May 2013
1   2   3   4   5   6   7   8   9

To the memory of my grandmother, Julia, who instilled a love of language, reading, science fiction, and mysteries in me from a very young age.

ACKNOWLEDGMENTS

The usual massive thanks to my epic Gang of Four: my amazing editor, Sheila Gilbert, who managed to keep me calm and writing when my deadline moved up and I was nowhere close to done, and fit in some great brainstorming at the same time; my wonderful agent, Cherry Weiner, who always knows when to nudge me and when to leave me alone and keep everyone else away, too; my awesome crit partner, Lisa Dovichi, who managed to do all her crit partnering and then some while writing and drawing and launching her first series; and my great, longtime main beta reader, Mary Fiore, for reading a long book and catching a plethora of little errors in record time. So glad the four of you are with me on this journey, 'cause I don't think I'd be sane (or as close to sane as I get) without you.

Love and thanks to all the good folks at DAW Books and all my fans around the globe. To my Hook Me Up! Gang, members of Team Gini, all Alien Collective Members in Very Good Standing around the world, Twitter followers, Facebook fans and friends, and all the wonderful fans who come to my various book signings and conference panels, I have but this to say: You complete me and I love you all.

Special shout outs to: my distance assistant, Colette Chmiel, who continues to keep my sanity safe from the pirate hordes trying to destroy it; Tammy Baker for doing me the ultimate honor and naming her youngest daughter after Jamie Martini; Hal and Dee Astell for massive fan support and being such good owners of the Travel Poof; Mary Rehak for coming all the way from Chicago to be with me when Alien vs. Alien released; Nicole Snyder and Edward Pulley for making me the loveliest warm pink scarves I wear all the time (many times together); awesome authors Weston Ochse and Yvonne Navarro, for saving me from evil spirits; all the good folks at the Greenway branch of the

United States Post Office for having supported me since well before *Touched by an Alien* came out, and who continue to make every trip to the USPS one I look forward to; my Sister in Insomnia, Kelsey Rowe, for helping keep the giggles going when we're both up far too late while being far too stressed; The Poisoned Pen bookstore, for throwing such an awesome release day party for *Alien vs. Alien*, which was made doubly special by being my first "on release day" signing ever; and ever-wonderful author, BFF, and sister in crime Marsheila Rockwell, for always being there when I'm having late night author panic attacks and only ribbing me a little bit about how an outline might have forestalled whichever dilemma I'm having before helping me figure out how to fix it.

Last, but never least, thanks to my wonderful husband, Steve, and fabulous daughter, Veronica. I love you both more than I can say (yes, Veronica, even more than the cats), and I wouldn't trade you for anything, not even A-C talents.

AS ANY PERSON WHO'S ever had to hide a huge secret about themselves knows, being outed before you're ready is one of the things you fear the most.

Whether your secret is that you're gay, in a country illegally, the wrong religion at the wrong time and in the wrong place, a space alien living on Earth, or that you hate popular shows, have been bitten by a radioactive spider, or have mutated due to giving birth to a half-alien baby whose father was supercharged by an evil bad guy drug, being outed can mean terrible things.

The people you're hiding amongst can turn against you in cold and scary ways. They can run you out of town with torches and pitchforks. Your loved ones can become targets for all sorts of bad guy schemes. You can lose everything.

There's nothing like a huge, interstellar invasion to really point out to the regular folks that aliens exist. And in our history, there's been nothing like the huge, interstellar invasion we had, complete with Flying Space Dinosaurs and their really bad attitudes. At least, nothing anyone living in modern times can remember or compare to.

The term "nowhere to hide" pretty much summed up the so-called fun. As did the terms "we're so screwed" and, happily enough, "take me to your leaders." It looked like evacuation time for My Favorite Centaurions, if they got that lucky.

But sometimes people surprise you.

Speaking of surprises, they keep on coming for me. In

addition to being Megalomaniac Girl and Wolverine with Boobs, I'm also now Dr. Doolittle. Because I like to be as diverse as possible in my worldview and talents.

But as I wasn't really saying, my talents tend to lie in areas most people ignore, like talking to space animals and catching on to whatever the crazed evil geniuses have going before it's too late.

It's been quiet for a few months, relatively speaking, which is nice and all, but tends to make me a little jumpy. Because quiet rarely means things have settled down. Quiet—in the almost three action-packed years of my experience with the A-Cs of Earth—means that the bad guys are readying for the Execution Phase of the next major conspiracy to take over the world or worlds and destroy everyone I know and love.

So I'm paying attention, because they're not going to catch us with our pants down, so to speak, while I'm still on duty. Of course, I don't always look for evil bad guy conspiracies. But when I do, I make sure to look everywhere.

That's right. I *am* the most interesting, bad-guy-foiling, sometime-superbeing-exterminating, mutated diplomat for an outer-space principality in the world. Okay, in the galaxy. What can I say? I get around.

CHAPTER 1

"THIS IS THE THIRD representative to become incapacitated in as many weeks," the TV announcer's voice shared.

"This is the only one incapacitated," Jeff corrected, presumably for my benefit, seeing as the TV announcer wasn't going to hear him unless said announcer had the best hearing in the galaxy.

"What do you mean?" I paid as much attention to the news as I did to the inner workings of the common housefly, which was to say, not at all. Hey, just because it was sort of my job to pay attention to the news didn't make me excited about it. I had a husband who seemed to live to stay on top of things, after all.

"I mean the first two are dead. This one's in the hospital."

"Anyone we know? Knew?"

"Yes." Jeff sighed the sigh of a husband who's required to stay on top of things because his wife refuses to. "The two who died were from Alabama and Oregon, and they died in a car crash. This latest one is from Montana, and he's got an extreme case of pneumonia. Because he's in his late eighties, the prognosis isn't good. You've met all of them at one time or another. I'd tell you their names, but I don't have the desire to play your version of Name That Tune."

"Why don't you find a *Love Boat* or *Fantasy Island* marathon going on? You'll enjoy those so much more than the constant barrage from CNN and C-SPAN."

"This is part of the job of being the Head Diplomat, baby."

I managed not to say that it was the boring part. There were lots of boring parts to our jobs now. They were interspersed with lots of terrifyingly exciting parts, the most recent of which had exposed the fact that aliens lived on Earth to the majority of the world's population. Change, it was good for you, right?

There was a knock at our door. Seeing as Jeff was engrossed in the afternoon news, and seeing as I didn't want to have to catch him up on whatever he'd miss in the minute and a half it would take to answer said door, I dutifully trotted out of our humongous living room to do the job. Helpful, that was me all over. Since we lived on half of the top floor of the American Centaurion Embassy, this also wasn't me taking any kind of risk. Whoever was knocking lived here.

Opened the door to find our top floor neighbors standing there, otherwise known as Christopher and Amy Gaultier-White. True to form, Christopher was glaring. Patented Glare #5, to be precise. "Have you heard the news?" he asked as he strode in past me and headed for the living room and his cousin, my husband.

Amy sighed. "He's a little stressed."

"That's his natural state of being. But, shocking one and all, yes, I've heard the news. If the news is about dead and dying politicians."

Amy looked shocked for a moment. She was one of my best friends from high school, so she knew about my "love" of the news. She recovered quickly. "Oh. Jeff told you?"

My turn to sigh. "Yes, yes, fine. I was busy."

"Doing what? Jamie's at daycare right now."

"I was wrapping her presents." Our daughter's first birthday loomed, and, since she was born on Christmas day, I felt it was unfair to do combo presents, meaning I had a lot of things Jeff felt were far too much for a one-year-old to be wrapped, bagged, tagged, and hidden.

Sure, as the daughter of a Jewish father and Catholic-yet-also-former-Mossad mother, I'd grown up sort of waving at the December holidays. And Jeff, being an alien whose parents were born on Alpha Four of the Alpha Centaurion solar system, didn't celebrate the majority of the available human holidays.

However, we were in Washington, D.C. now, and certain

things were inevitable. And demanded. There'd been a lot of demanding in recent months.

Amy and I joined our men in time to hear Christopher ask what was becoming a very common question. "Are they going to try to blame this on us?"

Jeff ran his hand through his hair. "No idea. So far, I haven't heard about any anti-alien groups trying to pin a bad car crash and an illness on us."

"Just give it time." Christopher shook his head. "Either that or they'll be asking us to revive the dead and save the sick."

I'd stopped making really inappropriate jokes about this months ago. Because, sadly, Christopher wasn't wrong.

During the excitement that ended up with us all being outed, we'd discovered that our old friends, the wackos from the anti-alien Club 51, were still around and active, albeit with new leaders we had yet to ferret out.

Once the general population knew about us, however, we got the fun of seeing just how many anti-alien groups there were. Turned out, there were a lot.

Turned out there were also a lot of groups who sincerely believed Jeff, Christopher, and their extended family were here to save us all and show us The Way.

In some ways, of course, they were. The A-Cs, as they called themselves, had been showing us the way since the 1960s, particularly in the areas of math, science, and technology. And they'd been protecting the Earth constantly from all the bad things from space that wanted to drop by to kick us or take over. There had been some human bad guy thwarting, too.

I'd been involved with the gang from Alpha Four for about three years now. I had a natural affinity for handling the weird and mind-melding with the psychos and megalomaniacs we routinely tangled with. Hey, it's nice to have special skills.

However, the special skills I didn't possess were those of diplomatic decorum and the ability to pretend to like people I detested.

"Will it affect tonight's dinner party?" Amy asked. "I don't know if this means we should cancel or carry on as if nothing's happened, or something in between."

Amy having come from money meant she was supposed

to have been our go-to girl for all the formal affairs, fancy table settings, and keeping the rest of us from saying the wrong things to the wrong people. In other words, in the perfect world I didn't live in, I should have been asking that question and she should have been answering it.

Sadly, she'd spent her first few months with us dealing with the fact that her father had been one of the megalomaniacs we'd had to deal with in a very permanent fashion. So while she was good enough to pass muster almost anywhere in the shoulder-rubbing circles we now traveled in, her confidence had been somewhat shaken and she'd flipped over to my side of the house—the kick butt first and take names later side.

Our diplomatic day had been saved by one man. A man of taste, breeding, and the ability to get anything done, at any time. A man who was now our Embassy Concierge Majordomo and potentially the most competent man on the planet. A man I decided it was time to call.

"Com on!"

"What can I do for you, Chief?"

"Walter, can you tell me where Pierre is? We need to ask vital questions only he can answer."

"Yes, Chief. Pierre told me to tell you that if you needed him, the event tonight will go on as planned, with a moment or two of silence for the two representatives who died last week, and a short, silent prayer for the representative in the hospital."

"He told you all that?"

"Yes, Chief. Five minutes ago. He said you'd want to know. He also said he'd be in the Ballroom, and would appreciate you and Chief Martini stopping by. Oh, and Commander Reader is about to join us on premises. He says he'll meet you at the Ballroom."

"Gotcha, Walt. Com off."

We looked at each other. "Is Pierre psychic, or part A-C?" Amy asked.

"No on the A-C, don't think so on the psychic," Jeff replied.

"He's just really, really good. I thank God every day that James brought him out here to save our Embassy."

"Speaking of which, I guess Kitty and I are going to the Ballroom. You two want to join us?"

Christopher shook his head. "We can't. We have to do a . . . thing. Before the party."

"A thing? Dude, you're normally more verbal than that."

"He's trying to be discreet, but I don't know why," Amy said. "It's taken forever, due to so many reasons, most of them highly classified, but my father's estate is finally being settled. We need to meet with my lawyer."

"Why so, Ames? You're his only child, and LaRue's dead and she had no children. At least, I sincerely hope she had no children." LaRue Demorte Gaultier had been Amy's father's mistress, and then his second wife. She'd ended up redefining the term "wicked stepmother" before getting shot by her own side during the big space showdown that I called Operation Destruction. "Who else could possibly be contesting the will or expecting to inherit?"

"The Board of Directors for Gaultier Enterprises. They want to have full control of the company." Amy had a look on her face I was familiar with—her "nothing's gonna stop me" look. "But I'm not going to let that happen. I believe the legal papers will prove that I'm the majority stockholder. And that means I'll be taking over Gaultier Enterprises."

CHAPTER 2

"AMES, GO YOU!"

"I know she can do it," Christopher said, as he put his arm around Amy and hugged her. "But it's going to take a lot of focus. And her being married to an alien isn't helping. At all." In a move that made me just a tad nervous, Christopher wasn't glaring—he looked worried.

"Whatever." Amy hugged him back. "Being married into the A-C clan isn't as much of a detriment to the Board as you think it is. Us not being evil psychos who want to destroy and rule the world? That's a bigger issue for the Board."

"Fabulous. While you guys are tangling with them, don't forget to eyeball who might be the next Bad Guy du Jour. 'Cause you know that no matter how many times we knock one down, another one's always ready to take his or her place."

"We will do," Amy said. "My money's on Ansom Parker, Janelle Gardiner, or Quinton Cross. With my father gone, they've all been jockeying to become Chairman of the Board. But the corporation and his will were set up so that if he died, LaRue was the instant successor. With both of them missing and presumed dead, the corporation, the Board, and I have had to get my father and LaRue both declared legally dead, and we only have an interim Chairman."

"Yeah, the problem with our jobs and lives is that we do a lot of things we can't tell anyone about."

Amy shrugged. "Better this than what we'd all go through having to explain how all these horrible people 'disappeared.'"

"As long as it doesn't get discovered," Christopher said, looking even more worried.

Amy kissed his cheek. "As far as anyone knows, accidents have happened and we're all very sad we haven't been able to recover bodies." She winked at me as they left, Christopher still looking concerned.

"Think Amy will actually take over Gaultier Enterprises?" Jeff asked.

"I think it's really likely, yeah."

"Think anyone's going to question the official causes of death on our long list of now-dead enemies?"

"No idea. I'm just hoping they don't question you, Christopher, or just about any other A-C."

"I know, I know. We can't lie. It's a good trait."

"In a husband, absolutely. In a politician or when being questioned by people who can't know the truth? Maybe not as helpful." I sighed. "I, however, have a more urgent problem. I need to finish wrapping Jamie's presents, but Pierre needs us, and James is on his way."

Jeff grinned and kissed me. He was the best kisser in, by my estimate, the entire galaxy, and his kiss did to me what it always did—made me forget about anything else other than getting our clothes off.

He ended our kiss and laughed. "No, baby, we don't have time for me to make you that kind of happy. But give me a second, and I can solve a different problem."

That Jeff knew I was ready to go was based some on experience but mostly on the fact that he was the strongest empath in the galaxy. Therefore, I knew he was aware of my disappointment.

Which quickly turned to joy, as he used hyperspeed to wrap the remainder of Jamie's gifts. I had hyperspeed now, but I didn't trust it for delicate stuff, and wrapping little girl gifts was definitely on the delicate side of the hyperspeed house.

Jeff finished up and we hid the presents in a closet in one of the many rooms of our penthouse that we didn't actually use. "You don't mind that I finished the wrapping?" he asked as we headed for the door.

"No. I wrapped half, you wrapped half. I'm glad you got to do some of that, even if it was quick."

He hugged me. "Me, too."

Since the Embassy went up seven floors and down several, ignoring the underground Secret Lab Level that led into the recently discovered Tunnels of Doom, most of us chose to save the energy and used the elevators to get up and down. Well, the human members of the Embassy staff did. For the A-Cs, all of whom had hyperspeed, stairs were almost always the faster option.

Because it had been some time since we'd told Walter we'd be right down to the Ballroom, we didn't use the elevator. Instead, we zipped down the stairs from the 7th floor to the 2nd.

We reached the Ballroom. And stopped dead in our tracks. I couldn't speak for Jeff, but I was stunned. Frankly, I couldn't speak at all for a few long seconds.

"Um . . . wow."

"Yeah." Jeff cleared his throat. "What's the proper thing to say at this moment?"

"You're asking me?"

"You're human."

"As if that matters for the current situation?" We were standing at one of the two entrances to the room. I took a quick look around. "Okay, Pierre's not here. So, we tell each other, really fast, what we actually think, and then we come up with the right way to tell *him* what we really think."

"I really think there's too much pink in here."

Couldn't argue with Jeff's sentiments. The ballroom of the American Centaurion Embassy was adorned in pink. And sparkles. And balloons. And that was just the ceiling. "Maybe Pierre thinks we're hosting an off-site visit from the folks from *Dancing with the Stars*."

"Maybe he's lost his mind." Jeff didn't sound like he was kidding.

"It's pretty," I said lamely. It was, if you were so into the color pink that you wanted all other colors banished from the face of the Earth. No one I knew was *that* into the color pink. Well, Pierre was, apparently, but this was news to me.

"Wow. Girlfriend . . . what's going on?" Reader joined us. "I mean, I thought I knew what was going on. Now I'm not so sure."

"See?" Jeff said to me, as if I'd been the one who coordinated the ballroom's decorations.

"See what? I see a hell of a lot of pink."

"Me too," Reader said. "What's the occasion? I ask because the occasion can't be the reason I'm here. I wasn't invited to Pink Fest."

"It's for our little princess' first birthday party," Pierre said as he zipped into the room. "I realize you're all in shock from the sheer overwhelming feeling of being in a cotton candy factory, which is why I wanted you to see it now, but, trust me, it's necessary."

"It is? Why?"

"Jamie loves it," Pierre said. "And she *needs* to love it. Her party is going to be televised, I'd like us all to recall."

"I'm still unhappy about that," Jeff growled.

Reader sighed. "Who isn't? But, let's be honest. If the way we keep everyone else in the world calm about the fact that there are a whole lot of aliens from the Alpha Centauri system living on Earth is to show how much like regular folks our Embassy personnel are, then we do it."

Jeff ran his hand through his hair. "I know, James. We had this argument months ago, and it made sense then, too. It's just . . ." He looked around. "It's just so damn *pink*."

"I have a bigger concern." The three male heads all swiveled toward me. "We're hosting a dinner party. Tonight. And, call me crazy, I thought we were hosting it in this room."

"You're crazy," Pierre said nicely. "We don't host dignitaries in the ballroom unless we are dancing, Kitty darling. We host them in the formal dining room and attached parlors for appetizers, and then we're all going to the Zoo for the actual dinner."

"Oh. Well. Then that's alright. I guess." I cleared my throat. "You know, Jamie's birthday is on Christmas. And since we're having her party on Christmas Day, I kind of thought, therefore, that the party would have a Christmas-y theme."

"Did you?" Pierre asked, as he fussed with some fake pink flowers that were marked as stand-ins for the real flowers that were to arrive on the actual day of the party. "I can't imagine why."

"Christmas-time. That's why."

"None of you celebrate Christmas officially, for a variety of religious reasons." Pierre looked at all our expressions and heaved a sigh. "You're allowed to be different, darlings. Your differences make you interesting to the general populace. The areas where you're just the same as everyone else make you comfortable to them. We want to ensure that everyone continues to think you're both comfortable and interesting."

"I feel like a reality star without the desperate desire for fifteen minutes of fame."

Pierre shrugged. "I'm sure you do. However, this week's festivities are among the most important of any you've had since we were all exposed to the world as being just a trifle more special than the average."

"I'm cool with being better than the average bear. I'm not sure I'm excited about single-handedly making pink the new black." I hadn't wrapped her presents in a lot of pink. Now I wondered if that was going to end up being a Total Mommy Fail on my part.

"I remind you that Jamie loves it and we will now leave it at that." Pierre shooed us out. "I plan to have the ball room closed off for tonight's festivities, so no visiting dignitaries should be offended by the sheer beauty of the room."

"I feel so much better," Jeff muttered. He heaved a sigh. "Okay, so what's our game plan for tonight?"

"Not spilling anything on anybody."

Reader chuckled. "That's always a good choice, girlfriend. But we do need to be coordinated. This is a good chance to show how important we are politically while also showing that we don't shove in our own agenda."

"We don't have an agenda beyond 'don't make us go back to Alpha Four,'" Jeff pointed out.

"And don't make us the War Division," I added.

Reader heaved a sigh. "Yes. And we need to ensure that these things are understood at a level where the majority won't ask for everyone to be exiled."

"You mean exiled again," Jeff said. "But yeah, James, we get it."

"Good," Pierre said. "Because based on your comments from only a few moments ago, I, for one, am not convinced you do indeed 'get it.'"

Before anyone could respond, the doorbell rang. The Embassy was large and the doorbell made an impressive sound that was piped through all the lower three floors.

Pierre made the exasperation sound. "No one should be arriving yet. The party doesn't start for at least another two hours."

He zipped off while the three of us exchanged a glance. "You think it's just a delivery of some kind?" Reader asked. "Or someone dropping by to visit?"

"Most of those who we want to see drop by via a gate. Or they call first."

Before Jeff could add in his two cents to this discussion, Walter's voice came over the intercom. "Chiefs, Commander Reader, you're needed downstairs."

CHAPTER 3

"**ROGER THAT,** Walt. Leaving Planet Pink pronto. But, to keep the theme going, why don't you pipe "Pink" by Aerosmith through the sound system."

"On it, Chief." The melodious sounds of Steven, Joe, and the rest of my boys sailed into my ears. It made the sparkly pinkness seem more appropriate. At least to me.

Jeff shook his head. "Only my girl. Shall we?"

"Stairs or elevator?"

"Stairs," Reader said firmly. "For those of us who know the two of you well, being in an elevator with you makes us feel like we're interrupting your sexy times."

"Hilarious. Accurate, but hilarious." So Jeff and I still took every opportunity to do the deed, especially in elevators. So what? It was part of the foundation of a good marriage, at least in my opinion.

Reader flashed the cover boy grin. "Besides, it's only one flight down. If we were going up to the top, I'd ignore my delicate sensibilities and vote for the elevator."

Three years ago, if anyone had suggested to me that I'd be living in the American Centaurion Embassy as one of the Co-Head Diplomats, I'd have asked who American Centaurion was before laughing my head off.

If they'd also mentioned that I'd be married to an alien from the Alpha Centauri system, along with having been a superbeing exterminator, then the Head of Airborne for Centaurion Division, or that I'd have saved the world multiple times, I'd have fallen on the floor, rolling around, begging them to stop being so funny.

Of course, if they'd told me my parents and best guy friend from high school had masqueraded as normal while actually leading secret lives drenched in espionage, or that I'd also be besties with a former top international male model, I'd have probably had to go to the hospital from hilarity overload.

We walked to the first floor with said former male model and went to the front door to find said best guy friend from high school, Charles Reynolds, head of the E-T Division for the C.I.A., chatting with Pierre.

Chuckie wasn't alone, however. Cliff Goodman, the current Head of Special Immigration Services reporting directly to the Secretary of Homeland Security, stood there with him. With Jeff and Reader here, we had a lot of power standing in our foyer.

"Why are you both here so early?" Reader asked. He sounded mildly annoyed. This seemed to be the Standard Reaction Mode for whoever was the Head of Field for Centaurion Division when dealing with Chuckie.

"Not that it isn't great to see you both," I added. Hey, I was the Co-Head Diplomat and I tried to practice my diplomatic skills whenever it was convenient and easy. "Unless you're bringing news of doom and gloom, and then come back later, okay?" I also didn't like to overdo the practicing.

Chuckie grinned. "No, for once, not coming by to share how the world's going to end tomorrow."

Good. I wouldn't have to tell Walter to spin "Paint it Black" by the Rolling Stones. Though I had Stones songs on the playlist for tonight's festivities because the British ambassador was supposed to be in attendance and I wanted to play more nicely than I had before and pretend I thought the Stones were sort of in the same league as Aerosmith, even though Aerosmith was the greatest and the Stones were merely good.

Cliff nodded. "Under the circumstances, the Department wanted to ensure that you and we feel your Embassy is secure. I decided to come by with Chuck, as opposed to sending a team here."

"Thanks, we appreciate that," Jeff said. "So, what do you need to see?"

"Any common areas the guests will be in," Cliff replied. "This is really just a formality, not a white glove test."

"Excuse me?" Jeff sounded confused, which wasn't a surprise.

"Earth saying. Your mother would understand it." This I knew for fact. Happily, the A-C Operations team, who I called the Elves because I never, ever saw them perform their wondrous and magical duties, handled the cleaning of every A-C facility, including the Embassy. If the cleaning was left up to me, we'd be decorating in the finest of Washington, D.C. dust. I didn't hate housekeeping, but we weren't exactly best buds forever, either.

Jeff grunted. "So, where do we start?"

"Basement," Cliff said. "Let's do this quickly so you can all get back to prepping for the party tonight."

"You all go on ahead," Chuckie said. "I need to talk to Kitty for a minute."

Jeff gave us both a searching look, shrugged, kissed my cheek, and he and the other men trotted off. This was the result of massive personal growth on Jeff's part, much of which had happened because he'd finally caught on that Chuckie was no longer in love with me and was, in fact, in love with Naomi Gower, who was one of Jeff's cousins.

I waited until the others were out of earshot. "Okay, what's going on?"

"I need to run some things by you, and I don't want an audience for it."

"Is this about the two dead representatives and the one really sick one?"

"No." He gave me the "you so crazy" look. I got that look a lot. "Why would those incidents, however tragic, be related to tonight's party or any of us in any way?"

"Dude, I figured it was safer to ask. You know how they teach you how to spell 'assume', right?"

Chuckie shook his head with a laugh, and led me down the hall into Jeff's office, closing the door behind us. He sat at the edge of Jeff's desk. "I need you to talk to ACE."

ACE was a collective superconsciousness I'd managed to channel into Paul Gower what seemed like eons ago but was, in reality, only about two years prior. Gower was not only one of Chuckie's future brothers-in-law, but he was also the current Supreme Pontifex for the A-Cs, or, as I liked to think of it, their Pope With Benefits.

"Why don't you ask Paul whatever it is you need to ask ACE?"

"I have. He says that ACE doesn't want to talk to me."

"Huh." ACE had never had any issue with Chuckie in the past. "What do Naomi and Abigail think?" The Gower girls were the most powerful of the talented A-Cs, to the point where no one, not even Chuckie and the girls themselves, knew the full extent of their powers.

At least, they had been. Until the interstellar invasion.

Naomi and Abigail had used their powers to protect all the various D.C. monuments at the National Mall—and all the people inside them. They'd managed to preserve our nation's capital and history as well as many thousands of innocent people, but it had come at a cost. They'd had to use so much power for such an extended period of time, it had burned them both out. No one was sure if the burnout was temporary or permanent. The girls seemed to be handling this well, but I wasn't as intimate with them as Chuckie was.

Chuckie shook his head. "They haven't talked to ACE since . . . right after the invasion attempt."

"Operation Destruction was pretty hard on everyone."

"Yes, it was. We test Mimi and Abby all the time. They still have no more powers than a non-talented A-C."

"I know you'll get mad at me for the suggestion, but have you considered giving them a Surcenthumain boost?" Surcenthumain had been created by a whole host of our enemies, Amy's late father foremost among them, and it was the reason Jeff, Christopher, and Christopher's "lost aunt" Serene all had beyond-expanded powers. It was also the reason I wasn't fully human anymore, Jamie having done the mother and child feedback that turned me into a semi-alien.

Chuckie sighed. "All moral and ethical issues aside, Mimi and Abby aren't handling being 'normal' as well as they think they are, so I've thought about it. But I don't want to risk it without some sort of confirmation that it would actually work."

"What does Tito think?"

"Doctor Hernandez isn't convinced that we have enough

data to safely guess, and none of us like the idea of using Mimi and Abby, let alone anyone else, as test subjects."

Chuckie was giving me a look that said I was asking stupid questions. I decided to take the logic leap. "So that's why you want to talk to ACE."

"Finally. Yes."

"Does Paul know why you want to talk to ACE?"

"Yes."

"Huh. Well, okay, let me give it a shot." I'd been the one who'd figured out what was going on with ACE when we'd first "met," and therefore ACE had a soft spot for me. As Reader put it, ACE cared most about me and Gower.

Because I never wanted ACE to feel that I took him for granted, I only contacted him when it was important. Nothing had been Earth-shattering, either literally or figuratively, for these past months, so I'd left ACE alone.

I sat in one of the chairs in Jeff's office, closed my eyes, and thought in my mind. ACE, are you there?

I waited. ACE?

I waited a bit longer, while doing my best to hold down the panic. Maybe leaving ACE alone hadn't been a wise plan.

ACE? ACE, are you there, are you okay?

Waited a few more long, silent moments. Opened my eyes, cleared my throat, and shared the scary news. "He didn't answer. And I . . . I couldn't feel him."

CHAPTER 4

CHUCKIE NODDED. "That's what I was afraid of."

"Do you think ACE has left us? Or . . . died?" I didn't know if ACE could die in the ways a human would understand, but I did know he could be injured, and we'd dissipated a similar superconsciousness, so ACE wasn't invulnerable.

"I don't know. I do know, based on the intel we got from Richard White, that if Gower were killed while ACE was joined with him then the PPB-Net that represents ACE will collapse in on itself and destroy the Earth. I'd have to guess if ACE were to . . . die that it would negatively affect Gower, perhaps even kill him. Gower's alive and well and we're all still here, so I don't know that ACE is dead, at least as we'd be able to comprehend it."

White was Christopher's father and the former Pontifex, who now also resided at the Embassy and was my partner whenever we got to kick evil butt, which happened with a lot less frequency these days. "Have you asked Richard about this?"

"No. The people who are most likely to get a reply from ACE are you and Gower, Mimi, Abby, and Serene. Serene's tried to reach ACE, as have Mimi and Abby. None of them could get a response. Mimi and Abby put it down to their talent loss. Serene thinks it's because she's not as close to ACE as the others."

"But you don't think that at all."

"Of course not. ACE has never shown himself to be

unwilling to talk to any of them. And he was talking to you well before you gained any kind of A-C talents."

"Yeah, he's always there for his favorite penguins."

"I'm worried that our benevolent observer has left us, and if that's the case, Earth is back to being very alone, lonely, and vulnerable."

"Why so? Alpha Four are our friends, and so are the rest of the planets in that system."

"Yes," Chuckie said patiently, "they are. And how do we contact our friends when we need them?"

"We ask ACE to connect us. Crap." I felt sick to my stomach. I hadn't worried about ACE much. I'd checked on him after we'd all survived the Dino-Bird alien invasion attempt, of course. "The last I spoke with ACE was when we were doing cleanup after Operation Destruction. He told me he was tired and needed to rest, just like the rest of us did."

"There's a possibility that ACE left us in case he was going to die, so he wouldn't destroy the Earth."

"There's also a possibility that he's so hurt that he can't talk to us. I have no vote for which one of those ideas is worse, by the way, but thanks so much for choosing to have this conversation with me right before I have to entertain a bunch of politicians."

He shook his head. "We've become reliant on ACE. If he's not there for us any more, we need to be prepared for it."

"Why are you discussing this with me and not Jeff or James or anyone else?"

"Because Gower isn't willing to admit that ACE isn't chatting with him on a regular basis. As far as I can tell, he hasn't told Reader." Reader was not only the Head of Field, but he was Gower's husband. "And if he hasn't told Reader, then he hasn't told anyone."

"Yeah, I can agree there." Chuckie was the smartest person in any and all rooms, so it didn't shock me that he'd figured out what was going on. "So, you think Paul knows, or suspects something's wrong with ACE and is hiding it to avoid mass panic?"

"Yes, nice of your brain to join the party."

"Blah, blah, blah. Does anyone else suspect?"

"No, I don't think so, mostly because no one else really

understands how we work with ACE, and most don't know that he exists, in that sense."

"What about Naomi, Abigail, and Serene?"

"I told them I didn't want to bother the Pontifex with my request. When they couldn't reach ACE, I said I'd talk to Gower about it. Mimi and Abby can no longer tell if I'm lying, and Serene can only do it if she's touching a picture of me, and I gave her no reason to race out to grab a camera."

"Not dissing the skills, Secret Agent Man, just checking. Have you talked to Cliff about it?"

"Absolutely not, and you shouldn't, either. I don't even want you talking to your husband about this. This is the highest security issue we have right now, and it affects the entire world."

"Well, I can do my best to take this news to my grave, but where have you missed the fact that, since his special Surcenthumain boost, Jeff can pretty much read my mind when he wants to?"

The door opened and Jeff came in, closed and locked the door behind him. "And I also pick up when she's stressed, simply by being the strongest empath on the planet. Though, I get why you don't want this spread around," he said to Chuckie.

"Can you feel ACE?" Chuckie asked him.

Jeff shook his head. "No. I've never even thought to try before, so I wouldn't know what ACE would feel like emotionally, even if I could access him."

"Can you get Gower to tell me the truth about what he knows?" Chuckie asked.

"Possibly, but not tonight. The party has to take precedence unless you're going to tell us to declare a state of emergency."

"No, I agree." Chuckie rubbed the back of his neck. "The last thing I want is anyone actually knowing that we have no idea where ACE is, in that sense."

The com sprang to life. "Excuse me, Chiefs," Walter said. "Missus Lewis asked me to remind you that it's almost time for Jamie to have dinner."

"Thanks, Walt, we'll be right there."

"I'll relay, Chief." The com went dead.

Chuckie's eyes were narrowed. "Think he was listening in?"

"No. If the com's on, you can hear that little white noise sound, and eavesdropping is *not* Walter's thing." Walter was the youngest A-C agent to ever get assigned to be Head of Security for any facility. As such, he was incredibly dedicated, and eavesdropping was frowned upon when we weren't in emergency situations. I looked at my watch. Sure enough, Jamie's dinnertime was in thirty minutes. "Denise has Walter do these reminders when we're busy, so I don't forget."

"It's redundant," Jeff said. Of course, Jeff never, ever forgot Jamie's dinner time, lunch time, or breakfast time. Or anything else related to our daughter. He was the best daddy in the world. He insisted I was the best mommy, but Denise was quite aware that I got distracted, at least occasionally.

"Whatever. So, what do we tell everyone about this powwow? Because I can guarantee they're going to ask what we were talking about."

"Wedding plans," Chuckie replied. "Discussing the wedding party."

"Still?"

He rubbed the back of his neck again. "Yeah, well, our wedding party isn't set yet, and every delay means things move around even more, so it works as a cover."

"Yeah, well, I can relate. Sort of."

"We went in the opposite direction, baby," Jeff reminded me.

This was true enough. We'd had to move our wedding up by several weeks in order to foil one of the many Bad Guy du Jour plans. However, the delays Chuckie and Naomi were going through weren't anything any of us could avoid.

What with all the invasion drama and whatnot, the powers that be—which included the President and many other major countries' leaders, including Australia's, where Chuckie normally lived half the year—all felt that what would help solve many issues was a good ol' Royal Wedding Extravaganza.

Jeff and I having already done said Extravaganza was good, because the *World Weekly News* had the pictures—courtesy of our favorite paparazzo, Mister Joel Oliver—and was re-running them regularly. But Christopher and Amy having had the nerve to forego a big wedding meant that

Chuckie and Naomi, being the next in line to get married, were now the "It" couple for the big to-do. I didn't envy them. At all.

A large part of my lack of envy was that they were probably the least involved bride and groom ever, in terms of what kind of say they were getting in regard to their own nuptials. I mean, I'd been uninvolved, in that sense, but Reader had handled everything, and done it well, and I'd actually had veto power.

Every decision Chuckie and Naomi made had to go up through both the A-C and U.S. governments. And then, and only then, could they actually run said decisions by their families. And then any changes the families wanted went right back up the chain. Needless to say, this took time, which added to the overall frustration factor.

Wedding By Committee was no one's idea of a fun time. That neither one of them had killed anyone yet was a magnificent testament to the fact that they were, apparently, the most patient couple on the planet.

"So, what's the issue Jeff and I are helping you solve, wedding party-wise?"

Chuckie sighed and looked slightly embarrassed. "I still don't have my side chosen, and that includes the best man."

"Paul's performing the ceremony, right?" Jeff asked. It was sad that we actually had to ask, but who was marrying Chuckie and Naomi had changed at least six times so far by my count.

"Yes. That's been finally and officially approved and, God willing, nothing's going to change it. And Reader, as his husband, is a groomsman, and so is Michael." Michael was the fourth Gower sibling. He was younger than Gower, though like his older brother he was big, black, bald, and gorgeous. Michael was older than Naomi, with Abigail holding down the baby of the family slot.

Michael was also an astronaut and the A-C Player of the Year, Every Year. "Having Michael must be kind of like a double for whoever's making demands, right? I mean, an astronaut has to be a decent draw or coup or whatever it is they're looking for."

"True enough. And while Reader's joyfully taken over the role of Reynolds Hater that your husband here held so happily for so long, I don't have any objection to him being in the wedding party."

Jeff laughed. "Just took getting to know the real you."

Chuckie snorted. "Whatever spin makes you happy."

"So, you have two dudes so far. How many girls are on Naomi's side?"

"Abigail, of course, and she's Maid of Honor. Also confirmed and, please God, not changing. Then you, Amy, and Caroline."

"Really? I hate to sound really stupid and out of it, but Naomi hasn't actually asked me." And I had to figure if she hadn't asked me, then she hadn't asked Amy or Caroline, either.

Chuckie gave me a major "duh" look. "You're the human face of American Centaurion. Even if we all hated you, you'd be in the wedding. Besides, you're my best friend. Mimi's always planned to have you in the wedding party."

"Well, you know, happy to and all that. Will she be mad that you've told me?"

"No, I think she assumes you already know. She's having trouble with not being able to read anyone, so she's choosing to believe that everyone else is now reading her."

Interesting. "Okay, so you need a couple more guys, right?"

"Oh no, I need more than a couple. Remember how your husband was inviting everyone to be a groomsman when you were engaged?"

"Vividly." I'd had to pull in gals from the Alpha Centauri system to fill my side. Conveniently, they'd been on Earth helping us handle a much smaller invasion than the one we'd just gone through. We'd done better with Invasion Lite than we'd done a few months ago, but Earth still being here and populated by humans and our Earth A-Cs was absolutely one for the win column.

"Oh, it wasn't that bad," Jeff said, sounding a little hurt. "Besides, it was nice to have everyone involved in our special day." That Jeff could say this with absolutely no humor in his voice showed how much more romantic than me he was. Because I couldn't think of our wedding as "our special day" without having to control my Inner Hyena.

Chuckie shook his head at Jeff. "Again, whatever spin you like, but it boils down to the fact that Mimi's doing the same thing. Serene, Claudia, and Lorraine are back on bridesmaid duty, there are a couple gals I've met twice and I don't think you actually know invited, and she's not done."

"Why so many? Of course, I'd have been okay with just you and James up there with me, but I know I'm different."

He grinned. "Yeah, you are. And I think she's asking what feels like half the world because everyone's encouraging her to do it. By everyone, I mean on the political side. Her parents and brothers have pretty much given up and just smile and nod whenever Mimi suggests anything."

"What's Abigail think?"

"She tried sanity for a while, got tired of being snapped at, and has joined the rest of the family in the smiling and nodding department."

Okay, so Naomi was turning into a freaked-out Bridezilla. Understandable and no worries, we could get that under control. I hoped.

I'd seen some of this over the past months, but even though I'd made both Gower girls our Cultural Attachés, they hadn't really done much since losing their powers, including stay at the Embassy. Wondered now if I should have forced them to work to keep their minds off of what they'd lost. As with the situation with ACE, nothing I could do about it at this moment. Tabled the worry for another time.

"Okay, so, who else have you asked to be on your side of things?"

Chuckie sighed. "No one."

CHAPTER 5

"**W**HY THE HECK NOT? Is there something wrong you haven't told me?"

Chuckie snorted. "No, if we ignore that we have world governments involved in my wedding plans, nothing's wrong. But ... I have exactly two friends, Kitty. You and Cliff. And that's it."

"That's not true, not any more at any rate."

"I suppose."

"King Alexander's your friend. I'd count Councilor Leonidas, too. And I can promise the other dudes we know from the Alpha Centauri system like you, too."

"Fine, but without ACE we can't contact them, so I can't mention them, or what we actually want kept secret will quickly be all over the news and give our enemies free rein to try whatever they want."

"Surely you have more options than this. I mean, what about Brian?"

"Really? Your ex who's now married to Serene? The guy who hated me all through high school? Why don't we see if we can bring Antony Marling back from the dead and have him in the wedding party, too?"

"Airborne always stands ready. The flyboys live to be in wedding parties, and I'm sure Tim, as the Head of Airborne, would love to be involved."

"I don't know that I'd go with the term 'love' for any of this," Chuckie said dryly. "But I suppose they're options. But none of them are best man material."

"Seriously, I'm in the room," Jeff said, now adding annoyed onto the hurt in his tone. "I think, after all we've been through together, I count in the friend department."

Chuckie put his poker face on, but I knew him well, and I could tell he was shocked by this. I couldn't blame him. "Dude, I realize the Martini-Reynolds Bromance only officially started during Operation Destruction, but Jeff's right. You have more friends than you realize."

"You want Goodman as your best man, don't you?" Jeff asked, and I could hear disappointment, hidden, but there.

Chuckie shook his head. "Based on the political reactions to everything we want to do, I'm worried that if I ask Cliff to be involved in any way that I'll then be forced to have other politicians involved. Standing up with Cliff is one thing. Having some of my worst enemies in my wedding party is another."

"What does Cliff think about that?"

"He's disappointed, but he's clear on all the myriad political ramifications."

Jeff cocked his head. "Then it's decided. You'll have American Centaurion and Centaurion Division personnel with you. You know, the ones you can trust, even when they don't like you right away. Right, Kitty?"

"Um . . ." I had no idea why Jeff was tossing this one to me.

"I mean, it would make sense for someone high up in Centaurion to be the best man. And since we can't ask Alexander to come over from Alpha Four, one of us here will have to do." Jeff had what I'd come to think of as his Happy Diplomat smile going strong.

"Um . . ."

"And, since the world is watching, perhaps one of the highest ranking A-Cs would be the right choice, right, baby?" Jeff was clearly trying to lead the witness, but I was clueless as to where he was going with this.

Chuckie started to laugh. "Wow. I never thought I'd live to see the day. But, yeah, Jeff, if you'd be willing and it's not against some A-C custom, it'd be great if you'd be my best man."

"Now see?" Jeff asked, clearly pleased beyond belief. "Was that so hard?"

It was rare when I was rendered speechless, but, as with

the Ballroom being turned into Planet Pink, this had managed it. Speechless twice in one day. Had to be a record.

"Kitty, you okay with that?" Chuckie asked me.

Managed to recover. "I'm still in shock and wondering when the calm, pod-people parasites landed on the two of you, but I'm happy with the outcome. So, yes, absolutely, great choice."

"Good. Of course, tomorrow, this could all change," Chuckie reminded us as we left the room, heading back toward the front door.

"No worries. We'll just call it Musical Wedding Chairs until the actual minute the ceremony starts."

"Oh," Reader said as he and the others came up from the basement level. "You're talking about the wedding party situation. Yeah, it's a nightmare. Paul won't even discuss it with me, he's so frustrated."

Chuckie shrugged. "It is what it is."

"It's keeping people calm and focused on positives," Cliff said. "So, all the pain will be worth it."

"If, you know, anyone ever lets Chuckie and Naomi actually tie the knot and consummate the marriage. Jeff, you and Chuckie get to join everyone else on the rest of the tour. I'm going to get Jamie taken care of."

Jeff looked like he was going to argue. Pierre cleared his throat. "We *are* looking to ensure all's in readiness for the event tonight."

Jeff sighed and nodded. "Good point. If I'm not upstairs by then, call me when it's time for her to leave for the sitter, baby."

I leaned up and kissed his cheek. "You got it."

The men headed off into the kitchen. I was about to head upstairs when there was a knock at the front door. Pierre was busy and I was right here, so saw no need to keep whoever waiting. Besides, it might be the UPS man—he'd been delivering a lot of packages, most of them for Jamie, and we were all on a first name basis with him by now. And because the doorbell was the loudest on Embassy Row, out of kindness to us and their own eardrums, our delivery folks tended to knock first and only ring the bell if the door didn't get answered right away.

Sure enough, a familiar man in the brown UPS uniform

was standing there when I opened the door. "Hi Ted, what do you have for us today?"

He smiled. "You mean, what do I have for you again. Found a package I missed earlier today." He held out a small box. "Sorry about that. Been happening a lot today. I've pretty much done my route twice."

"Oh, bummer for you, but cool for us, so thanks!" Took the box and was about to look at it when something caught my eye. From where our front door was, I could easily see our street and a good part of Sheridan Circle. Sure it was the part with a lot of foliage, but it was quite visible.

My enhancement had improved my vision, so I was able to spot what I probably wouldn't have before Jamie was born—there was a man standing among the trees.

Being someone now very used to having enemies attack at all times, I didn't dismiss this. I took a better look, though I made sure I wasn't staring straight at the guy in the trees. From the corner of my eye, the lurker looked familiar.

In point of fact, he looked like someone I was pretty sure was dead.

My eyes could easily be deceiving me, but if they weren't, Clarence Valentino, A-C Traitor at Large and presumed deader, was hanging out in the bushes across the street.

CHAPTER 6

THE MAN IN THE CIRCLE who might be Clarence returned from the dead hadn't caught me looking, at least
I figured he hadn't because he hadn't disappeared. Wanted
to be sure of what I was seeing before I alerted anyone, so
I needed a better look.

I smiled at Ted. "So, you think we should search your
truck, in case anything else for us turns up?"

He laughed. "You can come take a look if you want. My
route's almost done. Again."

We chuckled together and I went down the walk with
him to his truck. I didn't care if we had ten more packages
Ted had missed or nothing at all left in his van. This angle
meant I'd have a clear enough look to be able to tell if I was
seeing things or not.

Ted took me to the back of his truck and opened the
doors. "Not much left, but I'll triple check it if you want."

"Sure, if you have the time." I lounged against the back
of the truck, so that I could look around while seeming to
be not paying attention. While Ted rummaged, I observed.

It was hard to be sure if the man in the foliage was actually someone I knew and not just some random lurker. But
considering one of the last times I'd seen Clarence had been
when he was trying to lure the Gower girls into the trees by
the Lincoln Memorial, I felt I was on the right track.

"I don't see anything else for you," Ted announced.

Turned to look inside the truck. It was in a decent state
of disarray. "How do you find anything in here?"

"Normally? No problem. Today I must have turned a corner too fast or driven over a bump I didn't notice, because about midday I get to a stop and bam, all my packages are on the floor or on top of each other."

Our UPS man didn't normally get involved in high speed car chases, and there was no way he could have gone over a bump big enough to toss everything on the floor without his knowing. Ted might be lying, but I doubted it. An A-C moving at hyperspeed would be invisible to the naked human eye, and I had a good bet an A-C had done this. A specific A-C, in fact. The one hiding at the Circle.

Why was the big question. I didn't have a good answer. Yet.

Said good-bye to Ted and watched him drive off. No sign of anyone chasing him at hyperspeed. Of course, if this *was* Clarence, he was enhanced. Which might be how he'd survived.

Turned to face the Circle. This time, whoever it was seemed aware I was looking at him. He disappeared.

I didn't stop to ponder—I took off running. At hyperspeed.

Christopher had been working with me a lot on control, so I didn't slam my face into a tree. I reached the edge of the Circle and stopped. Then I trotted around at human level. I was quite proud of myself. Pity no one was around to see and rate this performance.

"What the hell are you doing, Missus Chief?"

Okay, someone was around. Point of fact, it was Malcolm Buchanan, aka the P.T.C.U. operative assigned by my mother to be my permanent shadow. Couldn't complain—Buchanan had saved my life more than once already. He was also a big, tall, good-looking, muscular guy with deep blue eyes and brown hair. I never complained about that, either.

"Hey, Malcolm, I thought I saw—" Clarence, and I saw him again, about a block away. I wasn't dressed for dinner, so I was in my usual jeans, today's concert shirt featuring Van Halen, and my Converse. I was good to go.

I could grab Buchanan and take him with me, but hyperspeed was hard as hell on humans and even though I felt Buchanan possessed Dr. Strange powers, he wasn't going to be up to a lot of hyperspeeding.

Took off and decided I'd beg forgiveness later.

Clarence saw me coming and he ran off as well. I wasn't too far away, and was able to keep the distance apart fairly close. This meant Clarence wasn't moving at the super-fast speeds Jeff and particularly Christopher could now hit, but he was still going at a good clip for an A-C. Whether this meant he couldn't run that fast any more or was leading me somewhere I didn't know. But I'd been a sprinter in high school and college and I'd been working on my stamina for the past few months, so he could run around all he wanted—he wasn't going to lose me.

We went back and forth around the Embassy Row area. Clarence didn't seem to have a destination in mind other than "away." Could mean he was trying to tire me out or trap me, could mean he hadn't expected to be seen, could mean something else.

Clarence ran across the Parkway. We both weaved in between the cars like they were standing still. He jumped off and crossed Rock Creek—we were both running fast enough that we splashed across the top of the water but didn't go in—and headed for the Oak Hill Cemetery. It was an older, well-forested cemetery, and Clarence lost me quickly.

Stopped running and considered my options. They seemed slim and I had an important dinner to hostess, a stealth bodyguard to reassure and apologize to, and a daughter to pick up from daycare. And, as I realized it, a package still in my hands.

Took the moment to look at said package. It was addressed to me, but the return address was also the Embassy.

The chances of anyone at the Embassy sending a package to me via UPS rather than handing it to me were pretty slim, bordering on none. Meaning this was a package that was potentially dangerous.

Thought hard and quickly. Ted's truck had been ransacked, most likely by an A-C. But if that was the case, was that A-C Clarence or someone else?

Decided to vote on it being Clarence. Sure, I'd seen him when I'd answered the door, but I didn't normally answer our door, Pierre did. And he'd never seen Clarence except possibly at my wedding, and I doubted the memory would have been top of mind for Pierre, especially not today.

So, Clarence, or whoever was pulling his strings, wanted a package delivered to us today and was likely watching to ensure it was delivered. But why?

Looked at the box. We were having a freaking huge party tonight loaded with the political elite. How hard was it to guess why tonight? Get the package into the Embassy, and then release whatever the hell was in it.

This presented me with a new problem. What to do with the box.

Curiosity might have killed the cat, but this cat wasn't stupid enough to figure the box was safe to open. I was more concerned with what kind of bomb it was, or if it maybe contained venomous spiders or something. I put nothing past The Bad Guys League.

I was, however, the least equipped person on staff to identify whatever it was, short of opening and therefore triggering the badness.

My phone, which I had in the back pocket of my jeans, chose this moment to ring. I put the box down, walked a couple steps away, and answered the phone, ready to run if this was the trigger for the bomb. "Hello?"

"Miss Katt?"

There weren't a lot of people who called me Miss Katt anymore. And I recognized the voice. It was my "uncle," Peter the Dingo, also known as the most dangerous and effective assassin alive.

CHAPTER 7

"YES, 'UNCLE' PETER? What can I do you for?"

"You can tell me where you are."

"Ah, why would I want to do that?"

"Because I believe you are holding something very dangerous."

Huh. The plot thickened. Or rather, just got weirder, which was pretty typical for my life these days. "How dangerous?"

"Causing much pain and suffering, and death, kind of dangerous."

"Well, I guessed as much, honestly. But how do you know about it?"

He sighed. "I have been watching your Embassy."

"Why? Or rather, who in it or coming tonight is on your hit list?"

"No one."

"I'd fall on the ground laughing, only I want to be able to run away should whatever's in the plain brown wrapper go boom."

"Truly. This is . . . a favor."

"For whom?"

"For you."

"Why?"

"Because someone is being a . . . sore loser, I think you'd say. He was told to move on, but has chosen the path of revenge. Revenge is not a good choice for people in . . . my line of work."

Thought fast and furiously again. During Operation Assassination, there had been two assassination teams assigned to get us, me in particular. One had been Peter the Dingo Dog and his cousin. The other had been Bernie and her husband/partner Raul. Buchanan had taken care of Bernie, but Raul had been arrested. I'd never seen Raul in person. But I knew he'd seen me.

Our enemies were released from prison all the time, because we had very powerful enemies. So Raul likely being out wasn't much of a shock. And Buchanan had killed Raul's wife to save me and Jamie, and that meant Raul had the best revenge reason in the world to disobey the Dingo's cease and desist order.

"Okay, so where's Raul?"

"You are so much smarter than you like to appear." He sounded incredibly proud. The idea that the Dingo might actually be thinking of me as his niece, as someone to protect, crept up and waved quietly.

"Thank you. Um . . . so, I appreciate you warning me. Should I dump the package into the river?"

"You're close to the Potomac? Again?"

"Yes. Though like you and your cousin, I don't want to go swimming in it again any time soon. How is he, by the way?"

"Very well. He is also watching."

"To protect me or to finish the job? Or for a new job?"

The Dingo sighed again. "Understand that there are . . . rules in our line of work. If there were no rules, then we would have anarchy, yes?"

"Yes, right."

"When someone chooses to break the rules for personal reasons, those reasons must make sense."

"I hate to say it, but revenge makes sense."

"No, not for our line of work. The risks are high, but so are the rewards. Unprofessional behavior is for terrorists, for amateurs." The way he said it, it was clear that the Dingo was only in favor of professional terrorists.

"You're worried that your business will dry up because if Raul offs me and potentially a lot of your customers, then word will get out that it wasn't a paid hit but a revenge hit, and the Assassination Union will raise the rates or something."

"Something like that, yes. So, where are you?"

"I ask again, why?"

"I wish to find you and disarm the package."

Package, not bomb. "What's in the package?"

"Something very bad."

"I guessed. Tell me more."

"I don't have to." The voice wasn't on the phone any more but behind me.

Spun around to see the Dingo and his cousin, Surly Vic, standing there. They were both in dark suits and appeared unarmed, but I was positive they were both packing more heat than I could hope to count. Still had that Smooth Criminal Who Could Be From Anywhere look, but since I knew, I could spot the little bits of East Slavic in them both.

Hung up my phone and shoved it back into my pocket. "Your GPS tracking is really good." My phone started buzzing—someone was texting me. Decided that being rude right now would be the stupidest move of my life. Whoever it was could wait.

The Dingo shrugged. "Yes." He nodded to Surly Vic, who went and got the package.

"Are you sure it's safe for you to handle?" My phone rang. Ignored it.

"We will exercise care and I appreciate your concern." The Dingo smiled at me. "Please give my best to your sister, when it is appropriate. She was a lovely young lady, and I hope she's doing well?"

He meant Caroline Chase, my sorority roommate and bestie. The Dingo had been dating her, sort of, during Operation Assassination, though she'd had no idea he was an assassin. Our lives were just that kind of glamorous.

"Um, will do, and yes, she's doing great. I'm sure she'd tell me to say 'hi' for her. If, you know, she knew you were here and we were chatting." Maybe. Anything was possible, after all. "So, what do I do now?"

The Dingo shrugged. "Return home, have your party. We will deal with your problem."

Shook my head. "I don't think it's just Raul." My phone continued to ring. I continued to ignore it and hope whoever was calling would take the hint.

Both assassins looked at me. "How do you mean?" Surly Vic asked.

"Someone had to help him get the package into the UPS truck. And I'm here because I was chasing someone I thought was dead. Raul may actually have a paying assignment."

They both shook their heads. "He does not," the Dingo said vehemently.

"Oh, so it's the old 'the enemy of my enemy is my friend' ploy, right?"

The Dingo beamed at me, looking all proud. Even Surly Vic seemed impressed. Nice to know that I was considered Top of the Class by someone. It was always the folks on the wrong side who thought so, but better to be appreciated than not at all, right?

"You must be cautious," Surly Vic shared. Wow, clearly I'd moved into that "family" spot for him, too. I was lucky that way.

"I'll do my best. But isn't it kind of bad for you guys to be back in town? I realize Operation Assassination went down months ago, but you're still on everyone's most wanted lists."

They both shrugged and seemed completely unfazed by my name for the big event. For all I knew, they were flattered by my naming choice. "We have work to do," the Dingo said. "Not work you will care about, I must add."

"You're sure?"

"Positive. I would not lie to you about that."

"Why *not*?"

They both chuckled. "You are ... special," the Dingo shared. "You have honor. And, therefore, you deserve the truth. We are not here on assignment for anyone you would care about."

"You're here to off Raul."

"And other enemies. Of ours and yours." Surly Vic shook his head. "We need to take this and disarm it. We have time. I believe it's set to go off in a few hours if it's not opened."

"Are you that amazingly good—and don't for one moment think I'm insinuating that you couldn't be, because nothing you two can do will surprise me—or is that just a really good guess?"

Surly Vic smiled at me. I managed not to faint or let my total shock show, but it took effort. "Just a really good guess. Based on a great deal of experience."

"What is it, just out of morbid curiosity?"

"Most likely a small bioweapon," the Dingo replied. "It would explode, killing and maiming some, but it would also spread a dread disease amongst all there, and within the building."

"A raze the building to the ground kind of disease?"

"Most assuredly."

"Um, you know, my letting the two best assassins in the world walk off with a scary bioweapon bomb is, well, not sounding like a good idea."

Surly Vic shrugged. "We could let you take it with you, and then, when someone who did not know how to disarm it triggered the bomb, you and your family and friends could die. Or we can remove the danger."

"Gosh, when you put it that way . . ."

The Dingo came to me and patted my shoulder. "We both give you our word—this bomb will not be used against anyone. We will dismantle it and deal with its creator. In the meantime, exercise caution and open nothing remotely suspicious." He handed me a phone. "This is the phone I used to call you. It is programmed with only one number. Use it if you need our help or even think you need our help."

The top international assassination team in the business had just given me their version of the Bat Phone. Didn't know whether to be flattered or freaked out. Settled for both.

"Thank you. I assume this is a burner phone and so is the one it will call. I won't let anyone know." I hoped. Jeff might already know, of course, but only if he was monitoring me. Wasn't sure if I'd given off enough stress vibes for him to have noticed otherwise.

"Yes. We will be in touch if necessary. Keep this and your regular phone with you at all times, even when sleeping."

"I will do. Hoping that this isn't also a bomb or a trigger of some kind."

They both chuckled again. "You are wise to always question," Surly Vic said. "But, as my cousin has said, we give you our word—we are here to protect you, and that phone is part of that protection."

Surly Vic nodded to me, Peter the Dingo Dog patted my shoulder again, and then they both took off. They were out of sight fast.

"Thanks," I called to no one. Well, likely no one. For all I knew, they were close by and would appreciate my being polite.

So, I had two new fairy godfathers who were going to protect me by killing people. I'd have questioned how my life had gotten this bizarre, but I already knew—I was just lucky this way.

CHAPTER 8

DECIDED CLARENCE WAS probably long gone and I'd better do what my new BFFs, the Assassination Squad, said. And, as Christopher always shared with me these days, any chance to practice was time well spent. He usually snarled that at me, but it was still probably sound advice. And I was sure Peter the Dingo Dog and Surly Vic would agree with the sentiment.

My phone was still massaging half of my butt with its nonstop buzzing that traded off with nonstop ringing. Pulled it out to see a lot of texts and missed calls from Buchanan. Decided not to read them because I could guess what they were saying and figured I could talk faster in person.

Took one more look around, saw nothing and no one, and took off for home.

Went back to Sheridan Circle, to find Buchanan there, trotting around the park, looking completely freaked out.

"Malcolm, what's up?"

His expression went to relief. "Where the hell did you go? You've been gone for well over fifteen minutes. And you didn't answer any of my calls or texts."

We were about seven minutes from the cemetery by car, less if you hit lights and traffic right, so that meant the Dingo had been tracking me before he'd ever called my phone. Not a surprise, really. That Buchanan hadn't spotted the Dingo and Surly Vic was more surprising. Wondered if he was feeling alright.

"Did you alert the Embassy?"

"No, I was too busy trying to find you. But if you'd been gone another minute, I would have. And then I'd have had your mother start GPS tracking you via your phone."

Was glad the Dingo had sent me home. "I wasn't paying attention to my phone, I'm sorry. I ran after Clarence." Wasn't sure if I should mention my visit with my "uncle." Buchanan reported to my mother, and Mom would *not* enjoy discovering I'd let the Dingo get away. Again. No wonder the Dingo Dog and Surly Vic were fond of me.

"Clarence Valentino? He's dead."

"He's not. We never found his body, remember?" We hadn't found Ronaldo al Dejahl's body, either. However, they weren't the only bodies that had been missing at the end of Operation Destruction—the supersoldiers and superbeings had done a lot of damage, some of which had ensured that there were a lot of folks listed as missing who were, sadly, probably dead.

"There were a lot of . . . partial bodies, if you recall."

"I'd rather not think about it." This was quite true. Thinking about the aftermath of Operation Destruction always made me want to cry and hurt evil people who were already dead. Then again, I was now pretty sure that one of those people wasn't actually dead. "But I saw him. Clarence was here, in the Circle, and then he ran off. I followed him, but lost him in the cemetery."

Buchanan shook his head. "I didn't see him, or anyone who looked like him."

"He helped get the package with the bomb delivered."

Buchanan went into Alert Mode. "What package?"

"Um . . ." The package I no longer had, and which, point in fact, I'd given to the assassins I didn't want to mention to Buchanan. "I got rid of it."

Buchanan went from Alert Mode into Skeptical Mode in the blink of an eye. "Where?"

"The river?"

"Really. Who was the package from?"

"I don't know."

"What was in it?"

"Don't know."

"So, you got a mysterious package and decided, what, to throw it in the river? Was this before, after, or during the time you were chasing a dead man through the streets of D.C.?"

"After. I think." Was about to ask if Buchanan didn't re-member that I'd been holding a package right before I ran off. Realized it would then take us right back to me having to lie to him some more. Stopped myself from speaking, but this left my mouth hanging open.

Buchanan gently closed my mouth and then put his hand on my forehead. "You don't seem to be running a fever."

"Ha ha ha."

He heaved a sigh. "This isn't funny, Kitty. I realize you saw something, I could tell by how you were acting. But you shouldn't be running off without someone else along." Bu-chanan didn't look angry; he looked worried. Felt bad—I didn't want to make him worry or feel like he wasn't doing a good job, and I wasn't enjoying lying to him at all.

"Sorry. Next time I'll take you, okay?"

"Yes, the next time you run off chasing figments of your imagination, please make sure I'm along for the ride."

"Okay, um, I'll just get back and keep things rolling for tonight. And, you need to be careful, okay?" If Raul was after me, he might also be after Buchanan.

He sighed. "I'm always careful."

Buchanan walked me back to the Embassy. No one seemed to be looking for me, which was well and good. So either Jeff wasn't emotionally monitoring either me or Bu-chanan, or he'd felt that I had the situation well in hand and would grill me for details later. Issue tabled for now, then.

Took the stairs up, in part to practice, because Christo-pher lived to ask me how much practice I'd put in each day and I obviously couldn't share my recent exploits without breaking my promise to the Dingo. Why I cared about that I couldn't say, but I'd been taught to go with my gut, and my gut said the Dingo was telling me the truth.

And if Buchanan, who'd been there, hadn't believed me about Clarence, would anyone else, even Jeff? I had no real proof, after all, and truthfully I'd never seen the man up close enough to be a hundred percent sure. Decided I'd ta-ble this issue as well.

I was great with my A-C powers if I was enraged and channeling She-Hulk or racing after presumed-dead ene-mies. However, I still had to work at using my talents when things were calm.

Well, my hyperspeed and superstrength talents. I'd

scored other talents, and those I never seemed to have issues with.

Which, as I left the stairs on the fourth floor a little fast, was a good thing. Two huge birds that looked like peacocks on steroids appeared out of nowhere. The Peregrines each grabbed one of my wrists and lifted me into the air. My speed slowed to normal and they put me down gently.

"Thanks Bruno and Ken." I gave liberal scritchy-scratches to our Royal Avian Protectors. "Lola and Barbie guarding the kids?"

Bruno cooed and looked at me. Yes, their mates were on Nursemaid Duty. This was, as had been proved a lot during Operation Destruction, a really good thing.

A soft mewing sounded and then there were balls of fluffy cuteness on my shoulders. "Harlie, Poofikins!" The Poofs were small balls of fluffy fur, with black button eyes, cat ears, and tiny paws. They could also go Jeff-sized if danger threatened, meaning that we'd seen the Poofs large and in charge a lot since we'd found out they existed.

Chose not to ask why no Poofs or Peregrines had shown up for an assist earlier. Because the danger hadn't been all that great was my guess. And I hadn't called for them.

The Poofs were also Royal Protectors, only we'd had them a lot longer than the Peregrines, since they arrived as part of Operation Invasion and ended up being the best wedding gifts anyone could get.

Well, we'd had some of them longer. The Poofs were androgynous and mated whenever a royal wedding was imminent. Apparently the Poofs felt that many more people were getting married, they'd stocked up due to the Dino-Bird Invasion, or else they'd decided all of American Centaurion and our military and research side, Centaurion Division, were part of the Royal Family, because we had Poofs up the wazoo.

Not that anyone minded, me least of all. Poofs for everyone and more Poofs for me was my motto.

The Poofs and Peregrines had some rivalry issues, but our flock of a dozen mated Peregrine pairs and our massive pack of Poofs had chosen to listen to me and get along with each other.

Yes, they listened to me, literally, and I could understand them, at least somewhat. Because the A-C "talent" I'd got-

ten by benefit of the Surcenthumain Boost was the ability
to talk to the A-C animals. Dr. Doolittle had nothing on me.
I hadn't told my parents, Jeff, Chuckie, or Reader yet, but I
was getting pretty good with our Earth dogs and cats, too. I
wanted to save it for when I was sure someone had a camera handy, so I could preserve their expressions forever.

Of course, the Peregrines were the reason we had a Zoo
to go to tonight. Because Pierre wasn't going to shuttle all
our guests to the Washington Zoo. He meant the five-story
building next to ours, which had taken severe water damage
several months ago. It had been my idea to buy it, fix it up,
and turn it into a zoo to house the Peregrines and anything
else that might show up from the Alpha Centauri system.

This idea, originally scoffed at by most if not all of my
nearest and dearest, had turned into a goodwill gesture and
publicity stunt that was working really well. The Peregrines
were, like the rest of us, "out" as being aliens, and they went
on display a couple of times a week. We kept said times
random for security reasons.

The Poofs had been spotted during the invasion, too, so
some of them did Zoo duty as well. We had every toy man-
ufacturer in the world in a bidding war over who was going
to get the Poof licensing rights. Chuckie, by dint of his business acumen and ability to multitask like no other, was handling all of that "fun."

We'd also built an enclosed walkway from our second
floor to the Zoo's second floor, as well as kept the top three
floors of the Zoo for regular people use. Which, apparently,
included tonight's dinner party. The idea made sense, so I
wasn't surprised that Pierre had come up with it.

Thusly escorted by my exotic feathered and fluffy
friends, I entered the daycare center. Before we'd taken
over the Embassy it had been an exercise room, and much
of that, the pads on the floors in particular, were still around.
But Pierre and Denise Lewis had really done it up nicely
and it was now totally safe for children, Poofs, and Peregrines. Dogs and cats, too, since my parents' pets were still
housing with us and, per Jamie, were lonely without her.

Speaking of my favorite bundle of cuteness, she saw me,
and ran to me, squealing, "Mommy!"

I picked her up and gave her a big kiss and hug. "Good
job, Jamie-Kat!" She was working on moving at human

speeds, and doing well with it. Jamie was, in point of fact, doing far better moving between human and A-C speeds than I was, but I chose to look at it as her being gifted and super-special.

She was just days under a year, but Jamie was moving fast in terms of development. All A-C babies did some things faster than humans, but Jamie was beating the normal A-Cs. She'd said her first word at the end of Operation Destruction, and in the months since then, had moved from baby talk to little kid talk. She'd started standing on her own at the end of our last fracas, too, and wasn't toddling so much as being kind to the adults and human kids and not really going for it in terms of all-out running and such unless the circumstances were dire.

No sooner than Jamie was in my arms, than the tide of canines hit us. "You sure having them here isn't a problem?" I asked Denise.

"Oh no, they're very well behaved and the children love having them." She had the cats in their carrier, and trundled it over to me. Due to Jamie's demands that the cats go everywhere with her in the Embassy, their carrier was now an extra-large luxury deal on wheels with a handle for pulling.

The cats seemed okay with their Feline Winnebago, probably because they liked traveling in style and with their own band of Poofs along. I wasn't positive, but it seemed to me that Sugarfoot, Candy, and Kane had Poofs that they considered theirs, just like the rest of us. For all I knew, the dogs had their own Poofs, too. There were certainly enough Poofs in there with the cats to accommodate every Earth pet we had and then some.

"Where are the rest of the kids?" I asked, as the human kids, Raymond and Rachel Lewis, trotted over, too. These days, we had several other hybrid children at the center— all those who had parents working at the Embassy, on Alpha, or Airborne—and I was used to seeing them and getting daily hugs and kisses.

"Picked up already. You're a little late, but that's never a problem. We all like spending extra time with Jamie."

Decided not to offer any excuse for why I was late since Denise didn't seem to care. Besides, getting rid of the Bomb of Badness was a good thing, right?

Raymond was a serious little boy of six and his sister was a sweet little girl of four. Their father, Kevin, was a gorgeous black guy with bags and bags of charisma. Denise was a gorgeous blonde with her own bags of charisma. Both of them had fantastic smiles with fantastic teeth on top of everything else. They were pretty much the perfect couple, and you couldn't hate them because they were also incredibly nice.

Surprising no one, their children were also gorgeous, with fab smiles and their own little bags of charisma. I wasn't sure if Raymond was too old for Jamie, but I was willing to go for the arranged marriage idea, because in addition to all their other fine qualities, the Lewises were also all smart. Hey, I wanted my daughter to marry well. Sure, after she'd grown up and found herself a career she enjoyed, but it was never too early to plan, right?

After I got my requisite hugs from the Lewis kids, Raymond gave me a very serious look. "I'm not sure this dinner party is such a good idea."

CHAPTER 9

I GAPED AT RAYMOND. "Um, why?"

"Daddy says that he's concerned about the security." Raymond was dead serious, and he looked ready to go downstairs and join the other men in the verification of our Embassy's safety set-up.

Of course, Kevin was my mother's right-hand man, meaning he was second in command of the Presidential Terrorism Control Unit, or P.T.C.U. Until I'd run into the gang from Alpha Four, I hadn't known this government agency existed, nor that my mother was the head of it. The past three years had been full of fun facts like this one.

Kevin and his family had taken up permanent positions at our Embassy, so Kevin had the "fun" of reporting in to two different bosses and doing two different jobs. He handled it smoothly, because, well, he was Kevin and smooth was his natural state of being. In the Embassy, he was our Defense Attaché. Denise was running the daycare and Embassy School because she was both qualified and didn't want to be bored every day of her life.

Denise shook her head and laughed. "One stray comment and *someone* thinks he knows better than his father."

"Is Kevin worried?"

She shrugged. "It's his job to be worried, and to act on those worries. Don't you worry, though, Kitty. Everything's under control. And Gladys will be with us, babysitting."

"Oh, good news." It was. Gladys was the head of all Security operations for Centaurion Division, and that included the Embassy, Pontifex's residences, Martini Manor, where Jeff's parents lived, and any other big A-C owned or operated facility. I'd still never met Gladys. Because I was kind of afraid of her. She was considered one of the most formidable, if not *the* most formidable, of all A-C personnel, and she had sarcasm down to an art form.

"So, you get Jamie's dinner taken care of, then let me know when she's ready for fun times." Denise tickled Jamie's tummy, as Jamie squealed with laughter.

"You're getting out of the uncomfortable formal affair *again*?" Was this woman's luck truly never-ending?

Denise winked. "The perks of being the Daycare Mom. I have to do it because it's my job."

"You are *so* lucky."

"I know. Believe me, I like going to fancy things as much as the next gal, but not these kinds of things. I'm much happier with the kids and Gladys is really fun to hang out with, and these are the only times I get to see her."

Gladys was someone Denise *wanted* to hang out with? Never a day went by when I didn't score new information like this. Decided it was in the interests of my longevity to not mention aloud that I found it hard to believe Gladys was a party animal. "Where will all of you be, here?"

Denise shook her head. "We're going over to the Pontifex's residence. That way, no one can sneak out to see their mommies or daddies." She shot Raymond an amused but exasperated look.

"Just trying to help," he said under his breath.

"And we appreciate your efforts." Hey, I had no issues with Raymond questioning our safety. In most cases, he was probably wise to do so.

I considered my options. I could try to get all of our animal kingdom and my daughter back upstairs alone, or I could call for help. "Com on!"

"Yes, Chief?" Walter asked.

"I need Len and Kyle here to help me. Like now."

"They're advised and on their way, Chief."

"You're the best, Walt."

Len and Kyle were human C.I.A. agents permanently assigned to be my driver and bodyguard, respectively. They were also young, cute, and former members of USC's Trojan Football team who'd come into my orbit during the excitement surrounding my wedding. Instead of pursuing pro careers, they went straight from college to Chuckie's side of things and, therefore, were swept right back up into my orbit.

Len had been the quarterback and Kyle had been on the line, which was why when it came to who got to handle what, Kyle got the four dogs and Len got the Feline Winnebago. I kept the cute little girl because I could.

"You boys ready for tonight?" I asked as we squished into the elevator. The dogs ensured that they took up a lot of room.

"Yes," Len replied. "It's supposed to be a fun night. And we'll have friends attending."

"I know. Olga doesn't want to miss any hilarity that might ensue."

Olga was the wife of the Romanian ambassador. The Romanian Embassy was across the street from ours, and through a variety of circumstances, we'd become close with Olga and her granddaughter and personal assistant, Adriana. That Olga was former KGB and training Adriana in all the skills was a secret we were all happy to keep.

Olga was suffering from multiple sclerosis, so she was mostly confined to a wheelchair. This didn't stop her from somehow knowing everything that was going on in D.C. and many other places as well. My personal goal was to surprise or know something, anything, before her. It happened, but very rarely. Hoped that she wasn't aware that the Dingo was in town, but I wasn't willing to bet on it.

"Since Pierre's been here, we haven't had any really disastrous social events," Len reminded me.

"True enough. I'm thankful for Pierre every day." I chose not to mention that an interstellar invasion definitely counted as a disastrous event.

We reached our floor and entered our palatial suite. I was adjusting to living in a portion of a huge building that was larger than the house I'd grown up in, but I still wasn't a hundred percent comfy with it, and I didn't know if I ever would be. Had we not had the Elves, I'd have hated this place based solely on having to keep it clean.

But we had the Elves and they'd prepared Jamie's dinner for me. Because the Elves wisely didn't trust my food prep skills. I didn't always make the smoke alarms go off, but I was close to batting a thousand.

The boys let the cats and Poofs out, and then I sent them to take the dogs for walkies. The Peregrines had their own areas, courtesy of the Elves, both in our rooms and at the Zoo, where they did their business, so to speak. They were really good at acting unlike every other bird out there and holding it until they were in their Dump Zone. I was grateful for this for a variety of reasons, Jeff's reactions to the idea of casual bird poop dropped in his home being number one.

Jamie was midway through both her dinner and the recounting of her exciting day spent with the letters of the alphabet, the colors of the rainbow, and the numbers one through ten when the boys and dogs returned, bringing Jeff along with them.

"Daddy!" Jamie was still in her highchair. Or rather, she'd been in it. But I blinked and she was out of it and in Jeff's arms. Her plate and cup hadn't moved. At least not that I'd seen. Meaning she'd used hyperspeed.

Heaved a sigh. Had to determine if this was a battle worth fighting while Jeff gave Jamie tons of Daddy Kisses and she started telling him about her day—at hyperspeed.

When A-Cs talked at their normal speeds, it made the humans in attendance woozy. While I was enhanced, my hearing had yet to catch up and I got nauseous fast. I could tell the boys, cats, and dogs weren't enjoying it either.

"Slow down, Jamie-Kat," Jeff said soothingly. "We need to talk slowly so we don't make everyone else here feel sick."

"Too late," Len said quietly. He sat down at the breakfast bar. Kyle followed suit. "You know, has anyone considered you guys just talking at what you'd call normal speeds as a viable weapon?"

Jeff and I looked at each other. "No," he said slowly. "But it's an interesting idea."

"Bad idea if publicized," Kyle said. "It makes you scarier than you already are. I mean, I'm not scared of you guys, but that's because I'm on your side and you know it."

Jamie looked at all of us, a worried expression on her little face. "Sorry."

I got up, took her from Jeff, and gave her a snuggle. "It's okay. But that's why we have to practice being more like Mommy than Daddy sometimes. Okay?"

She hugged me. "Okay, Mommy. I'll talk to the kitties and puppies more."

"Um, the kitties and puppies don't like it when you talk fast, either, Jamie-Kat."

Jamie shot a look toward me I was becoming familiar with—her "oh, Mommy, you see but you do not *observe*" look. "I meant like you do, Mommy. In their minds."

CHAPTER 10

HAD TO SAY this for Len and Kyle—they knew, absolutely, when it was time to make a hasty retreat.

"We need to dress for dinner," Len said as he stood quickly.

"Right," Kyle agreed. "Call us when you need help getting the animals over to the Pontifex's residence."

With that, the two of them took off. They didn't run, but they definitely didn't stroll, either.

The front door closed and Jeff and I looked at each other. "You talk to the animals in their minds?" he asked finally.

"I guess."

"I mean, not giving verbal commands you thought of, but by thinking at the animals without speaking and them understanding you?"

"Um, sorta."

"Sorta?" Jeff sounded like he was working to keep his voice nice and calm. "And is Jamie saying that this talent has extended to the Earth animals, too?"

"Ah . . ."

"You know you do, Mommy," Jamie said patiently, while I did my best to ensure that my expression, body language, and upper level thoughts didn't betray how freaky it was to be having this conversation, with this level of language clarity, with my almost-one-year-old. "Just like you talk to Fairy Godfather ACE."

"Right." Now I had to hope my worry about ACE wasn't

getting through to Jamie. Prayed Jeff was doing some sort of mind block or something, though he looked like my Dr. Doolittle-ness had sent him to Freaked-Out Land with me.

Jamie shook her head. "Fairy Godfather ACE is tired and busy. You shouldn't worry, Mommy. He'll never leave us."

"We can't talk about this with other people, Jamie-Kat," Jeff said quickly. "Daddy doesn't want you to talk about ACE unless it's only with Mommy or Daddy. And the same with Mommy being able to talk to the animals, that's just for us to talk about."

"I know, Daddy." Jamie looked back and forth between us. "Are you mad at me?"

I hugged her tightly. "No, we're not. Mommy and Daddy have been worried about Fairy Godfather ACE, that's all. And other things."

"Other things you don't need to worry about," Jeff said quickly.

"Okay, Daddy. Mous-Mous wants everyone to come with us tonight." Mous-Mous was Jamie's Poof, which, at the sound of its name, appeared from wherever it had been to perch on Jamie's shoulder and purr loudly.

"Everyone?" Jeff asked. "Daddy and Mommy have to entertain the other grownups."

"No Daddy, Mous-Mous wants all the other pets to come."

Jamie's saying that it was her Poof who wanted the other animals along was actually normal. Lots of little kids said their stuffed animals or favorite pet wanted to do the thing the little kid themselves wanted to do. Mom claimed that I'd used the cats they'd had when I was born, Sugar and Spice, as my excuse for anything and everything.

Now, however, I wasn't sure if Jamie was just being a little girl or if Mous-Mous was actually weighing in on the evening's animal arrangements.

Didn't matter, because all roads led to every animal we had heading over to the Pontifex's residence anyway. "No worries, Jamie-Kat. Every furred and feathered beast we have will be with you and Mous-Mous tonight."

"Yay!" Jamie gave me a big hug, which was always nice.

Jeff got her settled and her dinner finished up. Then it was bath time, and into a Minnie Mouse pajama set. The A-Cs loved black and white and Armani. However, Reader had managed to ensure that Jamie's baby shower registry had contained actual color. I didn't know how long before she'd be put into the white oxford shirt and black slim skirt that was the female uniform of A-C choice, but I was going to do my best to ensure that day was a long time coming.

Jeff finished getting Jamie ready to go while I fed the dogs and cats and packed Jamie's bag. She'd potty trained herself a month ago. Per Denise, Jamie had asked about it, Denise had explained the concept, and Jamie had done her thing. It made some things easier, but I almost dreaded what she'd do weeks, months, or years ahead of schedule next.

However, among the things it made easier was packing her for babysitting gigs like this one. All the room diapers and wipes would have taken up in the still awesome and reasonably pristine diaper bag was filled with changes of clothes, toys, and, as I looked inside, Poofs.

The cats were herded back into the Feline Winnebago along with whatever Poofs weren't in the diaper bag. The dogs went back on their leashes. We called for Denise, Len, and Kyle. And then I called for the Peregrines. As Jamie had said, in my mind.

"Whoa!" Jeff jumped as twenty-four big birds just sort of appeared. "I hate it when they do that."

Contrived to look innocent. "Yeah. It's sort of freaky."

Jeff gave me the hairy eyeball. "You called them, didn't you?"

Considered lying. Knew he'd know. "Yes. It's easier. You're handling this really well."

"I'm screaming and freaking out on the inside, but am trying to avoid having a huge fight with my wife about things neither one of us can control right before we have what is, according to James, the most important dinner party of our lives."

"Oh. Go you."

"But if you *want* to talk about all of this, feel free. I can handle it. I think."

Chose to circumvent the chat about my newly ex-panded Dr. Doolittle abilities and looked to Bruno. "So, we expect the flock to head over to the Pontifex's residence. Your thoughts?"

"I married the smartest girl in the galaxy."

Bruno winked at Jeff, then cooed, fluffed his feathers, did the weird, fast head bob thing birds seemed to love doing, and clawed, gently, at the carpet.

"Huh. Okay."

"What did he say?" Jeff asked. "And he winked at me, didn't he? Why does that bird wink at people?"

"Yes. Despite your misgivings, Bruno's your counterpart and he likes you. He only winks at a select few. Anyway, they want some of the flock with the kids, and some here, on duty. All the girls are going with the kids; all the boys are staying here on duty. Bruno says we won't even know they're there unless they need to be seen. Or need to save the day."

"There's not some kind of chance I can win an argument with them, is there?"

"No, not really. And, all things considered, it never hurts to have the Peregrines along in stealth mode."

"How many Poofs are staying behind?"

Managed not to look guilty. "A few. You know, same thing, just in case."

Jeff ran his hand through his hair. "We live in a zoo. I'd ask how this happened, but I know. I just don't always believe it." He heaved a sigh. "Okay, fine. Keep the Poofs and Peregrines out of sight. We'll figure out something if they're seen."

"Fake it 'til we make it?"

"As you like to tell me, baby, whatever works."

Denise and the boys arrived, we handed Jamie over with lots of kisses, then she and the pets were trundled down to the basement level to take a gate to the Pontifex's residence.

During Operation Confusion, before we'd moved in as the new Heads of the Diplomatic Corps, I'd been certain we'd find another gate in the Embassy. But searching had turned up only the one gate in the basement level. Everyone else had dismissed this as being normal, even Chuckie after a thorough search had turned up no additional gates.

But the feeling that there were other gates here we just hadn't found yet still tickled me now and then, and this was a now moment.

"Jeff, what if there's a gate we can't see because it's hidden with the same sort of technology used to hide all those underground rooms in the Earth?"

"Then Reynolds, your mother, our NASA Base Team, our squatters the hackers, or someone else would have identified it, based on the new information we have since the invasion." He said it patiently, which was yet more proof that he was a wonderful husband, because I knew he was tired of me worrying about this.

"Hacker International isn't squatting here."

"They're living on the top floor of the Zoo, rent free, with our Operations Team taking care of them like they do the rest of our facilities. I call that squatting."

"They're performing useful services."

"You mean they're playing around. Because that's all the useful I see out of their services."

"Let's not do this, especially because I know we're doing it because we're both nervous. Like you said, we need to avoid fighting before this event. Let's get dressed for the party neither one of us wants to be hosting and hope that nothing explodes."

Jeff stroked my face. "True enough. But I have a better idea."

"Yeah?"

He got the expression on his face where he looked like a big jungle cat about to eat me. I loved that look.

"Yeah," Jeff purred. "Let's get undressed first."

CHAPTER 11

WE WERE MOSTLY NAKED, I was in Jeff's arms with my legs wrapped around his waist, and he was doing wonderful things to my breasts, when the com activated.

"Chiefs, you're needed downstairs."

I stopped yowling like a cat in heat. "Why? No one's supposed to be here for another couple of hours."

"Actually, the first guests are set to arrive in forty-five minutes or less, and Pierre wants everyone prepped on what's going on where. Commander Reader also wants to ensure that we have the right teams assigned to the right politicians."

Jeff sighed. "We'll be down shortly, Walter. Just have to change into our formalwear."

"Yes, sir, Chief, I'll advise."

The com shut off. "You know, I can remember Gladys interrupting us like that, all the time. Is it just some Head of Security thing, or are they watching us on a spy cam so they can interrupt at rotten times?"

"I don't think so," Jeff said with a chuckle. "Though I admit, I'd rather be making love to you than going downstairs." He pulled my head to his and kissed me deeply while he let me slide slowly to the floor. By the time our kiss was done, I was ready to go for it and tell the rest of the gang to handle things in our absence.

But, such was not to be. Jeff patted my bottom and then we got down to the business of getting dressed.

Since I'd done some running around earlier, I took a fast

shower. Proving his dedication to the Diplomatic Corps, Jeff refused to shower with me. Decided to make him pay for this after the party was over, hopefully for hours.

Shocking no one, Jeff put on what he always put on—a black Armani suit, white shirt, and black tie. Despite being promised that diplomats had to wear casual clothing, somehow Jeff had avoided such and I was still impatiently waiting to see his butt in jeans again. A handful of times in three years wasn't enough, really.

I had put my foot down and demanded a dress that wasn't black, white, or black and white. Thanks to Pierre, our Embassy had its own designer on retainer, and Akiko had listened to my pleas. She'd created a lovely green cocktail dress that was slinky without being overtly sexy, and festive without making me look like a badly wrapped present under a Christmas tree.

Akiko also handled all our accessories, so I had lovely shoes that matched without being matchy-matchy, and a larger-sized handbag. Yes, we were in our own home, so I didn't need to carry a purse. But my experience told me I always needed to have my purse on me, if only to grab my Glock, or the adrenaline harpoon Jeff far-too-often needed slammed into his hearts.

I transferred my necessities from my standby big, black, cheap leather purse—aforementioned Glock and harpoon, iPod, earbuds, external speakers, cell phone, special assassin-issued burner phone, hairspray, brush, cash, and I.D. Hey, just because we were supposed to stay in the Embassy complex didn't mean we *would*. I was savvy to the ways of my life now, and it was always better to be prepared.

The handbag had a long strap, allowing me to put it over my head. The dress had been designed for this, so the bag's strap looked like part of the dress' trimming, and the bag itself looked like it belonged right where it was hanging. Yeah, Akiko was that good.

I wasn't big on makeup, so I didn't apply any. Gave my hair a good brushing and decided to go with putting it up in a fancy banana clip. Easy, yet looked like I'd put some real time and care into the 'do.

"You look gorgeous, baby," Jeff said as I finished up. He kissed my neck.

My neck was my main erogenous zone, and he knew it. "Mmmm, you do that any more and we're going to call in as too horny to attend."

"Not an option." He kissed my neck once more, then took my hand and we headed downstairs.

Pierre and Reader kept us all busy handing out assignments and ensuring we all knew what not to say to whom, so much so that the time flew by. Painfully, sure, but at least the ordeal went quickly.

Doreen and Irving Weisman also added in with suggestions and tips. Doreen was the daughter of the former heads of the Diplomatic Corps and Irving was her human husband. Because she'd grown up in this life, Doreen was our most experienced member on staff, and because he was a guy who'd scored a Dazzler—meaning he was incredibly smart—Irving had paid attention and was now as good as Doreen at saying the right things at the right time.

Doreen's parents, Robert and Barbara Coleman, along with the rest of the former Diplomatic Corps, had been eaten by the Poofs, on my order, during Operation Confusion. Doreen had loathed her parents by that point, so she wasn't holding a grudge.

Also, my order or no, the Poofs held a great deal of political sway on Alpha Four, meaning that if the Poofs ate someone, most A-Cs went with the idea that said someone deserved to be Poof Chow. There was polite mourning and then everyone went on about their business. I chose to never argue when my alien relatives by marriage had some whacked out belief that meant they didn't hate me.

Of course, most of the A-Cs had no idea what had happened to said former Diplomatic Corps—though I was sure some had a good guess. The party line was that they'd disappeared and we were still searching for them.

However, Doreen had certainly deserved to know what had happened to her parents. That the Poofs had agreed to chow down had given her a reason to not feel guilty for not feeling bad that her parents were dead. We were all about the silver linings these days.

Doreen had just finished reminding us that smiling and nodding were great, but laughing at bad jokes was better, Pierre had reminded us that our New World Order had created some happy politicians and some tense ones, and

Reader had just finished up stressing how the politicians from our home states were probably the most vital to keep happy, when the doorbell rang.

"Places, everyone," Pierre said. "It's show time."

Walter, who was, as always, on the com, turned on my music mix. The happy sounds of "Party Rock Anthem" by LMFAO met my ears.

"Really?" Jeff asked.

"You all said I should create a tasteful party mixtape."

Jeff looked at Pierre. Who shrugged. "I've learned, Jeff darling, to let Kitty win on the musical choices."

While Jeff grunted and muttered something about classical music and why it was good, Len and Kyle went with Pierre to station themselves as our Embassy's bouncers. Of course, they were bouncers with all the special C.I.A. toys that allowed them to easily spot bugs, hidden firearms, and other pleasantries.

Jeff and I headed to what we called the small salon. As the Co-Head Diplomats, we had the job of initial paw shaking and such. Once our guests had been properly greeted, Pierre led them into the dining room, which had been converted into a cocktail party area, albeit without the cocktails. A-Cs being deathly allergic to alcohol meant we were a teetotaler nation, and because we were on our own land in the Embassy, we enforced that rule as a "religious custom."

Happily, Pierre brought in the most welcome guests—my parents.

"You didn't take a gate?" I asked as I hugged my father, who was in a nicer suit than he normally wore. Appreciated him dressing up for the occasion.

"No, kitten. Your mother felt it would better if we were seen arriving."

"Just glad you're both already here, Sol," Jeff said as he let go of Mom and hugged Dad. "Always nicer when you and Angela are with us." He meant it, too. I'd truly married a great guy, and my parents agreed.

I got my mother's breath-stopping bear hug. "You look perfect, kitten."

"Thanks, Mom. Air . . . need the air."

She released with a laugh. "Sorry. Just been a long week."

"I'll bet." I studied her. She was in a simple black velvet dress that looked great on her. But Mom normally didn't hit me with the bear hugs unless one of us had been in extreme danger prior. "What were you working on?"

She grimaced. "Can't tell you. But, happily, that's because it doesn't involve any of you."

"Well, that's good." I hugged her again, praying the whatever that didn't involve any of us had nothing to do with the Dingo. "Glad you made it through safely, Mom, whatever it was," I whispered in her ear.

Got another bear hug, but this one was shorter. "Me too."

"I do hate to break up the mother and child reunion," Pierre said. "But more guests are coming, and I believe Angela and Sol have assigned duties."

"We do," Dad said. "Lead on, and we'll get to work."

Pierre and my parents headed off as the doorbell rang again. It was going to be a long night.

Unsurprisingly, our nearest neighbors were the next to arrive, in part because most of them had walked across or down the street. By now we knew most of them, and Pierre had a laundry list of their quirks, habits, and dislikes, as well as who was cheating on and with whom.

When we'd first moved to D.C. I'd been forced into the Washington Wife class. I'd hated every moment of it, but, shocking one and all, I'd actually picked up some tips and decorum along the way.

Therefore, I did all the greetings to foreign dignitaries properly. Oh sure, not as well as Jeff did them, but I made do. Of course, I didn't have to give Olga or Adriana any fancy greeting other than a big hug, but I did pull out all the stops and give Olga's husband, Andrei, a decent curtsey. Hey, he was the Romanian ambassador and his wife and granddaughter kept me informed and, in at least one case, alive, so I figured he deserved a good showing from me.

"Don't Get Mad, Get Even" from Aerosmith was playing. "Excellent song choice," Olga said with a wink. "I heartily agree with the sentiment."

As our local neighbors headed to the main room, "Ray Bands" by B.o.B came on. Jeff winced. I ignored it. I had a nice tune from ELO coming right after this one, and that'd teach him for telling me that I had to have some bands other than Aerosmith playing during this party.

Sure the song was about someone trying to get goodies

based on another person's fame. But that was appropriate for D.C. Besides, it was especially fitting considering who I could see on our near horizon.

Sure enough, the invitees that excited me the least were here—the Cabal of Evil had arrived.

CHAPTER 12

I DIDN'T WANT HALF of these people in my home, but Cliff had overruled any and all objections with a very simple point—these people were important enough that slighting them would cause us far more problems than if we just played along and pretended to like them. He'd been saying this to us for months, and we'd listened and played along and, honestly, liked a few of them now. But not all of them.

Of course, many former members of the Cabal of Evil were dead or in prison, all thanks to us. Our importance in the grand scheme of things was proven by the fact that the rest of the Cabal went on as if their former members' deaths or imprisonment had merely been unfortunate circumstances we'd had no choice but to help facilitate. Washington, it really had the best people.

It also had pretty much all the same people it had had before Operation Destruction. What Pierre called our New World Order was simple, but somewhat scary as well. This year was supposed to be an election year, for the House and a third of the Senate. However, due to the massive alien invasion, and terrifying proof that there was a lot of life on other planets—much of it paying attention to Earth—the President had requested that elections be suspended.

It was unprecedented and, per many protesting groups, unconstitutional, but the President wasn't asking for total control. No one was sure Earth wasn't going to be invaded again tomorrow, and the President wanted to ensure that the U.S. government remained stable. And that meant keeping anyone who was holding elected office in place an extra two years, which was when his second term would be ending anyway.

Shocking everyone, Congress and the governors of all fifty states agreed. Most of the countries worldwide were doing the same thing. This probably had a lot to do with what the "visiting dignitary," also known as King Alexander from Alpha Four, had said when he was cleaning up the intergalactic mess. Alpha Four was all about stability, and Alexander had definitely shared that he didn't want to have to come right back with his huge space battle cruisers and explain the Alpha Centaurion position to new folks any time soon.

So protests happened, we were blamed or praised, depending—but mostly blamed—and everyone who'd been elected stayed elected. All of them seemed happy about the extension of power and being able to stave off a re-election campaign for another year or so. But my hopes of one or more of the Cabal losing their seats were definitively dashed. Always the way.

As usual for the Cabal, they all arrived together. Operation Destruction had shifted power in the group, however. Senator Vincent Armstrong had moved from Senator Being Somewhat Manipulated to Big Man on Cabal Campus. He'd made this move because he'd aligned himself with us. That Armstrong owed us favors, as we did him, was something I'd managed to accept over the past few months, albeit unwillingly.

Accepting that Armstrong was planning his run for the Presidency wasn't as hard, because I'd realized that was coming during Operation Destruction. Armstrong had become an extremely pro-alien politician over the past many months, meaning he was considered a Friend of American Centaurion, title totally implied and important. We needed friends, and powerful ones were, these days, good to have.

His wife, Elaine, was with him. I'd gotten to know her over these past months and actually liked her. Sure, she was a career politician's wife, but she wasn't odious, obnoxious, or even overly fake. Mom liked her, too, which was the final seal of approval I required.

Barely had a chance to say hello to the Armstrongs when

the unofficial spokesperson for the Cabal came toward us, smile beaming. On some people this would be pleasant. On Lillian Culver, it was horrific. The woman was attractive, but only at first glance. Longer looks shared that she was all bones and angles, a well-dressed skeleton with skin on. She also possessed the widest mouth this side of a top super villain. I called her Joker Jaws to myself for a reason.

Culver was all in red, including dramatic red lipstick, which just made her look more like the Joker in drag to me. Managed to control my impulse to jerk away from her outstretched paw—I was pretty sure she didn't have an electroshock buzzer hidden in her palm, though I'd never have bet money on this.

However, Culver was a powerful lobbyist for a variety of defense contractors, and therefore a bad person to be overly rude to.

"Kitty, you look amazing," Culver said.

"You, too." Hey, I was amazed with her resemblance to the Joker.

Culver's husband, Abner Schnekedy, self-proclaimed artist, Most Influential Spouse of Someone With Actual Power on Cabal Campus, and odious twit, grinned at me. "Happy Holidays, Kitty."

"To you, too." I was doing great with the short, polite replies, and they were doing great with the not saying anything obnoxious. So far, this part of the event was a success.

My ability to remain monosyllabic was instantly tested. Always the way. Eugene and Lydia Montgomery were the next from the group to come within speaking distance. Lydia was the junior senator from New York, and Eugene was her husband. She was racing as fast as she could into the power centers of D.C. He was dull and normal and an actuary by profession.

When we'd first moved here, Eugene had been my only friend in the Washington Wife class. That friendship had been strained to the breaking point when I'd discovered that he'd been using me as a front for his affair with Nathalie Gagnon-Brewer, who I could see standing with her husband, Representative Edmund Brewer, right behind the Montgomerys.

Nathalie was a French expatriate and a former international model. But unlike Reader, who was a faithful spouse to Gower, Nathalie didn't enjoy her husband's preoccupation with being a fast-tracking politician. She'd been happy being married to a successful California vintner; not as happy married to a political animal. Couldn't blame her, of course.

Meanwhile Eugene had felt ignored and shoved aside by Lydia. Opposites had attracted and she and Eugene had started a passionate affair, which I'd discovered during Operation Assassination.

Over the past months Eugene had moved into the Cabal with what appeared to be ease. Oh, sure, he was clearly Low Man on the Cabal Totem Pole, but he was accepted as one of them now, which meant he was dead to me.

He also kept trying to repair our friendship, but I wasn't having any of it. In part because I couldn't trust that he wasn't trying to renew the relationship in the hopes of yet again using me as his excuse for when he went off to do the deed with Nathalie. Or even worse, for some new, nefarious Cabal plan.

"Hi, Kitty," Eugene said. "It's great to see you."

"Yes." Focused on keeping to the single syllables. I couldn't get into trouble with those, could I?

Lydia nodded. "We need to get together and do a couples' date sometime."

My gaze traveled to Nathalie without benefit of my brain's approval. "Ahh, sure . . ." My only other single syllable options were "No," or "No way in hell," neither of which seemed diplomatic in any way.

Jeff disengaged from Abner and Joker Jaws and rescued me. "We'd love to. We'll need to coordinate schedules." Jeff flashed his Happy Diplomat Smile. "Of course, it's not appropriate to do so tonight."

"Of course not," Lydia said with a bob of her head. "Whenever it's convenient for *you*, Ambassador."

The Brewers stepped up and we were suddenly outnumbered two to one. Brewer and Armstrong had been having a lot of meetings with Jeff over the past months, and Jeff actually seemed to like Brewer. He certainly wanted me to like Brewer, though I'd resisted all the "couples date" ideas Jeff had forwarded. They did the manly handshake-hug-backslap thing and Jeff's smile looked genuine.

Jeff had also tried to get me to hang out with Nathalie,

but while she was, after Armstrong and Elaine, the least objectionable member of the Cabal to me, I couldn't get past the adultery thing. I didn't want to talk about her sleeping with Eugene, I didn't want pretend I didn't remember that she was sleeping with Eugene, I didn't want to hear about why she was sleeping with Eugene, and I saw no way to avoid any of this if she and I went to lunch or tea or whatever. So whenever Nathalie tried to set something up, I had Pierre explain how busy, busy, busy I was.

"You're a vision, Ambassador Martini," Brewer said to me after he and my husband had finished being all Washington Gangsta.

"So are you," Nathalie purred at Jeff.

My mind chose this moment to note that Lydia, like Nathalie, was giving my husband goo-goo eyes. Brewer was giving me an appraising up and down glance. Eugene looked bitterly at Jeff and Brewer, then shot me a Sad Panda look.

My mind chose this moment to query as to whether I thought Lydia was hitting on my husband, suggesting a foursome, or, just for grins and giggles, if perhaps she knew about Eugene's affair and wanted to go for a Tri-Couple Tournament. My mind also wanted to know if the Brewers might be thinking the same thing. Sometimes I hated my mind.

Before I'd met the Cabal of Evil I'd never entertained thoughts like this. Sadly, so many of them had suggested so many different "fun" ideas during Operation Assassination that I now associated them equally with World Domination Dreams and Triple-X Porn.

While I wondered if brain bleach really existed, Eugene moped at me and Lydia and Nathalie continued to check Jeff out. Brewer continued to do the same with me while talking to Jeff about wine and how Christmas differed in D.C. from California—not as much snow in Brewer's part of California was the shocking reveal. Jeff shared the equally shocking news that it was the same in our parts of Arizona and New Mexico. Wondered if they had some Bro-Coded Message thing going, or if they were both somehow enjoying this conversation.

Right before I was ready to call the Poofs and ask them to eat everyone, the evening got just that much better. Guy

Gadoire and his husband, Vance Beaumont, moved into the salon and shoved Eugene aside.

Gadoire was a lobbyist for the tobacco industry. Vance spent his time lounging around in fashion-forward outfits ripped right out of the pages of *GQ*. Unlike Reader, he didn't carry them off perfectly, but he made do. To say they weren't my favorite couple was, potentially, the understatement of the year.

"My darling Missus Martini," Gadoire said as he grabbed the hand I wasn't offering and did his customary slobberfest that passed for kissing in his world. Gadoire spoke in a French accent all of us were sure was faked—he sounded far more like Pepé Le Pew than Maurice Chevalier. He didn't possess an iota of the charm either one of those famous French actors had, either. That Nathalie hadn't called him on his faking being from her native country was either a testament to her kindness or lack of interest.

"All Over the World" by ELO ended and "Sexy and I Know It" from good old LMFAO came on. I knew I hadn't put it onto the mix, so I assumed Kyle had told Walter to play it in honor of "Monsieur Love" as I called Gadoire in private. Made a mental note to hurt Kyle later while I did my best to control the Inner Hyena.

Somehow during Operation Destruction Gadoire and Vance had convinced Senator Armstrong and themselves that they were my besties. They still seemed to believe it, all evidence of my dislike to the contrary.

Vance broke protocol, pulled me away from Guy, and gave me a big hug. "Kitty, you look gorgeous."

Before I could escape or reply, Vance bent down and whispered in my ear. "Something's going on, something bad, and I think we're all in danger."

CHAPTER 13

THE LAST TIME Vance had shared a dramatic "we're all gonna die" message with me had been during Operation Assassination. He'd actually been right, even though it had been a ploy to get me to "share a bed of love" with him and Gadoire.

I didn't get a chance to ask Vance any questions, though, because Senator Zachary Kramer and his wife, Marcia, moved up for their Happy Hellos. They were the remainder of the Cabal and were both clearly displeased with being last in the Shake the Paws line.

"Your dress is amazing," Marcia said to me without preamble. "I don't know what you're paying that designer, but she won't design for anyone else in the Beltway."

"Akiko's very loyal." She was. A-Cs had plenty of money, the Diplomatic Corps in particular—since we were the showcase and lobbyist faction for the entire A-C community—and we paid well. Akiko wasn't on an exclusive retainer to our Embassy, but she was particular about the clients she took, and she'd told me in private she didn't care for Marcia. Needless to say, I felt Akiko was a girl of taste and refinement.

Marcia sniffed. "Well, we *should* all be wearing black."

"We should?"

She nodded. "Poor Wendell passed away an hour ago."

Had no freaking idea who Wendell was. Now had the entire Cabal staring at me, obviously waiting for me to say something appropriate.

"That's too bad." It was lame, but at least coherent and hopefully didn't give away the fact that I had no clue as to who or what we were talking about. Times like this, I really missed killing superbeings for a living. It was so much easier.

"We'd hoped Representative Holmes would have pulled through his illness," Jeff said smoothly, with just the right amount of sorrow in his tone. The man was incapable of not being great at any job you gave him. What a pity his wife wasn't as smooth.

"Ah, yes," I agreed, desperately hoping my tone matched Jeff's. "Should we cancel the party?"

"Oh, no," Marcia said with a tiny laugh. "The show must go on."

"Must it?" Whoops. My brain had allowed my mouth to share what I was really thinking.

Kramer nodded. "Wendell would understand, and want it that way."

"He would?"

"Oh, yes. Wendell served for decades—he, better than most, understood how the process can't stop just because we've lost a valued member."

We faced death on a regular basis, so I'd given this idea some thought over the past couple of years. Upon my untimely, or even long-awaited, death, I expected my friends and co-workers to be sad, and sobbing uncontrollably while tossing themselves onto my coffin wouldn't be going too far. In all the "my death" daydreams I'd ever had, seeing the gang partying had never entered the picture, but then again, I wasn't a career politician.

Saved by the bell. "I must move you lovely people on," Pierre said. "I'm sure the Ambassadors will find time to converse with you once the party's in full swing." As Pierre indicated the door, "Get the Party Started" came on, so, per Pink, she'd already handled that for us.

Several A-C agents—recognizable in their black Armani suits, crisp white shirts, and all-around hotness—escorted the Cabal to their next stop. Wasn't sure if this meant Pierre had called in reinforcements or if the agents were always on the roster. Pierre tended to keep the little things from me, which I appreciated.

"Jeff, while we have a moment alone, Vance just shared that the game was afoot and we were all in danger."

Jeff sighed. "I didn't get fear from him. I got excitement."

"Oh, so it's his usual 'I'll concoct a wild danger theory so Kitty will be so impressed she'll sleep with me and my love, Le Pew' ploy?"

"I'd assume so. But I had to put my blocks up so—"

Before Jeff could finish the next folks to arrive were ushered in. Making for a nice change, it was people we'd always liked and who I was glad would be around at least two more years—Senator and Mrs. McMillan. "Ambassadors, good to see you."

"Good to see you, too, Don." Jeff grinned as they shook hands while Kelly—who was, though older than me, a sorority sister—and I did our sorority's not-so-secret handshake and such before we hugged each other.

McMillan laughed. "I'm sure it is. You ladies done with your high-fiving?"

"For now," Kelly replied. "Who's assigned to ensure we're enjoying ourselves?"

"That would be Michael." Caroline, who was McMillan's Girl Friday, joined us. Now probably wasn't the time to tell her that Peter the Dingo Dog had fond memories and wanted me to say "hi" for him. I'd save that for a bathroom trip or something. "He's waiting for us. Impatiently."

"He can wait a minute longer," Kelly said with a sly grin. "Good to keep him on his toes."

Caroline laughed. "I suppose." Now that she was here, the three of us did the sorority secret stuff required for three or more. Hey, it was a rule, and one of the few I liked to follow all the time.

"Love the music," Kelly said when we were done, as "The Farm" by Aerosmith came on. Hey, just because I couldn't have it be all Aerosmith all the time didn't mean I couldn't make it a lot of Aerosmith with other cool songs added in.

"And I love you for loving it."

"Kit-Kat always has the best tunes," Caroline said.

"And the best clothes," Kelly said with a laugh. Unlike Marcia, she didn't seem bitter about it, but then, she looked gorgeous and was a more normal, secure person than Marcia. Not that this was hard to achieve.

"Sometimes I clean up nicely."

Caroline snorted. "You look great. And I know I do, too.

I love being considered part of this Embassy—Akiko's awesome."

"Caro Syrup, you're so modest these days. Must be from having the A-C Player of the Year panting after you."

Caroline grinned. "That never hurts."

McMillan chuckled. "I approve of Mister Gower so much more than anyone else you've shown an interest in, Caroline."

"And your approval is the deciding factor," Kelly said with a laugh. "Don, you're such a romantic meddler."

"Hey, he was right not to like Peter the Dingo Dog." Hoped I said this with the right joking, casual tone, and in a way that didn't indicate I'd seen said Dingo only a couple hours earlier.

Caroline nodded. "I'd rather date someone you approve of, Senator."

"And that's why she's indispensable," McMillan said. "Our Caroline thinks I'm always right."

Kelly winked. "I pay her extra for that service."

We all laughed, then they headed off to find Michael, Caroline leading the way, as Pierre brought in the next arrival. "Ambassadors, I believe you should move into the general areas now," he said as he handed off a man about my age. He had the typical younger politician look, but I guessed his heritage as Latin/Mexican and American Indian.

Because of this instruction from Pierre, I knew who we were talking to. "Representative Reyes, it's so good to finally meet you."

Reyes flashed a smile worthy of Jeff or Kevin. "Please, Ambassador, call me Santiago. I prefer to be on a first name basis with the most important constituents from my District."

Reyes was the newest member of the House of Representatives. The former rep from New Mexico's 2nd Congressional District had died in office a few months ago. The only new elections allowed this year were to fill seats opened due to the death or disablement of a congressman. Reyes had won the special election and had arrived in D.C. at the start of December.

Normally that would have meant he'd have had about two weeks to unpack and shake hands and then head back to New Mexico for the holidays. But of course this year, no one in the world was functioning on "normal."

An additional presidential decree—added as a coda to the main suspension of general elections decree—and plain old common sense had held all of Congress in Washington for most of the year, holidays included.

Congress hadn't complained, much, because they knew without a shadow of a doubt that all the planets in the Alpha Centauri system were watching us, along with God alone knew who else. The last thing the U.S. or other world governments wanted was to look like they weren't busy, efficient, and, most importantly, paying attention. Stable and hardworking, those were the current Earth Government Watchwords.

"Oh, I don't know that we're the most important, Santiago," Jeff said as he and Reyes shook hands. "But it's always nice to be appreciated."

Pierre's unsubtle hint was also to remind us that Reyes was our "assigned" politician. Now that he was here, we could stop being the Reception Committee and focus on our one dude. Reyes had run on the "Aliens Are Our Friends" platform, and we wanted to be sure he still felt that way after the party.

We left the small salon and joined the others in the dining room, exchanging the usual chitchat that was expected in these situations. Jeff excelled at it, God alone knew how. Me, I focused on smiling a lot and not allowing my body to move to the beat. Hey, Pitbull's "International Love" was on.

Pierre and the Elves had moved things around so the room now looked easily as nice as any fancy hotel ballroom. A-C agents, both male and female, were mingling with the guests, some in serving capacities, some functioning as our version of Booth Babes at a trade show, all focused on security. We had a complement of Security A-Cs around, too, but they were being very obvious. The agents were blending in nicely. So far, so very good.

One of the agents who was on server duty came by with fruit juice cocktails. Pierre and the Elves had come up with a variety of drinks that were so good you didn't really care that they didn't have vodka or rum in them. "Tempt you to something completely nonalcoholic, Congressman?"

"Santiago, please, Ambassador Katt-Martini. And yes,

thank you. I don't drink, either. It's nice to be at a party where that's celebrated."

Personally, I missed having a drink now and then, but I'd gotten over it. Kissing Jeff was so much better than any alcohol in the world.

"Okay, Santiago," I said, as we sipped our drinks. "And it's Kitty."

He smiled. "I'd been told you weren't the, ah, formal type."

We were being eyed by the Cabal. Tried not to feel like a zebra being appraised by a pride of lions, or a pride of perverts, which was probably a more accurate description. Failed.

"Depends on the situation, Santiago." And my level of nerves, which were, on the scale of ten, heading toward eleven. Prayed I wouldn't spill anything on my dress—it would make Marcia far too happy. Apparently, though, nervous meant I was giving the short, politically correct answers. Score one for nerves.

Reader and Tim, who were both in different parts of the room, came over as soon as they saw us. "Santiago, good to see you," Reader said.

"I second that," Tim said as Reyes shook their hands.

"Great to see you, James, Tim. Nice to get to visit how the other half lives."

Reyes, Tim, and Reader chuckled over this. I took it to mean they already had an inside joke. Did my best not to feel a tiny bit betrayed and more than a little left out. If I'd still been the Head of Airborne, I'd be in on the joke, too.

It shouldn't have surprised me that they all knew each other. Just because Reyes was newly elected didn't mean he was new to dealing with Centaurion Division.

"So, Ambassadors, what do you think is the most important thing we can focus on to make your people feel more at home on Earth?" Reyes asked.

"Excuse me?" Jeff sounded confused.

"They've been here since the nineteen-sixties," I replied. "They feel at home on Earth. Most of them were born on Earth, my husband included."

"Ah, what Kitty means," Jeff said, recovering quickly, "is that we just want to be accepted like any other residents of this planet."

Reyes grinned. "James told me that would get a rise out of you." He, Reader, and Tim all had another group chuckle.

"Yeah, thanks for that."

Senator McMillan joined us, as did Senator Armstrong. Their wives were together, being entertained by Michael and Caroline. "Ambassador Katt-Martini has a good sense of humor, Santiago," Armstrong said. "But you can't blame her for being a little touchy."

McMillan nodded. "We really need to get the latest alien issues settled, preferably once and for all."

The men all looked somber now. Took the leap. "What's just happened that all of you know about but I don't? And I'd better not hear that it's above my security clearance."

"Never again on my watch," Armstrong said seriously. Considering what had gone down during Operation Destruction, it wasn't a total surprise that Armstrong was backing me on the clearance issue.

"We have some legislation being proposed in the House," Reyes said. "The wording's such that it could lead to restricted freedoms for 'illegal aliens.'"

"Let me guess. The wording is also such that it puts into question whether or not the A-Cs on Earth are here legally, doesn't it?"

"I married the smartest girl in the galaxy. However, that bill's a long way away from passing, at least from what I've been told." Jeff looked at Reyes intently. "So, what haven't I been told?"

CHAPTER 14

I PREPPED MYSELF for words of doom and destruction.

"Not much." Reyes shrugged. "But anything can be sped through when the right incentives are given or applied."

Managed not to say that Reyes really had a way with the anticlimax, but decided I was happier with his answer than the one I'd been expecting.

"Well, that's all mysterious. Want to share what incentives are being tossed around, or are we just shooting the general blah, blah, blah right now so that Jeff and I get to spend the rest of the month not sleeping due to worry?"

"It's the usual political maneuvering," McMillan answered. "Some see the current state of affairs to be beneficial, some want to take advantage for their own reasons, both good and bad."

As "Everybody Wants to Rule the World" from Tears for Fears came on, someone touched my elbow. Jeff shot an annoyed look at the toucher.

Turned to see a tall, slender, incredibly handsome guy with black wavy hair who looked Indian but I knew to be a pure-blooded A-C. I knew him in part because he was in the Armani fatigues just like all the rest of the A-C males, but mostly because we'd spent a lot of time with Rajnish Singh since Operation Destruction. He wasn't full-time at the Embassy yet, but it was likely only a matter of time, because Jeff's charm needed more of an assist than the rest of the Diplomatic Corps were providing on a regular basis.

The A-Cs had the same number of skin tones and body types as humans did. When they'd arrived on Earth they'd all been housed in the U.S. Once world governments were advised and the right approvals given, the A-Cs expanded out and created bases all over the world. The A-Cs with the most appropriate looks and body types went to the countries they'd blend in with the best, took appropriate names and surnames, and increased each host country's overall hotness level. Raj was from New Delhi Base.

This base wasn't the biggest or even most active of the worldwide bases; superbeings weren't as common in that part of the world as they were in America, go U.S.A. for the ick-factor win. And while there were plenty of smaller bases all over the world, Euro Base, which was located in Paris, and Moscow Base handled or took the lead on the majority of the international incidents.

So the agents from New Delhi Base tended toward two types—the laidback and low-key and the extremely driven to prove they could run with the big dogs. I still hadn't figured out which one Raj was.

"Hi, Raj, what's up?"

Raj shot me a smile that gave Reader's cover boy smile a run for its money. "Excuse me, Ambassador," he said quietly. "But there's a gentleman at the door requesting you."

Normal sentences, made to sound incredibly thrilling. Yep, Raj was a troubadour. It wasn't the most popular of talents within the Field and Imageering sides of Centaurion Division, but it was a godsend in terms of the political side. We needed more troubadours, but right now, Raj was splitting his time between us and New Delhi Base, with us getting about ninety percent of him.

"New boyfriend?" Jeff asked, only half-joking.

Shot him the "really?" look while Reader rolled his eyes and Tim snorted. "I doubt it."

"Why does someone want to see Kitty and not me?" Jeff was pushing the worry.

"Are you picking up anything negative?" Everyone we were with was aware of Jeff's empathic talents, so asking wasn't revealing anything classified.

"No, not really." He looked slightly uncomfortable and I gave myself a duh. He'd told me he'd put his emotional blocks up and with all the people in the Embassy right now, he had to have them set to high. So he could get the strong, rage-level emotions, but he wasn't going to be picking up nuanced emotions at this time.

"It's someone who said he isn't invited to the party and doesn't wish to crash it, Ambassador. He says he has an important, private message for Ambassador Katt-Martini."

"Maybe it's more dirty pictures."

Armstrong choked on his fruit juice cocktail while the other men laughed. "Please God, not that again," Armstrong said when he could breathe.

Frankly, I doubted dirty pictures were waiting for me. Figured it was probably Buchanan—if he'd remembered that he'd seen me holding the package I'd told him I'd disposed of, he might want to talk to me alone.

"You're sure it's okay, Raj?" Jeff, who wasn't laughing, asked.

"I'll stay with her, Ambassador."

Jeff kissed my cheek. "Don't be too long with your boyfriend Buchanan. I get jealous." Nice to see Jeff had made the same assumption as me.

"Really? You? Who'd believe that?" I kissed his cheek as well, then let Raj lead me off to the front door. "What does Malcolm need?"

Our foyer was remarkably empty, considering how many people we had in the Embassy right now. I heard Pierre call everyone to dinner, meaning that the elevators and stairways were going to be busy while everyone headed for the second floor and the walkway to the Zoo.

"I have no idea, it's not Mister Buchanan at the door."

Stopped walking. "Raj, just who is at the door? In fact, why did you get the door instead of Pierre?"

"I took over for you and Ambassador Martini at the initial greeting stop so you two could spend time with Representative Reyes. I took over the door for Pierre so he could keep the party moving along." He cocked his head at me. "Am I frightening you for some reason?"

"Depends on who's at the door."

Raj sighed. "Someone who said it was vitally important that he speak with you immediately. Just as I told the ambassador."

Looked around. "Where are Len and Kyle?"

"Outside, with your visitor."

Wasn't sure that this was an improvement on things. Wasn't sure if I was overreacting to the entire situation, either. Only one way to find out.

I opened the door.

Len and Kyle were nowhere to be seen. Neither was anyone else.

CHAPTER 15

"**R**AJ, what in the hell is going on?"

"They were right here!" He sounded shocked, but troubadour talent meant he was one of the best actors out there. Raj could have been faking it, or he could be as shocked as he sounded. I didn't know him well enough to be sure.

"Come inside, close the door, and be quiet." Buchanan's voice was behind us, meaning he'd been inside the Embassy. Knowing Buchanan, he'd been inside from the moment he brought me back this afternoon and none of us had noticed him. My Dr. Strange theory seemed amazingly sound.

Since it *was* Buchanan talking, I did what he said. Turned around to see that he was not only inside but in an Armani tux. Buchanan wasn't quite good-looking enough to pass for an A-C, but he came close.

He also looked to be quite alone. "Where are the boys?"

Buchanan rolled his eyes. "I moved them and your visitor inside before we had a horrific incident on our hands." He gave Raj a derisive look. "You know, what the Junior Ambassador here should have done."

"Ambassador Martini doesn't want just anyone allowed inside," Raj said, voice clipped. "I saw no reason to go against his wishes."

Buchanan shook his head, spun on his heel, and started for the stairway to the basement. Raj and I followed him.

Went down the stairs to find the boys with guns trained on a third man. He was older, with short gray hair, gray eyes, and a stocky but muscular build. He stood ramrod straight, as if he were standing at attention, but he was in a regular suit, not a uniform. I didn't recognize him at all. "Who's Public Enemy Number One here?"

The man looked straight at me. "I'm Colonel Marvin Hamlin."

"You're the infamous Hammy?" He didn't look like a man who would appreciate a nickname of any kind. He looked like a man who wanted to be called "sir," not Hammy.

"To my friends." He cleared his throat. "I know we aren't friends, but . . . I need your help."

Colonel Hamlin had been in charge of Andrews Air Force Base right up until a couple days before Operation Destruction. He'd left Andrews for lunch and never been seen since. He was Cliff's former boss, and he was also, per Cliff and everyone else, very anti-alien. This was one of the reasons Colonel Arthur Franklin had been moved over to take charge of Andrews. Hamlin's disappearance had sped up the process, but that was probably good, because Franklin was a friend and had worked with us to save the day.

Pulled out my phone. "Let me get Cliff, Chuckie, and Jeff down here."

"No!" Hamlin jumped toward me, earning a nice body slam from Kyle that sent him into the wall.

"Why don't you want them called?"

Hamlin regained his balance. "Because I don't know who I can trust. I've been on the run for months."

"From who?" Buchanan asked. "And why?"

Hamlin shook his head. "I'm not sure who. People have been trying to kill me is why. But I believe I know why they're trying to eliminate me."

"And that reason is?" Really wanted to get one of the guys down here. But under the circumstances, with four of my guys here already, I could probably wait for the full explanation. I dropped my phone back into my purse.

Hamlin noted this and relaxed a bit. "I believe I've found the trail that will lead to the highest-level government conspiracy."

"There are a lot of those." So far in my experience, there was a high-level government conspiracy being hatched every week.

Hamlin nodded. "Yes, there are. But I believe they all stem from a single source."

"You mean one group's pulling all the strings?"

"I believe it's a single individual, with the right connections. And the brainpower to think well ahead of the rest of us."

"If that's true, then how is it you're still alive?" Len asked.

"Training, experience, and not a small amount of luck. I've been in hiding for well over a year."

"Wait a minute. You disappeared from Andrews the Friday before Operation Destruction started. That was less than a year ago."

"Excuse me?" Hamlin looked confused.

"She means the alien invasion that was stopped by the very aliens you don't like," Buchanan said.

"Ah. I don't know who was pretending to be me, but I actually disappeared last year, in November. Right after I'd discovered some discrepancies with a variety of Titan Security contracts."

"That was just before Jamie was born." None of the men in the room with me had been on our team at that time. Meant I was either on my own or needed to bring someone down from the party.

Hamlin nodded. "Your child was indicated as being an important factor."

Decided to forge on, based on the fact that, blocks or not, Jeff might be able to pick up the fact that my anger had spiked. People trying to steal, hurt, use, and terrify my daughter did that to me for some reason.

"What else?"

"I almost don't know where to start." Our expressions must have told Hamlin to pick a spot and start running his yap. "There are a variety of underhanded actions going on, or there were. Supersoldier projects in Paraguay and France. A super-drug to be tested on schoolchildren, also in France. Bioweapons. Assassinations. A variety of world domination schemes. Coordinated anti-alien activities designed to wipe the Alpha Centaurions off the face of the Earth. Just as many plans to force them to act as U.S. or world military."

"We know about, as in have stopped, most of those,

though probably not all. What about an alien invasion from a planetary system other than Alpha Centauri?"

Hamlin nodded. "And more besides. Some of the schemes were clearly set up to fail. Some seemed to exist as either a smokescreen or as a backup plan. I'd only begun to scratch the surface when I realized I had to run for my life."

"How did you know to disappear?"

"There was an assassination squad waiting for me at my home. I know how to spot them. It didn't take much for me to realize I'd been set up for assassination because I'd discovered the start of the real trail toward the Mastermind."

Wondered if said squad was made up of Peter the Dingo Dog and Surly Vic. They were right in the fact that I wouldn't care about Hamlin. At least, five minutes ago I wouldn't have cared. Now, I wasn't so sure.

"And no one noticed you were missing?" Raj asked.

Hamlin shrugged. "I have no idea how they could have had someone impersonate me for so long. For a short time, yes. But not for months."

Len looked at me. "They could have if they put an android in his place."

"I agree, but why have that android leave right before Operation Destruction?"

"To discredit me," Hamlin said before anyone else could answer. "To make me the fall guy."

"He has a point," Buchanan said.

"I knew I'd truly found the start of the trail to the Mastermind the moment no one started looking for me once I'd disappeared. So, why not have whoever, or whatever, was impersonating me disappear at a crucial time? It would be the last nail in my coffin."

Buchanan nodded slowly. "Colonel Hamlin has been discredited. And at least half the powers that be feel he was the other 'captain' involved in the invasion."

True enough. We'd spent time wondering if Hamlin, who was described by one and all as anti-alien but a good man nevertheless, was also the "good man" the late Antony Marling's beloved parrot, Bellie, had been talking about. Bellie now lived with Mister Joel Oliver, our personal paparazzo. Oliver wasn't invited to tonight's event because he tended to make politicians very nervous. But I wondered if I needed to give him a call.

"Based on the word of a parrot. The accurate word, but still."

"A parrot?" Hamlin asked weakly.

"It's a long story. But Malcolm's right—you certainly stood out as the likely 'captain' in place to cover the Parisian part of the supersoldier offensive or lack thereof for Operation Destruction."

"Well, I wasn't the 'captain,' but I agree that my 'disappearing' when you thought I did would make anyone believe I was involved."

"What happened to his android, then?" Kyle asked. "Mister Reynolds got a full listing from King Alexander of all the androids involved in the battle—Colonel Hamlin wasn't one of them."

Unpleasant thought occurred. "How do we know Hammy here isn't an android?"

"Short of killing him?" Buchanan asked. "Not too sure. Emotional readings won't matter. Perhaps one of the imageers could read a picture of him."

"No imageers. No empaths." Hamlin sounded emphatic. "I don't trust them."

"We don't trust you, so that makes us even. Right now, we can't be sure you're really a human being."

"By that token, how can I know you're human beings?" Hamlin asked. He looked at Raj. "Some of you aren't."

"That's it, I'm done acting like an ambassador. You get the real me, lucky you. Stop insulting the people with me or I'm going to kick you so hard in the balls we'll know for sure if you're an android or a real person."

Hamlin tried the stare-down. Always hilarious, since the only people who could win this against me were Mom and Chuckie. "Agreed. And . . . I apologize."

"Smart man. Accepted. For now. Look, we didn't invite you in here to insult any of us or just to hang out and shoot the breeze. You don't like us, you don't trust us, and you're on the run. So why are you here?"

"I came to talk to you, Missus Martini."

Chose to ignore him not using my official title. I'd kind of told him not to, after all. "Why so?"

Hamlin looked straight at me. "Because you were identified as Enemy Number One by whoever's behind everything. And that means you're the only person I can trust."

CHAPTER 16

LET THAT SIT on the air for a bit. Due to Operation Confusion, we all knew I was considered Enemy First Class by the League of Evil Super-Geniuses and Crazed Megalomaniacs. But if Hamlin knew this, too, that might mean he was telling the truth.

"Okay, Hammy. May I call you Hammy?"

"If I say no will that stop you?"

"Wow, no, it won't."

He shrugged. "Then by all means. What should I call you?"

"Kitty will do. So, let's belay the human or android worry. We have a variety of excellent doctors on staff who can probably determine your status in a fast and safe way. Let's go back to your disappearance. You were sniffing around. Why?"

"There were discrepancies with some of the Titan Security contracts, as I said. I pulled their records, and then started looking into any business even tenuously connected to Titan."

"And you found what?"

"Strong ties to a variety of companies. Gaultier Enterprises and their subsidiaries, the philanthropist Ronaldo Al Dejahl and his many businesses and subsidiaries, a host of other, less influential businesses. They have ties to a variety of organizations, including Club Fifty-One, which, due to your, ah, fine work, we know to be a widespread anti-alien organization. But there were plenty of others, including organizations thought to be benign."

"The Al Dejahl terrorist organization?"

"Yes, absolutely."

"Fabulous. So, Titan pretty much has or had less than Six Degrees of Kevin Bacon with, what, everything and everyone?"

"Pretty much, yes. Obviously, some of those connections were legitimate and not underhanded. But not all. At first I thought everything stemmed from Titan. But further digging showed that Titan was taking direction from someone else."

"Name who you think was in charge."

"I have no idea." Hamlin sighed. "Antony Marling and Madeline Cartwright were both influential. I believe Madeline was the brains of their operation, however. John Cooper was definitely involved with the Al Dejahl Corporation, as was Esteban Cantu. Herbert Gaultier was in bed with all these people and many more, including the late Leventhal Reid whom I know you knew."

Repressed the shudder thinking of Reid always gave me. "Go on."

"And before you tell me, I know four of those people are now dead and Cantu is in a very severe form of custody, I also know you haven't learned anything useful from him."

"How do you know that?"

"I haven't survived on the run and in hiding because I'm without survival skills, young lady. I also happen to possess computer skills."

"You mean hacking skills."

"I mean skills that were important in my career."

"Colonel Hamlin was in intelligence before he took a desk job," Buchanan said.

"Ah, so you have spy skills. Okay, works for me. So, what else did you learn, Mister Former Spy?"

"I learned that most of these activities were being protected and hidden by very high level clearances."

"Legitimate or forged clearances?"

Hamlin shook his head. "I have no idea. I wasn't able to dig far enough before I was discovered. I can say that I expected a full military investigation over my disappearance, but I haven't been pursued or investigated by the military."

"Not even after Operation Destruction?"

"No. There is no military investigation going on that is even remotely interested in me."

"That's bizarre." Thought about his wording. "But some-one's after you and investigating you, right?"

"Correct."

"My mother would be for sure, as would Chuckie. As in, the P.T.C.U. and the C.I.A."

"It's not them. I mean, I know they're investigating me, but they're not the ones sending hit men and similar after me."

Figured I might as well ask right now. "The Dingo, by any chance?"

"He was after me for a while. But he stopped his pursuit earlier this year." Interesting. Wondered if that pursuit was back on. Well, I had a way to find out. But I couldn't call my "uncle" and check right now.

"Probably after you brokered that deal with him," Bu-chanan said to me. He knew? How did he always know? I hadn't told Mom about that. Wondered if Buchanan had. Decided to worry about this later.

"Deal?" Raj asked.

"Not important now," I said quickly. "What we need is to determine if we believe Hammy here, and, if we do, what we're going to do to help him."

My phone chose this moment to ring. Dug it out of my handbag again. "Where are you?" Jeff asked, voice low. "We're about to sit down to dinner and you and Raj are noticeably absent."

"We're not having sex, if that's what you're worried about."

"Ha ha ha. This is me laughing about the silly reason you have for not being here yet." Jeff didn't sound like he was enjoying this "joke."

"Gotcha. We'll be right there. I'll fill you in once we have a moment alone." We hung up. "Malcolm, we need to get upstairs. Raj and I in particular, but since the boys are also supposed to be at the dinner, them too. Are you okay with Hammy here?"

Buchanan didn't look happy. "I suppose." Knew he wasn't happy being limited to the basement of the Embassy when we were going over to the Zoo.

"I'm open to other suggestions."

"I'll come up with something, Missus Chief. You head off and be diplomatic. Don't spill anything on your dress."

"*Just* when I was starting to feel for you, Malcolm. Hammy, we'll be back, um, somewhere in the nearish future. Please give Malcolm whatever other information you have so we can get rolling on your problem sooner as opposed to later. You should be safe in here."

"I hope so. Ambassador," he said as I turned to leave, "I know you want to share this with others. Please don't. You have friends who could be the Mastermind."

"You mean Chuckie." Controlled the anger, but it was difficult.

"I do mean Mister Reynolds. I also mean Cliff. Sadly, I also mean your mother. While none of them are at the top of my suspects list, they're all positioned well enough and, most importantly, brilliant enough to be doing this."

"My mother isn't trying to kill me at every freaking turn."

"I'm sure she's not. But you need to be thinking in this way. Whoever is behind all of this, and it's a vast network of conspiracies and threats, is someone unsuspected, because none of the people I named have the slightest idea who was pulling their strings."

"Okay. I don't like it, but I understand what you're saying." Knew Jeff was waiting beyond impatiently, but had to ask one last question. "What about Leventhal Reid? Was he unaware?"

"I don't know," Hammy answered slowly. "He's been dead long enough that I didn't spend as much time on him as I did some of the others."

"Huh. Well, if there was ever a man who wanted to perpetrate evil on the world for grins and giggles, it was him."

"We'll go over it, Missus Chief. Head off before your husband tries to kill all of us out of jealous frustration."

"I don't think it's jealousy right now, Malcolm, so much as my current and total entertaining failure."

"We'll fix that," Raj said confidently.

Buchanan, Len, and Kyle all exchanged a look that said they didn't believe this was possible.

"I currently like Raj more than all of you. Put together."

Buchanan grinned. "Then I'll make a note to expect the Junior Ambassador to become the new focus of Mister Chief's jealousy in about five minutes from now."

CHAPTER 17

ON THAT NOTE of potentially prescient doom, Raj, the boys, and I left. I took Len's hand, Raj grabbed Kyle, and we used the slow hyperspeed to get to the walkway section on the second floor. The boys only gagged a little when we stopped.

"Good job, Kitty," Len managed. "We didn't overshoot or hit a wall or anything."

"Christopher's been making me practice." A lot. And I was doing it because these days he was at Evil Personal Trainer From Hell levels. But it had paid off all day today, so that was one in the semi-win column.

We walked quickly down the corridor. It was nicely done, very sturdy, with bulletproof glass on either side, so you could look out onto the street and Sheridan Circle without the risk of a sniper killing you—a design perk I personally appreciated.

Both ends of the corridor could also be sealed off, again with strong doors whose windows had bulletproof glass. We might not be housing in the Bunker district of D.C., but we were going to ensure that we couldn't be easily overrun or overtaken.

The Zoo's street level was where our animals "housed" when they were on display. Because we'd had to gut and redo most of this building, we'd actually left the second floor as mostly open space with a full, top-of-the-line and giant kitchen, as well as a whole bank of bathrooms. Per A-C regulations, only one stall had a gate in it.

The fourth floor was for extra Embassy personnel and staff, as needed. Some on a rotating basis, some, like the A-Cs assigned to walk our dogs, were sticking around until they could score a better job. The fifth floor now housed Hacker International, along with their fantastic state-of-the-art computer center and our stationary floater gate, which was much less of an oxymoron than Military Intelligence.

Stairs were the only option from the first floor to the second floor. A-Cs could all move faster than any elevator, and we didn't want the general public having easy access to the upper levels. Once on the second floor, however, there were two elevators that handled the rest of the floors. We waved to the A-Cs and humans on food prep duty—I chose not to ask what world famous chef was shouting orders at everyone as we went by—and got into one of said elevators.

Pierre had set things up so that we could alter the second floor any way that we needed or wanted to. However, he'd also ensured the third floor would be a showcase.

The elevator doors opened and for a moment I wasn't sure if Jamie had had a hand in the decorations. The place glittered, though it wasn't glittering in pink, so that was one small one for the win column.

The floors were shiny marble; the walls were covered with fine art interspersed with fine sculptures. We had a blown glass ceiling filled with celestial bodies, including a glass bas-relief of the Alpha Centauri system.

I was used to all of this, though I still questioned the wisdom of these very expensive, very breakable things being housed in the Zoo. But Pierre insisted that's what insurance was for.

For tonight's festivities, Pierre had added small, white, twinkling lights all over the place. It was like stepping into a fairyland.

A fairyland that was doubling as the Correspondents' Dinner Lite. We'd discussed it, and while one long table sounded extremely royal, common sense said that round tables seating ten would probably be more practical. So the third floor looked like the prettiest, glitteriest convention ballroom ever.

Jeff was at the very far end of the room, naturally. Pierre had the room laid out like an obstacle course, too. It was impossible to go in a straight line from the elevator to any table beyond about one. There were a lot of people to get past and tables to wind through before I could reach my husband and my seat.

We'd assigned Embassy and Centaurion Division personnel to each table, so our team was spread out, some with only their spouse or date, some with a wingman, but none of the tables were all A-C only.

"We're going to weave through, being sure to hit every table," Raj said quietly to me. "Len, Kyle, once we're talking to the first table, you two find your seats." The boys looked at me.

"Why?" I didn't want to hit every table. I wanted to get to my husband, smile, and not spill anything on me or anyone else.

"We're late so you have an opportunity to say hello to everyone you might have missed at the reception. Trust me, this will ensure no one minds that they're waiting for you."

"Works for me. Boys, do what Raj says."

"You'll thank me later," Raj said with a chuckle. With that, he put on a beaming smile, offered his arm, which I wisely took, and we stepped out.

First table was headed by Tito and Abigail, who had a bunch of people I didn't know with them. They were also sitting across from each other, presumably so they could cover more diplomatic ground. This boded, and not well, for where I was going to end up sitting. Whenever we reached my seat. Did a fast count of the number of tables in the room. It was gonna be a while before Raj or I sat down.

"So sorry we were delayed," Raj said to the guests at this table. "Ambassador Katt-Martini wanted to ensure that the dinner will be perfect."

I smiled brightly. "It will be. Chef says all's well in hand and you're going to love the meal." It was a safe bet that whoever was running things went by the term and I could get away without saying a last name, indicating the sex of the unnamed kitchen whiz, or sharing I had no idea who was actually in charge downstairs.

The guests all beamed right back, Tito nodded, and Abigail gave me a thumbs-up where no one could see. Apparently I was, for once, getting Good Wife and Ambassador Points. I decided that I loved Raj.

We snaked our way through the room, never missing a table, laughing and chatting with everyone along the way. Raj ensured he was never more than one person away from me, so he was always nearby to fix any slips. By midway through the room we'd passed the majority of the guests I didn't know at all or know well.

Which meant we were getting closer to the people I did know and who would, therefore, be not only watching me closely but be ready to comment on any mistakes I might make. Goody.

My parents were hosting folks from the Bahraini and Israeli Embassies, or as I preferred to call them, my Middle Eastern Contingent. To the rest of the room, this was a high-pressure assignment filled with diplomatic intricacies, and any missteps would result in, at best, another war in the Middle East.

In reality, these people all got along now, in great part because of how Operation Destruction had gone down. In other words, Mom and Dad had scored the cool table with no actual stress or pressure involved. Wondered if it was too late to ask to sit with my parents. Figured it was. Always the way.

I kissed my mother on her cheek, and did the same with Mona Nejem, the wife of the Bahraini ambassador, and someone who was now second only to Olga in terms of ambassadorial spouses I loved and trusted.

Got introduced to Mona's husband, as well as the Israeli ambassador and her husband. Khalid was next to Mona—he was to her as Buchanan, Len, and Kyle were to me. Oren and Jakob were here, too, as was a young woman I'd never met before who, like them, looked to be in her mid-twenties.

Leah was sitting between Oren and Jakob, so I assumed she was with the Israelis, and, therefore, with Mossad, just like they were. We had the head of the P.T.C.U., Bahraini Army, and Mossad representing, all sipping their water and fruit juice cocktails while at the same time keeping their eyes on every part of the room. This was, without a doubt, the safest and deadliest table we had.

Len and Kyle were at a nearby table with Olga and the rest of the Romanian Embassy personnel and some of our closer neighbors. As with my parents, they had a low-stress table. Same with Lorraine and Claudia, who, with their husbands, were each hosting nice people at their tables and apparently having a great time.

Lorraine and Claudia were Dazzlers, which was what I called the female A-Cs, at least to myself. They were also both Captains in Centaurion Division and as such, I'd have thought they'd have been closer to the head table. That they weren't was disappointing for me—they were my best A-C girlfriends and some days it felt like I never saw them any more.

"You look guilty about something," Lorraine said quietly when I gave her a hug.

"Do not."

"Well, not to regular people. But I know you and I want the scoop the minute we can be alone."

"Will do." Guiltily scurried off to Claudia's table.

"What are you up to?" Claudia whispered as we hugged. "You look like you're ready for something to happen. Do we need to take a bathroom break?"

"Yes, but not right now." I extracted myself as fast as possible. Dazzlers really had it all in terms of beauty and brains, Lorraine and Claudia especially. I knew I could trust them completely with everything that was going on. And the idea of telling them what and who I'd seen today was appealing. Only I couldn't do so here and now.

Tim and his wife, Alicia, had a lot of Top Brass types, including Colonel Franklin from Andrews Air Force Base and his wife, sitting with them. The three single flyboys and their Dazzler dates were also running really fun tables. None of them asked me what I was hiding or feeling guilty about, either. I was willing to hang out in this section of the room for hours.

Sadly, Raj wasn't having any of that, and moved us on to our next stops. And our next ones. And on and on.

Interestingly enough, the Cabal of Evil was spread out at different tables, which I guess meant the evil was somewhat contained. Chuckie and Naomi had scored sitting with Joker Jaws and Abner, Monsieur Love and Vance, and some normal people I knew from our neighborhood. Lifelong friendship or not, wasn't sure if Chuckie was going to forgive me for this setup, even though I'd had nothing to do with the seating plan.

"How's things going?" I asked Naomi quietly as I gave her a hug.

"Okay. Do I have to invite these people to my wedding?"

"Probably."

She grimaced as I moved toward Chuckie. "You owe me," he whispered in my ear as I bent to give him a hug. "Big time." Yep, not forgiving me for this one.

"Blah, blah, blah. Duty calls." I raced off to catch up with Raj—who was moving us on to the next stop—before Chuckie could note my looking guilty or something.

We were closing in on the head table. It had only taken what seemed like forever.

Doreen and Irving were at a table sort of in front of the head table loaded with presidential Cabinet members and their significant others, including Marion Villanova, who was the chief aide to the secretary of state, and Langston Whitmore, who was the secretary of transportation.

Villanova and Whitmore, who were both closeted, had been duped into having romantic relationships with two of Antony Marling's best androids. They'd made the best of the loss of their creepy significant others and were now "dating" each other. In Washington, this was considered a brilliant strategic move and they were the new Power Couple. I figured they might even get married.

While neither one had ever been my favorite person, for the most part, we'd gotten along in that Smile and Bob Heads from a Distance way. And Villanova still seemed content with this.

Whitmore, however, gave me a dirty look. Had no idea why, unless maybe he was hungry. "I'm sorry about the delay, Secretary Whitmore," I offered, in the hopes that he'd stop glaring. He wasn't up to Christopher's standards at all. "We just want to be sure everything's great."

"That's the line you people like to use all the time, isn't it?" he replied.

"Yes," Raj said, as he took my elbow. "We at American Centaurion like to do the best we possibly can." He shot the table a beaming troubadour smile and headed us off quickly. Tabled concerns about what Whitmore's damage was for later.

Christopher and Amy were at the table on one side of

the head table, along with White and Nurse Magdalena Carter, aka White's main squeeze and our Embassy staff nurse. Tito being at the back table now made a little more sense—with Lorraine and Claudia in the room, we had medical personnel spread throughout the floor. Always a wise choice for us.

Christopher's table was holding court with politicians from Arizona and New Mexico I didn't know personally. I'd met too many people, my stomach was beginning to grumble, and my feet were starting to hate being in heels—the names were one long blur which nicely matched the faces, which were also blurry. Hoped I wasn't giving off the same vibe as Whitmore and focused on smiling. Thankfully, I'd gotten really good at saying, "Chef says you're going to love what's coming." It seemed to suffice.

Reader and Gower were at the table on the other side, with Cliff, the Kramers, Eugene and Lydia, and Serene Dwyer. Alone. Without her husband, who, as I thought about it, I hadn't seen anywhere.

"Where's Brian?" I asked her quietly as I gave her a hug.

"With Patrick and the other kids," she whispered back. "Tell you why later."

I could understand why Brian might want to be overseeing Patrick, who'd been born right after Operation Destruction. Like Jamie, Patrick was exhibiting some new and frighteningly impressive A-C talents and abilities. But babysitting was supposedly being taken care of by Denise, Patrick's regular daycare provider, and no less a person than Gladys. So why wasn't Brian here instead of at the Pontifex's residence?

He'd been in the Embassy at the start of this shindig. Brian not being here now was unsettling, but I knew better than to ask questions at the moment. Also didn't know who was handling their assigned table, since Serene, as Head of Imageering, should have been holding court at a table different from Reader.

Took a better look at the seating. Serene was next to Gower. So was Reader. This was a break from every other table. Something had happened while I was in the basement. But now wasn't the time or place to find out what.

This table had an empty seat which I assumed was for Raj. Assumption confirmed after we'd said hello to everyone, because Raj took his seat, giving me a smile that said I was surely competent enough to get to my own table three feet away. Loved his optimism.

The head table had Jeff, the Armstrongs, the Brewers, and the McMillans, along with Reyes and someone I hadn't seen in a very long time—Camilla, our A-C double, triple, and potentially quadruple agent.

I gaped as Camilla smiled. "Kitty, it's so nice to see you." She leaned up, clearly for me to do the cheek-kiss I'd been handing out all over the room.

Bent down to oblige.

"Wipe the shocked look off your face, for God's sake," Camilla hissed in my ear. "I'm filling in as Reyes' 'date' and working. Be happy I'm here, something's going down tonight."

CHAPTER 18

KISSED CAMILLA'S cheek on autopilot. It was amazing how I was suddenly laser focused and extremely alert.

As with every other table, my seat was across from Jeff's. I'd seen every dude in this room, and I could confirm that, as always, he was the hottest looking guy around. He also looked pleased and like he was suddenly glad Raj was around, too. Jeff shot me a proud look. "Everything fine in the kitchen?"

"Absolutely. Chef has things well in hand."

All the men at my table stood, and Jeff looked like he was going to leave his seat to help me into mine. But I had Representatives Brewer and Reyes on either side, and they both reached for my chair. "Allow me," Reyes said with a smile for me and Brewer, who laughed and sat down.

The way the tables were arranged, Nathalie Brewer's back was to Eugene's. This should have meant he wasn't paying any attention to what was going on, unless he was ready to share his affair with his wife.

However, this wasn't the case. Before Reyes could do anything else, Eugene leaped up from his table and somehow beat Reyes to my chair.

"Here, Kitty, let me help you," Eugene said, almost slamming the chair into my leg.

"Thank you, but I've got it," Reyes said, giving Eugene the look normally reserved for the crazy aunt in the attic. Couldn't blame him.

"No, no, please let me." Eugene seemed strangely intent on being weirdly chivalrous. This didn't compute.

Worried for a moment that Reyes and Eugene were going to fight over my chair. However, Reyes chose the path of least resistance and shrugged. "Okay, if it means that much to you."

I looked at Jeff, to see if he had a clue as to what the hell was going on. Received the "what the hell?" look back. Clearly he had no idea what Eugene's damage was, either.

As Eugene clumsily shoved me into the table, he accidentally banged against Brewer, which ended up rocking the table. Fortunately nothing much went over, though Reyes' water slopped around and Brewer had to catch Eugene who almost fell over onto the table.

Eugene blushed, but was still intent to help me get properly situated. "Kitty, I'm so sorry," he whispered as he moved my chair back so my stomach wasn't shoved into the side of the table.

What was it about this party that everyone wanted to whisper to me? Were all Washington dinner parties like this and, if so, could I hope to avoid them in the future?

But once Eugene had stumbled back to his table, things went more smoothly. Being between Reyes and Brewer wouldn't have been my first seating choice, but Brewer was always good for winery talk, and Reyes was big on New Mexico's wineries. I was able to add in here and there, but the men were doing the conversational heavy lifting.

Camilla was chatting with Senator McMillan, Jeff was chatting with Senator Armstrong and Kelly McMillan, Nathalie Brewer was engaged with Elaine Armstrong. So far, so good.

Glanced around. The other tables all seemed fine. I spotted Caroline and Michael close by and they were the only A-C insiders at their table. How we'd missed stopping by that table was beyond me, but Whitmore's bad attitude had clearly thrown off Raj's groove as much as mine.

Considering that Caroline worked for McMillan and Michael was an astronaut, they should have been with another couple from our side of things. Ergo, using my brilliant deductive reasoning, they were acting as Serene's replacements. Wondered if I should get up to go say something to their table, but the possibility that Eugene would try to "help" me again seemed high, and one experience of that weirdness was enough.

We had a five-course meal coming, which was great because by now I was starving. Appetizers were served, each person receiving an artfully arranged plate filled with bite-sized works of art. I almost didn't want to eat mine. Did, however, and enjoyed. Chose not to agree with Brewer that a glass of wine would have gone nicely. We had a variety of sparkling water and juices that were covering the beverage side of things.

The soup arrived, and it was delicious. My promises to every guest about the greatness of the meal seemed to be coming true, for which I thanked God and Pierre.

It was during the salad course that Reyes started choking. The bad kind of choking. And after a few moments, it was clear he wasn't getting any air.

"Drink some water, Santiago," Brewer suggested. Others offered similar ideas, and Camilla patted him on the back. Nothing was helping.

Everyone looked concerned, but my high school had prepared me for this. I shoved my chair back, went behind Reyes, and did the Heimlich on him, being careful not to squeeze too hard—I wanted to open his airways, not crush his ribs.

Performed the maneuver perfectly and a crouton popped out of Reyes' mouth. My high school gym teachers would have been proud.

"Thank you, Kitty," he gasped. "My God, I seriously thought I was going to die."

"Do you need water?" Camilla asked.

Reyes' glass was empty. "Here," Brewer said, "take mine, haven't touched it." He winked at me. "I only like the hard stuff, like my virgin piña colada here."

Reyes took Brewer's water and drank it gratefully. "Thanks, Ed." He took a deep breath and let it out. "Whew. Dinner *and* a show, huh?"

We all laughed, I sat down amid a small round of applause, and we finished the salads. Everyone at our table moved the croutons to the side.

Talk turned to lifesaving and such, and I was called upon to explain my prowess with the Heimlich. Good schooling got interspersed with lifesaving as the main course arrived.

As with everything else, this part of the meal was amazing, and I started to relax and enjoy myself. Once you've popped a crouton out of someone at your fancy dinner party, really, there's nothing to worry about from a decorum standpoint.

The conversation went from lifesaving to what we were afraid of. Shared my fear of snakes, which got a firm agreement from Nathalie, Kelly, and Elaine. Brewer claimed a fear of heights; Reyes felt that choking to death in public was now his fear; McMillan said that after war what he feared were closed minds, which got a lot of impressed nodding. Armstrong said he feared making his wife angry, and Jeff jumped on that bandwagon to a lot of laughs.

Camilla said she worried that the wrong people would be in office. Figured this wasn't a real fear of hers, but a great way to move the conversation toward something where she wouldn't have to reveal a weakness. I was impressed, because it worked like a charm at a table full of politicians, especially since one of them was indeed running for the presidency.

Our table agreed that Armstrong was a great presidential choice. Considering our current Commander in Chief was at the end of his second term, the idea of a President we were on good terms with wasn't a bad one. McMillan was extremely pro the idea of Armstrong taking the highest office in the land and, as with so many other things, his vote of confidence made me feel much more inclined to support Armstrong.

Because the incumbent VP wasn't interested in seeking his time at the top, the field was wide open. "You're sure to get the nomination, aren't you?" I asked.

Armstrong shook his head. "Nothing's sure until the national convention, and that won't be until the year after next. As you well know, Kitty, a lot can happen in a short period of time, let alone in more than a year."

"True enough. So, will you end up having to ask someone who spent months running against you to be your vice presidential nominee, or do you get to choose from a wider range of options?"

Armstrong shrugged and McMillan laughed. "We're powwowing on that. I'm helping Vincent sift through his options. None of which are me, by the way."

"Why not?" Jeff asked. "You'd make a great team."

"Oh, we do make a good team," McMillan said. "But I don't have the drive to survive a campaign, at least not right now. As long as someone I believe in is running, I'm happy to help and remain where I am." He winked at me. "I like going home to Arizona too much to give that up willingly."

"But to answer the ambassador's question," Armstrong said with a smile, "Don and I are trying to figure it out. There are a lot of options."

"Not me or Santiago," Brewer said with a laugh. "We're too new."

"Nothing wrong with new," Armstrong said with a grin. "Nothing wrong with old. The issue is where you stand *on* the issues, and who you'll protect or sell out, and why."

The others nodded and the conversation was off onto what was good and bad about politics.

"Jeff, you should consider running for office," Reyes said, after the discussion of what made a good politician had been going for about five minutes. The other men at the table chimed in with their agreement, while the wives nodded theirs. I kept what I hoped was a poker face on and focused on my potatoes.

Jeff looked shocked. "I've never considered it." The way he said it, I knew he also didn't want to consider it.

"You're a natural," Brewer said.

Managed not to mention that in our Embassy that was probably considered an insult.

"You would have a lot to offer," McMillan said thoughtfully. "And you're a U.S. citizen, so there's no issue with eligibility."

"I don't want to run for any office. Why would I need to run for office?" Jeff sounded confused and a little stressed.

"For the good of your country and fellow men," Armstrong said without missing a beat. "Could be good for smoothing over certain . . . issues."

"I don't see how my being a politician would make anyone happier that we A-Cs are here. Besides, there are no elections for two more years, so no point in thinking about it right now." Jeff's tone of voice said that, as far as he was concerned, this topic was done. The expressions on the faces of the politicians at our table said that it was only done for right now.

Reyes grinned. "Aw, c'mon. You'd be great, and if you ran

for something, then I wouldn't be the new kid on the block any more."

Jeff managed to laugh as a nice distraction arrived—dessert. We were treated to individual-sized Baked Alaska, all beautiful to behold. "I only thought they served that dessert on cruises," Reyes said.

"I don't tell Chef what to make and Chef doesn't tell me how to perform the Heimlich." I was managing not to drool, but it took some effort.

Reyes laughed as we were served. The dessert was really yummy and it was nice to get to have it basically in our own home. Decided having a gourmet chef around wasn't a bad trade-off for having to host the party.

"Are you alright to have a dessert like this?" Nathalie asked. "It *is* made with alcohol." She sounded worried, not nasty.

"It only has alcohol in it if it's flaming." I knew this because the only part of the meal I'd been interested in was the dessert course, and Pierre had already reassured me that we weren't going to be setting the Baked Alaska on fire, and therefore all the A-Cs could eat it in safety.

Everyone dug in and the conversation slowed a bit and turned toward who'd been on a cruise and where they'd gone. Shocking no one, everyone had hit a cruise somewhere along the way, so there were a lot of sea experiences to cover. Coffee and tea were served, or another round of sparkling water or fruit drinks, depending on preference.

Armstrong was regaling most of the table with a rather hilarious story about their first cruise ever, when he and Elaine were in a cabin so small he couldn't stand up straight, when Reyes put his hand on his stomach. "Excuse me a minute," he said quietly to me. "Think I need to go to the powder room."

"Are you okay?" He looked a little pale. Tried not to worry that something in the food had made one of our most important guests sick. Failed.

"I don't think I should have had another fruit drink with the Baked Alaska." He grimaced. "That'll teach me not to like hot drinks with dessert. I'll be right back. One floor down, right?"

"Right." Tried not to contemplate how Reyes getting

sick at this party would get spun by everyone, Marcia Kramer in particular. Failed again.

"I'll go down with you," Camilla said. She shot me a look.

"I'll join you both. Group trip." Reyes didn't argue and no one else was really paying attention. The three of us got up quietly. "Bathroom break," I said softly to Brewer when he turned to give me a questioning look. He nodded and turned his attention back to the Armstrongs.

The three of us either had to work our way through the room in order to get to the elevators or we could take the stairs on this side of the room, which meant we only had to walk past one table. Offered Reyes the choice. "Stairs," he said firmly.

We moved quickly past Reader's table and headed downstairs. Reyes was sweating, was definitely pale, and, when my hand accidentally brushed his, felt clammy. This was so not good. The heck with the party—Reyes was clearly not doing well. Didn't know what to do for food poisoning, but Camilla was trained in medicine, and Tito, Nurse Carter, Lorraine, and Claudia were only a floor away.

"Santiago, did something in the meal disagree with you?"

"Maybe. Not sure. Maybe I'm coming down with the flu, which would be the worst timing in the world." He shook his head. "I'm sorry, Kitty, I don't want to wreck your party."

"That's okay, I just don't want you to feel bad or get sick. Are you allergic to anything you might have eaten?" I smelled garlic on his breath and tried to remember which of the courses had had a lot of garlic in it.

"No, no allergies to anything." He swallowed hard. "I really think it's either the flu or the combination of the fruit drink and the dessert, that's all."

"I'd say botulism," Camilla said. "But we had nothing that would have been suspect and, as far as I saw, no one else seemed to be in distress."

We reached the second floor and got Reyes into the stall closest to the stairs, which didn't have the gate in it. We were the only ones racing someone to the bathroom, so Camilla's impression that food poisoning wasn't to blame seemed potentially correct.

The individual stalls were unisex and each one was large

and nicely appointed. In addition to the usual amenities, Pierre had installed small couches in each one, in case someone wanted to lie down. He insisted these were necessary. I'd let him win that one, because I was much more excited about the fact that we had stacks of real hand towels, not paper ones, in the bathrooms. Hey, it's the little things you treasure.

The stalls were also really soundproof, which everyone considered a good feature.

All this was great for Reyes, but made getting to talk to Camilla alone in the bathroom awkward. "Do we talk out here or do we share a stall?"

She rolled her eyes. "I don't actually need to go. If you can hold it, we can sit on a couch." She looked around. "Or we can just stand here. The kitchen staff isn't near enough to hear anything."

"Okay, so, what's going on?"

She dropped her voice. "We think one of the 'captains' from the invasion has infiltrated and is nearby. Not sure who or what his target is, but we figure it's either the Pontifex, the hybrid children, or you."

CHAPTER 19

THERE WERE A LOT of responses I wanted to give to this statement. All of them related to Colonel Hamlin who was, if all was well, being guarded by Buchanan in the basement of the Embassy.

Or course, my experience said things rarely went well. "Um, can you hold down the fort here for a couple minutes?"

Camilla was a rarity among the A-Cs—she could lie believably and well. She'd told me the few A-C liars that existed were found early and trained in the various arts of spying and such. We were all still alive because Jeff's father, Alfred, had put Camilla in place when Jamie was born, and Camilla had done her triple agent duty perfectly, helping us thwart Operation Confusion.

Chuckie had put her on assignment to sniff out which A-Cs were traitors, or, in their minds, which A-Cs were Purity of the Race Patriots still supporting either their former leader, Ronald Yates, or the former Diplomatic Corps. So I hadn't seen Camilla for a good long while.

However, the reality was that the flip side of Camilla being a world class liar was that she was also world class at spotting liars. Her eyes narrowed. "What are you up to that no one else knows about?"

"Oh, um, some others know about it. Look, we're on the same side." I truly hoped. "Give me about five minutes, or less, and then we can bring each other up to speed."

She nodded. "Fine. One of us has to stay here until Representative Reyes feels better anyway."

"Right." I took off, using hyperspeed. I wasn't enraged, but I was really, really stressed, and that seemed to be working for me in the same way rage did—I was in control of my A-C talents.

Zipped from the Zoo, over the walkway, through the Embassy, and down into the basement, without hitting into anything. Which was good, because no one was there.

Resisted the impulse to curse. Buchanan had moved Hamlin before; maybe he'd moved him now. Where to was the question. Dug out my phone and hit Buchanan's speed dial button.

It rang and went to voicemail. Hung up and called again. Same thing. Tried this three more times. Either Buchanan was somewhere where he couldn't hear or see his phone, or something bad had happened. Or both.

Had a lot of options, but decided freaking out really couldn't be one of them. Instead, I called Christopher. Thankfully he answered.

"Hi, Kitty, why are you calling me right now?"

"Too much to explain. First, a question—is anyone at the party acting sick?"

"Uh . . . no, not that I can see."

"Great. Next, can you find Malcolm Buchanan?"

"Right now?"

"It's important right now."

"Excuse me, have to take this." I could hear Christopher get up and leave his table. "Okay, now that I've rudely taken a call and left in the middle of a senator's discussion of alien rights, let me search for your lost love."

"Geez, does Jeff routinely ask you to handle the jealousy for him if he's busy elsewhere?"

"No. That's . . . weird."

"I'm gonna hate this, aren't I?"

"Yeah, I can't find him. Should I search the cosmos?" This wasn't Christopher being snarky. Well, it was, but he could make good on the offer. Since his Surcenthumain boost, Christopher could "see" all the way to the farthest planet in the Alpha Centauri system.

"No, I have a horrible feeling he's somewhere in the tunnel system."

When we'd first discovered the deep and, it turned out, ancient tunnel system, it had been cloaked at least as well as the Crash Site Dome, and had been impenetrable via A-C talents. At the end of Operation Destruction we'd been able to see and map all the deep underground tunnel system—everyone had thought this was thanks to the Poofs finding and taking the Evil Flying Dino-Birds' myriad hidden power cubes.

Everyone had also assumed we'd be able to see and fully function within the tunnels and their connected rooms from then on. But within two weeks the tunnels had gone back to being cloaked, we couldn't get in and out of the rooms without a power cube, and tunnels and rooms both were once again impenetrable to the talented A-Cs, Jeff and Christopher included.

After the horrible discovery Chuckie had confirmed with me this morning, I now wondered if we'd been able to "see" the tunnel system because ACE knew we'd need to map it and also knew he wouldn't be around to help ensure we could continue to "see" the system whenever we might want.

Christopher pulled me back to the present situation. "Okay. So what's our next move?"

"I need you to see if Representative Reyes is sick or okay."

"Okay." There was a pause. "Oh my God!" Christopher hung up.

Decided that meant Reyes was really sick. Tabled the issue of where Buchanan and Hamlin were and ran like hell for the Zoo.

Christopher had beaten me and was slamming against the bathroom door.

"What's going on?" I asked as I joined him. Camilla was nowhere in sight.

"Reyes isn't sick. He's dying. I sent Camilla for Tito, Lorraine, and Claudia. Why the hell are these doors so damn tough to break down?"

"Pierre had them reinforced for the soundproofing. And they've got a lot of metal in them." I slammed into the door with Christopher.

Did the trick and the door flew open. Reyes was on the floor, vomit and other horrible bodily fluids all around him.

He was convulsing and if I'd thought he'd looked bad before, it was nothing compared to now.

There were footsteps behind us and Tito and the three women ran up. Camilla was holding Tito's hand. He gagged when they stopped, the usual human reaction to hyperspeed. Reyes started to vomit up blood.

"You didn't take your special Hyperspeed Dramamine?"

"I did, I take it every day now. But this is horrible. I'm a doctor but I wasn't prepared for this." Tito motioned to me to step out. "Christopher, can you help me with diagnosis?"

Christopher grabbed Tito's hand and touched Reyes. Because of Christopher's expanded talent, he could see inside someone. This particular aspect of his expanded talents had helped save a lot of us over the past year.

"Where's Nurse Carter?" I asked Camilla.

"Left her upstairs in case someone else was affected."

Tito shook his head. "I don't know what's going on with him. It's as if all his internal organs are trying to shut down." He looked over his shoulder at me and Camilla. "You two were the closest to him. What happened and when?"

We described Reyes' symptoms. "I thought it might be botulism," Camilla said.

"It's not, and it's not the flu, though the initial symptoms sound similar for both. Think. Give me everything, even if it seems stupid or unrelated."

My memory nudged. "Oh. Well, I smelled garlic on Santiago's breath. I don't remember us having garlic in any of the food, though."

"Oh my God. Arsenic poisoning." Tito started barking orders to Lorraine and Claudia, who were both working at hyperspeed.

Christopher and I looked at each other. "There's no way that's an accident," he said.

"We have to lock down the upstairs, and this floor. Everyone's food and dishes have to be searched. And no one can be allowed to leave." I'd seen enough cop shows to know the basics.

Christopher pulled out his phone and made a call. I couldn't focus on what he was saying—I was too focused on Reyes. Christopher hung up. "James is on it."

As A-C agents poured out of the bathroom stall on this floor that contained the gate and spread out, presumably through the Zoo and potentially the Embassy, a thought occurred. "Why isn't Jeff down here? There's no way he's missing this level of anxiety."

"He knows. I told him to stay and keep things calm upstairs. Kitty, what the hell are we going to do?"

"We need to get him to Dulce, STAT," Tito snapped.

"We can't," Camilla replied before I could say anything. "He's too high profile. This has to go through proper channels. Proper human channels."

"Then call nine-one-one," Tito said. "Because this needs more medical than we have here."

"Already handled," Camilla said. "But we're going to need police, too, I think. Because arsenic means a murder attempt."

"I know who to call." Pulled out my phone. Looked at the burner phone in my purse for a moment. Poison wasn't the Dingo's style. And he'd said no one they were after would matter to me. He wasn't stupid; he'd have to know Reyes would matter to me. So either the Dingo was lying to me—always a possibility—or he wasn't the assassin in charge of this.

The police wouldn't want anyone to leave. Only I didn't know where Hamlin and Buchanan were. Meaning at least two people technically with access weren't here now. Decided to worry about these issues later. Like as soon as I could tell Jeff later. Which wasn't now, however.

Scrolled through until I found the number. I didn't keep these guys on speed dial. Happily, phone was answered on the first ring. "Officer Melville."

"Hey, Herman, it's Kitty Katt-Martini." I'd stopped calling him Officer Moe, Ishmael, or Ishmoe. At his specific request. It was tough to do, but anything for our men in uniform.

"I know. I have caller ID. What can I do for you, Ambassador?"

"I need you and the rest of the K-9 squad down to the American Centaurion Zoo facility five minutes ago. I think someone just poisoned one of our party guests, using arsenic, I must add, and we are officially out of our element. It's time for you to repay the favors we did for you during Operation Assassination."

"You're sure?"

"As sure as I can be, based on what our staff doctor is saying. We've called nine-one-one, not that any ambulance with hunky, life-saving paramedics is here yet, but I'd like to see a friendly face right now, so please bring Prince along."

I heard someone talking in the background. "The information just came over the police and fire bands."

"American Centaurion is specifically requesting you and your K-9 squad. We're not asking for the rest of the police force." I could technically get away with this request, because we were on American Centaurion soil, so to speak.

"I understand. We're on our way."

We hung up and I fretted. Tito and the girls were working feverishly, but Reyes looked no better.

Christopher took my hand. "He'll pull through. Tito's the best doctor there is."

I wanted to be comforted. I wasn't. I knew ACE frequently gave Tito a little assist here and there. This didn't detract from Tito's medical awesomeness, but in cases like this—where the patient was close to death—it was a huge comfort. But ACE wasn't around, and I couldn't bet on him being able to help.

"Someone has to handle the door, whenever the paramedics get here."

"I will," Camilla said. "Lorraine and Claudia are better with medicine than I am. I've called for more medical support. I'll handle cops and paramedics. Only the K-9s in, right?"

"Right, at least for now."

She zipped downstairs as a slew of Dazzlers, including Melanie and Emily, Lorraine and Claudia's mothers, arrived.

Christopher and I backed out of everyone's way. Some of the Dazzlers were cleaning up around Reyes, but it was still awful to watch and hear. Reyes was in agony, and I wanted to do something, anything.

Steeled myself, let go of Christopher, and shoved into the room. Knelt down in a clean space and took Reyes' hand.

"Kitty, get out of here, you can't help," Tito said. Reyes clutched my hand.

"No. I'll move when you need me to, or do whatever you need, but I'm not leaving Santiago alone."

Tito looked at me, then at Reyes, and nodded. "Fine."

I ignored what the medical staff were doing and focused on Reyes. "Hang on, Santiago. We'll get you taken care of."

"The ... crouton ... was easier," he gasped out.

I managed a laugh. "Yeah." I squeezed his hand. "Tito's the best. You'll be fine and we'll be laughing about this in a couple of days."

Reyes convulsed again and I stopped talking, though I didn't let go of his hand. The Dazzlers got him completely out of his clothes, because his clothes were covered with blood, vomit, and other less savory fluids. Three of them lifted him onto a gurney while the others ensured he was cleaned off. Sheet pulled up to cover his lower body.

I wasn't looking at any of this much; I was focused on holding his hand, on keeping him connected to someone during what had to be the most terrifying moments of his life. I was terrified, and I wasn't the one going through this.

Tito, Lorraine, and Claudia had been working on him nonstop through all of this. I had no idea what they were doing. I was just aware that it didn't seem to be helping.

Paramedics arrived; Tito briefed them on the medical procedures so far enacted for presumed arsenic poisoning. Took a quick look and saw Melville standing with Christopher, his dog, Prince, sitting at attention. Prince sniffed toward us and whined. I figured that didn't bode well for Reyes.

The paramedics' conversation with Tito wasn't boding well, either. I heard phrases like "massive amount of arsenic for these reactions" and "you've done all the right things." If we'd done all the right things, then why didn't Reyes look better?

The paramedics joined the Dazzlers, but didn't have most of them move off. More medical things were perpetrated on Reyes. He still looked awful.

"Kitty," Reyes gasped. "Promise me ..."

"Yes?" I leaned closer to him. "What do you need, Santiago? Whatever it is, I'll handle it."

"Promise ... my desk ... you'll clean ... it out. You ... not ... someone else."

"I promise." Wondered just what kind of porn Reyes had hidden he didn't want the press or other politicians getting their hands on. "Do you need anything else?"

"Like to . . . see tomorrow." Reyes managed a twisted grin. "Dinner and . . . a show. What a way to . . . go."

"You're not going anywhere, Santiago. Other than to the Georgetown Medical Center."

He squeezed my hand again. "Tell James . . ."

"Yes?"

"I hope . . . he's . . . right and . . . ready."

"Right about what? Ready for what?"

Reyes didn't answer.

CHAPTER 20

REYES WASN'T LOOKING at me any more, and his hand felt limp in mine when he'd been holding tightly only a moment before.

Someone put their hands on my upper arms and moved me gently away as the paramedics started slamming the pads onto Reyes' chest and doing the electroshock thing to make someone's heart start beating again.

A few minutes of this dragged on. Then Prince threw back his head and howled. The rest of the dogs in the K-9 squad took up the cry. I'd heard this before, during Operation Assassination, when Prince had determined one of the squad and his dog had been killed.

While Prince and the other dogs were howling, the head paramedic and Tito had a brief, quiet conversation. The head paramedic shook his head. Tito slid his hand over Reyes' eyes, closing them. The paramedic covered Reyes with the sheet. The dogs quieted.

"He can't die. He can't be dead. He's a good guy."

"Even the good guys die, baby," Jeff said softly. I realized he was who was holding me. "I'd like American Centaurion personnel accompanying the body," he said to the paramedic in charge.

"We can't allow anyone to leave," Melville countered. Prince strained against his lead, but Melville kept him under control.

"We've locked off this floor from the walkway and the Embassy," Jeff said. "Security personnel aren't allowing anyone to come or go, other than authorized police and paramedics, who are already inside. However, we don't have a morgue here, so we need to have the . . . body removed for examination."

"That's what the paramedics are for," Melville said.

"No offense to them, but I want someone I know I can trust protecting Representative Reyes' body." Jeff said this calmly, but his tone insinuated he wasn't going to take no for an answer.

"We can have agents from another base come over," I suggested. "Our people, but who weren't here at any time."

"I want people we can trust witnessing the autopsy," Tito added. He looked grim and upset. Lorraine and Claudia looked ready to cry. The rest of the Dazzlers looked no better, including Camilla, who looked more upset than Tito. Had a feeling she felt she'd just failed at her job.

"It's irregular," Melville said.

"We're on American Centaurion soil." The positive about being angry was that it stopped me from crying. I pulled out of Jeff's hold and turned on Melville. "Someone murdered Santiago in our home, and they did it in a way where he suffered horribly. And that someone probably wants to frame American Centaurion for this, too. I called you for help. You either help or you get out."

"You can stop snarling at me," Melville said calmly. "Irregular doesn't mean 'no.' It means we need to make arrangements, that's all."

"And you'll make them quickly, and quietly, without advising the press," Chuckie said, voice set at his deadly level, as he joined us.

Melville didn't even bother with trying to stare Chuckie down—he'd already lost that battle during Operation Assassination. "Fine. I assume we're giving the C.I.A. jurisdiction on this one?"

"No, the P.T.C.U. The head of which is upstairs already organizing the questioning of the witnesses and ensuring no one touches anything. Helped by A-C Security."

"Does everyone know?" I asked. Because if they did, inevitably someone upstairs was texting to the press.

"Yes, because Camilla gave me and Angela the head's up and your mother knows how important ensuring all the attendees are rounded up and held is to an investigation. The dogs' howling made it clear we have murder, versus attempted murder, on our hands, which is why I'm down here. Your mother already confiscated all cell phones and other PDAs, so we'll have a short time before the press descends on us." Chuckie looked at Jeff. "You need to get back up there."

"Not until I know Santiago's body is going to be protected and we have assigned Centaurion personnel guarding his body along with Doctor Hernandez and his medical staff." Jeff almost never called Tito anything other than Tito, and he never called Lorraine and Claudia "medical staff." However, times like this demanded official titles and I completely approved of the sneaking in of Centaurion Division personnel.

"They're suspects," Melville pointed out.

"How so?" Tito asked. "We were nowhere near the head table."

The head paramedic nodded. "Arsenic poisoning of the level we believe we have here would have taken no more than thirty minutes to react. From what the doctor's told me, you were all eating dinner by the time our victim would have been poisoned."

"That means kitchen staff, wait staff, and members of the head table," Chuckie said.

Melville cleared his throat. "Ah, that means the Ambassadors are suspects."

"Really? Because we'd be stupid enough to kill someone at our own dinner party, in our own Embassy? And kill off someone who wholeheartedly supported us to boot?"

"Perfect crime," Melville said. "If you got away with it." Everyone shared looks of outrage as Melville put his hand up. "I'm not saying you're involved. I'm saying that I'm the head police officer on the scene and you're suspects. I can allow you to wander off, and then people can question, or I can treat you as suspects right now, get your statements, search you, and let you go on about your business."

"Do it, quickly," Chuckie said.

Melville had two of the other K-9 officers pat me, Jeff, Chuckie, and the others down. Thankfully, none of us were hiding bottles of poison on our persons. Fast statements were taken. They all corroborated each other—nothing had

seemed amiss, no one had acted oddly, particularly toward
Reyes, and no one else's food had caused any kind of reactions other than gastronomic happiness.

Wanted to tell Jeff about everything that had happened
now, more than I had before, but this was absolutely not the
time or place to mention Clarence and his mystery package,
assassins lurking about, the return of Colonel Hamlin, or
the disappearance of Hamlin and Buchanan. None of them
were the likely murderers, either, though Clarence would
have had the best shot of getting inside without being spotted. But why would he want to kill Reyes?

"Who besides the servers came by your table once you
were seated?" Melville asked.

"No one came by our table once we were seated, not
even before Kitty arrived," Jeff answered.

A bad thought occurred to me. Someone had indeed
come by, in that sense. "And he said he was sorry . . ."

"What? Who?" Chuckie asked.

Prince whined and nudged against me. I looked down,
Prince whined again, louder. We were on the same wavelength. "Ah . . . Prince wants to, um, smell the body. Please."

"What?" Melville sounded shocked.

"Let him," Jeff said, and he had his Commander voice
on. He didn't use it as much these days, but he still possessed the ability to let anyone and everyone know he was
the man in charge in less than three syllables.

Melville handed Prince's lead to Jeff, who took it and
handed it to me. Prince and I went to the gurney, Prince
sniffing like mad. He put his front paws up onto the bed and
sniffed Reyes' body. Tito pulled the sheet back before I had
to ask him to, which was a relief.

"Be careful," I said quietly. "It can kill you, too, if you get
any on or in you."

Prince stopped sniffing for a moment to look at me derisively. I'd gotten this look from cats, Poofs, and Peregrines,
but it was a first from a dog. However, I got the point—
Prince was a highly trained professional and he knew better
than to put his paws, nose, or tongue onto a body that was
toxic, thank you very much. He snorted at me, then went
back to sniffing.

After a couple of intense sniffing minutes he got down.
"You can cover the body again," I told Tito, who did as re-

quested. Prince whined and looked around. "He wants to check out the room where this happened."

To everyone's credit, no one asked me how I knew what Prince wanted. One tiny favor in a night full of badness. Chose to enjoy the moment.

"You sure you're up to this, baby?" Jeff sounded worried.

"Yes. You figure out who's going to go with Santiago's body. Chuckie, you come with me and Prince."

"Me? Why?"

"I think you're going to be helping Prince make an arrest."

CHAPTER 21

WE HEADED UPSTAIRS. "Kitty, who do you think did this?"

"Tell you if Prince and I agree." It made no sense, and a part of me didn't want to believe it. But only one person had acted weird—weird on my scale, which was a pretty heavy-duty scale—all night.

"No, tell me now, so I'm prepared."

Chuckie had a point. "Fine. Eugene practically broke my chair fighting with both Santiago and Edmund Brewer to be the one to help me sit down."

"He wasn't sitting at your table . . . I can see why that could be suspicious. But how could he have poisoned anyone moving your chair in?"

"He practically fell onto Brewer, slammed me into the table, water spilled . . . it would take sleight of hand of some kind, but it would have been doable."

"This is Eugene Montgomery you're talking about, right?" Chuckie didn't sound convinced. Couldn't blame him.

"Right. I know, he's not exactly Mister Smooth, but maybe he got lucky."

"Or maybe he practiced. But what's his motive?"

"Beats me. We get to find out, if I'm right. And if not, we're back to square one anyway."

"Oh good. Routine." Chuckie opened the stairwell door for me and we headed back into what I hoped I wouldn't now always think of as the Pretty Room of Death.

I was surprised to see everyone still at their tables. Well, almost everyone—obviously some of the guests weren't in the room and we had a lot of Security A-Cs and most of the K-9 squad up here, but they were all hovering on the edges. The guests were seated, looking worried, bored, or outraged, depending.

People started talking. Not to me—at me. My name and title were being spoken, called, and shouted. Amazing how fast a relatively quiet room had gone to bedlam.

Looked at Reader for support. "Ignore the rest, do your thing, and let me know when, Kitty," he said softly as I went past. That I could hear him over everyone else was most likely because I was looking right at him, but it helped. Reader was being kept in his seat by Cliff—I could tell Cliff's hand wasn't merely resting on Reader's shoulder, but pressing down. Wasn't sure why, but assumed Cliff had his reasons.

Prince ignored all of this, and I chose to listen to Reader and follow suit. We aimed for the head table, which, in addition to the Brewers, Armstrongs, and McMillans, held my mother. Kevin was standing behind her. Mom had her In Charge and Pissed to Be Here face on. I couldn't blame her.

Reyes' seat was empty—Mom was sitting in my vacated chair. "You brought a dog?" she asked without preamble.

"I brought the Top Dog of the K-9 squad. Prince and I need to do some work, Mom."

"I'm not even going to ask. Do you need us standing up?"

"Only you. Everyone else is still in their original seats." Mom obliged as I brought Prince over to Reyes' seat. "Search and seizure time, Prince."

He sniffed Reyes' chair, then my chair, then he sniffed Brewer for a good little while. Initial investigation done, Prince jumped into Reyes' chair and started sniffing what was on the table. His nose reached one of the glasses and Prince snorted. Prince looked around the table, sniffing like mad. He sniffed the one glass again, snorted again, looked at me, tossed off a third snort, and jumped down.

"Wow. Mom, the poison was in that glass. And, I think, only that glass."

Mom motioned a couple of A-Cs over. "Find out who put that glass on the table."

"Run it for fingerprints, too," Chuckie added. Mom nodded approvingly. Kevin motioned for a couple of the K-9 cops in the room to come over.

I was going to pet Prince and give him praise, but he wasn't done. He started sniffing the floor around the table. He was moving fast, and I was in heels. Decided this was the best trained animal in the Zoo right now and dropped his lead. Prince didn't even seem to notice. He was intent on his sniffing.

It didn't take long—after all, the table in question was right by this one. Prince sniffed around Reader's table and ended up next to Eugene, who looked nervous and mildly terrified as Prince stuck his snout right into Eugene's crotch.

Eugene's expression went to fully terrified when Prince started to growl. Chuckie, who'd been hovering nearby, moved in his super fast and highly trained way that showed why he was able to take out an A-C if he had to and grabbed Eugene. "Let's see what the dog's upset about."

"N-nothing," Eugene stammered. "I'm not really good with dogs."

Prince backed off to allow Chuckie to stand Eugene up, but he started barking. This wasn't friendly barking. This was teeth-bared, fur up, growl-barking meant to indicate the barkee was bad news and should be taken out by the pack immediately if not sooner.

Chuckie patted Eugene down with great prejudice while Prince barked his approval and support. It was clear that, if Eugene so much as breathed wrong at Chuckie, Prince was ready to remove one of Eugene's limbs, at the very least.

"You're also not good with lying," Chuckie said as he took a napkin off the table, then pulled a small packet out of Eugene's pants pocket. He held it toward Prince, who barked his head off at the packet. Chuckie nodded. "Angela, I think we'll discover this packet contained arsenic."

There were gasps from a variety of people, Lydia foremost among them. "My husband would never hurt anyone!"

Apparently Kevin didn't agree, because he slapped cuffs on Eugene. "You want to search him some more?" he asked Chuckie.

"We'll strip search him later. We need to verify if he had any accomplices first." Chuckie eyed Lydia. "Such as his wife."

"Lydia didn't do anything!" Eugene exclaimed. "And neither did I."

Lydia looked shocked and confused, but Eugene looked trapped and panicked. He also looked guilty. I stepped up to him. "I get how you did it, sort of. I don't get *why* you did it, though. What had Santiago ever done to you?"

"Nothing! I didn't do anything to him. I don't know what that packet is—your friend here must have planted it on me."

Cliff let go of Reader, who stood up and came to our side of the table. He looked furious. "Right," Reader said as he reached us. "Of course he did. We'll listen to more of your lame and completely ridiculous accusations of innocent people later. You're on American Centaurion soil. And that means that, as Head of Field for Centaurion Division, I'm putting you under arrest—our kind of arrest."

"I want my lawyer," Eugene said weakly.

"Do you?" Reader asked with a pleasant smile. "That's nice. American Centaurion doesn't really do lawyers. And yours isn't allowed to come visit at this time."

"You can't do that," Lydia protested.

"Actually," Cliff said, "they can."

"Particularly when you, an American citizen, have perpetrated an unfriendly act on American Centaurion soil," Kevin added.

The room went quiet. Wasn't totally sure why. Assumed Kevin had said some code word that meant something to everyone else. Perhaps this information was in the Briefing Books of Boredom and the Diplomat's Handbook that was more like the Diplomat's New York City Phone Book. I'd been trying to read through them. Hadn't gone quickly.

"Are you officially stating that you believe an unfriendly act was committed by an American citizen?" Armstrong asked carefully.

No one spoke. I had no idea why, it seemed clear to me. "I think murdering Santiago Reyes, in our Embassy, in cold blood, counts as an unfriendly act, if anyone's asking me."

Chuckie and Cliff both winced in unison. Uh oh. Risked a look at Mom. She had the same expression as she'd had when I'd come home after two in the morning without calling her first. I'd never done that again, and I had a feeling I was never going to use the term "unfriendly act" again without a lot of thought attached to it.

"Um, what does my saying that actually, ah, mean?"

Reader shook his head. "Oh, nothing much, Ambassador. You just shared that American Centaurion is considering this to be an act of war. As in, we're considering war with the United States."

Whoops.

CHAPTER 22

"I WOULD LIKE TO offer Romania's good offices to help resolve and repair this matter," Andrei, Olga's husband, said before anyone else could speak. He ensured his voice carried.

How anyone had heard the prior exchange was beyond me, but I put it down to my luck being consistent. On the plus side, Olga was here, and I was sure that was why Andrei had reacted so quickly.

"Good offices?" I was sure I'd seen this term somewhere. Couldn't remember where, but was pretty sure it didn't indicate the penthouse suite of an office building.

"Means Romania's offering to help settle this dispute between countries," Chuckie said. "Thank God, and please stop speaking, Kitty," he added under his breath.

Really wasn't sure how to react to this. Didn't seem to matter. Andrei came to our part of the room and he, Reader, Cliff, and Chuckie started having a very fast, very high-level discussion. They managed to move in such a way that I'd have to shove in in order to hear or speak. Fine. I'd blown it, but I wasn't the bad guy here.

Speaking of whom, Kevin moved Eugene next to Mom. Mona and the rest of the Middle East Contingent had followed Andrei over to this part of the room, but they were with Mom. So I went over there—I was more used to being bawled out by my mother than Chuckie anyway.

"It's okay, kitten," Mom said softly. "As the ambassador, you have every right to declare this an act of war."

"If this had happened in our Embassy, we would have declared the same," Mona agreed.

Oren nodded his agreement. "Same for Israel. Any of us, really."

Jakob cleared his throat. "What, as good friends to American Centaurion, can we do for you right now, Ambassador?"

Had to say this for Chuckie telling me to shut up—I thought about the ramifications to whatever I was going to say to this question before I replied.

We were standing next to three powerful political couples. Now wasn't the time to share insider information. "Honestly, if you all wouldn't mind staying around, even after the police release you, I'd appreciate it so much. I feel very lost and alone right now, and could use some advice from all of you."

Mom shot me a look that said I was indeed actually as smart as she'd always suspected. Mona nodded. "Of course, Ambassador. Just tell us where you want us to go and we'll ensure that we remain to assist in any way."

"I'd say the fifth floor, once you're all cleared. Have one of the Barones come and escort you." Jeremy and Jennifer Barone were an A-C brother-sister team of Field agents who'd been permanently assigned to our Embassy after Operation Destruction. We'd had them remain upstairs with Hacker International tonight, to ensure no one wandered up there and to have A-Cs right there to advise and alert in case the hackers found anything of significance going on. Clearly the impending murder of a representative hadn't hit their airwaves. Had no idea what this might or might not mean.

"Absolutely, Ambassador," Khalid said. "Is there anyone else you would like to join us?"

Everyone seemed so much more on top of things than me right now. Thank God. "Yes, please ask the Romanian ambassadress and her assistant if they'd be so good as to join you. It looks like the Romanian ambassador is going to be here for some time, so it would be nice for them to be able to wait comfortably for him."

"I'll make sure the police clear all of these guests first," Kevin said, as he handed Eugene off to Mom and headed toward the officers I'd nicknamed Larry and Curly during

Operation Assassination. They had real names, but for whatever reason, unlike Melville, they weren't attached to my using them. Ergo, I still called them Officers Larry and Curly. Either they didn't understand my Three Stooges references or they were flattered by them. Decided not to worry about it right now.

Jeff chose this moment to arrive, which was nice. But he was instantly pulled into the impromptu Kitty's Screwed Up Again meeting, which wasn't. Always the way.

Because of where we all were, Eugene was standing near to Brewer, who shook his head. "I can't believe you'd do something like this, Gene. We'll get it sorted out."

"Thanks," Eugene muttered. He looked at Brewer—his expression didn't say, "So glad I have a friend." It said, "I hate your guts." He wiped the look off his face quickly, but I'd seen enough to recognize it—it was reminiscent of the looks Jeff used to give Chuckie, gave Buchanan these days, and was currently shooting at Raj, presumably just to keep in practice.

Pushed aside worry about Buchanan's whereabouts for the moment—there were bigger fish to hook, gut, and toss to Pierre to have fried.

My brain nudged. Eugene was in the Cabal of Evil only because of two reasons—his wife had managed to get into the Cool Kids Crowd and had no intention of leaving any time soon, and he was sleeping with one of the other members. With Brewer's wife, to be exact.

Maybe Eugene hadn't changed as much as I'd thought. Or, rather, maybe he'd changed in a different way.

Stepped away from the group just a bit and examined our table. Not too much had been moved, Mom's doing no doubt. Reviewed what had happened from the point Raj and I had reached this part of the room. Then I looked at Brewer's place setting and the light dawned.

Rejoined Mom as Kevin came to take the Middle Eastern Contingent off to give their statements. Waited until Mom and I were alone. "I have a strong theory. Should I share it now, or do you want me to wait?"

"Wait one moment. Charles!" The way Mom said his name, there was no way Chuckie wasn't going to come right over. She'd definitely put the "you will obey me without question, young man" tone into one syllable.

He indeed disengaged immediately. "Yes, Angela?"

"Kitty has a theory. I'd like you to hear it."

Jeff had great hearing, yet another A-C trait enhanced by Surcenthumain. He joined us, too. "It's okay, baby, we'll get everything taken care of." He took my hand and squeezed it. I squeezed back.

"Good. And, thanks, Mom. I actually think Eugene's telling the truth. In a way."

"Really?" Chuckie didn't sound impressed or pleased that he'd been called over here.

"Really. I do think he's the one who put arsenic in the water glass, only Santiago Reyes wasn't his target."

"Shut up, Kitty," Eugene said desperately.

"No way in hell, you jerk. And, just in case you weren't sure, I'm never forgiving you for both murdering Santiago in such a horrible way *and* doing it on American Centaurion soil, regardless of whatever diplomatic thing is being facilitated by Andrei." Maybe I could insist that Eugene be executed in the public square, so to speak, as appeasement for American Centaurion's outrage. Unlikely, but still something to daydream about.

"Kitty, can you get to the point?" Chuckie asked in a pained tone.

"Sure, since we're on a schedule and all. Eugene wasn't trying to kill Santiago—he was trying to kill Edmund Brewer."

CHAPTER 23

MY ANNOUNCEMENT engendered lots of gasps of shock from everyone other than Eugene, Mom, and Chuckie. Even Jeff gasped. Enjoyed my Big Reveal moment. Knew everyone's being impressed with me wouldn't last long.

"Why do you feel that Representative Brewer was the actual target?" Chuckie asked, speaking quite slowly and distinctly. Reader, Cliff, Andrei, and the others from their table gathered 'round.

"Because Edmund Brewer didn't drink his water. He gave it to Santiago instead."

Everyone gave me polite looks that said I was either crazy or making no sense.

"See?" Eugene said, sounding slightly hysterical. "He's the one who did it! His fingerprints will probably be on the glass."

"Of course his fingerprints will be on the glass—it was his originally. But you're the one with the evidence on you, Eugene . . . and the motive." Was glad Jeff had a firm hold on my hand, because I really wanted to tackle Eugene and throttle him.

"Give us the full explanation, girlfriend, because we need the clarity," Reader said. Nice to see I was back on his friend, versus formal, speaking mode.

Shot a glance in Nathalie's direction. She caught my eye and nodded. Hoped that meant she was okay with my spilling the beans.

"Okay, Eugene is jealous of Edmund."

"Why so?" Cliff asked.

"Because Eugene has been having an affair with Edmund's wife, Nathalie."

"It's in the past," she said quickly. Really? As always, I was the last to know.

Brewer nodded. "Nathalie told me about the affair months ago, and broke it off. We made some . . . adjustments in our work and private lives." He took and squeezed her hand. "All's forgiven between us, and I chose not to confront Gene because it would have hurt Lydia."

Lydia, who was standing next to Cliff, definitely looked hurt and more than a little surprised. But she rallied. "I still don't see how Eugene could have done this."

"Good Stand By Your Man attempt there, Lydia. And, while all might be okay on your side, Edmund, Eugene's not on your side." I'd seen how he'd looked at both Nathalie and his wife. "You have one of the women he wants and I'd bet Lydia's spent a lot of time with you, learning the ropes."

"Yes, of course. That's what you do for your friends and associates." Brewer shot Lydia a warm smile. I'd never realized he was as good a politician as Armstrong, but I was impressed with his ability to give off a completely caring vibe.

Lydia smiled back gratefully. Eugene's eyes narrowed. Wondered if Eugene was really as stupid as he seemed to me right now. Tabled the decision for later.

"So you're also monopolizing a lot of his wife's time."

"We were out as couples quite a lot," Nathalie said quickly.

"Fine. Meaning Eugene gets to see his former mistress happily back with her husband *and* gets to watch his wife look up to his romantic rival at the same time. After a while, he can't take it any more and he plots his revenge, and it's dependent on getting close to you in a situation where anyone could be the murderer."

"This is the first truly big event we've gone to in months," Nathalie confirmed.

"Lucky us. So, we had servers passing around drinks, and lots of them, meaning that someone could have spotted Eugene dropping arsenic in your drink. Dinner would have to do, and it wouldn't have been a problem only we had a seating arrangement that put him close, but not close enough, to you. So he had to do something to get closer."

"That's why he was so obsessed with helping you to sit," Jeff said.

"Yes. And he did a terrible job with it, too. Knocking into Edmund, slamming me into the table, and sloshing water all over. It was really well done, because no one caught him emptying the contents of that packet of arsenic into Edmund's glass. Because there were only the ten of us and everyone was more focused on me and what Eugene was doing to me than what he was doing on or over the table."

"Let's say all that's right," Reader said. "But you need to explain how Santiago ended up drinking that water."

"I gave it to him," Brewer said, and he sounded horrified and saddened. Wasn't sure if it was genuine, but I had a feeling it was. "After he'd almost choked to death and Kitty saved him. He'd drunk all his water and I hadn't touched mine."

"Right. And no one could have predicted that Santiago would choke on a crouton, or that you'd give him your water. But Eugene was a double failure, because he put the arsenic in the one thing you wouldn't touch."

"I was told to!" Eugene said, then slammed his mouth shut.

"Don't try for the insanity defense," Chuckie said. "Your motive seems crystal clear."

Everyone else nodded, but I didn't. My impression wasn't that Eugene was going for the crazy plea. Maybe because of what Hamlin had told me earlier, I wondered if what Eugene meant was that he'd been hired or coerced to perform this assassination.

Raj was standing behind Lydia and he was a tall guy. I could see his face easily. He caught my eye and raised his eyebrow. So he had the same thoughts I did.

"Good work, Kitty," Cliff said. "Depending on whether or not Centaurion Division will allow the police to take Mister Montgomery or not, you've given them, or your own authorities, all they'll need to make this an open and shut case."

"Well, Prince had a paw in this, too."

Upon hearing his name, Prince trotted over from wherever he'd been. While Cliff, Chuckie, Reader, and Mom started to discuss where they were going to take Eugene and who would or wouldn't be allowed to see him, I gave Prince his well-deserved pets. I also used the time to think.

A lot had gone on today, and that usually indicated the Big Plan was in action somewhere and somehow. I needed to figure out what was going on, but to do that, I needed to run my mouth, and it would be nice to run it with someone who'd listen and add in.

Per Hamlin, Chuckie, Mom, and Cliff were out, and that meant Kevin was out, too. Buchanan was God knew where. If I went with Hamlin's warnings, frankly, Buchanan could be the Mastermind. Anyone could. At least, anyone who wanted to destroy and control the A-Cs. And if they were good enough, they could be fooling anyone, including me.

That meant there were three people I knew for sure I could and should talk to. Happily, they were the three people I wanted to talk to anyway.

I took Prince's lead, backed up, and shoved Jeff back gently, then tugged on his hand, while nodding to Raj. "Raj and I need to talk to you," I said quietly.

"You and the new boyfriend want to share your affair in public, too?"

"Jeff, oh my God, the jealousy crap is so not funny, particularly right now." I needed to talk to someone who I knew I could trust with everything I'd done and seen and learned today, and who would hopefully listen and not freak out at me. But if Jeff was going into Major Jealousy Mode right now, he wasn't going to be that someone.

He squeezed my hand. "Sorry, baby, I was teasing you. Bad timing for it, I should have realized."

"Yes, you *should* have." Blocks or no, I was getting worried. Jeff didn't seem to be picking up anything emotionally, from me or anyone else, and that boded badly.

Raj joined us. "Ambassadors, I think we need to talk, somewhere very secure." His voice was low but his expression remained very amiable. He was good.

"I agree. I'd like you to get Richard White, and have him join us, please, Raj. And do it as unobtrusively as possible."

"Unobtrusive is my middle name. Where should we meet?"

Considered our options. They were limited. I heaved a sigh. "Let's all go to the bathrooms on the second floor."

"A good choice." Raj shot us the Troubadour Smile and moved off to where White and some of the other Embassy personnel had congregated.

"Is it?" Jeff asked.

"Well, is Christopher still down there?"

"Yeah, I told him to stay and keep that floor under his guard."

"Then, yes, the bathrooms are a good choice."

Jeff sighed. "Only my girl. We're taking the dog, too?"

"Absolutely. Prince is a hero. Plus Officer Melville is downstairs."

Jeff took Prince's lead from me. "Then let's go walk the dog, baby."

CHAPTER 24

WE TOLD MOM and Chuckie that we were going to back out and let them and the Head of Field handle things while we returned Prince to his rightful owner. Got a suspicious look from both of them, but they let us go without comment. Reader and Cliff, assisted by Andrei, were tossing off a lot of comments about my unintentional declaration of war and what to do with good old Eugene, so that might have been why we were able to get away easily.

The three of us went downstairs. As Christopher joined us, Prince bounded over to Melville, who bent down to give his dog a big hug. "Were you a good dog?" he asked Prince, who licked Melville's face in reply.

"He was a hero and definitely caught the bad guy."

"Glad he did his duty," Melville said. "We've sent your medical staff and a large number of security personnel from your East Base with Representative Reyes' body. They're at the Georgetown Medical Center, and Doctor Hernandez asked me to tell you that Nurse Carter has gone with them as well."

"Good to know." It was. Nurse Carter had been working at the Georgetown Medical Center when we'd met her, so she'd know the people working there and could smooth things over where needed. The thought occurred that she also knew the Dingo and Surly Vic on sight, and that meant she could easily be in danger. The need to get all the things I knew shared with others was getting overwhelming. "So, do we still need to keep this floor secured?"

Officers Larry and Curly joined us and pulled Melville aside. He came back quickly. "We've cleared all the kitchen and wait staff, and based on what you and Prince found, I think we have our killer well in hand. We're almost done taking statements upstairs, too."

"That's pretty fast."

Melville shrugged. Christopher graced me with Patented Glare #3. "We had our personnel help. Since this is our jurisdiction."

"Oh, go us."

Melville smiled at me. "Yeah, it was helpful. And I'm sorry if I upset you earlier, Ambassador. Our unit takes our positive relationship with American Centaurion very seriously. And, based on the killer being caught essentially red-handed, you can relax the guard here. Good police work, by the way."

"Thanks." Wanted to bask in the glow of a job well done. Had a funny feeling in my stomach that said this wasn't the end, but merely the soup course.

Raj and White arrived on the floor and stood in front of the bathroom that had the gate in it. Melville went with Larry and Curly to handle some more police business, and the three of us trotted over. We waited for a few moments, then entered the stall using hyperspeed.

"Okay, what's going on?" Jeff asked once the five of us were inside and we had the door locked.

Tried to figure out where to begin. "I need to tell you things. Many things. But I need you to promise me that you're going to listen to everything and not go racing off until I tell you I'm done."

"When have I ever done that?" Jeff sounded hurt. "I always listen to you, baby."

"I always listen, too," Christopher added. "When don't I listen?"

"Actually, both of you tend to react much faster on occasion than Missus Martini might like right now," White said. "I, on the other hand, am always the picture of patience and good, attentive listening."

"This is so very true. Anyway, Jeff, Christopher, I need to tell you guys things that I guarantee are going to make you mad, and you have to promise me you won't get mad and do anything until I tell you I'm done with my recap." I wanted to add "especially not mad at me" but decided to let the general "don't be mad" cover.

"You're acting like I ignore you," Jeff said. "I always pay attention to your theories, baby."

"She knows," Raj said soothingly. "But I agree that there's enough going on that you need to listen to all of it without passing judgment."

"And Raj doesn't even know everything I'm going to tell you."

"Oh, I think I know more of it than you realize."

"How so?"

Raj shrugged. "I'm waiting for some goods I ordered to be delivered. And we're meeting here, not in the basement."

"Gotcha. Raj, you impress me with your Soul of Discretion-ness."

"I live to serve, Ambassador."

"This is touching," Christopher snapped. "But all you've told us is that you two have a secret that, one day, you might share with the rest of us."

"Why should we be meeting in the basement?" Jeff asked, eyes narrowed. "What's there?"

"Nothing anymore, and that's part of the problem." Took a deep breath. "I'm going to give you the high-level bullet points. Then we're going to discuss them. Then, after that, we're going to talk about and agree on what we're going to do. Promise?"

The men all nodded. "Jeff and Christopher, I want to hear you promise." They both mumbled something. "You either promise and do whatever death swear Alpha Four has, or I'm only going to share what's going on with Richard."

Jeff sighed. "Fine, baby, I promise to listen to everything you have to say and discuss it like a grownup, and then abide by what we all decide to do."

"What Jeff said," Christopher said. "I swear, or whatever will make you happy."

"Works for me. I know I don't have to drag this out of Richard."

"No, I believe I stand firmly on the side of the only person with the track record for success when running off half-cocked, Missus Martini."

"I'll hurt you later, Rick, honey."

"Oh, it's catsuit time again?"

"I think so, yeah. Right now, you four are the only ones I can talk to about this. If Raj hadn't been with me earlier, he wouldn't be in this exciting Inner Circle, but it's got to stay among the five of us only for now."

The men all nodded. So far, so good.

Checked to make sure my thoughts were organized and in chronological order. Knew I had to leave out anything about our lack of ACE. Not a problem. Jeff knew and everything else I had to share was easily as stressful.

"Any time, Kitty," Christopher snapped.

"Oh, cool your jets. Fine, I'm ready. Remember, bullet points, and none of you speak until I'm done." They all nodded. "Okay, first off, I saw Clarence Valentino today. He's alive, can't verify how well, but he was watching the Embassy from Sheridan Circle."

Jeff opened his mouth.

I put my hand up. "You don't get to speak yet. Our UPS man's truck was ransacked and he had to essentially do double deliveries today. Our second delivery was a package, addressed to me, but with the Embassy's return address. I had the package in my hands when I spotted Clarence and went after him. Malcolm was watching me, but he didn't see Clarence."

"Was it a bomb?" Christopher asked.

"Did I say I was done? No, I did not. You don't get to talk yet. I chased Clarence into the Oak Hill Cemetery, where I lost him. Then my phone rang, and an old friend called. And no, it wasn't Sheila or one of my sorority sisters. It was Peter the Dingo."

"We need to put everyone under guard," Jeff said.

"Stop it! I am not done!"

"Jeffrey, you promised," White said. "And, frankly, since your wife is standing here, alive and well, obviously there's more to it than we know yet."

"Thanks, Richard. Okay, so I think the Dingo is actually sort of thinking of me as his niece, or at least as someone to protect. Surly Vic, too. They're here because Raul the Other Assassin is out of Guantanamo or wherever he was stashed and is coming after me to avenge the death of his wife, Bernie. Which means he's also probably after Malcolm, if he realizes Malcolm is the one who killed her. The package we

were sent was indeed a bomb, Christopher, presumed to be
a bioweapon of some kind, and the Dingo took it from me
in order to defuse it. They, ah, also swore me to secrecy. And
gave me a burner phone so I could call them if I needed
their help."

"Wait, the two top assassins are here to protect you? Seriously?" Christopher sounded like he couldn't believe me.
Couldn't blame him, I could barely believe it, either.

"And you let them take a bioweapon?" Jeff asked,
sounding like he could believe it but was hoping he'd heard
wrong.

"Yes and yes, but we're still at my telling you all what's
gone on and you shutting the hell up. So, I went back to the
Circle, but Malcolm hadn't seen Clarence and he didn't remember I had a package. So I didn't push it, because I didn't
want to have to lie to him."

"I believe Mister Buchanan missed Clarence, and much
of the ambassador's exploits, because they were both using
hyperspeed more than perhaps the ambassador herself realizes," Raj said.

"If you saw Clarence why didn't you say something?"

Raj shook his head. "I'm truly expecting a delivery that
was guaranteed to come today, so when I spotted the UPS
truck making a second round, I kept an eye on it. My office
is near the front door; I thought I'd save Pierre a trip. But
you answered the door first. So, I watched you. I spotted the
man you think was Clarence Valentino about the same time
I believe you did."

"What do you mean 'I think' was Clarence?"

"I've never met him, but I also didn't have a clear
enough view to be able to pick the man out of a lineup let
alone a crowd. I know he was an A-C because of how fast
he was moving. I chose not to mention it because you returned safely and it was clear from what I overheard you
saying to Mister Buchanan that you didn't want to tell anyone."

"So, you think Clarence is the one who actually poisoned
Santiago?" Jeff asked.

"No. I have no idea what Clarence is up to, but I think
he's the one who planted the package in the UPS truck. The
Dingo felt the bomb or weapon or whatever it really is was
set to go off during the party or when it was opened. But

wait, there's more. Remember that I had a visitor when we were all having mocktails, a person you and I both thought was probably Malcolm."

"Yeah, Raj got you, I remember."

"The visitor was actually Colonel Marvin Hamlin. Malcolm spotted him and moved him, Len, and Kyle into the basement. Raj can back me up on all of this, as can the boys, but Hamlin says he's been on the run a lot longer than we'd think—longer than the start of Operation Destruction. Since before Jamie was born."

Jeff's eyes narrowed. "If that's true, who was impersonating him, an android?"

"That's our suspicion, yeah. Anyway, here's Hamlin's big reveal—he thinks that everything that's going on, and I mean *everything*, is the work of one Mastermind. A person who's been pulling the strings and manipulating all the other bad guys. He has the background in military intelligence to make us believe he knows what he's talking about, but he also has no guess who it is, but it's someone well connected and, per Hamlin, brilliant. And also per Hamlin, I'm the only one he can trust because I'm still identified as Enemy Number One by whoever's in charge."

Here it came, the part I wasn't going to enjoy sharing.

"So, Colonel Hamlin suggested you not share any of this with either Charles, Clifford, your mother, or any other number of people you'd normally turn to," White said without missing a beat.

"Wow, Richard, were you there or did Raj fill you in?"

"No, it just makes sense. If Colonel Hamlin is telling the truth, a Mastermind of that level would have to be brilliant. And we have a great number of brilliant people in our circle."

"We do. We're missing two of them, though. We left Malcolm and Hamlin in the basement. Malcolm seemed to have everything under control, but when Santiago was first sick, before I knew how bad it was, Camilla told me why she was on-site, so I went to check on Malcolm and Hamlin. They're both gone, I couldn't reach Malcolm on his phone, and Christopher couldn't find him."

"I didn't search the cosmos, but Kitty thinks he's in the tunnel system somewhere."

"I think they both are. They have easy access to it from

our basement. I'm worried that one or both of them are more than gone, though."

"You think someone killed them?" Jeff asked.

"Hamlin feels there are assassins after him, and while Malcolm is amazing, he's not invulnerable."

"He's also brilliant and capable enough to be the Mastermind," Raj mentioned.

"And before we head down that path, I think Eugene said something that could be related. When he said he was told to poison Brewer's water—I realize everyone thinks he's trying for the crazy defense, but what if he was manipulated by the Mastermind?"

Jeff ran his hand through his hair. "What would the point be of having Eugene kill either Santiago or Brewer? From a Mastermind's perspective, I mean."

"We probably don't have enough information yet," Raj said before I could. "But I think we have more urgent concerns."

"So many I'm losing count."

"Such as what Camilla told Kitty," Jeff said. "I wasn't advised about anything going on."

"Ah, sorry, missed a bullet point. James' side of things got wind that one of the 'captains' from Operation Destruction was coming here, most likely to hurt Paul, our children, or me. If the 'captain' was Hamlin, then that's correct intel but, as far as we know, incorrect plan, so to speak. But if there's another captain out there, then he or she could still be gunning for any of us."

"But if Colonel Hamlin overpowered or hurt Mister Buchanan, that intelligence could be completely correct," Raj added.

"Wonderful. No chance we can grab everyone, head to Cabo, and forget about all this, is there?" Jeff asked.

"Sadly no. Oh, Santiago asked me to personally clean out his desk. He also had a message for James. And I want to talk to Eugene to see if he'll tell me if he was given the idea or coerced or something. Did you get anything from him emotionally?"

Jeff shook his head slowly. "Not a thing, actually. And you'd think I would have, even with my blocks up. Eugene's not a cool, relaxed killer. He'd have to have been nervous, excited, something."

"Jeff, you haven't felt anything much tonight, not since the guests started showing up, I can tell. Can you humor me and take your blocks down for a minute?"

He gave me a long look. "I hope you're wrong." He closed his eyes. "They're down." Eyes opened, looking straight at me. Jeff had an expression in his eyes I wasn't used to seeing—fear. "I can't feel you, baby. I can't feel anyone."

CHAPTER 25

I REALLY WANTED TO PANIC. However, that didn't seem like a good plan. Besides, Raj beat me to the reaction punch.

"Ambassador, if I may, could we please search you?" Raj asked politely.

"Why?" Jeff looked freaked and sounded upset. Couldn't blame him.

"I have a theory. It's one I don't want to forward until we've searched you, and then the rest of us, honestly, probably starting with Ambassador Katt-Martini's purse."

Figured out where Raj was going with this. And I never had a problem forwarding a theory. "You think someone slipped Jeff an electronic mickey?"

"A what?" Christopher asked.

"A who?" Jeff asked.

"Yes," Raj replied with a smile.

"You actually know what that meant?" Jeff asked him.

Raj chuckled. "We're much more media and pop culture focused at New Delhi Base."

"Great," Christopher grumbled. "Someone else to encourage more Kitty-isms."

"Raj, this could be the beginning of a beautiful friendship. Christopher, I'm ignoring you."

"Our enemies have certainly used electronic bugging on us before," White said possibly in an attempt to get us back on topic. "I'd say we all need to be searched." He began patting himself down.

Raj and Christopher did the same, while Jeff and I did each other. It didn't take long—I found a small disk in his outer suit pocket. Dumped my purse out—nothing I hadn't put in it.

"Okay, let's see what this thing I found on Jeff does when I smash it."

"Wait!" Raj grabbed my hand. "If it's what we think it is, it needs to be reverse engineered so we can determine how to guard against it."

"Good point, and nice save." Clearly Jeff wasn't the only one upset and not necessarily thinking straight. I was normally smarter than this. Wondered if I'd missed some Electronic Brain Slower disk in my purse somehow. Decided I was still understandably upset over Reyes dying in front of me while I was holding his hand and cut myself a break.

Jeff stared at Raj for a long moment. "You're hired. Full time. Have the Operations Team send the rest of your stuff, you're staying with us."

"Wow, this emotional blocker thing seems to do wonders for your ability to reason logically."

"Hilarious. I'd like to know if whatever you're holding is actually what's blocking me, though."

Christopher took the disk from my hand and disappeared.

"Still feel nothing," Jeff said. He jerked. "Oh. No, everything's back." He blinked. "Hang on, I need to put my blocks back up, fast."

My phone rang. Dug it out. "Jeff feeling things again?"

"Yes. You can come back now, Christopher."

"Why don't you come to me?"

"Why? And where are you?"

"Why? Because, unlike you, I don't want to hang out with four other people in a bathroom any longer. For where, I went to the farthest point from Jeff I could get. I'm in the basement. And yes, I'm alone."

"Gotcha. Are we sure it's safe to have the walkway opened up for everyone?"

"I told Walter to put the shield up over the buildings. He said he'd done that as soon as all the guests were inside."

"He's so good."

"Yes, but why arc we still talking? Oh, wait, it's you. You really like it in the bathroom, don't you?"

"Blah, blah, blah. See you shortly." Hung up and gave everyone a bright smile. "Christopher's in the basement. He suggests we join him."

"I'm fine with that," Jeff said. "I'll monitor myself to see when I stop feeling anything. But what about everyone upstairs?"

"Let's get all my news dealt with first, okay? Because until we do, I don't know what to do about anybody upstairs."

Jeff nodded and took my hand. Raj opened the door for us, and we all hypersped out and down the walkway, which was indeed no longer blocked. Reached the basement quickly. Sadly, Christopher was indeed alone.

"I stopped feeling people the moment we got into the Embassy," Jeff shared.

Christopher nodded. "I monitored your mind when I left. I needed to be a good hundred yards away before I could tell you started to pick up emotions again."

"That's a football field. It would have covered everyone at the party and part of the Embassy, too. So why didn't you notice?"

Jeff shook his head. "I don't know. I could pick up some emotions, but they were faint and none of them alerted me to anything going on. But I suppose because I could pick up some emotions, I wasn't alerted to the fact I wasn't getting any nearby."

"So, you might have noticed, only you had your blocks up high."

"Which anyone who knows Jeffrey would know he'd have to do at an event such as we had tonight."

White had a point. "Which means whoever slipped this into your pocket was here tonight and knows us well."

"No," Raj said. "The person who planted this doesn't have to know any of you well or even at all. He or she just had to plant a bug. Whoever created this is the person who knows you well enough to know how to block the most powerful empath we have."

"My money's on the Cabal of Evil doing the planting, it's one of their go-to moves. Hell, could have been Eugene, if he was really taking orders from someone."

"If he was," White said slowly, "then that person could easily be in the Zoo right now."

"You think they're going to do a Jack Ruby on him?"

"What?" Jeff and Christopher asked in unison.

"Jack Ruby assassinated Lee Harvey Oswald before he could stand trial," Raj replied without missing a beat. "Then Ruby was killed. It's one of the reasons a conspiracy theory surrounds President Kennedy's death."

"Raj, did you also go to human schools?"

"No, we just really like the History Channel at New Delhi Base. Along with all the other channels. But I believe you're correct to worry."

"So, what do we do?" Christopher asked.

"We do what Kitty wanted, and think about what's going on, determine what our options are, and plan accordingly." Jeff was back to full on Commander Mode. Which was alright with me.

"The way I see it, we have the usual three different plans going on," Christopher said. "Whatever's going on with the assassins and why they're really here, whatever Clarence—if it's really him Kitty saw—is up to, and the murder tonight and whatever else might be going on around it."

"Trust me, it was Clarence. I'm sure of it." Well, I was pretty sure, and my hunches were usually right, so I was sticking with Clarence unfortunately being alive and well. "What about Colonel Hamlin's warning, and Buchanan and whatever's happened to them? And we also have this emotional inhibitor that someone planted on Jeff. Even if it's related to Eugene's insanity tonight, that indicates a much higher level of tech savvy than I know Eugene's capable of. And that makes, what, five different plans?"

"I'm sure they're connected in some way," White said.

"Well, yeah, Richard, they usually are. But which is related to the other and in what way?"

"Does it matter?" Raj asked. "There are five of us, that means we can each explore one of the situations and see where it leads."

"Not alone," Jeff said firmly. "Whatever's going on, it's deadly. We just lost a friend less than two hours ago. I don't want to lose anyone else."

"We've already lost Buchanan and Hamlin," I pointed out.

"We'll find them," Jeff said confidently.

"Potentially not without help." I wasn't being Polly Positive right now, but facts had to be faced.

"But we can't trust anyone else, can we?" Christopher asked. "I mean, based on what Kitty was told. *If* it was true, that is."

"Let's assume it was," White said mildly. "At least until events prove otherwise."

"Richard, you sound really calm."

"It's part of my charm, but yes, I'm not as panicked as you sound, Missus Martini."

"Do I sound freaked? I don't feel freaked."

"Yes, you do, baby," Jeff said, as he pulled me to him and hugged me. "You're handling it really well, but we just went through a hugely upsetting experience, and you had a busy day well before then. Your stress is off the charts—you're the main reason I had to put my blocks back up. Though, no one else in the entire Embassy or Zoo is feeling a hundred percent normal."

"You're sure? About everyone else." I knew he'd be sure about me. "I'm asking because if someone's feeling triumphant or too relaxed, it could identify our Mister Big."

Jeff and Christopher looked at each other. "I could kill two birds with one stone," Christopher said.

"Take Uncle Richard with you," Jeff said.

Christopher walked over to the cloaked switch that turned the basement into the Jolly Green Giant's elevator. We started moving down.

"Is now really the time for Christopher and Richard to search the tunnel system?"

"We're here and I can do it faster than anyone else," Christopher snapped.

"That you can, son. But I can't."

"Good point," Jeff said. "I can handle the faster speeds, but that defeats one of the purposes of Christopher going into the tunnels in the first place. And I have to insist that I don't want any of us doing anything alone right now."

Considered our options. They seemed slim. If I wanted to focus only on humans or A-Cs. But it was me, and I didn't.

CHAPTER 26

"HANG ON A MOMENT." Concentrated. In a few seconds, Bruno appeared, along with Harold, who was the male half of Christopher's set of Peregrines.

Jeff jumped. "Geez, I hate how they do that. And just where the hell were you when people were being murdered?" he asked Bruno.

Bruno ruffled his feathers and warbled.

"Ah. Um, none of us were in danger, per Bruno."

"Santiago died," Jeff said flatly.

Bruno cawed at him, and he sounded pissed.

"Um, Bruno's job isn't to protect visiting dignitaries. His job is to protect the Royal Family and their Retainers. And, um, I'm quoting here. Bruno's also got the Poofs' backs on this one—it's not their job, either."

"What the hell?" Christopher snapped. "Then what good are they if they can't stop someone from being killed in our home?"

Bruno squawked indignantly and Harold started in, too. I had two seriously pissed Peregrines facing off against two seriously annoyed men. Not good. Especially when Harlie, Poofikins, Christopher's Poof, Toby, and a variety of other Poofs appeared, and started jumping up and down and mewling in a very angry manner.

I cleared my throat. Loudly. The Poofs and Peregrines quieted down. "Jeff, Christopher, let me explain something for you. The Peregrines and the Poofs are animals. Alpha Four animals, to be sure, but animals. They have very clear

reasoning, therefore. They have been bred for thousands of
years with one job and one job only. Deviation from that
job isn't in their makeup."

Bruno squawked and nudged up against me, as Harlie
and Poofikins jumped onto my shoulders, rubbed against
my neck, and purred.

"What do they say?" Jeff asked tiredly.

"Bruno says that if I'd known to ask for them to watch
for someone trying to kill a stranger, they'd have done their
best. But that order would have had to have been given, and
understood, in order for them to have taken action. And
now, both of you need to apologize to the Poofs and Peregrines."

"What?" Christopher practically shouted. "Why?"

"You've insulted them and hurt their feelings. I'd like to
mention that insulting the animal that's willing to take a
bullet for you isn't a good idea. It's not their fault that we're
expecting them to think like people." It was, point of fact,
probably my fault.

"You're right, baby. And it's not your fault, either."

"I thought the blocker was blocking you."

"It's blocking me from reading your emotions, but your
expression's crystal clear. And I'm sorry we got mad at the
Poofs and Peregrines. They're right—their jobs aren't to
protect our party guests. That's our job."

"Actually," Raj said, "it's the job of Security and Centaurion Division to provide protection for all of American
Centaurion's Diplomatic Corps and their guests."

Something about what Raj said struck me, for the first
time since we'd moved in here. "Christopher, apologize,
right now. I need to ask something."

He shot Patented Glare #4 at me, but Jeff nudged him,
hard. "Fine. I apologize to the Poofs and Peregrines for getting mad at them."

Toby sniffed and pointedly jumped onto my shoulder, as
Harold came and stood on my other side. "Wow, they can
totally tell when you're lying."

Christopher rolled his eyes. "Why is this relevant?"

"You want to search the tunnels? Then you're taking
Bruno and Harold and Toby with you. If they decide to forgive you, that is." The elevator stopped, but no one kicked
the wall plate to open the door.

White cleared his throat. "Why don't the three animals in question go to the other side of the room with Christopher and straighten things out that way?" He shot Christopher an extremely parental "do what I say and shut your mouth" look. Christopher sighed and stepped away.

"Go on," I said gently to Bruno. He, Harold, and Toby went over, unwillingly if I was any judge. "Okay, while they sort all that out, I have to ask—who did Security for the Embassy before we were here? Walter walked into a fully functional mini Command Center, so someone had to be doing the job."

"Interesting question," White said. "I honestly don't know."

Jeff looked at me. "We need to know, don't we?"

"I think we do, yeah. Because we've already established that some of the human drivers who worked for the former Diplomatic Corps are still loyal to them. What about their Security team? Were they part of the horrible Gaultier's Zombie Monsters experiments, or were they one with the cause?"

"Thing were so chaotic when we moved in, it never occurred to me to ask," Jeff said. "And Gladys never said anything about Walter replacing an existing agent."

"Maybe they'd gotten rid of Security, but I think we need to know, and soon."

Christopher rejoined us. "I think I groveled enough to be forgiven. So, I'm going to check the tunnels. But before I go, do you think Hamlin was a human or an android fooling you, Kitty?"

"Love how you put that. We hadn't determined before Jeff called me and Raj to dinner."

"I'd bet on the real one," Raj said.

"I think it'll depend on what shape Malcolm is in if and when you find him."

"Fine. I'll search the system within a hundred mile radius. There's no way they could get farther than that even in this time."

"If they're both really human, I don't think they could get a quarter of that distance in the time since Raj, the boys, and I left them, but that'll give us a good cushion. You won't burn yourself out? That's a lot of running."

"I had a big meal, I'm good."

"I believe the ambassador should unblock before Consul White goes. That way the ambassador can tell the moment he can feel again."

"Call me Jeff, Raj, please. The formality when we're in private meetings is killing me."

"Good plan," Christopher said.

"Well, it is if Jeff's going to be okay doing it. I'm trying not to be stressed, by the way."

"Yeah, baby, I'll be fine, even if your stress is still high. Just give me a minute." Jeff relaxed against me, took a deep breath, let it out, and relaxed some more. We were all quiet for a good couple of minutes. Couldn't speak for anyone else but being silent that long was certainly hard for me. "Okay."

"Before I go, let's get a baseline—what can you feel?" Christopher asked. "Anything?"

"Yeah," Jeff said finally. "Can't feel any of you, not even Kitty, but I can feel the people over at the Zoo. They feel faint, but readable. I'm not picking up anything I shouldn't. Then again, I wasn't picking up anything earlier, including the fact that my wife was having visits from the presumed dead."

He had a point. I wasn't good enough to hide much from Jeff in the first place, and that he'd missed that I'd visited with two assassins, chased Clarence, and chatted with Hamlin seemed so unlikely as to be impossible.

My brain nudged—nice to know it was still with us. "You know, what are the odds—if someone could create an emotion-blocker that works to make Jeff empathically deaf, dumb, and blind—that this same someone couldn't create an emotions-controller? The androids that Marling created were so good that they gave off human emotions and fooled Jeff and the other empaths. Good enough that we're questioning if the Hamlin we met was the real deal or not. What if someone altered that technology and made it so that a person would give off specific, normal emotions, but not the biggies, like gloating and murderous intent?"

"I'd believe it's quite good, Ambassador."

"Raj, seriously, I'm with Jeff, start calling me Kitty. And I agree. We need to get that disk reverse engineered pronto."

"Can we trust the reverse engineers?" Christopher asked. "I'm going to keep on coming back to this until we have some better answers than 'I don't know' and 'we'll find out.' If Colonel Hamlin is right, who, besides the five of us, can we actually trust?"

"Technically, you can't trust me," Raj said. "I haven't been involved with any real activities until recently."

My stomach sank. Raj was right. "What if we can't trust anybody?"

CHAPTER 27

❝I'M NOT SAYING you can't trust me, Kitty," Raj said patiently. "I am saying that based on Colonel Hamlin's warnings, and speaking somewhat modestly, I fall under Colonel Hamlin's area of concern."

"So, if you're brilliant enough to be the Mastermind, why were you hanging out at New Delhi Base all this time?"

Raj shrugged. "My skills don't fall toward medicine, mathematics, or science. I'm a good investigator, and I've been asking for a Centaurion Division Main post for years. Until the invasion earlier this year, I was told that since Centaurion Division wasn't into creating entertainment no one needed troubadours and I should enjoy myself and catch a few more Bollywood movies."

"Christopher, that was very rude." This earned me Patented Glare #5.

"How do you know I'm the one that said that? It could have been someone else."

"Was it?"

"No. But it could have been."

Jeff sighed. "Christopher, we have to figure out what to do with that disk. I need to be able to function."

"I don't want it lost or stolen," Christopher said, while sharing Patented Glare #2.

"We need some leaded casing to keep Superman's Kryptonite from draining his powers. But the person we'd ask for this stuff is one of the people we're no longer supposed to trust." I was really hating this, in no small part because my mother and oldest friend were supposedly on the untrust-worthy side of the house.

"Let's determine who we *can* trust," White said. "Before Christopher goes in search of Mister Buchanan and Colonel Hamlin. Then Jeffrey can read Rajnish and we can continue on with the unraveling of the latest attempts to ruin our lives."

"Succinctly put. What Richard said. Let's start with the obvious—there's no way Paul or any of the Gowers are against us."

"Gladys could be," Raj said.

"Why so?" Jeff asked a tad belligerently.

"Because she's only Former Pontifex White's half sister. Her loyalties could lie with her late father."

"Rajnish is correct to bring it up," White said quickly, before Jeff could get angry. "But I can assure all of you that Gladys, like every other Gower, is definitely not on the side of my late father, the Purity of the Race Contingent, nor the War Division group."

"Richard, I'm so proud. You used all my Bad Guy Group names."

"I've decided the battle against them is fruitless."

"Wise man takes the path of least resistance. Okay, so Claudia and Lorraine, and their parents, I know they're trustworthy. James for sure. Tim proved himself way back when, so he's in. Same with the flyboys. And Tito."

"So, you think the core team when Jeff, you, and I were the heads of Centaurion Division are all cleared?"

"Yes, because we all went through too much. Honestly, I realize that Hamlin suspects Chuckie, but I go back to what Amy said during Operation Destruction—no one, no matter how brilliant, would allow themselves to be that close to real death. There was no way Chuckie could have guessed Christopher's Surcenthumain boosted talent level, or known that Richard, the Poofs, and I would arrive in time or be able to do anything."

"I agree, especially because I was there. And I think the idea that your mother is trying to do anything to hurt you is insane, baby. No matter what Hamlin may have said."

"I would see most of our key personnel as being cleared," White agreed. "Kevin and Mister Buchanan as well. I agree wholeheartedly with Jeffrey, and I include your father in that as well. It's impossible to believe that your mother would have allowed anyone even remotely suspect to be this close to her only daughter and grandchild."

"Mom's been fooled before. Chuckie, too."

"But only because of governmental protections," White countered.

Raj cocked his head. "Washington."

"Excuse me?" Jeff asked.

But I got it. "The people we probably can't trust are those we've come to know since changing jobs and moving here. The former Diplomatic Corps may have been friends with them, but they were one with both the Purity of the Race and the War Division plots, so for all we know, they'd know exactly who was behind this." Only the Poofs had eaten them.

"Doreen is suspect, however," White said, apparently on my wavelength. "While I don't for one moment doubt her loyalty to us, the fact that we did kill her parents could easily make her a double agent."

"It was self-defense and she hated them. But yeah, you're right. It's a stretch to see her as the Mastermind, though. Not because she's not brilliant enough—both she and Irving are certainly smart enough to make that cut—but because she's too young."

"Camilla is a spy," Jeff said. "And she's worked as at least a double agent for us already."

"Triple, really. And yeah, your dad hired her, but I agree, we probably can't trust her implicitly. And she'd also be smart enough, and she's older than Doreen, so she also has Mastermind potential. Though she's the only reason we're all still alive."

"Who else?" Jeff asked. "Of our closer personnel, I mean."

"Pierre, Len, and Kyle. I think they're all clear, honestly. Especially if we accept the fact that there's no way Chuckie's the Mastermind."

"Magdalena," White said. "We're intimate, but that could be her getting close."

Christopher shot his father Patented Glare #1. "There's no way you mean that."

"I don't mean that I don't trust her. I mean that, based on this particular exercise, we need to move her into the Mastermind potential group."

"Don't take this the wrong way, but is she smart enough?" Dazzlers were, without question. Nurse Carter was pretty damn smart, but I wasn't ready to declare her a genius on Chuckie's level.

"If she's truly the Mastermind, we wouldn't know," White replied. He seemed completely unperturbed.

"Richard, you're finding this funny in some way, aren't you?"

"In that sense, I suppose I am. In part because I believe Rajnish has hit the nail on its proverbial head—these actions against us are coming from someone who is a high-level Washington insider, therefore we need to look at high-level Washington insiders who we've only interacted with this past year."

"What about the freeloaders?" Jeff asked.

"Hacker International's loyalties are to Chuckie, and I've known these guys for years, especially Stryker. As long as we all agree that Chuckie's not the evil Mastermind, then I think it's safe to clear them. Olga and Adriana, too, really. I'm only alive because of them."

"What about the others you told to meet you in the computer lab?" Raj asked, using the nice name for where Hacker International hung out.

"The Middle Eastern Contingent falls into the same area as Doreen. Unlikely to be against us, but shouldn't be given full info until we're sure. Same with Cliff, who for sure is brilliant enough to be the Mastermind, although he's almost too young. Same with all the politicians and lobbyists we know, even Senator McMillan."

"Colonel Franklin?" Jeff asked.

Shook my head. "He was okayed way too long ago. The dude who was the head of Area Fifty-One is in no way going to be the evil anti-alien Mastermind. However, I don't know how much we want him, or Captain Morgan, involved. Similar to the K-9 cops, called in when needed but military, like police, tend to get in the way."

"I can agree with all that," Christopher said. "So, do I take the disk with me or leave it with all of you? If I run into trouble the disk could get damaged or stolen, and if Jeff can feel people in the Zoo, we've determined range."

"Put it in Kitty's purse," Jeff said. "That's where we store most of the bugs anyway."

"Ha ha ha, you are so funny." I took the disk and put it into the little zippered pocket on the inside of my handbag, hopefully keeping it safe from damage or theft.

"Okay, Jeff, I don't plan to be gone too long, but do your best to monitor me the moment you can. I know that'll be close to impossible because of the tunnels' shielding, but pay attention because for all I know, I'll find something that will lead me above ground." Christopher grinned. "So I won't block you."

Jeff laughed. "Will do. Be careful." He looked at Bruno. "I don't care if you're all still upset with him or not. He'd better come back safely—and I mean that with the idea of it being the most direct order possible—or else we'll be having stuffed Peregrine for dinner with a side of diced Poof."

The animals all shot me looks that said they knew I'd never allow that *but* they'd humor Jeff anyway.

White kicked the part of the wall that opened the door to the Tunnels of Doom and Christopher and his Alpha Four Animal Honor Guard took off.

CHAPTER 28

"DO WE WAIT HERE** for Christopher or do we head up and see about getting something done?" White asked. Months ago we'd identified where the elevator button was on the inside of the tunnels, so he wasn't suggesting stranding his only son.

"I don't think we have a clear enough idea of what's really going on yet to make a lot of headway in the done department. But if we're open to ideas, I really do want to talk to Eugene, especially if Raj is right and the Mastermind is in attendance. And then I want to give James Santiago's message and clean out his office like he asked me to."

"You also have several diplomatic couples waiting for you in the computer lab," Raj reminded me. "You need to see to them before you do anything else."

"And no one's going to let you into Santiago's office at this time of night, baby."

"Good point." Time of night brought up another, differently pressing concern. "Oh my God, what are we going to do about Jamie and the other kids? Serene told me Brian went to the Pontifex's Residence, I presume for the same reason Camilla was in attendance. But I don't want Jamie picking up anything that's gone on, and I know she will if we bring her home right now."

"Not to worry," White said. "The children, and all your pets, are all spending the night. I called Denise and Gladys as soon as your mother advised us we weren't to leave the room, but before my phone was confiscated. The Operations

Team will bring over anything that's needed and Gladys increased Security where they are as well."

"The Elves always deliver. But, really, Mom took your phone, Richard?"

"She took mine, too," Raj said. "We probably should get those back."

"So, we're going back to the Zoo. Jeff, did Mom take your phone, too?"

"No, I claimed diplomatic immunity and the likelihood that her daughter would try to call me. We can head back, but you all need to remember that we have to keep a lot of what we just discussed to ourselves."

"Mom and Chuckie are not going to want to hear that the Dingo's in town, for example." I knew they'd find out, somehow, and already dreaded their reactions.

"The assassins I'd like to tell them about, but I know you promised. However, when the Dingo shoots one of us, you may change your mind." Jeff didn't sound like he was joking.

"He said he wasn't after anyone I'd care about. I think he's clearer than many about who I care about." Why I was suddenly defending Peter the Dingo Dog I couldn't say, but when I'd been with him and Surly Vic I truly hadn't picked up any danger or animosity coming from them. Which was more than I could ever say when I was around half of the Cabal of Evil.

"You're giving a lot of credit to a man who spent all his efforts the first time you met him trying to kill you, me, and our daughter."

"He's got that weird sense of honor. I don't think he'll ever accept a job on us now. It's why Magdalena's still alive, too."

"Speaking of whom, I believe she should be, if not warned, then at least protected," White said. "And I'd like to ensure that our people at the hospital are well."

"From what Officer Melville told us, it sounds like we have a lot of people over there. Jeff, should we send someone with Richard?"

"I hate to say this, but the farther I am from the blocker in your purse, the more use I'm going to be."

"Great, so once everyone's phones are back in their possession, Jeff, you and Richard will go to the hospital, and Raj and I will go upstairs and visit Hacker International. I'm sure Ravi will leap at the chance to reverse engineer something easier than an android."

Jeff heaved a sigh, but he hit the switch that took us back up. He pulled me to him and hugged me. "A night when Jamie's having a sleepover should mean we never leave the bedroom," he murmured as he nuzzled my ear.

"Mmmm-hmmm." I couldn't talk—anytime his mouth was near me like this I had to focus on not grinding against him.

He chuckled and hugged me tighter. "Nice to see you returning to sort of normal." Jeff kissed the top of my head. "Remember, what happened to Santiago isn't your fault any more than it's Ed Brewer's. Regardless of who did or didn't give him directions, Eugene's the one who murdered someone tonight, not any of us."

I leaned my head against his chest and let his double-heartbeats soothe me. Jeff was right, and I knew it, but it had been nice to be focused on something, anything, other than having watched Reyes die in front of me.

"Are we sure that Representative Brewer was not involved?" Raj asked.

So much for soothing. "I'm not sure."

"I am," Jeff said. "We need to search him and his wife. If they aren't wearing any emotional blockers or whatever, then they're clean. I can still feel people over at the party. And I've gotten to know Ed over the past few months. He feels right."

"That's not necessarily enough for us to go on," I pointed out.

Jeff sighed. "Fine. Here's what I'm getting. Ed's ripping himself up right now for giving his water to Santiago. Nathalie's blaming herself for having had the affair with Eugene in the first place. Ed's furious with Eugene and regretting not telling Lydia before tonight. Nathalie's terrified that Ed's going to blame her for what's gone on and she's also worried about everyone else's reactions. They're both so upset their emotions are as clear as yours normally are, baby."

"As soon as we can, I'll have Security search everyone 'as

a precaution,'" Raj said as we reached the basement. "But those don't sound like emotions you'd automatically have programmed in."

"Who knows what the latest crazed evil geniuses consider normal emotions?" We zipped upstairs. Decided to verify all was really well over here before we went back to the Zoo. "Com on."

"Yes, Chief Katt-Martini?"

"Walt, how's everything over here? Are we secure and do we have personnel in the Embassy again?"

"I have the shielding up on the Embassy, but have had to open shields on the Zoo, or else no one could get in or out. However, per my discussion with Consul White, I've closely monitored the walkway doors between buildings and have only opened for authorized personnel."

"Walter, who, besides Christopher, myself, Kitty, Raj, and Richard, have you let through?" Jeff asked.

"Only Camilla, Chief. She said she needed to check something out on Mister Reynolds' order."

We looked at each other. "Um, Walter, where did she go when she was in here?"

"She stayed in the lower levels, Chief Katt-Martini. Second and first floors."

"So, she didn't try to go into the basement?" Jeff asked.

"No, Chief. Wouldn't you have seen her in there?"

My brain kicked. "Walter, you monitor the basement, right?"

"Of course, Chief Katt-Martini. The basement is set up to be monitored. The tunnel levels less so, but that's because most of the tunnels are now monitored from the computer lab, per Mister Reynolds' order."

They were monitored using human-created sensors and roving cameras, but I'd forgotten that I could have asked Hacker International if they'd spotted Buchanan and Hamlin in some way. Well, I'd do that when Raj and I went up there in a bit.

"So, what happened to Malcolm and the, um, visitor we had down there?"

"Oh, Mister Buchanan told me he was taking your guest somewhere safer. They left via the tunnel system before you'd sat down to dinner. He didn't say you didn't know," Walter added, the worry clear in his voice.

"We've just been a little worried about where Malcolm went is all. Missed the communiqué from him, but all's well if he told you he was taking our guest somewhere." I sincerely hoped.

"Thanks, Walter," Jeff said. "Go back to monitoring."

"Yes, Chief." The com went dead.

"So, what do you think Camilla was doing over here?" Jeff asked as he pulled out his phone and sent a text, presumably to Christopher to let him know that Buchanan was in control of the situation when they'd left the Embassy.

"You want to search or you want to ask her?"

"I want to do both. Wait here." Jeff zipped off at the fast hyperspeed. He was back momentarily. "Nothing seems missing or out of place, at least not in my office, or anywhere else. Raj, you might want to check yours."

"Yes, sir." Raj zipped off and was back even faster than Jeff. When you got right down to it, hyperspeed was really great. "No, Ambassador, nothing seems to be disturbed."

"Jeff. You called Kitty by her first name. Do it with me, too. That's an order, if it helps."

Raj grinned. "It helps . . . Jeff."

"We both tend to prefer informality, Raj," I added.

"No one prefers it more than you, baby, but that's part of your charm."

"So you claim. Now that that's settled, let's find out what Camilla was doing. We're only jumpy because of what Ha—, ah, our guest told me."

"Nice save, baby. If we're assuming our absent guest is right, however, we need to remain jumpy."

"What if, despite our beliefs to the contrary, Mister Reynolds is actually involved?" Raj asked carefully.

"Then we deal with it. Because I don't believe Chuckie's involved in anything that's working against us, at least not consciously or willingly."

"We need to determine if Camilla was really in here on his orders," Jeff said. "And we need to find out what she was looking for and why, whether she came in here on his orders or not."

"Asking directly may not be wise," White pointed out.

"Then we'll be sneaky about it." Took Jeff's hand. "Let's get over to the other side."

Zipped through the Embassy and over the walkway.

Stopped before we hit Grandmother's House, but only because we had to. A part of me was really willing to just run out of the Zoo and keep on going. But most of me wanted to know what the hell was going on and get it stopped.

We hadn't been gone all that long, so we still had a lot of official people milling around on the second floor. Camilla and Chuckie were not among them. But this proved nothing, one way or the other.

I resented the fact that even a little part of me was wondering if Chuckie could be the Mastermind. I'd gotten over a lot of my hatred of D.C. but today's events were threatening to bring it all back, and then some.

Of course, if I were the Mastermind, I'd want to be sure I focused blame on some easy targets. And there was no target easier or more obvious than Chuckie. Therefore, my job, as his oldest and best friend, was to ensure that I didn't fall for the scam, and that I figured out who was behind it. No problem, I was Megalomaniac Girl—this was right there in my wheelhouse.

My internal dilemma solved, I turned back to the matters at hand, the first of which was calming Pierre down, because if I was freaked, he was freaked to the tenth power.

Time was spent in hugs, reassurances that no one in their right mind could hold him responsible, and confirmation that there was still no one better at being our Majordomo Concierge and he was, of course, not going anywhere other than to bed to relax and then to his offices to craft our clever PR response.

We'd easily spent as much time comforting Pierre as we had discussing evil plots against us, so by the time we were done, the K-9 squad were all together and had joined us, Prince nudging in between me and Jeff to get a double dose of petting from his two favorite ambassadors. His words, not mine.

"We're ready to clear out, Ambassadors," Melville said. "We have our killer caught and in custody, have everyone's statements, and Centaurion Division's agreed to let us take possession of the prisoner and book him."

"Is Eugene still on the premises?" I asked.

"He's downstairs in a secured car," Melville said. "Some of your people are there."

"I want to talk to him. Before he leaves."

Melville shrugged. "Fine with me."

"Don't go alone," Jeff said.

"I won't be alone." I took Prince's lead from Melville. "You okay with me snagging your dog again?"

Melville grinned. "Nope, he loves you two."

"I meant take another person." Jeff looked worried.

"No." I leaned up and kissed his cheek. "He may not talk if you're there. Prince will rip Eugene's throat out if he tries anything."

"Promise?" Jeff asked.

Prince wuffed. "Yes, we both promise. Wait here until I'm back, though, please and thank you."

Prince and I trotted downstairs. There were a lot of Security A-Cs around. Had a feeling they'd been called in from most of the Bases worldwide—the only time I'd seen this many in one place was at the Dome. I knew none of the Dome personnel had been pulled away. But even so, there were a lot of big, hulking, handsome guys hanging around in black Armani suits.

They all nodded to me and let me through. The police van taking Eugene away was easily spotted—it was surrounded by squad cars and a lot of men in SWAT gear. I chose not to question.

"I'd like to speak to the prisoner before he's taken away," I said to the nearest official looking guy. His name appeared to be Dier. Especially after looking at a bunch of A-Cs, he was pretty ordinary looking, other than the uniform.

"Authority?"

I checked. Yep, they were in our circular driveway. "You're on my country's land."

He cracked a smile. "Go right ahead, Ambassadress."

"She's an ambassador. Get it right or get out of the way." Tim shook his head as he came to get me. "Amateurs."

"What are you doing down here?"

"Airborne's escorting the prisoner. Just in case."

"All of Airborne?"

We walked around to the back of the van, and sure enough, the five flyboys were all in attendance. Tim was in the standard Armani suit all agents, human or A-C, wore, and the flyboys were still in their Navy dress whites. Eugene was going to have the best-looking and best-dressed honor guard going.

"Hey, Kitty," Jerry Tucker, my favorite flyboy, said. "Been missing our girl. Going to kick this guy in the nuts before he's taken away?"

"Contemplating my options. Can Prince and I go inside?"

Tim nodded to one of the SWAT guys, who opened the doors. I was almost shocked to see Eugene inside and alive.

"Kitty, I'm sorry."

"Sure you are. Guys, a little help?" Joe Billings and Randy Muir, aka Lorraine and Claudia's husbands, each took a side and lifted me into the van, while Prince gave a great example of an effortless, majestic leap. Matt Hughes and Chip Walker climbed in with us. "Um, I kind of want to talk to Eugene alone."

"No," Hughes said calmly.

"Sorry, Kitty," Tim concurred. "My orders. If you're in here, you have guards. Period."

"Oh, fine, fine. Can the doors be closed?"

"Absolutely not," Tim said flatly.

"Chip and Matt will with be with me, and I'm not going to do anything to Eugene anyway." I glanced at our prisoner. "And you have him well-shackled, so unless he's taken a course in how to become an escape artist, I think we're all good. Besides, I have Prince."

Tim sighed. "It's you, Kitty. The bizarre finds you naturally. That's an expensive dog you're trying to carry around in your purse, but he's not enough. The doors stay open, Matt and Chip go inside, and we'll all wait for the explosions."

"Thanks for that and you're hilarious." Tim and the others backed away from the doors. But all of them were watching, the SWAT guys with guns at the ready. Didn't know whether to feel safe or totally in the line of fire. Settled for both. "Guys, can you stay back here while Eugene and I have a quiet talk?"

"Sure," Walker said. "But we'll be watching."

"Never had a doubt." Went to Eugene, who managed to combine a glower along with pathetic hopefulness. It was an interesting combo. "You said you'd been told what to do," I said softly. "What did you mean by that?"

Eugene nodded. "Come closer," he said quietly. "And I'll tell you what I mean."

Prince growled, low in his throat. "Ah, no. I think I'll stay right here and you can tell me what you mean."

"Fine. You're right, I was jealous of Ed. But I wouldn't have killed him, except it was the only way."

"You didn't kill Edmund Brewer, you killed Santiago Reyes. And only way for what?"

"The only way to save the world. You'll see, Kitty. I'm a hero."

CHAPTER 29

HAVING HELPED TO SAVE the world more than a couple times myself, this didn't exactly impress me overmuch. I was also well aware that saving the world and being considered a hero did not necessarily go hand-in-hand.

"You need to come across with more factoids and less bluster. Because I don't buy how killing your sorta romantic rival would save the world."

"He's not who you think he is, Kitty." Eugene dropped his voice. "He's a robot."

My responses to this statement were limited, mostly because there was a fifty percent likelihood this was correct. After all, I'd seen more than my share of really excellent androids over the past year. Or more, depending on who might be still passing as human or A-C instead of identifying as an evil sleeper android.

Went with the safest reply. "Right."

"He is," Eugene said desperately. "Look, Kitty, I didn't know what was in that packet. I was told that it was something deadly to a robotic but that wouldn't hurt a human. Or an alien," he added quickly.

"So, who gave you the packet and your marching orders?"

"I don't know."

"So, it was voices in your head?"

This earned me a dirty look. "No. I was contacted by mail. The situation was explained, and I was asked to help."

"Who approached you?" Chose not to ask why Eugene

thought anyone would approach him for hero work. Most people tended to think of themselves as willing to answer when the call came, after all.

"The C.I.A. The information came to me from Pia Ryan."

"The late Jack Ryan's wife?" Or, as I thought of him, one of the first casualties of Operation Assassination. Eugene nodded. "So, Pia's who gave you all the stuff?"

"No, she gave me an envelope that had been delivered to her. But it was addressed to me. Pia said she figured someone had sent it to her because they knew she knew me."

"And you believed her?"

"She seemed to be telling the truth. She gave it to me at a party, in front of everyone else."

"You mean a party with all the people you used to despise?"

He glared at me. "Yes. Sorry, but I like having some friends."

"You used me and lied to me. That ends friendships in my world."

"Does it? You have a lot of liars around you, Kitty. Maybe more than you realize."

"I'm sure. So, Pia gave you the packet and instructions?"

"No, she gave me an envelope that had another envelope inside it. This was also addressed to me and it was sealed. Inside was a full disclosure briefing about how we have a lot of robots masquerading as important politicians. They're going to activate and take over, soon, unless they're stopped."

Interesting. This was, point of fact, basically true. But we'd found a lot of them during Operation Destruction. However, we all knew we hadn't found every one.

Of course, the idea that some mysterious do-gooder had chosen Eugene to be his or her Instrument of Righteous Annihilation seemed more than a little farfetched. But it was a great way to get someone just gullible enough convinced to do your dirty work. And for sure we had people willing to do things like this prancing all over.

However, it was my turn to talk. Went, again, for noncommittal. "You're high."

"No, Kitty, I'm not. I saw the numbers, the information. I'm an actuary, this is what I *do*. There was a lot of information, and I read through all of it. Ran all the numbers. It all added up. Our people are in danger, mine *and* yours. I had to do something."

"Going to the authorities wasn't an option?"

"There's no one I can trust there. The robots have a lot of control."

It was actually bugging me that he was calling them robots instead of androids. Chose to not correct him and get over it. Presumably whoever was in charge had their reasons for telling Eugene he was dealing with a robot versus an android.

"I'm sure they do. So, you decided to cowboy it all on your own and kill someone accused of being a robot without, say, verifying first?"

"You can't tell they're a robot until they're dead."

"Really." Did my best to get a lot of sarcasm into those two syllables.

"It's true. All the data was in the briefing I got."

"Okay, so where's the information?"

"I can't tell you."

"Look, Eugene, let's pretend that I believe you and don't still want to just kick your shin so hard that it'll never stop hurting. If you really got instructions and information like this, they are the *only* thing that could have a prayer of clearing you of murder in the first. And I'm probably the only one willing to go find this evidence, since I don't see Lydia hanging around telling you she'll wait for your cheating ass even if you get life in prison."

"Why should I trust you? You said you aren't my friend anymore."

"Because to the entire rest of the world, you appear to be a crazy, cheating, and above all, *stupid* murderer, who just killed a public official in a gruesome manner only because you missed your actual intended target, who you wanted to kill so you could have his wife and yours, too. To me, however, you appear to be someone who might be telling the truth. On a Truthfulness Scale of one to ten, I have you at a two right now, but I'm prepared to go into the negative numbers unless you come across with something concrete."

The reality of this seemed to strike him for the first time. "But . . . I didn't know what I put in the water was deadly to anyone but a robot. Killing anyone human was an accident."

"And just who, exactly, do you think is going to believe that, versus calling this extremely premeditated murder? Anyone? Bueller? Right, I only hear the sound of crickets chirping, Eugene."

"What's going to happen to me?" He wasn't really asking me, since he was looking off into space in the terrified manner of someone who just realized they aren't asleep after all and they really are standing naked in front of a huge auditorium filled with everyone they've ever known in their entire life.

"Gas chamber? Firing squad? Lethal injection? I'm not clear on what they do to you around here for this kind of horrific act of violence. But I know what *we'll* do to you, and I doubt that we've relinquished all authority to the D.C. police and local legal system. Tell me where the hefty briefing papers and so-called anonymous instructions are. I'll get them, and if you're telling the truth, I'll make sure the proper authorities know about it."

He nodded. "I kept them hidden. So Lydia wouldn't find them. Just in case."

"Hidden where?"

"Somewhere safe."

"Super. Where, exactly, is this safe place? Your office?" He shook his head. "Security deposit box?" Another head shake. "Bus locker?"

"No. Why would I go to the bus station, ever?"

"Pardon me for sullying your pristine reputation. So, where the hell did you hide these instructions from a mysterious person that you both believed and obeyed?" I'd worry about why he was so stupid later. Like once I'd found this information later. If it was real, we had the means to be able to have a hope of tracking where, and possibly who, it came from.

"I kept it at work."

"Your office?"

"No, I've been free—" Eugene was interrupted by two things. The first was the shriek of a Peregrine that appeared between us and shoved me just a little to the right.

The second was the arrival of a bullet through his brain.

CHAPTER 30

AS BLOOD SPLATTERED, Prince slammed into me and George the Peregrine. I went down, to be quickly covered by Hughes throwing himself on me and, by association, the animals.

Men were shouting, and I heard more shots being fired along with the van doors being slammed shut, even though the shots didn't appear to be coming toward the van. Anymore.

"You okay, Kitty?" Hughes asked.

"Yeah. Can we get up yet?"

"No," Walker replied. "You stay down. Matt, stay on top of her." He sounded tense. Couldn't blame him.

"That bullet was meant for me, wasn't it?"

"Yeah," Walker said. "I think it was. Good thing the Peregrine showed up when it did."

Gave George a nice scritchy-scratch between his wings and petted Prince while we all lay on the floor of the van. A lot of things were running through my mind, not the least of which being that I had a really good guess as to who'd just shot Eugene: Raul the Assassin with a Grudge.

This line of reasoning raised many more questions than it answered, of course. Like where were the Dingo and Surly Vic, what was really going on, and what was the rest of the sentence Eugene was going to speak? I was most interested in the last one, since it was the only way to find whatever he'd been sent.

The shooting stopped. Someone banged on the van

three times. Hughes got off me. "The shooter might have been aiming for both of you," he said as he helped me up.

"Yeah." Walker was examining the part of the van behind what was left of Eugene's head. I pointedly looked at the big hole in the metal, versus the big hole in Eugene. Realized that I'd sort of asked for Eugene to be executed in the public square and this had been pretty close to matching my request. "I think it was an armor-piercing bullet, meaning it would have gone through Kitty and into Montgomery here, too."

"Intentional double-duty or just didn't care about who else got killed?"

"Depends on who hired him," Hughes said. "I mean, we all agree this was the work of a professional, right?"

"Seems like it to me." Hoped this was noncommittal enough that neither one would ask the obvious question.

"Which assassin that's tried to kill you before do you think did this, Kitty?" Walker asked.

So much for noncommittal. "Tell you guys later when we do the team debrief I just know we're going to have." Looked down at my dress. Sure enough, there was blood and dirt all over it. "My dress is ruined."

That said, I burst into tears.

The van doors opened and someone had their arms around me in record time. "I'll take it from here," Jeff said as he picked me up. "One of you take the dog and get him inside the Embassy safely. The bird can take care of itself I'm sure."

I buried my face in Jeff's neck as he zipped us out of the van and into the Embassy. At least I assumed that's what he was doing. I was too busy crying like a baby. Though Jamie rarely cried like this, truth be told.

Heard a door close and lock. Jeff sat down with me in his lap. "We're back in the bathroom, baby." He cleared his throat. "And the bird's still with us."

"Good." Maybe I could wash my face and attempt to not look like a bright red Christmas ornament. "George is just making sure we're really okay. How'd you know to come get me?"

"One of the other Peregrines showed up and started pecking at me while a couple Poofs did their jump up and down and mew in an authoritative manner thing."

"You can understand them now?"

"No. I just figure that when the animals are acting up like that, it has something to do with you being in trouble. So far, the theory's never been wrong." He hugged me. "Thank God you're okay."

"I don't know why I'm crying."

"I do. It's been a hell of a day. Who was the killer aiming for, you or Eugene?"

"Matt, Chip, and I think it was me or both of us, based on the bullet being used. I think the shooter was Raul, by the way."

"Makes sense. Nice to see your supposed 'uncle' was on the job." Jeff's sarcasm knob was definitely turned to eleven.

"Who knows what's really going on? Not me." Pulled my face out of his neck and pulled myself together as much as I could as I sat up. Harlie and Poofikins appeared in my lap and started purring. Having the Poofs there helped a lot. Having Jeff hugging me helped more. "I'm a mess, aren't I?"

"You're always the most beautiful girl in the galaxy to me, baby." Then Jeff kissed me deeply. His kiss always drove everything else from my mind, and I enjoyed it for the kiss itself and the momentary removal of worry about anything else other than getting naked as fast as possible.

Jeff ended our kiss slowly. "We still have lots to do tonight, baby. With this attack, Richard's worried even more about our people at the hospital, and I am, too."

"You two need to get over there. I got some information from Eugene, but he was killed before he could give me all of it."

"Nice to see our luck remains consistent." Jeff hugged me again. "I don't want to leave you alone here."

Shook my head. "I'm inside the Embassy now. No sniper's going to shoot in here, and I'll stay away from windows." Put the Poofs gently onto the couch, gave George another scritchy-scratch, got up, and washed my face with cold water. It helped a little. Focused on the nice fluffy towels we had as I used one to dry my face. We really didn't have time for me to go Basket Case on everyone.

Took a deep breath, let it out slowly. Felt a little more in control, but I still looked like I'd been crying. Fine. I'd looked worse.

There was a knock on the bathroom door. Jeff looked at

me, I nodded, and he opened the door. White came in. "I approve of this as our new office. That way, no one can claim needing to use the facilities to get out of a boring briefing session."

I burst into laughter. "Thanks, Richard. What's up, you heading over to the hospital?"

"Yes, because there's now another body going over. The SWAT team has declared the area devoid of snipers, so I'm going over with Airborne and the entire K-9 division, which should provide me with more than enough protection. Jeffrey, you need to stay with my partner and take care of her until I'm back."

Jeff grinned. "Yes, sir, Uncle Richard."

White came over and hugged me. "Anything I should know before we go? Other than the fact that, apparently, Raul is a sneakier person than the Dingo expects."

"Or he has help the Dingo doesn't." Heaved a sigh. "Eugene got orders telling him Brewer was a robot. Robot, not android, by the way. If we can find those papers, then we can maybe figure out who put Eugene into *La Femme Nikita* Mode. He said they weren't at his home to protect Lydia. I asked about other places. He said he kept them at work, but not his real office. He was mid-word when he was . . ."

"Regardless of what he thought he was doing, he murdered someone, and tried to murder someone else, without doing due diligence," White said gently. "That he's dead instead of you is a blessing. What word was he saying?"

"He said he was free and then bam, George knocked me back and Eugene was dead."

"Was he working for free?" Jeff asked. "As in, volunteering somewhere?"

"No, he didn't make it sound like that. We'll figure it out, I'm sure. I'm still shaken up, so my Megalomaniac Girl skills aren't kicking in."

"I'm happier than I can say that your Doctor Doolittle skills were in top form," Jeff said, as he gave George a pat.

"Well, as you said, we'll figure it out," White said with calm confidence. He hugged me again. "I'm going to ensure that all our personnel are brought safely home, and as soon as possible. I believe we want everyone safely tucked away."

"Speaking of which, where's Christopher, does anyone know?"

White and Jeff both shook their heads. "I haven't picked him up at all," Jeff said. "So I think he's still in the tunnels. I sent him the news that Buchanan appeared to have made the decision to go underground, but I haven't heard back, so I don't know if he got it or not."

"If he's not back by the time I return from the hospital, we'll worry," White said. "Otherwise, he's a big boy and, frankly, quite competent enough to dispatch anyone or anything he might need to."

"He likes getting to cut loose," Jeff added. "We get to do it so infrequently now."

Chose not to voice any worries. Because I could tell both men were saying these things so they could hide the fact that *they* were worried. "You're right. Christopher will be fine." Chose also to not mention that the last time someone had disappeared, Jeff and Chuckie were gone for far too long a time.

White kissed my cheek, gave Jeff a hug, and zipped off.

"Ready to leave the bathroom, baby?"

"In a second. George, Harlie, can you two please ensure we have at least a couple Peregrines and some Poofs going with Richard in Stealth Mode?"

Harlie mewed and George squawked and did the head bob thing.

"Oh, good initiative!"

Jeff sighed. "Translation?"

"Samson, who is Richard's Peregrine, is with him, as are his Poof and several others. Poofs are already at the hospital because they're with their people, so we're good. Everyone's on high alert, so to speak."

"Good." Harlie and George both turned and looked at Jeff. "Err, good jobs, everyone." Harlie purred, George squawked in a friendly manner. "You're, ah, welcome."

"See? You can get what they mean. So, let's head upstairs and see what Hacker International thinks of the bug in my purse."

CHAPTER 31

OF COURSE, it wasn't that easy. We had to work our way through our party guests who were finally being allowed to leave, albeit slowly.

Security had a system going—the elevators were off and all guests were being filtered down one set of stairs only, with A-Cs posted everywhere along the way. We found Abigail at the stairwell on the second floor, checking guests off a master list, and talking into a Bluetooth.

She halted the flow of people trying to leave to give me a big hug. "Hang in there, Kitty. Sis and Michael are downstairs, verifying that whoever I say has come past me is also going past them, no more, no less."

"Where'd you score the headset?"

"Came down from upstairs," she said with a grin. I knew she meant Hacker International. "Chuck's handling the third floor, by the way, same verification system." She looked away from me. "Yes. Yes, the Ambassadors are coming upstairs. Good." She looked back. "Chuck's holding the rest so that when this group passes, you two can go up without a problem."

"No," Jeff said. "Let our guests leave first." This earned him big smiles from the people who were nearest on the stairs.

Abigail shared the news, and the guests began moving down again.

On the plus side, my looking like a wreck who'd been crying was actually taken as a show of how distraught we were over Reyes' death and the party being pretty much destroyed. Since we were actually distraught, this was a good thing. Most people were incredibly kind and supportive, and more of them took the time to pause and talk to us than I'd have figured.

We'd had a lot of guests, so this took some time. I used said time to calm down, so by the time the last couple had hugged me, shaken Jeff's hand, told us they'd loved the party and it wasn't our fault someone had gone insane during dinner, and then said in a while it would be a great story to tell albeit with a sad ending, I felt in control enough to be able to think and do my mind meld with the psychopaths.

Which was good, because among those guests who were refusing to leave were the Cabal of Evil.

Abigail had warned us that there were several guests who weren't going to budge until we were back on the third floor, so it wasn't a total shock to see the remains of the Cabal sitting around. Villanova and Whitmore were with them—I'd wondered if they'd hung around with the rest because of their former android significant others, but clearly they were happy to continue filling in the Cabal's ranks. Lucky us.

The McMillans and the Israeli ambassador and her husband had also remained, along with the folks I'd expected to see here—my parents, Andrei, the rest of our Embassy staff, Cliff, Reader, and Gower.

Andrei and the Israelis weren't going anywhere until we got up to the fifth floor. So that meant getting rid of the Cabal. Easier said than done. Especially when Reader and Andrei pulled Jeff into another discussion with Alpha Team, Cliff, Chuckie, and Senators McMillan and Armstrong. Even though I was technically part of Alpha Team, I was pointedly asked to deal with everyone else so the powwow wouldn't be interrupted. Always the way.

Of course, Lydia was a mess. Someone had advised her that Eugene had been shot and she was alternating between ranting about inefficient police and sobbing on Gadoire's ready shoulder. Apparently she was also Pepé Le Pew's type. I wasn't flattered.

Vance came over to me. "Told you something was going down," he said in a low voice.

"Did you know what Eugene was up to?"

"No, but I don't think he and Santiago are the first to die mysteriously and I doubt they'll be the last."

Again, it struck me that Vance, for all his odiousness, was a hell of a lot smarter and more intuitive than I, or anyone else, would give him credit for. "Duly noted."

He sighed. "Look, Kitty, I know we got off to a terrible start way back when. I pretend to Guy that we always got along, but I'm not stupid—I know you hated me in the Washington Wife class, and I can't blame you. At all. But I really hope my standing by you when those pictures arrived shows that I consider and want you as a friend."

"Thanks. I think." The fact that I'd handled the pictures without Vance's assistance wasn't really the point. He and Gadoire really had come to support and help out, and, in a town like this, that probably meant more than him being a complete twit when we'd first met.

"I know there's more going on. Guy thinks I'm crazy, and I'm afraid to talk to too many people about what I'm putting together, for a lot of reasons. I've seen what you and your friends and family accomplish. I think I've seen a bigger picture than anyone's paying attention to. I want to help, and I want to stay alive. Near as I can tell, teaming up with you will be the best way to achieve both."

"Oh, I don't think we do that much," I lied.

Vance gave me a look I could only think of as snide. "Right. And your husband's not the hottest thing on two legs, either, right?" He shook his head. "I'm smarter than I act. You of all people should be able to relate to that."

"Fine, fine. You win. While I try not to be offended about your most recent insinuation, would you mind hanging out here for a while, even if the others leave?"

"Sure. I think Guy's going to have to take Lydia home anyway, and I'd rather miss all her hysterics if I can."

"I hear you on that." Realized what I'd said. "I mean, I feel awful for her, but there's a lot going on."

"I don't care for her much either," Vance said with a grin. "She's nice enough, but there's something about her that rubs me the wrong way. Anyway, anything I can help you with while I wait?"

"Help me get the rest of your gang to leave."

"They won't until they've talked to you and ensured you still think they're your best friends forever." This was said with an incredible amount of sarcasm, at least nine on the scale of ten. With very little effort, it was clear Vance could turn his sarcasm up to eleven. Maybe, despite all the prior evidence, he *was* one of us.

Or he was playing me. Only one way to really find out. "Okay, I need to do something upstairs. Can you stall everyone or entertain them or whatever until I'm back?"

"Sure, what excuse do you want? Checking on the baby isn't going to fly because we all know your kids are off-site."

Interesting. Wondered how much else everyone knew. Figured I was keeping Vance around partly to find out. "Just say that I had to calm some things down upstairs and check on the Romanian ambassador's wife, to make sure she's feeling well."

"Sounds good." Vance headed for the rest of the Cabal, and I slipped off to the stairs. No one tried to stop me. Wasn't sure if that was good or bad. Like so many other things, tabled for later.

"Where are you going, kitten?" Mom's voice was behind me on the stairs. She sounded tired, pissed, and resigned. Okay, so no one had tried to stop me in an obvious way.

Stopped and turned. She was on the landing. "Handling some stuff. You want to come?"

"Do I?" It wasn't asked sarcastically. Mom was giving me the chance to choose to give her plausible deniability or ask for backup.

"Nah. Just checking on Olga and Mona."

Mom smiled. "That's my girl."

She went back to the others; I used the slow hyperspeed and went up. Time to visit Hacker International and get at least one of the million answers we needed.

CHAPTER 32

HACKER INTERNATIONAL CONSISTED of the five best hackers worldwide. They all had other talents, too, and were pretty much Best in Show for anything scientific or similar they were interested in, including alien linguistics and reverse engineering.

Chuckie had found these guys and become friends with them when we were in high school, so I'd known them since then, too.

Stryker Dane, whose real name was Eddy Simms, was their sort of leader. He was kind of an underground celebrity and also ran a pretty popular website and an even more active blog. He was also a U.F.O. and extraterrestrial languages expert.

In addition to his other talents, Stryker wrote the *Taken Away* series, where he claimed to have been abducted by aliens and shared his exploits and experiences. His sales had skyrocketed since Operation Destruction.

For some this would mean they'd have bought a palatial estate, gotten a haircut, hired a personal trainer, visited Neiman Marcus, Macy's, or Express and invested in a decent wardrobe, and given overall personal hygiene serious consideration.

Stryker being Stryker, the only change had meant he had an even bigger set of what he, and admittedly I, would call collectibles and everyone else would call really expensive dolls or sculptures of Darth Maul. Otherwise, he was still overweight, undergroomed, and dressed in khaki shorts, flip-flops, and a vintage *Star Wars* T-shirt.

Big George Lecroix was tall, skinny, and black, and he wasn't an author, but otherwise, he was a whole lot like Stryker. He came from France and was Europe's best hacker. He was also fluent in twenty languages.

Ravi Gaekwad, also known as Ravi the Geek, particularly when we were mad at him, was India's best hacker, because the best only associated with each other in the world Hacker International lived in. In addition to having a normal-person build, Ravi was also into both the software and hardware sides of the house and was the best reverse engineer around, which had been amply proved during Operation Destruction.

Dr. Henry Wu was small, scrawny, and bald. He came from China, covered all the languages Big George didn't, and was also a software expert, even better than Ravi, which was saying a lot. Needless to say, in order to be in the club, he was his country's best hacker.

Last but in no way least was Yuri Stanislav. Yuri was blind and had earned the nickname of Omega Red, mostly because he was Russian and therefore the others didn't feel he could be called Daredevil. Omega Red was killer with audio cryptology as well as hacking and other pursuits, which included working out, making him the rarity of the group in more ways than one.

They were all dressed like Stryker—shorts, flip-flops, and T-shirts—even though we were in the dead of winter. Hacker International preferred to stay indoors, and since they lived on this floor as well as worked on it, and had the Elves taking care of their every need, they hadn't left the premises since pretty much they'd arrived. Hence why Jeff considered them squatters.

The other four were in *Star Wars* shirts, too. I'd made a half-joking comment that they clearly wore a specific science fiction shirt for each day of the week and, instead of proving me wrong and tossing on a polo shirt once in a while, they created a Shirt of the Day chart. Today was *Star Wars*. Tomorrow would be *Star Trek*. Had to hand it to them—they were organized and efficient within their ranks.

Of course, all the hackers had good money tucked away, some under their mattresses. Their skills were such that they were paid to do things, to stop doing things, and to stop other people from doing things. When we'd discovered them housed at Andrews Air Force Base they were working for the U.S. Government. Now they worked for American Centaurion.

Because Andrews had been attacked and their underground bunker had been destroyed, we'd moved Hacker International and their government equipment into the Embassy. Jeff had handled them being in our ballroom for exactly a week and a half and had then insisted they get moved. They had nowhere to go and were working on things we needed done, so Pierre had put them in the Zoo. It seemed to be working out.

Raj was already here, as was Camilla. She was busy having Stryker and Big George look something up. Big George was definitely turning on the charm for Camilla, at least as far as he was able to.

His French accent had helped Big George with the ladies in the past—insofar as any of Hacker International could be helped romantically—but Camilla seemed intent, not interested, and since A-Cs really had no issues with skin color at all, I knew it wasn't because he was black. This was a first for any Dazzler next to someone as smart as Big George was. Maybe Camilla had grooming standards, which would explain her disinterest in the brain trust nearby.

Raj came over to me. "Camilla asked me to ensure that we have the entire Embassy scanned for bombs, bugs, and other hostiles. She said that's what Mister Reynolds asked her to search for. She found nothing on the first or second floor, but she told me she's uneasy and doesn't believe our buildings are clean. While you were gone I did ask Mister Reynolds if he'd sent her over, and he confirmed it. He's as uneasy about it as she is."

"Did you ask for Dulce to scan?"

"Yes, I've already taken care of that, and advised Walter. No one's found anything yet. It could be that Camilla and Mister Reynolds are both as jumpy as the rest of us right now, so are seeing things that aren't there."

"Or they could be listening to their guts that say we always have someone trying to bug us." I dug the disc out of my purse. "You know, like now."

Raj nodded. "Not saying they're wrong. But your mother

had everyone searched before they were allowed to leave, ostensibly for packets of arsenic, but we were looking for discs like that. None were found on anyone, and scans have shown nothing."

I looked at the disc. "Maybe our scanners can't pick up whatever these are. Did Gladys or Walter say they picked up anything in my purse?"

"No." Raj sounded impressed. "And that hadn't even occurred to me." He pulled out his phone. "Hello, Gladys. Yes, once more, please. Just the room where I am. Yes, I'd like to hold." He waited for a few moments. "Good, thank you." Raj hung up. "You're right, our equipment can't find this. They show nothing at all here within the scans."

"It so figures. Ravi, got a job for you."

"Wow, Kitty, nice to see you to, how've you been?" Ravi, like everyone else in my circle apparently, had a sarcasm knob.

He also had Jennifer Barone. They'd met during Operation Destruction and had had a courtship almost as fast as mine and Jeff's. Ravi was brilliant, and brilliant nerdy geeks didn't delay when any woman showed clear romantic interest, let alone a Dazzler. And Jennifer, unlike Camilla, possessed the Dazzler weakness for brains and brainpower.

They'd been engaged for months. Jennifer had been ready to get married within a week of meeting Ravi but they were waiting because his parents would be scandalized if he married someone without a courtship and engagement of a decent length.

Apparently his parents weren't clear on the fact that when your son, who's never had a date in his life, scores an incredibly hot and brainy chick, the best thing to do is have them sprint down the aisle to wedded bliss.

"Oh, blah, blah, blah, Ravi."

"She's been through a horrible night," Raj said, troubadour tones of compassionate outrage on full. "More than one person has been murdered in front of her. And we need your help, Ravi."

"Oh, sure, Raj. Kitty, you know I'm just teasing. You okay?" Ravi liked Raj, in part because they were both from India, and in part because if a troubadour wanted you to like him, you liked him. And clearly Raj wanted the people in this room to like him.

"I do and I am. Besides, you'll be apologizing in a second anyway." I handed him the disc. "We found this on Jeff. It's blocking his ability to feel people. Has a range of pretty much however far it is from here to the basement of the Embassy. And our incredibly complex scanners can't pick it up."

Ravi whistled. "That's strong, and if our scanners can't pick it up, cloaked impressively." Chose not to comment on the "our". As far as I was concerned, Hacker International were part of the "us" that made up American Centaurion now.

"Yeah. So call me exceedingly concerned."

He examined the disc. "Doesn't look like much. Small, so it's using some kind of miniaturization along with or within its mechanization. Maybe nanotech." He kept talking. My ears turned off.

Ravi's mouth stopped moving. "Super duper. Can you reverse engineer it?"

"Am I breathing?" Ravi jumped out of his chair at his impressive computer setup and trotted over to the impressive laboratory portion of the computer lab.

Because he was dating Jennifer, Ravi had gotten the full tour of the Dulce Science Center, a fact Jeff still regretted. Because Ravi had come back and then taken the rest of the hackers over for a visit. They'd come back to D.C. with a slew of Dazzlers panting after them and even more equipment.

So while the Zoo's computer lab wasn't up to Dulce or NASA Base's levels, it was the next best thing. It should have made me feel like I was back in the Science Center. But being in here just made me miss Dulce, the Lair, and what our lives had been like. So I didn't visit here much unless I felt like having fun riling up Hacker International. Hey, I liked to keep in practice.

Ravi had the disk under a magnifying lamp while he fiddled. He was talking to someone over at Dulce while he was so fiddling. "Are you live with me and receiving all data?" Apparently the answer was yes. "Good. Do you have enough to analyze to be able to track? Huh. Okay. Well, we'll just have to deal with it. Removing the outer shell now."

Couldn't say what made me do it. Jeff would call it

feminine intuition; my mother would call it my gut. I called it being Megalomaniac Girl. Regardless of why, I knew, without a shadow of a doubt, that something bad was going to happen the second Ravi removed the shell.

Which is why I tackled him to the ground as the disc exploded.

CHAPTER 33

THERE WAS THE USUAL BEDLAM. It was stopped quickly. Because we had a troubadour in the room.

"Everyone, calm down!" Raj had total calm authority going in his tone. I'd only heard a few people sound more authoritative, and I was married to one of them. Mom would have been proud. Everyone shut up immediately. "Kitty, Ravi, are you alright?"

"I am. Ravi?"

"If you get off of me, I should be fine."

"Most people don't complain."

"Most of their fiancées aren't in the room."

"Good point. A little help?"

Raj got me to my feet, then helped Ravi. "Is everyone okay?" he asked as Jennifer flung herself into Ravi's arms. I'd never seen Ravi look so proud, happy, or smug.

Took a look around as everyone else said they were fine. There were less everyones than I'd been expecting. And I'd just noticed this room was short about ten people I'd been thinking I'd see here. I was not batting even close to a thousand tonight. "Where's Olga and Mona and everyone?"

"Under the circumstances, this didn't seem to be the best place for them to wait," Jennifer said as she extracted herself from Ravi and went back to being professional. "Len and Kyle agreed. Jeremy took them to the fourth floor. There's a nice sitting room there, where they could be comfortable."

"And where Mossad and the Bahraini Royal Guard

couldn't check out what the boys are doing here." Camilla sounded like she thought whoever had sent them up to this floor was an idiot.

"It seemed like a good idea at the time," said idiot replied. Without too much resentment or defensiveness in my tone. At least, I hoped.

She shook her head. "We're under attack. That means everyone's a suspect, and everyone's a potential enemy."

"I don't normally think that way." Well, I didn't normally think that way. Thanks to Colonel Hamlin's visit, I was thinking that way constantly tonight.

"Time to start." She was examining where the disk had been.

Chose not to share that Camilla could be proud I'd already started on a full-blown case of paranoia and also had her on the Suspects List. She might be pleased or might be pissed, and since it was a fifty-fifty shot, I chose discretion as the better part of valor.

"Jeremy's staying with the guests on the fourth floor, just in case a fast exit is needed. And Len and Kyle are with them, too," Jennifer said, sounding worried. "Was that alright?"

"Yes, that's great, Jennifer. Don't let Camilla throw you. She's still working on her people skills."

Camilla snorted a laugh. "Takes one to know one."

"No argument. So, what do you think? Of what just happened, the explosion, I mean. I'm clear you're not happy with our lack of distrust and stealth."

She was quiet for a bit. "As explosions went, it wasn't a very big one," Camilla said finally. "But it was powerful enough. I think it would have taken Ravi's hands, and possibly his head. So that means it was a contained explosion, and that takes skill." She turned to me. "How did you know it was going to blow?"

"No idea. I just did. And I know that sounds totally lame, but it's all I've got, sorry." I wondered where the Poofs or Peregrines had been. This seemed like a time when they should have intervened.

Then again, I hadn't been in danger, and maybe they didn't consider the hackers to be part of our Embassy. Except I knew that Jennifer and Ravi had Poofs. We had so many Poofs, the rest of the hackers probably had them, too.

And the Peregrines loved Omega Red for whatever reason and they were warming up to Big George, too. Couldn't speak for the Poofs or Peregrines, but my cats thought Henry was da bomb for whatever reason, and that meant the Poofs would think he was okay, too. And my dogs loved Stryker, presumably because he always smelled like food and was a crumb smorgasbord. So, the animals certainly considered the hackers part of that which made up "us."

Maybe it was a simple reason—this wasn't something that keen animal senses could have picked up. When someone's about to shoot they give off physical and mental clues, small and many times almost imperceptible, but not if you're an animal trained for thousands of years to protect. Even a highly trained assassin would give off some smell or vibrations that were different.

But the disc had just been a piece of equipment. It wouldn't have told an animal it was going to go boom.

So why had it told me?

"Kitty's reason is fine with me," Ravi said as he joined Camilla. "I'm happy to still have my hands and head."

"Is there anything left?" Raj asked as Ravi examined where the disc had been.

"Nothing." Jennifer brought his Bluetooth over from wherever it had gone when Ravi and I had hit the ground. He put it back on. "You still there? Yes, sorry, had no idea it was going to explode, either. No, the ambassador saved me. Kitty. Yes." He turned to me. "Serene says that next time you need to bring anything like this you find to her."

"Serene's your contact at Dulce?" Managed to stop myself from asking how she'd gotten there. She'd taken the gate in the bathroom and gone to work, was the obvious answer.

"Yes." He listened again. "Got it. Yes. Absolutely." He laughed. "I'll tell them." Ravi turned back to me. "They got a little before the disc blew. Serene said that she's going to look for explosive signatures and she'll let you know what she finds. She agrees with Camilla's assessment that it was a contained explosion, and she's got some ideas. She also said to tell you, Kitty, that she expects you to check in with her the moment you find another one of these discs."

"How did they get anything? That explosion was instantaneous."

Raj coughed. "Not for us."

"Oh, right." If you can move at hyperspeed, some things do indeed seem slower. I still wasn't seeing things in slow motion. Chose not to wonder if the A-Cs felt they were walking through gelatin every moment of their lives. Jeff had never indicated such, and when I could see people moving at hyperspeed it didn't make me feel like everything else was moving slowly, so maybe it was all in the perspective.

"Serene's an explosives expert," Camilla added. "If anyone could get something from what little we had, it'll be her."

"True enough. I wish I had brought it to her, because now we have nothing."

"I'm sorry, Kitty," Ravi said. "There were no outward signs of a bomb or a trigger. And I definitely looked."

"Well, this just goes under the 'our luck holds firm' heading. It wasn't really your fault, Ravi." It was mine, for not going straight to Alpha Team. And I knew I was going to hear about it from the rest of Alpha Team as soon as they found out, too. "I have a related question for you, anyway."

"Go ahead."

"If someone can make a device like what just blew up, that can stop the most powerful empath from feeling anyone within at least a football field radius, could that same person make a device that could put an emotional overlay or similar onto a person? So that, say, I could be furious and ready to kill someone, but all an empath would feel was that I was happy and thoughtful?"

"I'd think so," Ravi said.

"Absolutely," Stryker chimed in. "It's already been done, in that sense, with the androids."

"But the androids had the full range of human emotions. Jeff was able to find them based on things like murderous rage."

Big George shrugged. "So what? They were last year's model."

"We found them this year."

"It's a figure of speech, Kitty," Big George said. "And you know it."

Henry chimed in for the first time. "You always strive to achieve more, Kitty. To make something more effective, smaller but more efficient, and so forth. Think of cell phones. The first ones were bricks. Now you can get tiny ones, and even though the trend is going larger again, they're sleek and thousands of times more powerful than the first models."

"And they're always coming out with new models."

"Right. Every six months or faster. So, you see—"

I recognized Henry going into lecture mode. "Selling past the close, Doctor Wu. Cease now, I'm on board."

He snapped his mouth shut and gave me a dirty look. "You don't catch on as fast as you like to pretend."

True enough tonight. But I wasn't going to tell him that. "Oh, blah, blah, blah." Looked around. Omega Red was intent on his Braille keyboard and didn't seem to be paying attention. "Yuri, your thoughts?"

He didn't reply, but his fingers kept on moving,

"Yuri. Yuri Stanislav. Omega Red. Dude with the sunglasses on—what are you working on? Or are you asleep? Just please don't be dead, I've had enough of that tonight."

"Just a minute, Kitty," he said absently.

"Time's wasting, Yuri. We are busy people with a lot of horrible conspiracies to identify and thwart."

"Really?" Big George sounded incredibly thrilled.

"Really, but I want Yuri to chime in on our bug situation."

"I haven't been paying attention to that, Kitty," Omega Red said without any shame in his tone whatsoever.

"Are you kidding me? Why not?"

"Because I've been doing something else. It's related, so calm down."

"Tell me what you've been doing that's related and I'll think about not kicking you."

"You won't kick me, and not just because I'm blind and that would be wrong. I think I've found the company that's created something very similar to what you described."

"The bug or the overlay?"

"Both."

"Awesome. Let me guess, Titan Security."

"No. Gaultier Enterprises."

CHAPTER 34

"IT SO FIGURES."

As I said that, it occurred to me that there was one person I hadn't seen since I'd escorted Reyes to the bathroom—Amy.

Camilla looked at me. "Is Amy Gaultier-White around?"

Resisted the impulse to ask if Camilla was a mind reader. "No idea. Com on!"

"Yes, Chief?" Having the communications and sound system hooked into the Zoo had been costly, but oh so worth it.

"Walt, do you have any idea where Amy is?"

"No, Chief. She's not on premises."

Fabulous. "Any idea when she left?"

"No, Chief, I'm sorry, I don't. It was chaotic for a little while. Do you need me to see if Dulce can track her?"

"That's okay, Walt. I'll just call her."

"Yes, Chief." The com went quiet.

Pulled out my phone and dialed. Amy didn't pick up. Called a few more times, all of which went to voicemail. Sent a text. No reply. "This is too reminiscent of Operation Confusion," I said under my breath.

"Yes, it is," Camilla said. Dang, she'd heard me. "We need her tracked down, immediately."

"There could be a good reason for why we can't find her."

"There could be. There could be some very bad reasons, too." Camilla's expression softened. "I know she's one of your closest friends. She was a patsy before. Whether that means she was good enough to fake us all out, is a patsy again, is running down a lead, or is in mortal danger, we don't know. And we won't know until we find her."

"I know. I just . . . Christopher's not here right now."

"So? She's his wife, so either she's faked him out, or she could be in trouble. Either way, we need to know. Make the call."

Heaved a sigh. Hated it when the right thing to do seemed counter to what a good friend would do. "Com back on."

"Yes, Chief?"

"Walt, have Dulce track Amy, please. I can't reach her by phone and I want to be sure she's okay."

"Yes, Chief. Hang on." The soft white noise of the com played in the background while we waited for a couple of minutes. "Chief, I'm sorry," Walter said after what felt like forever. "But Dulce cannot locate Amy Gaultier-White anywhere."

"Ask them to keep on scanning for her." A thought struck me. "Tell Gladys I want her to scan for Clarence Valentino, too. Regardless of the fact that right now you want to tell me he's dead and regardless of the fact that's the first thing Gladys will say. Scan for him, and Amy, until you find them both."

"Yes, Chief."

Sent Jeff a text. Got a fast reply—Christopher wasn't back and he couldn't feel him anywhere, though he could now feel everyone else. Shared the fun we'd been having in the computer room. He replied that he couldn't find or feel Amy, either. We both agreed this sucked, big time.

Didn't know what to do, so I grabbed a spare chair and sat down. Tried to think, to piece things together. Got nothing much. Other than that I was missing obvious things like people not being where I expected them to be and my not noticing until it was really late in the game.

Ran through everyone I could think of. Most of our personnel were at Georgetown Medical Center, on the third floor, in the fourth floor sitting room, or here. But I hadn't realized Serene was off-site and I hadn't noted Amy was missing until just now. So, was there anyone else I'd missed?

"Are Naomi and Michael still downstairs?"

Raj sent a text. "No, all the guests who are willing to

leave have gone. They're back with the others on the third floor." He chuckled.

"What's so funny?"

"Abigail said that Naomi used the time downstairs to add to her wedding guest list, and that now that those two are back, Michael's offering his shoulder to Missus Montgomery. She said to tell you her sister's a Bridezilla and her brother's a wedding crasher. She said you'd get the jokes."

"I do." Chuckled for a moment, then my brain chose to share that there was something very wrong with this. Sat up straight. "Ask her where Caroline is, and did either she or Amy get checked off on any of the exit lists."

Raj texted at hyperspeed. "No, neither woman is on the lists. Abigail doesn't know where they are, has asked her brother and sister, and they don't, either. All assume Caroline went home or that she and Amy are both with the team at the hospital."

"No way. Amy wouldn't have gone for anything medical, it's not something she could help with and Magdalena was along so they wouldn't have needed anyone else to facilitate with Georgetown. Caroline's loyalty is to the McMillans. If they're here, she's here. Unless . . ."

Unless she'd seen something or someone, or they'd seen her. Caroline and Amy had become friends, and they'd come down without backup to help me take on androids and supersoldiers during Operation Assassination. If one or both of them had seen something or someone, then they'd have gone for it, especially if they were together. "Raj, contact Dulce and see if anyone can find Caroline."

Walter and Gladys were contacted. Caroline was also missing and unable to be found.

It was a safe bet they were together. So, people were dying and bullets were flying. When they'd left was probably key. Had to have left before the bullets, because after that Chuckie had put the Gowers on exit duty.

Who they'd seen suddenly seemed obvious. Caroline knew the Dingo on sight. Maybe she thought he was going to be shooting at our people, or at me, and she'd gone to stop him, to reason with him, whatever. Amy had probably gone, too. Meaning they'd gone up to the roof, because that's where all self-respecting members of the Assassination Squad loved to hang out.

Which roof? The shot that had killed Eugene had come from Sheridan Circle, and that was Raul's favorite perch. So the Dingo had been where? Either on top of Romania's Embassy, Ireland's Embassy, or on top of ours. Looking out the third floor windows of the Zoo you could see either one of those buildings.

This would also explain why the Dingo hadn't "shown up"—he'd been distracted by the girls. So, did that mean we couldn't find them because he'd killed them, or because he'd taken them? And if he'd taken them, had it been to hide them . . . or to protect them?

There was, as always, only one way to find out.

But there were people waiting for me, and Vance had a theory he wanted to put forward which I wanted to hear. No worries. I was the co-ambassador, and it was time to Delegate Some Authority.

"Ravi, work with Serene to see what, if anything, you guys can get that we can track on. Omega Red, you keep on tracking and give us everything you can on this division of Gaultier Enterprises and anything related to it. Big George, help Omega Red and see if you can determine any conspiracy theories related to Gaultier and Titan Security, too. There'll be a lot, look for theories I'd believe."

"What about me and Doctor Wu?" Stryker asked.

"I want the two of you looking for coded messages talking about anything odd or out of the ordinary for coded messages."

"Kitty, if a message is coded, it's going to be out of the ordinary," Henry said.

"Do you want me to start calling you Doctor Won't? Or worse, Doctor No?"

"No, that's the worst James Bond movie ever made," Henry muttered.

"Exactly. Positive damn mental attitude, dudes. This is why you live here now—find the ones that are *really* out of the ordinary."

Stryker sighed. "You know you can't reason with her when she's in this mood."

"Stryker, I have no problem hurting you."

"Yeah, yeah, I know. We'll scan the cosmos for the weirder than normal. We even have an official name for the level you're looking for—Kitty Weird."

"Raj, make a note on my calendar that, when this is all over, I need to really cause Stryker some pain. Jennifer, ensure that we're getting whatever cooperation we need from Dulce and advise me if you think anything seems even a little off anywhere or with anything the guys find. Raj, Camilla, you two come with me."

We trotted out of the room and down one flight of stairs. "Raj, I want you handling everyone here. They're going to want to be given an assignment. Have them help you research what happened to Raul the Assassin. I don't have a last name, but Len and Kyle were the reason he was arrested, so they probably know where to start. We want to track anything and everything he's done, particularly since he was arrested."

Raj nodded. "Anything else?"

"Yeah. Listen to what Olga has to say, or insinuates, with incredible attention. Coordinate whatever else is going on in the Embassy, and be sure that people keep me advised. If Camilla or I fall off the Dulce radar, Alpha Team needs to be advised immediately. Tell the boys that I'll have backup and I want them staying with you."

Raj went onto the floor and Camilla and I headed downstairs. "What are you planning?" she asked as we reached the third floor.

Looked through the stairway door's little window before opening it or answering. The Cabal was still here, clustered around Lydia. It was official—she was acting Kitty Weird. "Have a question for you."

"Okay."

"Are you married?"

"No. How is that relevant to anything?"

"Helps me determine how to phrase the relevant question. If Jeff were murdered, even if I was furious with him for cheating on and humiliating me, would you think I'd be hanging out or do you think I'd demand to go with his body?"

"Jeff's never going to cheat on you."

"Work with me on this one, will you?"

She peered through the window with me. "You're wondering what the hell game Senator Montgomery is playing, aren't you?"

"Yes, I am. She rubs Vance the wrong way."

"The pathetic momma's boy?"

"I think he may be less pathetic than we think."

"If you say so."

"Look, I don't want to go back in there, because if I do, power in the room shifts."

"Well, look at you, actually paying attention." Camilla's sarcasm knob went well past eleven. "But you're right. You want me in here, figuring out what's going on with a whole bunch of people who should be a hell of a lot more upset than they are, right?"

"Right. They'll do things around you they won't around me. But, I also need you to get Vance to meet me here, without having everyone else notice."

"Consider it done. Figure it'll take a little time, though, both to get the message to Vance in a natural way the others don't notice as well as to get the others to join me into their conversation, their real conversation, not the one they'd be having if you were in there. You want me going along off-site with those people if they suggest it?"

"If you can cozy up to them enough that they will—and I'm sure you can—then yes. Just make sure you leave a trail of breadcrumbs, because I don't trust any of them."

"You don't trust me, either."

"What do you mean?"

"You're giving off signs of distrust. Minor ones, but I know how to spot them. You're right to distrust me, by the way."

"Is this where you kill me?"

She chuckled. "No. I'm on your side. Still. But you only know me as a double agent."

"Triple, really."

"Whatever number makes you happy. I should be suspect to you, it's intelligent to distrust someone you know lies for a living. Keep in mind, though, that it's also intelligent to distrust others who lie for a living, as well as those who don't."

"So, what, distrust everyone?"

Camilla smiled at me as she opened the door. "Now you're catching on."

CHAPTER 35

CAMILLA MOVED CALMLY through the room while I contemplated how similarly she and Chuckie appeared to think. I missed what she did or who she spoke to, though, because my phone rang and I stepped away from the door to take the call.

"What are you doing?" Jeff asked in a low voice.

"Stuff. Why are you calling me?"

"Because you're hiding in the stairwell."

"Where are you?"

"In our favorite bathroom."

"Super. Remember to wash your hands after."

"Hilarious. I know you, and I can tell you're up to something and that it involves that Vance guy."

"It does. Look, we have a lot of ground to cover. You're stuck being political. I have the hackers working on a variety of things, same with Raj, who has the boys, Olga, and the Middle Eastern Contingent. Amy and Caroline are missing. I'm betting on one of them having spotted my 'uncle' and them both having gone to investigate."

Jeff cursed quietly. "I can believe it. They both think they're junior versions of you. I can't find either one of them emotionally, either. But it would explain why the assassin had such a clear, uninterrupted shot at you and Eugene."

"Right, because my 'uncle' was being distracted by the girls. So, I want to look for them. Yes, I'm taking Vance with me because he has some theories I need to get and I want to kill two birds with one big rock."

"I don't want you going anywhere alone. And before you protest, your new friend is not a fighter. He's frightened, but not ready to do much more than run screaming."

"That's his go-to move, I know from Operation Assassination. Time's of the essence, though."

"Yeah, well, there's more. And I need to talk to you before you disappear on me, too."

"I'm never the one who does the disappearing."

"So you say. Look, baby, I need my wife right now. Something major's come up and we have to discuss it. I need you to meet me on the third floor."

"No, I'm not going onto the third floor, because once on, it's clear I'm not getting out for hours. Can we do it over the phone?"

Jeff heaved a sigh. "Sure, why not. We're only fifty feet away from each other."

"Then use the superfast hyperspeed so no one can see you and come to me."

"You could just come down to the second floor."

"I could, but you're faster than me." I blinked and Jeff was there. Hung up my phone. "See? Was that so hard? You washed, right?"

"I wonder if it drives Jamie as crazy when you ask that as it drives me?"

"She always remembers."

"That's our good little girl." Jeff ran his hand through his hair, took my hand with his other one, and moved us up the stairs, about halfway between floors. "We've been given an interesting offer. And by interesting I mean something that I'm not happy about."

"Go on."

"Your mother contacted the President, so he knows what happened to Santiago, and to Eugene."

"Fabulous."

He shrugged. "The President doesn't care about Eugene. The police are on it, and that's not the political problem."

"Oh, political problems. Yay."

"Yeah. The district Santiago represented is now left, again, without a representative. Per your mother, a year ago, no one would have cared, they would have just done yet another special election. This year, however, they care, and not just because general elections have been suspended. There are a lot of bills going through the House."

"A lot of bills that Santiago insinuated deal with immigration and the definition of who's an illegal alien and who isn't."

"Right. It's a bad time to have a heavily A-C populated district unrepresented."

"And they know they have A-Cs worldwide who consider that their home district, too." All A-Cs, even those, like Raj, who were born and raised in another country, were U.S. citizens first. Those outside of the U.S. held dual citizenship where necessary—and they all called Dulce and Area 51 home.

"Right." Jeff swallowed. "So, the President is concerned because, as we know, they know more than the world is watching what goes on here now. The government can't afford to look like they're ignoring us or don't care about us, or how we interact, or whatever political spin it is they're all going for."

"They know at least an entire other solar system, plus God alone knows who else is paying attention to us. We can ask Mister Joel Oliver about the rest of the ramifications."

"Right. Glad he's on your speed dial, because there's more. The President and your mother called New Mexico's governor. Normally, the governor doesn't appoint an interim representative, but the President's point blank told him to make an exception."

"Okay. God, I hope it's not the guy who ran against Santiago, though it would make sense, since he's interested. But he's hugely anti-alien, and that will make things really uncomfortable for us."

"Yes, the governor pointed that out. Neither he nor the President want someone representing our district who isn't pro-alien, in no small part because Santiago won, and he ran on a very pro-alien platform, so that means the people who voted for him are pro-alien, and they're the majority. Santiago won by a wide margin."

"Check. So, what do the President and governor want us to do?"

Jeff cleared his throat. "Well, it's more what they want me to do, but you're going to be involved."

"Edge of my seat, so to speak."

Jeff nodded, and spoke in a tone of utter doom and gloom. "They want me to fill in as the new representative for New Mexico's Second Congressional District. Starting now."

CHAPTER 36

LET THAT STATEMENT sit on the air for a few moments. "Um, what did James and Paul say?"

"That my answer had better be 'yes.'"

"Oh. Serene?"

"Said that she'd been shoved into a high-level role with less preparation and I could man up and suck it up."

"Oh. Did you ask your parents?"

"Yes, in desperation. They're thrilled. I think my mother's already called the entire population to tell them about it. My father's proud, I can tell."

"Oh. What about our politically inclined guests?"

"Senators Armstrong and McMillan and Representative Brewer all agreed this was the right thing to do. Lydia even pulled herself together long enough to say she agreed as well. Your mother and father both are behind this idea a hundred percent, too."

"Oh." Contemplated all the things I wanted to say. None of them seemed helpful.

"Yeah."

We stood there in silence for a little bit. "Wait. How can you take this position when, like an hour ago, I essentially declared us in a state of war against the U.S.? I mean, I didn't do that on purpose, but it was noted and reacted to like it was very real."

"I asked that same question, baby. Andrei mentioned an obscure clause in the original A-C agreement with Earth, that states if one of our 'leaders' consents to take a 'political position of reasonable power' within the U.S. Government, then American Centaurion will shift to become 'closer to their new country of choice.'"

"Does that mean we become the fifty-first state or something?"

"No, but it alters our situation with the U.S. so that we can get mad, but we have to work it out in the same way Arizona has to work out arguments with New Mexico."

"Wow."

"Yeah. I have no idea how Andrei found that clause."

"Oh, I do. Olga. She's probably had that clause handy since we moved in. Maybe longer."

"Yeah. Good point. So, my taking the position means we just solved any war issues with the U.S., potentially forever. Andrei did say that we have escape clauses in case the government turns on us."

"Well, that's good. I guess."

"Yeah."

Stood there with a little more silence going. "You haven't even been the head ambassador for a full year."

"Co-head ambassador. Yeah, baby, I don't know what to do. Becoming a full-fledged politician is about the last thing on Earth I want."

"The President and the governor asked you to do this personally?"

"Yes, we were on the phone. The governor said he'd come out here, tonight, if he has to, in order to convince me."

"Let's avoid that."

"So you want me to say yes?"

Contemplated all our options. They seemed amazingly limited. "Well, it's just for now, right? Until they have time to do another election?"

We looked at each other. "Supposedly," Jeff said finally.

Contemplated some more. There was no way Jeff wasn't going to do an excellent job doing whatever it was representatives did. Civics and Social Studies had been a long time ago so I wasn't going to be a lot of assistance. However, we had a wealth of people who could teach him.

The light dawned. "That's why the Cabal of Evil is hanging around, isn't it? They want first dibs at influencing you."

"Yeah, I think so. Your mother called the President right

after Eugene was arrested, after we took the dog down-stairs. I think they knew about this plan before I did."

"Senator McMillan said to do it?"

"He said, and I'm quoting, that it was my civic duty to help guide and govern my country, protect all the citizens entrusted to my care, and answer when the call came."

"Yeah, he's a war hero all right. What did Armstrong say?"

"He's really happy about this. I'd be willing to describe him as giddy."

"Wow. Well, he's one of the few politicians we're legiti-mately close to. It has to be some sort of political coup to be able to say a presidential appointee is your dinner buddy."

"I suppose. I wouldn't call him my buddy."

"Five bucks says he does."

"I don't take sucker bets, baby." Jeff heaved a sigh. "I have to do this, don't I?"

I hugged him, tightly. He hugged me back even tighter. "It's not fair. It's never been fair for you, Jeff. But that's the problem when you learn how to be a good leader so young—you're stuck leading for the rest of your life."

"There's leading and then there's . . . this."

"Santiago would be proud to have you follow him."

Jeff was quiet for a few moments. "I suppose. We'll never know."

"He wanted you to run for office." I nuzzled against him. Who knew when I'd get to nuzzle again tonight? "So, who's going to be the Chief of Mission then?"

Jeff stopped hugging me and moved me away from him a little. "What do you mean?"

"You're taking a new job. I know for a fact there's no way you can be the Chief of Mission here and also be a congressman. Even if we wanted to go for it, it's against governmental law, rules, and regulations. So, who are we moving into the position?"

Jeff cleared his throat. "You, ah, don't know?"

"No. Do you want me to guess? We're in the middle of a huge lot of something going on that I think we'll need to get back to shortly. Besides, Vance is going to come to find me at any given moment. Do me a big favor and just spell it out for me as if I were Jamie. Or younger."

Jeff shook his head. "I'm just surprised you're even asking me, baby. It seems pretty obvious to me, and to everyone else, too."

"Does it? It's not seeming obvious to me, but I'll admit that I've been missing some obvious things tonight. So, again, throw a girl a bone and just tell me who's going to be our new Chief of Mission?"

"The same person who's Chief right now, baby. You."

CHAPTER 37

"YOU'RE ALL HIGH."
       Jeff chuckled. "Hardly. You're already fully versed in the job."

Put my hand onto his forehead. "No fever. I expected a fever because you're talking crazy talk and you know it. I'm not even through the Briefing Books of Boredom I got when I first started with Centaurion Division, and I'm having a worse time with the Diplomat's NYC Phonebook. You can't seriously think I can just waltz in and take over what you do. Can you?"

Jeff kissed my forehead. "I can and I do."

"We're doomed." A happy thought occurred. "There's probably some law or regulation that prevents me from being the ambassador while you're a representative."

"No, actually, and if there is, it's being waived under the circumstances, just like so many other things."

"What if people protest?" I asked hopefully.

"They won't."

"They're protesting about everything right now."

"So one more protest won't make any difference."

"What if I need to represent as the wife of the representative?"

"Then you'll do it, as the representative's wife who happens to be the ambassador."

"I see nothing but headaches on the horizon."

Jeff grinned. "I see opportunities to try to persuade Madame Ambassador to do things my way." His voice was a purr, and I was instantly ready to discuss the ramifications of our new positions while trying out some old positions.

But before we could actually do anything, the door opened and Vance stepped onto the stairwell. "Jeff, they're starting to worry that you're sick or dying in the bathroom. Precedent has been set for that tonight."

Jeff sighed and gave me a nice kiss, albeit a quick one. "Take someone, anyone, with you who can actually handle themselves in a fight. I'll be monitoring you. If you go into the tunnel system, let me know before you go in."

"I will do, on all of those." Somehow.

Jeff kissed my forehead, then zipped off. I didn't even see the door open or close.

"It's still amazing to see that," Vance said.

"See what?"

"Someone disappear in the blink of an eye."

"Yeah. So, Vance, you have some theories to forward?"

"Yeah, I do. Do you really want to have this meeting here?"

"Actually, no." I started down the stairs again.

"We're going to the second floor so we can go over to the Embassy to talk?"

I was about to say yes as long as no one else was there when I heard voices that sounded like they were on the first floor. "No." Went down the stairs faster.

"Hey, wait up!" Vance took the stairs two at a time. "You're really fast."

And I was also supposed to be a secret weapon. The world knew about the A-Cs, but it didn't know that I'd become sort of half of one. "I was a sprinter and hurdler in school."

"Ah, that's why you're in terrific shape." Vance sounded appraising. I tended to forget he and Gadoire were actually bi until moments like this.

However, Vance's sexual orientation was shoved aside by my having heard correctly. We did have people on the first floor. The group who'd gone to the medical center were all back. Sure they looked exhausted, but the game was afoot and I'd been point-blank told to bring some decent backup along.

"Hey, why'd you guys come to the Zoo instead of going to the Embassy?" I asked as we joined them. The whole lot of them. Good. I was going to be able to make Jeff happy and take someone other than just Vance along with me.

"James told us to," Tim said. "He said there was important news we needed to get briefed on as soon as we were back."

"Yes, there is. But I need you all working on something else." This earned me suspicious looks all around. Always the way. "Okay, fine. I'll just take Richard. The rest of you can troop upstairs."

Got more suspicious looks. Well, from everyone other than White. He looked amused, but he also looked worried. Yeah, his only child was still missing. Couldn't wait to tell him who else was gone.

"What are you up to, Kitty?" Tim asked, clearly speaking for Tito and the flyboys.

Lorraine and Claudia extracted themselves from Joe and Randy. Their dresses looked as bad as mine. I loved my girls.

"You know, our girl's been through a lot tonight," Lorraine said. "You boys go up and get debriefed. We'll stay with Kitty and help her out."

"Yeah, we'll keep her out of trouble," Claudia added.

Their mothers were at the back of the group, along with the rest of the Dazzlers who'd gone to the medical center. Melanie and Emily exchanged a look. "Kitty, do you need us, too?" Melanie asked.

"Hell yeah," Vance said under his breath. "Bring the dudes, too."

Had to weigh my options, and not only because I didn't necessarily want to have Vance hitting on everyone with clear intent to score. Of course, the only way to avoid that would be to take no one else with us.

A smaller group would be more manageable. And that way we'd have Melanie and Emily to call for backup. "Nah, I should be good with Lorraine, Claudia, and Richard. But keep your phones handy."

White gave Nurse Carter a kiss on her cheek. "Stay with the group."

She nodded. "Be careful."

All of Airborne were giving me looks that said I was keeping them out of the fun. This was true. Then again, I had no idea what fun we were going to be having, let alone how much Vance was going to be willing to say in front of

White and the girls. "I'll let Jeff and James give you the news themselves. Why spoil their big reveal?"

"Because that's your typical move?" Jerry asked.

"And here you used to be my favorite."

The guys all chuckled and some of the Dazzlers started up the stairs, and the rest of the team clustered around the stairwell to follow suit. As my smaller team gathered together, Tito came over, too. "You taking this civilian along?" he asked without preamble.

"Yes."

Tito nodded and pulled something out of his medical bag. "Take this," he said, handing a pill to Vance. "You'll thank me later."

"What is it?" Vance asked suspiciously. "Someone was poisoned earlier tonight."

"Not by me. It's a medicine you'll appreciate." Meaning it was Tito's specialized Hyperspeed Dramamine pill. Chuckie, Reader, Tim, and the flyboys now took this every day, too, because every human who worked with A-Cs appreciated being able to go fast without having to barf their guts out afterward.

"Take it," I told him. It would be nice to be able go to hyperspeed without worrying about Vance's physical reaction to it.

"Kitty takes one every day," Tito said reassuringly as I nodded cheerfully.

This was a flat-out lie, but I appreciated it, because Tito had just covered the fact that I wouldn't be bothered by hyperspeeding. He'd also reminded me to ensure I had a hold of one of the A-Cs if we needed to run.

Vance grumbled, but he took the pill as requested.

Good doctorly duty done, Tito followed the others up the stairs.

"So, what's going on?" Lorraine asked.

"Lots. More than lots. We have people dead, people missing, new assignments, political maneuvering, and more. It's been a great day. But first, let me mention to my man, Vance, here, that whatever you wanted to tell me you can tell Richard, Lorraine, and Claudia as well."

He looked uncertain. Well, he looked like he wanted to suggest a five-some immediately, but right after that he looked uncertain.

"Before we get into whatever the next stage of our fun and frolic is going to be, Missus Martini, could you share with us what the 'big reveal' is?"

"Oh, yes, yes I can." Considered how to broach the night's position changes and decided straightforward was the way to go. "Jeff's been appointed to fill the Congressional seat that was just vacated by Eugene's murder of Santiago, and I'm now the sole Chief of Mission."

Claudia and Lorraine both laughed. Loudly. "No, seriously, Kitty, what's going on?" Claudia asked.

"Sadly, exactly what I said. Along with our usual myriad deadly schemes focused against us."

"There's a bigger scheme that I don't think anyone's noticed yet, other than me," Vance said. "But Kitty's not joking. The President made the request, as did the governor of New Mexico. The move is effective tonight."

Lorraine and Claudia gaped at us. "You cannot be serious," Lorraine said finally.

"I'd assume they're very serious, young ladies," White said. "I can't think of a better choice than Jeffrey, to be honest."

"Richard, would you like to take over as Chief of Mission?"

"Absolutely not. I'm retired from public service. However, your friend here had something to tell us. It's nice to see you again, young man. During our first meeting you ran away."

"We were being shot at," Vance said flatly.

"True enough," White said pleasantly. "You ran away screaming, as I recall. Difficult to say a proper good-bye when that happens."

"Yeah, yeah, and then the next time I saw you was at the President's Ball where you shared that you and the rest of your mission were sleeping with Kitty. I get it, we're not exactly 'close.'" Vance looked at me. "Do I have to spend the rest of the night saying I'm sorry or what?"

"No, you're good to go. But we need to do double duty. Amy and Caroline have disappeared. Richard, I think they saw my uncle."

"Ah. That could be awkward," he said. I saw the realization of who we were talking about light in the girls' eyes. I loved working with Dazzlers.

"Yes. So we're going to be looking for them while Vance tells us about whatever connections he's made that have him worried."

"Very worried," Vance added.

"Where do you want to start looking?" Claudia asked.

"The last place Jeff wants me to go."

"Tunnels," both girls said in unison.

"Got it in one. I have to let him know when we go down there."

White looked at Vance. "I strongly suggest we take an alternate route."

"I know there are tunnels, deep, ancient ones, running underground," Vance said. "They were created by aliens, and not you guys. They were visible to Earth equipment for a short while and then they went back to being impenetrable. There's an entrance under your Embassy, as well as by the Lincoln Memorial."

We all stared at him. "Wow," I said when I'd recovered enough to speak. "Vance, you know a hell of a lot more than I'd have suspected."

He grimaced. "Look, it's an act, okay? You show you're too smart around here, you don't make a lot of friends." I could count Chuckie's friends that weren't from Alpha Four on one hand, so Vance had an excellent point. "I read the *World Weekly News*. I know what goes on. So you don't need to put a bag over my head or blindfold me. Let's just get going, because I really want to tell you what I think's going on."

"Why so?" White asked.

Vance shrugged. "Because you're probably the only ones who can stop it."

CHAPTER 38

"PEOPLE SAY THAT TO US A LOT." And they were usually right. However, I had BFFs to find. "Can you talk and walk at the same time, Vance?"

He shot me a very snide look. "At least as well as you can."

"So you claim. Okay, before we let Vance roll his theory, let's determine where we're going." I led the others outside to the Zoo's lovely circular driveway.

The Zoo was on the curving corner of Sheridan Circle. I stood pretty much where the van had been and faced the way its doors had opened.

I hadn't really paid attention earlier, in part because I was distracted by murder and mayhem, and in part because they'd been up for weeks now, but the Christmas lights on the trees in Sheridan Circle and on most of the buildings within view were quite pretty. No one was really overdoing it in this part of town, so most of the lights were white and sparkling. Ireland was the lone exception—they had green lights interspersed with white. All in all, the scene was quite beautiful; a sharp contrast to all that had been going on.

"Why are we here?" Vance asked, interrupting my perusal of the external decor.

"The bullet that shot Eugene came from that way," I pointed to the Circle. "Meaning that vantage point was taken. So, if you were going to be somewhere that would allow you to protect someone standing where I am, where would you go to perch?"

Everyone looked around. "We're looking up high, Missus Martini?"

"Yes, Mister White, we are."

"Assassins like the high ground," Vance said.

"Vance, you have hidden depths."

"I keep on telling you that. It's hard to see, but if I was trying to cover everything, honestly, I'd be on top of the building we were just in. Gives you the best vantage point for the whole area. Your Embassy is taller, but it's also a lot farther away from the action. And you don't have any Christmas lights on either building, so it's easier to hide in the shadows up there."

"I agree," Claudia said slowly. "Especially if they were trying to get someone here."

"No, actually, they were planning to protect someone here."

"Want to explain that?" Lorraine asked.

"Not at this precise time. So, okay, I can buy that who we're looking for was on the roof of the Zoo. But how would Caroline or Amy have spotted anyone if they were on the roof?"

"Oh, I wouldn't have just one man on the roof of the Zoo, Ambassador," a man's pleasant, and quite familiar voice said from behind me. "I'd have someone on top of Ireland's Embassy, too, lovely green and white Christmas lights or no. Which they did."

Spun around to see a tallish man with a full beard in an overcoat that, per usual, hid whether he was pudgy, muscular, or both. "Mister Joel Oliver! I'm so glad to see you."

"And it's always a pleasure to see you, Ambassador." As he came nearer, I saw there was something on his shoulder. A shape I recognized. And didn't care for.

Chose to ignore the shape and maybe it'd go away. Or just stay silent. "Jeff's going to need to talk to you."

"Jeff! Jeff! Jeff! Bellie wants treats!" Sure enough, the Parrot From Hell was along for the ride. My luck was always consistent.

"Hush, Miss Bellie. We'll visit Jeff later. And I'll be happy to give our nation's newest representative any help I can."

"Wow. You, as always, amaze."

"I do what I can."

"I think you know everyone here other than Va—"

"Vance Beaumont," he said, cutting me off mid-word as he leaped over to offer his hand to Oliver. "I'm your biggest fan. Beautiful parrot, by the way."

"Bellie likes Vance!"

"She is the biggest slut in the world, isn't she?" I asked whoever was in charge of my luck.

Oliver seemed stunned. "I have a fan?"

"Lots, but I'm the biggest," Vance said as he did indeed continue to act like the biggest fanboy in existence. "Your exposé on Titan Security should be required reading for all law enforcement and politicians. May I give your bird a treat?"

"Bellie likes Vance! Bellie wants treats!"

Oliver looked at me. "Is he for real?"

"Yes!" Vance said. "I can't believe I get to work with Mister Joel Oliver!"

Claudia and Lorraine sidled closer to me. "Is he serious?" Lorraine asked quietly.

"He seems serious." Seriously deranged.

"You find the most interesting people," Claudia said carefully.

"Don't I though? Yeah, um, Vance, let's let go of the nice reporter and remember that we are in the middle of something big right now."

"I can't wait to tell you what's going on," Vance said to Oliver, clearly ignoring me. "You may have already put it together yourself, but haven't had enough to go public."

"I think we're talking about different things," Oliver said, shooting me the "help me, help me" look.

"Vance!"

He dragged his head around to sort of look at me. "Yes, Kitty?"

"Vance, I'm speaking as both the ambassador of the property we're standing on and as someone who's more than willing to kick you in any number of places. Let *go* of the nice reporter, back away, and focus. We are not on a field trip, he is not Steven Tyler or Joe Perry, and you are not twelve. Pull it together, dude, you're embarrassing me in front of my cool friends."

Somehow, this got through. Vance let go of Oliver and looked embarrassed. "I just really think he's great," he mumbled.

"I'm flattered," Oliver said as he stepped closer to me and the girls. "Truly. However, as I was saying to the ambassador, I don't believe the assassins on either your roof or Ireland's are who shot Mister Montgomery."

"They weren't. Remember Operation Assassination?"

"As if it were yesterday."

"Well, the assassin who got arrested is out and gunning for his wife's killer."

"Oh dear." Oliver looked around. "I don't see Mister Buchanan with you."

"Yeah, we're missing Malcolm, Christopher, Amy, Caroline, and someone I'll tell you about when we're not standing in the middle of the street, so to speak. Now, back to it—were you on Ireland's roof?"

"Yes, investigating. I'd suggest that you didn't need to verify for yourself, particularly since none of you are exactly dressed for scaling a building, but I know you and imagine you'll want to see for yourselves."

"MJO, is this you telling us we *should* investigate, or is this you being resigned that we're going to waste time when you could just tell us what you found?"

"Ah, you've just come from spending time with the lovely Madam Olga?"

"Shockingly, no, I spared myself time in Remedial Class. But you and she do share some traits."

"Well then, no, I'm not trying to be vague and secretive while making you really work for the information so you'll remember it better the next time I'm not around to help out. I went up onto Ireland's roof; I can tell someone was perched there for a while. He never fired a shot. And then he left. I was heading to look at the roof of this building when you came outside."

"Super duper. I happen to know who was on top of that building, and therefore who was on top of the Zoo. However, I'd like to verify that we don't have dead bodies on the roof."

Oliver nodded. "It's easiest to access the roof if we go inside."

"It's also easy to see us and ask why we aren't powwowing with all the politicians."

"We could use the fire escape," Vance suggested, pointing to the metal ladder system that was on the side of the building where the walkway attached. The walkway was lit on the inside, and the glass meant it was very visible from the street. But that meant we could see well while climbing up cold, slippery, metal ladders.

"Now, see, *that* is why he's coming with us," I said to Lorraine and Claudia. They didn't look convinced.

White went under the bottom of the fire escape and proved that white men could indeed jump. One leap and he had the bottom of the ladder. Easily. His weight brought the sliding portion down, and he held it in place.

"Mister White, you're the man."

"I felt the need to show off, Missus Martini. No one's acted like I was important for at least a few minutes and my ego was getting terribly abused."

"I'll fawn over you some more in a bit. Who's going first?"

"I'd like to," Oliver said. "Chivalry and all that."

"You got it."

Oliver started up, then me, with Vance, Lorraine, and Claudia following, and White bringing up the rear. All of us other than Oliver were in evening dress. So much for not scaling buildings in our formalwear. Found myself hoping there were no other reporters hanging around.

Also found myself wondering why I'd been stupid enough to not take a coat. It wasn't the coldest winter—we had no snow, for example—but it was still cold enough, and I wasn't dressed for being outside. The few minutes I'd been out earlier I'd been inside the police van and preoccupied.

Vance and White were in suits, so they were probably fine, but by the time we reached the top, the girls and I were shivering. A-Cs originated on a world that had two suns, so they handled heat really well—to this day I'd never seen one of them sweat. Well, other than Jeff right before our wedding. However, cold was a different story.

"It's freezing up here, so let's make it snappy. MJO, do you see anything that says how many other people might have been up here, and where they went when they left, and Vance, do you want to share what the hell you think is going on?"

White started to take his jacket off, presumably to give it to one of us, but before he could, someone opened the door to the roof.

We all froze, literally and figuratively.

CHAPTER 39

JEFF STEPPED OUT, carrying coats. He was wearing a trench coat that made him look, if it were possible, even more handsome. I did love seeing him in coats, one of the advantages of being in this part of the country. "You all really need to plan a little better."

I was shocked that Bellie was silent. Shot a glance at Oliver—he had one hand holding her feet and one on her beak.

Jeff handed the coats out and helped me into mine while White and Vance helped Claudia and Lorraine into theirs. No one mentioned that all the women's coats were the same. I was just thrilled that the Elves had deigned to branch out and let us have fancy coats when we were dressed up. Once the girls were covered up, White and Vance put on the coats Jeff had brought them as well.

White's was also a trench—apparently they were Official Elf Issue For Cold But Non-Snowy Weather. Vance's was obviously his—a very trendy topcoat that I knew I'd seen in the *GQ* Fall Fashion issue. It looked great on him, but I knew it would look better on Reader. Reader, however, would undoubtedly have an Elf-Approved Trench. If he were joining us. Which I hoped he wasn't. I didn't enjoy him mad at me. And I knew he was mad at me already and would be madder to find me and the others out here.

Once everyone was covered up, Oliver let Bellie go. She screeched with joy and flew to Jeff's waiting hand. "Bellie missed Jeff!"

"Jeff missed Bellie," he shared with much love in his tone.

"She's the sluttiest parrot in existence," I muttered. My teeth were only chattering a little now. Jeff put his arm around me while Bellie moved onto his shoulder and started nuzzling him. "How'd you know we were here?"

"You mean aside from the fact that I'm tracking you and could emotionally feel what you were doing? I looked out the window. Fortunately, it was when I was being put on the spot yet again and everyone was faced toward me, so I don't think anyone else saw the six of you acting like Spiderman."

"I'm so proud of the reference. How'd you find our coats?"

"That's what the Operations Team is for."

"Okay, how'd you get out here?"

He sighed. "They all think I'm in the bathroom again."

"Well, at least it's a useful excuse."

"Yeah, it only lasts so long, however. Why are all of you on the roof? I haven't been able to give you my full attention because I've been too busy being told what my new job entails. It entails things I don't want to do, by the way."

"I'm sure. We're figuring out who was where when."

"Somehow, I think you think that was supposed to make sense. It doesn't, but I believe that you believe, baby."

"I don't see much that would tell us more than that there were people up here and they aren't here any more," Oliver said.

"Speaking of people who disappeared, Christopher's back," Jeff told me. "He found Buchanan." There was an edge to Jeff's tone I didn't like.

"Is Malcolm okay?"

"Well, he's alive, and appears to be in one piece, so that's good. He's in the infirmary—Tito, Magdalena, Melanie, and Emily are working on him."

"Oh my God, how badly is he hurt?"

"As far as any of us, Christopher included, can tell? Not at all. But he's unconscious and can't be roused." Jeff hugged me. "We'll figure it out, baby."

"Where was he?"

"In the tunnels. Alone. Miles, and I do mean miles, away from where he should have been. Christopher's pretty sure there was a motorized vehicle of some kind down there. No sign of your other 'friend'. But where exactly is really interesting."

"Can't wait? Where, exactly, was Malcolm?"

"Right under Gaultier Enterprises' research facility, positioned just out of sight of the cameras we have there."

"Wow, you're not kidding about being far away. I wonder if that's supposed to be a clue?"

"Maybe. Who knocks a guy out and leaves him as a clue?"

"Everyone we interact with."

"Good point. But what kind of clue?"

"Well, my 'uncle' said the special package I received had a bioweapon in it. What if someone's tested that on Malcolm?" Hated this idea the moment it came out of my mouth, because it seemed oh-so-likely to be right on.

Jeff hugged me tighter. "If that's what it is, baby, I promise we'll figure it out. Tito's created a cure for humans so they can move at hyperspeed and not get sick. He can figure this out, too."

"I hope so." Chose not to mention that Tito had had plenty of time to work on and perfect his Hyperspeed Dramamine, and no one was going to die if he hadn't created it just right.

It was late and I was cold and tired and needed to stop thinking about failure in any and all ways. We needed to find Amy and Caroline so I could check and make sure Malcolm was okay, and then go to bed.

Considered our options. They seemed slim. Well, I had one option left. Dug out the burner phone the Dingo had given me and dialed the one number on it. The phone rang, and didn't go to voicemail. But it didn't pick up, either.

Jeff stopped his Bellie snuggling with a jerk. "I hear a phone ringing."

"It's on the other end of my call."

"No." Jeff handed Bellie back to Oliver and took my hand. "No, it's coming from that way." He pointed to the Embassy's roof.

Contemplated our options. They seemed about as slim as our earlier options had been. "I guess we need to go back down and inside. And back out again."

Jeff looked over the side. "I closed the drapes on the third and fourth floors before I came up here. And the squatters keep their shades closed because they don't like to see moonlight, let alone sunlight."

"Why do we want to go back down via the fire escape?"

"Because there's a straighter line." Jeff pointed to the walkway.

White shrugged. "I know the walkway can handle our weight, Jeffrey. And the fire escape is near enough that I believe we can safely handle the leap."

"Leap?" Vance asked.

"We're not jumping down three floors, are we?"

Jeff snorted. "No. Just about half of one."

"Um, excuse me? Half of one?"

"Maybe all of one. C'mon, baby." Jeff started down the fire escape. He was about at the third floor level when he jumped off and over and landed on the top of the walkway.

I could stand up here, go inside, or support my husband's plan. Chose to go with the latter, in the hopes that he was right, we wouldn't all die, and I'd earn some Good Wife Points.

Hung up the burner phone, put it back into my purse, and started back down the stupid fire escape we'd just climbed up. Slipped a few times, but managed not to scream, only because I had my teeth clenched.

"Jump now, baby," Jeff said.

"I'm at like the fourth floor."

"When have I not caught you?" He had a point. Turned and jumped toward him. I only screamed a little. "There we go," he said as he caught me and put me down gently. "Safe and sound. Supposedly you do stuff like this all the time, even when I'm not around."

"I'm usually the one in the lead and in jeans and my Converse, not a designer cocktail dress, a velvet opera coat, and high heels."

"You're doing great as always, baby. And you look fabulous doing it, too. Next!"

Oliver insisted on going down next. He waited to jump until he was much closer to the walkway, despite Jeff's encouragement for him to go for it sooner.

Lorraine was next, and she jumped when Jeff told her to. Same with Claudia. Both girls seemed to enjoy the thrill. I'd really turned them into adrenaline junkies.

Vance was next, and if I'd been careful, he was caution

personified. He was so slow that White started off after him, jumped at the bottom of the fourth floor, and landed without Jeff's help, all before Vance had made it to the middle of the fourth floor.

"Show off."

White and Jeff both laughed. "It's not as difficult for us to land well," White explained, while Jeff cajoled Vance down the ladder.

"Who's going to catch me?" Vance asked.

"No one," I replied. "Because you'll like it too much."

"Bitch."

"You know it. Hurry up, Vance. It's going to be Christmas by the time you reach the rest of us."

He got to about where Oliver had jumped, whimpered audibly, and leaped. Lorraine and White grabbed his arms and pulled him fully onto the top of the walkway. "That was the most pathetic jump I've ever seen," Lorraine said.

"Whatever. My God, is this what you people do for fun?"

Jeff grinned and took my hand. "Buddy up with the humans," he said to Lorraine and Claudia. Then he took off for the Embassy. Showing judgment, Lorraine and Claudia both took a hold of Oliver. White grabbed Vance, and they all ran after us.

Since we were going at hyperspeed, we reached the Embassy in about two seconds. However, we now only had to get up five floors. The wisdom of this gambit was eluding me.

"There's the fire escape," Vance said. "And does that pill the doctor gave me kick in late or what? I want to barf."

"That's from you getting upset over the jumping," Oliver said. "You'd be much worse without Doctor Hernandez's cure."

"You have a bottle of pills, MJO?"

"I acquired some, yes."

Chose not to ask him how. "Super. Um, Jeff? What's the plan now?"

The fire escape wasn't as conveniently placed as the one at the Zoo. We had to leap over from the top of the walkway a good ten feet. I wasn't liking our odds.

"Who's first?" Jeff asked. "I think it has to be me or Richard."

"You go, Jeffrey," White said. "You're the strongest and

have the longest reach in case someone doesn't jump well enough."

Jeff kissed me and, without any hesitation, jumped to the fire escape. He made it without issue. "Come on, baby. Don't worry, I'll catch you again."

As I backed up, contemplated whether to keep my heels on or not, decided I should since it wasn't slippery here, and started to run, it dawned on me that Jeff was, despite the circumstances, having fun.

The leap wasn't too bad—my track coaches had ensured every one of us could do every event, and I'd been okay with long jump—but Jeff was there to grab and catch me anyway. It wasn't quite the same as when he caught me as I dropped from a great height, but it was still nice—two catches in one night. And, you know, the likelihood that I'd fall from up high was getting better with each passing moment. If I was clumsy enough, we could get a triple. Go us.

Started up the ladder as the others contemplated how to get Vance and Oliver across without worry. I reached the top while they were still discussing it. Conveniently, I had an easy answer.

"Hey guys! Someone went this way before and left us a path." A sturdy rope was tied quite well to some metal on the roof, right over the walkway. Clearly my Assassination Uncles planned well.

Tossed the rope down while Jeff climbed up the fire escape using hyperspeed and then helped me hold the rope and help the others up. Oliver had a little trouble—Bellie flew off his shoulder to perch on Jeff's, but apparently only so she could squawk enthusiastic encouragement.

Oliver up, Lorraine and Claudia went up next. They used hyperspeed and were up in no time. "This is so much more fun than that dinner party was," Lorraine said with sincerity.

"Totally," Claudia agreed. "Not that the party wasn't nice, Kitty."

"If you were into uncomfortable small talk and murder, it was great, yeah. What's the holdup?" I shouted down to Vance and White, though I had a good guess.

"I wasn't an athlete in school," Vance shot back. "This is giving me horrible flashbacks from the parts of gym I didn't like, which was all parts of it other than the locker room and showers."

"Time's wasting. Climb the rope or jump to the ladder. Or stay there and we'll get you later."

"You know, I think I want to stop being your friend."

"You're not actually in the Friend Zone yet, Vance."

"Something to motivate me." He started climbing up and either he was the best actor in the world, or he really sucked at this.

White shook his head. "This is embarrassing. Young man, let's go for a version of the fireman's carry, shall we?" He helped Vance down the whole two inches he'd managed to climb. Vance then got on White's back, and they started up.

"You're letting your uncle do the heavy lifting?"

Jeff shrugged. "He's enjoying himself."

"So are you."

Jeff grinned. "Yeah, I am." As White got nearer to the top, Jeff reached down and grabbed Vance's shirt and jacket, and hauled him up. White zipped up the rest of the way.

"This has been, without a doubt, the least fun I've ever had breaking and entering," Vance said. "So, now that we're here the hard way, what's next?"

"You know, I thought the Embassy was shielded. How is it we could climb up and are standing here?" Was so happy this had occurred to me now, as opposed to when we were on top of the walkway.

"It is," Jeff said. "The shield means we can't breach the building, not that we can't stand on it."

"If you say so." Pulled out my burner phone and dialed again. This time, I could hear the ringing, too. "I think it's coming from the other side of the roof."

We trotted over toward the sound. "There," Jeff said, as we neared the "room" that made up the roof entrance. There was a burner phone sitting on the ground where you'd see it if you opened the door from inside the Embassy. It was where the ringing was coming from, confirmed when I hung up my burner phone and dropped it back into my purse and the phone on the ground stopped ringing.

White grabbed us both before we could go to the phone on the ground. "There's something, or someone, on the other side," he said quietly.

Looked. Sure enough. Something was just visible at the "back" of the roof entrance room. Something that looked like it was hiding.

CHAPTER 40

JEFF SHOVED ME TO WHITE, motioned for all of us to get back, then ran over using hyperspeed. He stopped dead. He didn't look scared, he looked shocked. "What are you two doing here?"

The rest of us chose to take that as meaning it was safe and joined him. To see Amy and Caroline, trussed up like Siamese Twin Turkeys, effective gags included. They were sitting back-to-back, arms at their sides, torsos expertly tied together. Their legs were straight out, also well tied. It would be close to impossible to move, unless they were both world-class gymnasts, which they weren't.

"These knots are unreal," Jeff said as he checked their bonds. "Hang on, it's going to take a few minutes."

Vance sighed, dug into his pants pocket, and produced a rather impressive Swiss Army knife. "This should help."

"See?" I said to Lorraine and Claudia. "That's why he's along." They still didn't look convinced, but not as unconvinced as they had earlier. So that was something.

Jeff sawed the girls free in quick order, while Vance actually assisted with the gags. White picked up the burner phone and handed it to me. "This appears to be a phone. It seems your 'family' no longer wants you able to reach them."

"I suppose." Took the phone from him. Had a thought and checked. Sure enough, there was another number programmed in. "No. I think they wanted us to find Amy and Caroline."

"They did," Amy croaked. "Bastards."

"They could have killed you. They didn't. Call them Efficient Friends."

Caroline nodded. She didn't seem able to speak. White stepped away and made a call. I stepped away and tried to open the door to the roof.

I was enhanced, so I should have been able to rip it off its hinges if necessary. But I couldn't even get the knob to turn. "So, I guess the building's shield is really on."

"Yes, handling, Missus Martini," White said as an aside, still on his call. "The shield prevents you from entering, not touching, but it also repels intrusion. If you shove against the shielding you'll bounce off."

"I'll take your word on that, thanks. Vance, you want to give it a go?"

"Like every other thing we've done since we walked outside, no."

A thought occurred while White continued his quiet conversation I couldn't hear even though I was trying to. "Mister White, could the building's shield affect the scans? As in, we couldn't tell Amy was here because she's sitting *on* the shield?"

"It's very possible. I'm handling something else right now, but I'll check with Gladys once we have breathing room."

"Sounds good." Tried to let him continue uninterrupted. Failed. "If that's the case, we'll want a workaround."

"I agree." White hung up. "Ah, I believe we have our answer. Gladys just sent a text sharing the fact that she can see Amy near to me."

"How does that prove anything one way or the other?"

White smiled. "Because Gladys saw her the moment the shield was turned off."

The door opened and Jeremy Barone stepped out, followed by Len and Kyle. Jeremy looked surprised to see us all up here. Len and Kyle did not. Len and Kyle had worked with me a lot longer. Jeremy had two bottles of water, Len had two women's coats, Kyle had my Converse.

"I love you, Mister White," I said as I took my heels off and put my comfortable shoes on. The hell with fashion—if asked, I was bringing the tennis shoes and skirts look back.

While the girls were helped into their coats and drank their water, I decided it was time to figure out where My

Favorite Uncles were. They clearly hadn't left the roof via the Embassy's interior.

Dialed the number on the new burner phone. This time the phone I was calling was answered. But no one said anything. "Hello?" I said finally.

"Ah, Miss Katt. I felt it would be you, but wanted to be sure."

"Yeah, it's me. What's going on? Why was the phone I was supposed to be calling if I was in trouble left on the top of the Embassy?"

"I knew you'd find it."

"Wow, you have a lot of faith in me."

"I do. As do your friends."

"Yeah, about that . . ."

"They are, as you're surely determining, unharmed. Cold and uncomfortable, but unharmed."

"What if we hadn't figured out where they were?"

"If you had not called me within another hour, I would have called in an anonymous tip."

"Okay." I had no argument for this, since we'd found them and, per Jeff's giving me the thumbs-up sign, clearly both girls were indeed okay. Lorraine and Claudia were doing some medical-type things with Amy and Caroline, but no one seemed worried. "Raul almost killed me. At least I'm pretty sure it was him."

"Yes." The Dingo sounded pissed. Which was kind of nice. "Your friends distracted us at a very poor time. That has been explained to them. In detail."

"Great. I'd imagine they'll never make that mistake again. Who wants to sit on the roof tied up for half the night?"

"It's better than being murdered."

"Yes, I'm in total agreement with you. So, where are you?"

"We're somewhere very safe."

"Good to know. Just out of curiosity, do you have any idea where Raul is?"

"No. He missed you tonight and the area became quite . . . crowded. He left well before we did."

"Yeah, there were a lot of police all over the area."

"There were a lot of your agents as well."

Interesting. I hadn't known that. Because Alpha Team didn't tell us what we didn't need to know.

"Well, great. So we don't have to worry about Raul right now, then?"

"You should always be vigilant." He paused for a moment. "Are you still on the roof?"

Saw no reason to lie. "Yes."

"Why are you still on the roof?"

"We just found the girls and don't know where you are."

"We aren't on your roof." The Dingo had a point.

"True, but we also couldn't get inside until just now."

"Excuse me?"

"We climbed up from the outside."

"I see. How many is 'we'?"

"Seven of us. Well, now, really twelve of us."

"You must make quite an interesting picture, a dozen people standing on the highest building in your area."

"You just said we didn't have to worry about Raul right now."

"No, I said you needed to be vigilant. Standing outside on top of a high building is better than standing outside under a tall building, but not nearly as safe as being inside your very secure building."

"We couldn't get in. Before. But you'll be glad to know we can now. And all that." Vance tried to get inside. Jeremy prevented this.

"Someone's opened the door?"

"Got it in one!"

"Good. Get inside."

"Tell me where you are."

He sighed. "I don't want you bringing an army. It won't help. I've given your friends some instructions. They'll share them with you. Stay vigilant and keep your head down. We'll be in touch. And please get inside—it's going to rain soon."

And with that, the Dingo hung up on me.

CHAPTER 41

"BYE," I said to no one. Hung up and dropped the new burner phone into my purse along with the other burner and my actual phone. I looked like a cell phone hoarder. Or a drug dealer.

"What's going on?" Jeff asked.

"I honestly have no freaking idea, but my 'uncle' says Amy and Caro Syrup have intel and that we should get off the roof before we receive it. So let's do what he says and get inside."

He'd also said it was going to rain. Sniffed. Didn't smell like rain. Looked around. Didn't look like rain, either. Maybe he'd been being obscure. Or maybe he meant bullets were going to rain down on us. Or something.

"Oh, I know why I couldn't feel them," Jeff said, as he held out his hand. There was a disc in it. "Caroline had this taped to her. She said she was told to ensure that it was given to you."

"Emotional blocker or emotional overlay device. Don't try to open it; they're rigged to explode. Len, Kyle, who's where? We need to get this to Serene, pronto, but I want Ravi to stay in the loop. And someone needs to verify if Malcolm has a disc like this on him somewhere."

"Everyone but the hackers are with the Pontifex," Kyle shared. "And to say they're all kind of pissed at you guys for disappearing is like saying the Atlantic's a little wet."

"Fabulous. How'd you guys know we were here?"

"Mister White called me," Len said. "We didn't tell Alpha Team where we were going."

"Not that this meant anything," Reader said as he and

Michael joined us on the roof. Reader looked pissed. Michael looked worried. "Because I'm really aware when people leave a room I've told them not to leave."

Michael didn't bother to bawl us out—he headed straight for Caroline.

Len shrugged. "We work for the ambassador." Kyle nodded. So did Jeremy.

Reader let this pass without comment. Probably because he had other comments. "I'd love to know why American Centaurion's Prom King and Queen are playing around on the roof of their Embassy. Just asking." Reader didn't sound like he was just asking. He sounded angrier than he looked.

"Thanks for the lovely new title, James."

"That's not an answer, Ambassador." Wow. Ambassador, not my name or anything. Yeah, Reader was officially pissed off at me and apparently planning to stay that way. Joy.

"Scavenger hunt," Vance said. Happily, none of the A-Cs were actually facing Reader when this was announced. They were facing me. My ability to control my Inner Hyena was, therefore, being tested severely.

Reader stared at Vance. "A scavenger hunt."

"Yeah. It's something fun to do, breaks the ice. Everyone was feeling tense and down, Kitty and I thought, why not a scavenger hunt?"

Reader looked at me. "You suggested—after having one man poisoned at dinner, and then another shot in front of you, along with the announcement of Jeff's new assignment, and yours—that what everyone needed was to have a scavenger hunt?"

"Not everyone. Just a few of us." This was true. Sure, I hated lying to Reader, but by now I couldn't remember who we'd told what to any more.

"Ambassador, is there a good reason for why you're lying to me? I'm just asking, because it's been a hell of a long night and all, but in all the time I've known you, the words 'scavenger hunt' have never left your mouth."

"Ah . . ." Damn, lying to Reader didn't work. Had Mom been giving him tips? And he was still calling me ambassador. Wasn't sure if he was doing it to remind me that I was supposed to be more mature and in charge or because he was too angry to use my name. Decided now wasn't the time to find out.

Saved by the bell. Well, really saved by Michael who rejoined us, his arm around Caroline in a very protective manner. "James, I want to take Caroline home. She's been attacked, is freezing, and I don't want her getting sick or being in any more danger than she's been in already."

"M'okay," Caroline croaked out. "Jus' cld."

"Yeah, get her home. We can get all the information from Amy, right?" Reader asked her.

"R-r-r-ight. But 'm fine."

"Caro Syrup, you sound like a frog. You need some hot tea with honey or something."

"I'll take care of it," Michael said. "Everyone else might want to get inside, too." With that he bundled Caroline down the stairs.

Reader sighed. "Where were we? Or should I say, what were you lying to me about before we were interrupted?"

"Is this guy trustworthy?" Vance asked.

"Yes."

"The rest of them?" Vance waved his arm to indicate everyone on the roof.

"As far as I know, yes." I hoped, anyway. With Hamlin gone and Malcolm felled by some mystery ailment, Hamlin's intel became more suspect.

"Great. Then I'm going to tell everyone my theory, Kitty. Mostly because in the time I've been trying to tell it to you we've done everything other than discuss what I think is a lot more important than why we're on this roof, no offense to you or your friend intended," he said to Amy.

"None taken," Amy said in a tone indicating she was lying like a wet rug.

"Good." Vance heaved a sigh. "I think we have a high-level government conspiracy going on."

Everyone snorted, even Jeremy. "When don't we?" Reader asked. "Per Reynolds, we have at least a dozen active at any time."

"Well, there's one more, and I don't know that anyone else—other than Mister Joel Oliver for whom this may be old news—has put events together like I have."

"We're listening, Vance." Well, I was. Couldn't speak for the others.

"Great. I think someone is murdering members of the House of Representatives indiscriminately."

"Eugene's accidental murder of the wrong guy was indiscriminate but—"

"*No.*" Vance sounded upset. Reminded myself that he'd already told me that Gadoire thought he was an idiot for this idea of his. Also reminded myself that most of the time when I forwarded a theory I was told I was an idiot right up until the moment my theory proved to be correct. "It started earlier this year, and it's picking up speed."

Oliver shook his head. "This isn't something on my radar. Sorry to disappoint."

"It's real," Vance said, voice clipped. "And the longer it's ignored, the more people are going to die."

"Then why isn't this on anyone's radar?" Reader asked.

"Because every death looks natural or accidental. But they're starting to increase in number. It began with the representative who Santiago ended up replacing."

"Representative Bowers died in office," Oliver said. "Literally. Had a heart attack at his desk."

"Sure he did," Vance replied. "An assisted heart attack. The killer waited about a month, then there were more. A couple here, one there, a few more. This month alone we've already lost four. All seem natural or accidental. But they aren't."

Reader shook his head. "If the best investigative reporter out there isn't in on this, why should we listen to you? This just sounds like another crackpot theory."

"My theories tend to sound like this," I reminded him. "When I first put them out there."

"What, you've jumped on board this crazy train?" Reader sounded like he was warring between surprise and frustration.

"Maybe. I mean, Vance has done research. I think we should look at it."

"Yes, you should," Vance said. "If this goes on, every member of the House is going to die."

"Everyone dies," White pointed out.

"I mean prematurely," Vance snapped. "And you know it. You need to run the numbers like I have—once you do, you'll see a pattern, and that pattern is intentional."

Reader still didn't look convinced. Not a problem. "Look, Commander, you don't have to do the light reading." Hey, two could play the Title Game. "We'll have

Hacker International take a look. It should be an easy project for them. Then we can decide."

   "Make them do it fast," Vance said. "Right now, every
rep is in mortal danger." He looked at Jeff. "And that includes you."

CHAPTER 42

I'D BEEN TIRED and upset about Reader being upset with
me. Right up until the moment when Vance pointed out that
my husband, the newly presidentially and gubernatorially appointed representative from New Mexico, was, if his theory
was correct, in the line of fire. Now I was wide-awake and
could table Reader Issues for when Jeff was somewhere safe.

"Let's get inside," I said, tugging on Jeff's arm.

"No one's going to shoot at us, baby."

"You mean right now. Someone was shooting just a couple hours ago."

"Good point." Jeff made the "after you" gesture and the
women proved why they were smarter — Lorraine and
Claudia led the way inside, with Amy right behind. The rest
of us followed, with Reader making White, Jeff, and me go
in before him, Jeremy, Len, or Kyle.

Once inside, I tried to split up, but Reader wasn't having
any of it. We marched as a group back through the Embassy,
across the walkway, and into the Zoo. "I want to go to the
bathroom."

"No," Reader said flatly. "You and Jeff get to hold it until
we're done."

We took the stairs up, mostly because Reader seemed to
feel we weren't trustworthy in an elevator, and not for the
fun reasons this time.

Exited to see absolutely no one. "Wow. Glad you rushed
us back for this."

Reader pulled out his phone. "Where is everyone? Really.

Huh. Okay. Okay." He eyed me and Jeff. "Fine. Yes, get down here." He hung up. "Apparently the Romanian ambassadress felt that everyone was tired, herself especially, and insisted that everyone be escorted safely home, to reconvene another day."

"I love Olga. I'm just saying."

Raj joined us. "You should. She's very perceptive." He looked at my feet and smiled. "You look even more in the holiday spirit now."

"Blah, blah, blah. Look, I'm with Olga. It's late, we're tired. I'd like to check on Malcolm, get something over to Serene with the highest priority, get the Hackers going on Vance's intel, and go to bed."

"Call the hackers," Reader said. "They're up."

"I could go see them."

"No. You can call them or they can wait for their information."

Before I could argue more, Jeff spoke up. "Jeremy, why don't you take their instructions to them?"

"Yes, sir."

Vance cleared his throat. "Take me, too."

Jeff nodded. "I agree."

"Why?" I asked.

"Because I want to make sure they're looking at what I've looked at. And, as I told you before, Lydia's not my type."

"Dude. Her husband just murdered someone and was then murdered himself. You cannot think she's going to fall into bed with Guy."

"I don't think, I know." He held up his phone. "Just got the 'come home now or don't come home until tomorrow' text."

"It's using all my self control to not make a comment on your lifestyle."

"Yeah? Well, Guy and I don't climb and jump around on the outside of tall buildings for fun, either, especially not in good clothes. Different strokes for different folks."

Jeff nodded to Jeremy. "Take him with you, then make sure he has a secure room on the fourth floor here."

"Yes, sir," Jeremy said.

"He didn't call you Chief," I said quietly as Jeremy and Vance headed for the elevator. I was becoming hyper-aware of titles and their usage tonight.

"Because I'm not any more. There's only one Chief here now, baby, and that's you."

"Huh." Eyed Reader.

Who eyed me right back. "Don't even try it. I still out-rank you."

"You don't know me."

Reader laughed. "The hell I don't." He looked at Jeff. "I know you, too. Why did you want to get Jeremy and Vance out of the room?"

"Because we need to tell you what we know, all that we know," Jeff said. "And I don't know the Barones well enough to know if we can trust them or not." He held out the disc. "This is either going to be an emotional blocker or something that causes an emotional overlay. I think it's an overlay, because when I was around the blocker, I couldn't feel anyone, and I'm holding this and can still feel everyone in the room."

"It's also likely to explode," I added. "Since the blocker exploded already. Hopefully it'll only explode if someone tries to open it, which is what happened to the blocker. Oh, and this needs to get to Serene yesterday, under very reliable guard."

Claudia and Lorraine looked at each other. "We'll take it," Lorraine said.

Claudia nodded. "If the boys are home, then we need to go back to the Science Center anyway." They looked at Reader, who nodded.

"First, you need to know where Caroline and I got that," Amy said. "Or rather, from whom. And that's not going to take five minutes."

"There's more," White said. "I believe James needs all the details."

"I agree," Jeff said firmly. "And since the likelihood is going to be that what you take to Serene explodes anyway the moment she tries to access it, I'd like the two of you to hear what we've got to say."

The girls looked to Reader again, who nodded again.

"Nice to see that our various chains of command are all functioning at least semi-nicely. Can we sit? I may be in my Converse now, but my feet still hurt."

Reader looked around, heaved a sigh, and shook his head. "Were you this much trouble when Jeff was the Head of Field?"

"More," Jeff said with a grin. "Let's go to the Embassy. We have a nice living room with lots of things to sit on over there."

CHAPTER 43

READER WAS SOMEWHAT understanding about why we'd withheld information. Sadly, he wasn't any less angry with us for anything we'd done, particularly with anything I'd done. Though he kept the lectures to a minimum, he made it clear I was in the Centaurion Division Doghouse.

Lorraine and Claudia were a lot more relaxed about things, even about our withholding, potentially because they knew we'd cleared them immediately. And they weren't actually upset with me for anything else, either, so that likely helped as well.

Everyone agreed with Raj's assessment—that we could still trust those who'd been trusted team members prior to Washington. Len and Kyle were given their special dispensation based on there being no way in the world anyone could have planned out how they'd met me, which they were obviously pleased about.

Raj was given special dispensation because he knew everything that was going on anyway. He clearly found this amusing.

No one was happy that I'd been hanging out with the Dingo and not sharing, but Amy confirmed that the Dingo and Surly Vic had stressed that they were here to protect and serve, at least to protect and serve me, and that anyone who caused them to be distracted the next time they were trying to stop me from being assassinated would be killed with great malice aforethought.

Everyone also agreed that telling Chuckie or my mom

what was going on was both necessary and to be handled delicately. For some reason, I wasn't the Designated Delicate Delivery Person. Tried not to be offended. Failed.

No one was happy about Possibly Clarence running around, and everyone was less happy about Possibly Colonel Hamlin running around, either. Especially since I'd given the Dingo what he'd said was a bioweapon. Extra especially since Buchanan was still unresponsive.

Christopher joined us midway through our confessional meeting to share that Buchanan was still alive, Tito and the rest of the medical team still had no idea what was wrong with him, and that he hadn't had any kind of disc or other odd foreign object on him that anyone had found.

Thusly all caught up, Lorraine and Claudia headed back to the Science Center, disc in hand. Serene verified receipt and that she was in contact with Ravi. She also verified that all Dulce-based children who'd been at the Pontifex's Residence were back at home with their parents. Gladys was also back at Dulce, but was scanning our D.C. buildings every fifteen minutes.

Gower was back at his local residence along with the four Embassy kids, but he wasn't alone with just Denise and the children. His sisters and Chuckie were all there, too, as was Kevin, per my mother's orders. Reader felt that the kids, Jamie especially, were having a great time. Poofs and Peregrines were confirmed on site and on the case, so I managed to stop worrying about Jamie. A little.

I was able to give the lion's share of worry to Jeff. Because if Vance was right, then Jeff was in danger. Of course, it seemed like we were always in danger, but Vance's theory didn't appear to have anything to do with the A-Cs, meaning it was more random than we were used to.

The rain started right after Reader sent everyone else back to bed. "He was right," I said as I went to the kitchen window so I could check to be sure what I was hearing was indeed rain.

"Who was?" Jeff asked.

"My 'uncle'. He told me to get inside because it was going to rain soon."

"So he has a good weather app on his phone," Reader said. "You need to stop thinking of these men as anything other than dangerous assassins."

He was probably right. Only, Reader hadn't been the one talking to the Dingo and Surly Vic. "I'm more worried about Raul than the Dingo."

"Get away from the window," Jeff said. "Because you're an easy target right now."

"Not if the building's shield is still up."

Jeff grumbled but didn't argue.

Our penthouse took up half of the top floor, meaning that we had a lot of windows in the various rooms. Our half had a view of the Circle from most of the windows, though we could also see our street, the Zoo, and the heavy foliage behind us that wasn't actually part of our property.

From the kitchen I could see the street and the Circle pretty easily, as well as the embassies across from us. The rain was falling steadily now—not too hard, but you'd want to have a head covering of some kind if you were outside.

Couldn't see anyone outside lurking, on either rooftops or in shadows. Hard to tell at the park in the Circle, but no dangerous lurker stood out to me over there, either.

Memory nudged. "James, I forgot, Santiago had a message for you." Wanted to continue to call him Commander but just didn't have the energy for it. If he wanted to be mad at me, so be it. I was done with whatever fight we were actually having.

"He did?"

I swallowed. "Yeah. It . . . it was the last thing he ever said." Blinked tears away. I could cry now, but tears weren't going to bring Reyes back, nor were they going to figure out what was going on. Supposedly we'd caught his killer, but if there was someone behind Eugene's dementia, I wanted to ensure they paid for what they'd done, and soon.

"Ah." Reader's tone was very gentle. "What was it?"

"He said to tell you that he hoped you were right and ready."

"That's it?"

"That's it."

"Do you know what he meant?" Jeff asked.

"No," Reader said slowly. "I'll run over the last few conversations he and I had. Hopefully I'll figure out what he wanted me to know."

"Santiago also asked me, specifically me, to clean out his desk. Me, not anyone else. But that was before he gave me the message for you."

"Well, that'll be easier than you might think. Jeff's going to be moving into Santiago's old office."

"Oh. Good." Didn't relish this idea, but there was undoubtedly nothing that could be done about it.

"James, don't you need to go home and get some sleep?" Jeff asked. Pointedly, if my ears were any judge.

"I'm staying here tonight."

"We love you, James, but you're not staying in the room with us," Jeff said.

Reader chuckled. "No, I'm actually taking a guest room. But I have Walter on notice to wake me up if either one of you tries to get out of your rooms tonight."

"We're not going anywhere tonight," Jeff said firmly.

Heard movement, then someone put their hand on my shoulder. "Kitty," Reader said quietly, "stop looking for the bad guys."

"Why? They're out there."

"Yeah, they are." He turned me away from the window gently. "None of what's happened today is your fault." It was nice to hear, but I had a feeling Jeff had indicated that Reader needed to play nice with me.

"I didn't catch Clarence and none of you believe I saw him."

"True, you didn't catch whoever you saw. But I know Jeff and I both believe you saw someone. And if it wasn't Clarence, it had to be an A-C because no one else could outrun you. And that means it's likely someone spying for our enemies, because Alpha Team doesn't have someone spying on our Embassy."

"I gave a dangerous package to the world's best assassin."

"You did. If they were going to use it, they wouldn't have protected you."

"You really think so?"

"I really do."

"Santiago died at my dinner party, and Eugene took the bullet intended for me."

"You caught Santiago's murderer and you were with him so he didn't die alone. And thank God Eugene took that bullet instead of you. He was a cold-blooded murderer. You're not." Reader hugged me. "You're a protector. We all are. That does make it harder to deal when we feel like we've failed to actually protect."

"Like I have tonight."

"Like we all have tonight. But you haven't failed."

"Feels like it. Feels like I have no idea of what's going on anywhere, either. You all have private jokes—" Stopped myself before I sounded like a jealous, whiney baby.

Reader hugged me again. "I know you feel left out. But your job is to ensure the Diplomatic Corps functions as it's supposed to. Keeping our Diplomatic Corps protected is part of my job now."

"What about keeping Jeff safe? If Vance is right, he's now a target."

"*If* Vance is right. Look, I'm willing to give the guy the benefit of the doubt based on you telling me he's been hiding that he has a functioning brain, but right now, it's just another crackpot theory tossed out. But regardless, of course we're going to be protecting Jeff."

"Tell me how you're going to do that on the House floor. I'm dying to know."

Reader sighed. "We'll find a way, Kitty. I promise. When you and Jeff and Christopher were in charge you always found a way. Give the rest of us the credit of believing we're close to as good as you guys were."

Felt bad and like I'd hurt his feelings. "That's not what I'm trying to say and you know it."

"Yeah? Well, two people were murdered, basically in front of me, Tim, and Serene, and we weren't able to stop either death from happening. We had a tip that there was going to be a problem and still couldn't stop it."

I jerked. "Wait a minute. A tip from where or whom?"

"No one we know."

"No one I know, no one you know, or no one anyone knows?"

"It wasn't a straight tip, more of an assumption based on a lot of information. Intel came from Camilla, derived from the work she's been doing for Reynolds. I know we can't tell if we should trust her or not, based on the word of someone who might be the missing Colonel Hamlin, might be an android pretending to be Hamlin, or might be someone else who either lied to Buchanan or was in league with him."

"Why would Malcolm knock himself out the way he's knocked out?"

"In-fighting? No honor among thieves? There's really no

one main Mastermind? I can keep going. We don't have enough to believe anyone right now, Hamlin or Vance or Camilla. But precedent says that Camilla's brought us real, actionable intel. The other two are unknown quantities."

"And Camilla was right," Jeff said. "Something bad happened, and if Hamlin is the real deal, a 'captain' from the invasion did show up."

An idea formed. But it was small and somewhat vague and I was tired. Decided to sleep on said idea before I forwarded it, in part because I had a feeling only Vance would take it seriously. That I was connecting with someone I still thought of half the time as an asinine twit wasn't comforting.

"Okay, I'll stop worrying for right now."

Reader chuckled. "I don't believe that. But just remember that we're here to help and protect you, not to be avoided because we're going to get in the way or cramp your style." He hugged me again. Realized he was hugging me and I hadn't been hugging him back. Rectified that situation and felt Reader relax a little.

"You don't cramp our style, James."

He chuckled. "Right. I know you miss being an active part of Alpha Team. But you're doing your job as Head of Recruitment really well."

"So you claim."

"So I know. Now, get a good night's sleep, what's left of it, and I'll see the two of you in the morning."

Jeff walked Reader to the door. Heard them talking quietly, but not for too long. Then Jeff was back. "Ready for bed, baby?"

"What did you and James talk about where I couldn't hear?"

"I told him that I wasn't going to let you go anywhere alone, and reassured him that where we were both going was straight to bed." His eyes closed a little and he got the "jungle cat about to eat me" look on his face. "We might even go straight to sleep."

"God, I hope not."

CHAPTER 44

WE STARTED GETTING UNDRESSED, rather slowly. Not doing sexy undressing so much as helping each other get our clothes off in a relaxed manner.

I could have wallowed in feelings of guilt or remorse, but reality said that I'd have plenty of time for that tomorrow. Right now, being with my husband in a safe, intimate way seemed like the best idea in the world.

As I hung our coats up, I noted that there was a fedora hanging in the closet. "Huh, the Elves seem to think you're going to need headgear tomorrow."

"I don't wear hats."

"Oh, don't be a baby, try it on."

"No."

"Yes." I was now used to dealing with a little girl who already had opinions about her clothing. I put it on his head and took a good look. And kept on looking. "Um, wow. Keep it on."

"You like it?"

"Keep it on in bed."

Jeff looked at himself in the mirror. "Why?"

"Um, 'cause you look even hotter in the fedora, if such is possible to believe." Handed him his trench. "Put the coat back on."

"I swore to James we weren't leaving our rooms, let alone the Embassy."

"Am I wearing an emotional blocker?"

"No."

"Then pay attention and put the coat on."

He did with an embarrassed little smile. "Okay. So?"

"So, um, wow. Jeff, this is an amazingly good look on you. Like *GQ* cover model good. Like, never take this stuff off good."

Apparently Jeff was finally paying emotional attention again, because he started to blush. "It's just a coat and hat," he mumbled, though he looked pleased as well as embarrassed. "I've worn a coat before."

"Yeah, and you look great in them. But this one's different." Possibly because of the hat. Because I'd seen Jeff in the standard-issue trench before. Heck, I had one, too, albeit the girl version. On the roof earlier he'd looked totally hot, but I knew some of that reaction was because I hadn't seen him in a coat in a while.

But right now there was definitely something more electric about how he looked. Had to be the hat and trench combo. Resolved to ensure he wore this every single day, even in the summer.

"I don't get why you like this so much."

"Did you like my wedding dress?"

"Yeah," he purred.

"Remember how much I loved you in your wedding tux?" He grinned. "Then consider this the everyday alternative."

"Who knew you were this easy to please?"

"If anyone should, it would be you. Besides, I'm picky. I only take the hottest guy in the world to bed."

Jeff grinned again, and turned me around so he could unzip my dress. "Flattery will get you everywhere."

"As long as it gets me in bed with you still dressed like this, I'll flatter 'til the cows come home."

Jeff insisted my dress wasn't ruined for life, so I tossed it into the hamper instead of the trash. The Elves had saved worse, after all. Besides, I no longer cared. I had a living fantasy to get back to.

I was still in my bra, underwear, and thigh-highs. Jeff picked me up before I took any of them off. "If I'm staying dressed, you're at least staying partially dressed," he said, right before he kissed me. "At least for a few minutes."

Couldn't have told anyone where this particular fantasy came from, but it was incredibly hot to be mostly undressed while Jeff was more dressed than normal. Maybe it was a holdover from our wedding night. Chose not to question because questioning would mean talking and I had other things I wanted our mouths doing.

We were alone in our huge apartment, but we didn't move out of the closet. Of course, our closet was humongous, but that wasn't the point. Jeff shoved our clothes over and then shoved us up against the wall while I wrapped my legs around his waist.

"Mmmm," he growled as he moved his mouth to my neck. "What's a naughty girl like you doing in a place like this?"

"Ahhh." Hey, it was hard for me to talk when Jeff was on my main erogenous zone.

"You're a spy, aren't you?" he asked with a chuckle that sent sexual shivers through me. "You need to be interrogated." One hand was cupping my behind, keeping me up. The other one was toying with the other side of my neck.

"I'll never tell," I managed to gasp out, as Jeff's hand started to slide down my chest. He flicked my bra open with one well-practiced movement, then began playing with my nipples. In about three seconds my hips were thrusting against him.

He ground against me, making me moan. He was rock hard, and as he rubbed against me, tongue flicking all over my neck, while his fingers played with my breasts, I locked my legs around him and squeezed. He thrust against me again and an orgasm hit.

"See?" he said as my wailing died down. "I have ways of making you talk." He bit my neck gently and his fingers brushed the skin on my stomach.

Sometimes I couldn't maintain the sex play for even a couple minutes before I was at the begging point. Usually, by the time the first orgasm hit I wasn't able to do much more than ask for more of them. But today had been long and eventful and full of bad things, and all I wanted was to be taken away to someplace where only fun, sexy things happened.

"I'll resist." Three syllables *was* my resisting.

"Will you really?" Jeff said, as his fingers slid under my panties. "We'll see about that."

I gasped as his fingers slid in and over me. He was an

expert with this move, and started building me up again almost immediately. I grabbed his face and kissed him, all without losing hold with my legs or knocking his hat off.

Jeff kissed me back deeply and his tongue and fingers occupied so much of my attention that I didn't realize we'd left the closet until he put me down on our bed.

He removed my panties as he straightened up. "Now let's see you resist."

It was difficult because he looked incredibly sexy, like a gorgeous superspy or film noir detective. Maybe that was what I liked about the fedora and coat. Decided I was thinking far too much, as I sat up, grabbed him by the coat, and pulled him on top of me.

"Maybe you'll be the one answering the questions," I said as I nipped his ear.

He grabbed my hands and held them up over my head in one of his. The other hand went back to work on my breasts. "Tell me what organization you belong to," Jeff said with a wicked grin. "Or I'll take whatever I want."

"Do your worst, I'll never tell."

"If you insist." He grabbed my wrists with both hands again, only now he moved my arms so that he had my hands held on the bed next to my hips. "Last chance to tell."

I knew where he was heading and even if I'd really been trying to keep a secret from him, I'd certainly never share it at this moment. "Never."

Jeff chuckled as he knelt by the bed. "Then I'll have to make you talk," he said against my inner thighs.

Couldn't tell you what it looked like, him down there fully dressed, because the moment his mouth was on me my head was back and I was too busy moaning to look at anything other than fireworks going off behind my eyes.

As with everything else related to the bedroom, Jeff was an expert at this, and within moments his lips, tongue, and teeth had me wailing out a symphony of sound. None of it was coherent, but then again, I got my point—do it some more, don't stop, oh God that's so good—across anyway.

Jeff let go of my wrists and slid his hands up to my breasts. This was the last straw, and I went over the edge. A huge orgasm crashed over me and my entire body bucked.

As my body quieted, he stood up and undid his pants. I moaned. Sure, I'd just had two great orgasms. But the ones where he was inside me were always better. The jungle cat look was on his face again as he slid into me and my legs wrapped around him again automatically. "Tell me what I want to hear," he growled.

"Never," I gasped out, as he thrust into me, each movement deep and rhythmic. My hips moved in time with him, keeping up as he started to go faster. My hands clutched at his chest and I had to keep myself from ripping his clothes apart or off.

He kept up the growling questions and I managed to keep on saying I'd never tell, as our movements got faster and more frenetic.

"Who do you belong to?" he asked, as I got nearer and nearer to the edge.

"No one."

"Wrong answer." Jeff slammed into me and I moaned. The feel of him inside me and his clothes against my bare skin was highly erotic. Huge orgasm had just a little while ago or not, I was building up fast. "Tell me," he purred against my neck.

"Oh . . . God . . . Jeff . . ."

"That's the right answer." He kissed me and it was deep, strong, wild. My arms wrapped around him as he thrust even harder and I climaxed again. Jeff growled into our kiss as he joined me. As always, this made my climax spike in time with him, and our bodies shook together for a good, long time.

Finally our bodies quieted and Jeff kissed me again. "You fought a good fight."

"Oh, I can fight more." I nuzzled into his neck. "If you make it worth my while."

He leaned up on his arms. "Do I get to get undressed?"

I laughed. "One piece of clothing at a time."

"When does the hat come off?"

My turn to do a wicked grin. "Last."

CHAPTER 45

FOR AS TIRED AS I WAS, both physically and emotionally, it wasn't a shocker that I fell right to sleep once we
were done having lots more incredibly fantastic sex. Jeff
was even fully naked by the time we were done, too.

What was surprising was that I woke up early.

Put it down to the fact that I was now used to getting up
with Jamie. Of course, Jeff was still sound asleep, and he was
normally up before me.

Looked at the clock. 6:30 in the morning was earlier than
early for me, unless Jamie had woken up early for some
reason. And Jamie wasn't here.

Neither were the pets. Listened, but didn't hear any animal or bird sounds. Didn't hear much of anything, other
than Jeff's rhythmic breathing. So why was I awake?

Rolled carefully out of bed so I didn't disturb him. Gathered up my underwear, his clothes, and the now-beloved
fedora and went to the closet. Another fedora and trench
were in there. Presumably the Elves didn't want Jeff going
out in a dirty set, and also presumably they were clear that
I was going to keep him in that outfit as much as possible.

"Thanks," I whispered to the hamper. I doubted that was
where the Elves lived, but my bet was that it was their por-
tal. "Seriously, if you guys want cookies and milk or silver
dollars left in shoes or any other kind of bonus, leave me a
note where Jeff won't find it. I've got you covered."

Dumped the clothes into the hamper, put the "old" fedora on top of the hamper, and trotted into the bathroom.

Came out to find Jeff still fast asleep. Worry niggled. What if he'd been hit with whatever Buchanan had been hit with? What if Jeff wasn't going to wake up?

He grunted. "M'wake." Then he rolled over and went back to snoozing.

Worry abated, I contemplated what I should do with my wide-awake self. I could read more of the Briefing Books of Boredom or the Diplomat's NYC Phone Book. Decided those were only options if I wanted to go right back to sleep. Part of me did, because I doubted I'd had enough rest.

But I was awake, and maybe I was awake for a reason. After all, when the Peregrines had arrived, Christopher and I had been woken up first. Maybe we were getting a shipment from Alpha Four.

Waited. Nothing. So, that most likely wasn't the right answer. Checked my phone. No calls, no texts, nothing. Burner phones were quiet as well.

ACE? Sure it was probably useless, but I could hope, right? ACE, are you there? Do you need Kitty?

Waited, but no answer came. Heaved a sigh, but then it had probably been too much to hope for. ACE would let me know when he was back. I hoped.

It was still raining. Maybe there'd been thunder or a heavy raindrop or something. No matter, I wasn't going back to bed.

Put on a robe and went out to the living room, taking my purse and handbag with me. Turned on the TV while I transferred stuff from the handbag to my regular purse. Which was a mistake—turning on the TV, not moving stuff into my purse—because the news was filled with our disastrous party. Hadn't realized I was masochistic, but apparently this was so, as I morbidly flipped through the channels to find out who was covering the story. Everyone was. Go journalism.

Could wake Jeff up and share the "fun" with him, but that seemed pointless. Frankly, waking anyone up seemed pointless. They'd all see and hear about this soon enough.

My phone beeped with a text from my father, asking me to call him whenever I woke up. Well, Dad was up, and I was up, and I desperately wanted to talk to someone. Waited an entire two seconds before I dialed.

"Hi, kitten, you're up early."

"Um, yeah. Dad, have you looked at the news?"

"Yes. That's why I sent the text. Your mother's still asleep. She got in late and is thankfully sleeping like a rock. She needs it. You need it, too."

"Yeah, Jeff's still asleep, but I woke up and am really wide awake. And Mom's had a busy few days, hasn't she?"

"Yes, but I don't know all the details." Dad sighed. "How are you doing, really?"

"I'm okay."

"Kitty, don't lie to your father."

"I don't want to whine." Actually, I desperately wanted to whine, but felt that I was a little old for it.

"That's what I'm here for, kitten. You may be a big girl with an important job, and a husband and baby girl of your own, but you will always be *my* little girl and if I need to slay some dragons for you or defend you from the ravening hordes, then that's what I'm here for."

That was all it took—the floodworks started. "Oh, Daddy . . ."

Blubbered out a variety of things, mostly related to having Reyes die at my party while holding my hand, and then to have his murderer turn out to be inept and assassinated at the same time. Dad grunted sympathetically at all the right places.

Then I blubbered some more about nothing that really mattered—my dress getting likely ruined, our having thrown another disastrous party, the news asking if we were The Embassy of Death. Dad continued the sympathetic noises with the occasional "not to worry" tossed in.

Proceeded to then sob on about things that did matter— Jeff being forced to become a representative, my being forced to handle being the real, full-time ambassador, my fears about all the variety of unknowns we had going on, Reader being mad at me.

"And when we first moved here I thought Eugene was my friend but he wasn't and now it's like Vance is trying to be my friend and like James isn't and it's so weird and I just miss being a regular person," I shared as I was winding down.

Dad chuckled. "Kitten, you've never been just a regular person. Even before you met Jeff you were exceptional."

"Aren't you required to say that under the Parent's Rules and Regulations Code?"

"Maybe, but it's true. You were much more exceptional than you realized."

"I guess. But I just had a normal job and a normal life."

"Do you miss it? I mean truly, not just at this moment."

Considered this. Decided I owed my father honesty. "No, not really. But I miss what I used to do with Centaurion Division."

"Only because you had a bad day yesterday. You've been settling in well, and now your rhythm's being shifted again. I understand. But, honestly, kitten, as the saying goes, with great power comes great responsibility."

"Thanks for the Spiderman moment, Dad." I sniffled. "I know I have a great life, I really do. But right now, I feel like all my friends are doing other things. Not just James and Lorraine and Claudia. But Amy's taking on Gaultier Enterprises, and when she wins, that'll mean she's going to be running that company. Caro's always busy with the senator, especially now. Sheila and I are back down to a text a month to make sure we're both alive kind of thing."

"You see Charles at least every week, if not every day," Dad reminded me gently. "And every person you named would be there for you in an instant."

"True."

"James may be upset with you, but it's because he cares about you and doesn't want to see you get hurt. He's in charge now, and, as I said before, that means he has the greatest responsibility. That can wear heavy, especially when things go wrong, as they did last night."

"I guess."

"Let's be honest, kitten. You had two people you knew murdered in front of you last night."

"I've killed people, Dad. It's not like I haven't seen someone die before."

"But there's a difference between killing in battle, killing in self-defense, and witnessing cold-blooded murder. You were hosting a dinner party. People aren't supposed to die at dinner parties unless they're in Agatha Christie novels."

Sat up. "Say that again, please." The little idea I'd had the night before seemed clearer.

"It was just a little joke, kitten. I said people aren't supposed to die like poor Santiago did, poisoned in that awful way, unless they're in a murder mystery."

And suddenly I could see the forest of dense and confusing foliage for the distinct tree branches that were really there.

CHAPTER 46

"DAD, HOLD THAT THOUGHT." Let my mind settle for a moment. "You know, Dad, you are totally the best father in the world."

"Always nice to hear. You sound better. Are you?"

"Yeah, I am. Have Mom call me whenever she's awake and had her coffee. I need to go. I love you, Dad."

"I love you, too, kitten."

We hung up and I contemplated my options. Wanted to run theories by Chuckie, but he was with far too many people, my daughter included. Checked on Jeff; he was still fast asleep. Since I was in the room, I put on the standard-issue A-C pajamas of white T-shirt and blue pajama bottoms, got my slippers, and rewrapped up in the robe. Washed my face with cold water and ran a brush through my hair.

Through all of this Jeff remained asleep, but he was moving like he was dreaming, so I again concluded he was okay.

Decided the other person who I'd run to, in fact the person I'd gotten very used to running to until we'd been moved here, was in the building. Sure he was probably still mad at me and my feelings were still hurt about it. But the game was afoot and that meant we needed to work together. Sent a text. Got a fast reply. Yay, he was up early, too.

Went to the front door, opened it, and waited. Didn't take long. The elevator arrived and Reader came out. He was dressed like me. "I didn't think I'd woken you up," I said softly.

"You didn't. I was awake. Just hadn't gotten the drive up to shower."

"Me either." We went into the living room. I settled on the couch, he took the closest comfy chair. "Why were you up?"

Reader shrugged. "I got enough sleep."

Far be it for me to argue with that logic, since I had no better reason for being up to watch the sun rise. "I need to run a theory by you."

He flashed the cover boy grin. "Been a while since you've said that to me." He stopped smiling. "But before you start, were you crying about something to do with Jeff, or were you crying about last night?"

"Last night."

"Okay, that's an understandable reason. Just wanted to make sure I didn't need to intervene or provide marriage counseling."

"No, we're good." Well, Jeff and I were good. Possibly Reader and I were good, too. But I didn't want to ask right now. "I need to get this out before I lose my train of thought." He nodded and I went on. "I was talking to my dad before I texted you."

"So he got the tears?"

"In bucket loads, yeah. But anyway, as we were winding up or down or whatever, he mentioned that the only time people are supposed to die by arsenic poisoning is during murder mystery novels."

"Nice sentiment. Sorry we failed at that."

"No, listen. It made me think—what if we're looking at this the wrong way?"

"How do you mean? I don't even know that we're looking at it in any way specifically."

"Yes, we are. Colonel Hamlin, Clarence or whoever, the Assassination Bureau, all of these things are making us focus on threats against *us*, against American Centaurion and Centaurion Division."

"Because these are all threats against us would be the reason why."

"Yes, okay, fine. But let's, just for these few minutes, say that maybe Vance is on to something."

"Okay, since we're in the realm of hypothesis."

"Vance didn't come to us with a theory about how some anti-alien or purity-of-the-race group is attacking us. His theory relates to humans, regular people, who are doing specific jobs. He doesn't think that Jeff is in danger because he's an A-C. Vance said that Jeff was now in danger because he's just become a representative in Congress."

Reader's eyes narrowed. "Go on."

"So, let's take away the extra 'stuff' that's just our lives in general, which means we ignore whatever Hamlin told me, we stop thinking about the assassins and why they're here, we don't worry about Clarence and the mystery package."

"If we take the hypothesis that Hamlin's correct, though, there's a Mastermind, and that person would also be behind whatever Vance is talking about."

"Maybe, but who cares? When Sherlock Holmes solves a crime, it doesn't matter if it originated with Professor Moriarty. Holmes has to solve the crime *first*, and then, once that's done, then he can continue to trace the thread back to the evil Mastermind."

"Okay, then what do we focus on? You caught the person who committed last night's crime, at least the first murder. If I'm following your thought process, Eugene was killed by an assassin trying to hit you, so his murder we should ignore."

"Yeah, at least right now. Because we know who killed Eugene—Raul—and we're pretty sure of the why, which is that Raul was trying to kill me. The bottom line for last night, though, is that a representative was murdered. Supposedly the *wrong* rep, I might add. Eugene told me he was given instructions and was supposed to kill Brewer, not Santiago."

"He was lying to save himself, Kitty."

"Maybe, but he didn't seem like it, and I don't know how saying you merely killed the wrong guy removes your guilt or gives you sympathy from a jury. He said he'd been given written information, and lots of it, that he hid to protect Lydia from finding it. If we can figure out where he hid that information, then we can determine if he's telling the truth. And we want to so determine, because if Eugene wasn't full of it, then Vance's theory becomes much more sound and likely."

"Okay, let's say that you're on the right track, that your new buddy's got the goods. How does that change what we need to do? Because we still have assassins running around, in addition to people who may be Clarence and Hamlin, or may be androids, or may be something else."

"He's not my buddy."

"Right. You're forwarding his theories, you backed him up, he was running around on the roofs with you—he's your friend."

"Do I detect a hint of jealousy?"

Reader shrugged and looked slightly embarrassed. "No. I mean, you're allowed to have other friends. Even if they happen to be married gay guys who dress well and have a certain amount of class."

"Oh my God, you *are* jealous! Vance is not my replacement for you. But while we're on the subject, let me mention that you and Tim had all those little private jokes with Santiago, some of which were about me."

Reader grinned. "Yeah. We used to joke with Santiago that you were our little tiger and that once you were on the case, you'd never stop until you figured out what was going on and did your best to save the day." He sat up straight. "I think I know what that last message of his meant."

"That he hoped you were right about me?"

Reader nodded. "When Santiago got to D.C., he called me. He said he'd found some odd things, nothing he thought was too big a deal, but he was hoping to talk to us about them, just to ease his mind. He made it sound like it was policy stuff, nothing life-threatening or even all that urgent. I told him we'd take a look after the party and that if it was anything that needed our attention, we'd handle it."

"Santiago knew he'd been poisoned. Tito and the paramedics were talking about arsenic poisoning around him. They'd had no choice."

"So he was trying to ensure you'd be the person who cleaned out his desk because I'd bet that's where he left whatever it was that he found."

"And he wanted you ready, ready to back me, in case he was wrong, and whatever he found was indeed a big deal and connected to his death, right?"

"Yeah, I think so. I mean, I have to believe he'd want us to avenge his death if we possibly could."

"And we want to. At least I want to. And not just because you're mad at me." Hadn't meant to say that out loud. I looked down so I didn't have to see Reader's expression.

Reader got up, moved next to me on the couch, and put his arm around me. "I'm sorry I've been upset with you. I'm not really mad at you, Kitty."

"You called me Ambassador most of the night."

"Because we were in a very political situation, and you weren't acting like the ambassador—you were acting like the Head of Airborne. I can't blame you for it, and I don't blame you for it. You had to take over because we'd all failed at our jobs."

"That's not true. No one thinks you've failed."

"Well, Santiago's not able to tell us his thoughts. Which is the failure."

"I don't think you're a failure. You're doing a great job."

"Some days." He hugged me. "You're still my girl, Kitty. You always will be. And you're right—I am jealous. I barely get to see you, we rarely get to work together, and when we do see each other, we're at separate tables. And the person you were risking your life with last night wasn't me, it was some guy who seems like a substitute for me."

I laughed. "Vance could only be James Lite and that would be with a lot of work on his part. He says he wants to be friends, but he's not you. I hated him on sight. With you . . ."

"Yeah, I know." He chuckled. "Still ready for me to turn straight so we can run away from all this?"

"Every day. You ready to man up and do it?"

He kissed my head. "Sorry, still gay. And unlike your new buddy, not bi."

"Still breaking my heart as always."

We both laughed and I leaned on his shoulder. Just like always, it was a great place to be.

"It sucks that I don't see you like I used to, girlfriend, but I'm always there for you, you know."

Heaved a sigh. "I miss you so much sometimes, James. It's just not . . . the same. It's like the band got broken up, and each part started their own new bands, with new members, and we sometimes get together for reunion tours, but it's not like it used to be."

"Yeah. I know what you mean." He kissed my head. "But that's how life works. We've each hung onto friends from way back when, but only a few. You have Reynolds, Amy, Caroline, Sheila, Brian. I've got Pierre, who I'm not allowed to call Peter any more." Reader chuckled. "But you have more of him than I do."

"Sorry to hog, but I'm keeping Pierre."

"I'll let you. Because we're all still in the same band. We just have to spread out and play solo and separate gigs. But when it matters, we get the band back together again, with the new members, and we rock it better than anyone ever has or ever will."

"I was whining to my dad about how I missed being ordinary."

"Me too, sometimes."

I laughed. "Dad said I was never ordinary. And if I wasn't, I know for a fact you weren't, Mister I Started Modeling At Age Three."

"True enough. Trust me, you're not the only one longing for the good old days of a year ago sometimes."

"You miss getting to be the comic relief?"

"You've noticed? Yeah. Sometimes. There's a limit to how funny or flip the Head of Field can be before the troops start to worry and question. It's probably one of the reasons Jeff fell for you so fast—he could be himself, all aspects of himself, with you."

"I just don't stand on a lot of formality."

He laughed. "Understatement of the year. And I know you miss kicking butt."

"Every day. Well, honestly, not every day. But a lot."

"You're going to be fine as the ambassador."

"Now I know you're lying."

"No, you will be. You're really good at handling things without any training, experience, or background."

"Thanks, I think."

"It's a compliment. You roll with the punches, analyze quickly, and make good decisions. You come by that naturally—your mother does the same thing."

"Only with training, experience, and background to back her up."

"She didn't always have that."

"You've been hanging out with my mom a lot?"

"Yeah. I love watching her work."

"What went on earlier this week, that she was involved in?"

He didn't say anything for a few seconds. "I can't tell you. But she's fine, and so was everyone with her. We didn't lose anyone, we did what we had to, so in that sense, we won."

Decided to let this answer be enough. "Okay."

"That's it?"

"Yeah. If Mom wants to, or can, tell me, she will. Until then, I'll trust you that I don't need to know and that the lack of knowledge won't endanger me or anyone else I care about."

He hugged me again. "Now that's some personal growth."

"It happens to me occasionally." Hugged him back. "I love you, James."

"I love you, too, Kitty. And trust me, you're forever my girl."

"Good. Even though I now want to hear some Paula Abdul."

He laughed. "Sorry. So what's our next move?"

"I'm not. *Forever Your Girl* is a great album. But anyway, we need to clean out Santiago's office and figure out where Eugene hid the paperwork that will supposedly clear his name, in that sense."

"The office will be easy enough. We'll want to go over with Jeff anyway, and he needs to go today. He has to be sworn in."

"Joy, and I'm not even going to ask why that's happening today. But doesn't swearing in happen on the floor of the House?"

"Yes, but Santiago's office is in the Capitol complex. He was living there, too."

"Really?"

"It's not completely uncommon." Reader shrugged. "He didn't have time to apartment hunt. Anyway, if we're going to the Capitol, and we are, we might as well go through Santiago's office before someone else does."

"Okay, but let's work on Eugene's stuff first. Right before he was shot, I was trying to get the location where he'd stashed this info out of him. It's not at his home, and not at his office. He said he was free and then he was shot."

"He said he was free, as in, I'm out of jail?"

Thought about it. "No. He was trying to answer my question." Ran the events back over in my mind. "Wait. He said he had the papers at work. So I asked, again, if he meant his office. He said no, he'd been free ... but what if he was cut off mid-word? Free could mean—"

"Freelancing." Reader let go of me, got up, and pulled his phone out of the pocket of his robe. "Sorry, I know it's early there. Oh? Well, I slacked off and got a couple hours of sleep. Okay. Look, I need work history run on Eugene Montgomery. Yes, the guy who poisoned Santiago. Yeah, focus on the most recent trails first. Could have been under the table. Yeah, search financials. Great, thanks, Serene." He hung up. "She hasn't gone to bed, because you sent her the best Christmas present ever, I guess. She's excited about the explosive mechanism on the disc and the components making up the shielding."

"Someone should be."

Reader's phone beeped. He stared at it.

"What?"

"I'll give you three guesses where Eugene was freelancing. And the first two don't count."

CHAPTER 47

"I PLAYED THIS GAME with Omega Red last night. Let me skip my first two guesses and go for the answer he gave me. Gaultier Enterprises."

Reader nodded. "Got it in one. The research facility."

"Where Christopher found Malcolm, basically."

"Yeah."

"So, what do we do?"

Jeff came out of the bedroom, also wearing our Sleep-wear Standard Issue. "Now that you two have made up, we have a fast meeting, then we all get showered, get dressed, and get going."

"You were awake? All this time?"

Jeff grinned, came over, and kissed me. "Not the whole time. But with all the angst and worry going on in the living room, I woke up."

"Sorry," Reader said.

Jeff shook his head. "No, this was the most important thing the two of you could have done. Besides, gave me time to check on Jamie and everyone else who's staying with Paul. Per Abigail, the adults are all awake, something about the news being too 'good' not to share with everyone, and she told me everyone's fine. They're going to keep the kids there today."

"Denise isn't going to do daycare?" Decided we could talk about the news another time. Like never.

"She's doing it at the Pontifex's Residence. Gladys feels, since it's a smaller building with far fewer people coming

and going, that it'll be easier to protect everyone there.
Kevin agrees, as does Reynolds. Kevin's staying with everyone, though Reynolds and Paul will have to leave later today."

"They'll be with us at the swearing in?" Reader asked.

"Yeah." There was a knock at our door and Jeff went to
answer it. He came back with Christopher, Amy, and White,
all in their robes and PJs. We looked like we were either at
a group day spa or a psych ward. Chose not to share this
thought.

"Jeff said that something from last night was connected
to Gaultier Enterprises," Amy said as she plopped down on
the loveseat. "So, what do you need from me?"

As Christopher joined her, White took the chair Reader
had vacated, and Jeff started a pot of coffee, Reader and I
caught everyone else up on the thinking.

"We need to find two things at Gaultier—whatever Eugene had hidden there, and possibly whatever he was
working on, and information on whatever was given to
Malcolm, hopefully including a cure." Tried not to worry
about Buchanan. Failed utterly.

"Getting in is no problem," Amy said. "Legally, I can go
anywhere I want in any Gaultier facility. The problem is
finding what we need without giving anything away and before someone destroys whatever it is we're looking for."

"I don't believe we can all go," White said. "We discussed
it after Representative Martini called us to an early summit
meeting."

"Uncle Richard, that's not funny."

"No, but it's accurate. You need to get used to the title,
Jeffrey. I doubt very much that you're going to be allowed
to leave office as soon as you'd like."

"Wonderful," Jeff groaned. "Let's get back to Kitty's
murder mystery theory for a while, okay?"

"Okay, and my father's right," Christopher said. "I can
go in as Amy's husband, and we figure we can use the excuse that she wants to impress her father-in-law, so she's
giving him a tour."

"That could work, really. I mean, Richard's the retired
Pontifex, and that has cachet in more places than just with
every A-C."

Amy nodded. "That's what we were thinking. I'd love to

bring Chuck along, but his cover's been pretty much blown along with everyone else's, so if I walk in with the head of the C.I.A.'s E-T Division, you know people are going to pay far too much attention to what we and he are doing."

"Same goes for Cliff," Christopher added. "I know he falls under the 'met once we were in Washington' group, but even if he didn't, he's too high-ranking. But we need someone with higher-level skills than any of us have."

Considered the options. "Take Doctor Wu with you."

"You're kidding," Amy said.

"No, I'm not. Of the five of them, Henry's the best with software and you need someone who can hack in in less than a minute and find what you need in less than five."

"How do we explain him?" Christopher asked.

"*You* don't," Amy said. "Because you can't lie. At all. Richard, if I do the talking, can you believably pass Henry off as your assistant?"

White nodded. "I'm not up to Camilla's standards, but since you'll be assisting me, I won't have any trouble with it."

"Take Raj, too," Jeff said.

Christopher made a face. "What do we want with a troubadour?"

"Wow, will you stop hating on him and his talent? Raj is great for this—and no one can charm like a troubadour. Other than you, James."

Reader laughed. "Thanks, girlfriend. But I agree. I'd like to go to Gaultier, but honestly, my job is to protect you guys, and if we're still going with the idea that Vance is on to something, then I need to be guarding Jeff."

"Raj works well with the squatters," Jeff added. "They'll listen to him, and that means less whining from Wu."

"Raj can also run point between you guys and us, so no one asks why Amy, her husband, or her supposedly interested father-in-law are busy texting instead of paying attention."

"Okay, we're set," Amy said. "I don't know that we'll be able to be done with all this before the swearing-in, though. Will it matter if we're not there?"

"No," Reader said. "You could go, but Paul will be there, and as the Supreme Pontifex, his presence represents for every A-C, so you can be absent without it causing issues."

"The press will find a way," Amy said. "They always do."

"Speaking of which, should we invite Mister Joel Oliver along?"

"Only if you want to present him as your personal photographer," Reader said.

"Yeah, we do," Jeff said. "I want him around—we can actually trust him, and he's the one who will know who's lying and who isn't."

"You normally know that," Christopher said.

Jeff shook his head. "We can't count on that, on any empath, any more. With devices that can block or overlay emotions, being an empath becomes less of an advantage. Now I can be lied to in even more ways than the rest of you."

"Duh. I forgot. You guys need to search for three things. Omega Red found something like what we found—the emotional blocker that blew up—and the emotional overlay, but he found them not at Titan, but at Gaultier."

"Well, aren't I so proud to hopefully become the head of Evil Incarnate." Amy's sarcasm knob was definitely at eleven. "Does that mean we need to bring him along, too?"

"How do we pass off a blind guy as anyone's aide?" Christopher asked.

"There are ways, but I think he'll be happier staying home. Henry can connect to him, and that means we have someone downloading info here as well as there."

"What will the rest of you be doing while we go perform corporate espionage?" Amy asked.

"Searching Santiago's office for clues," Reader said.

"Prepping to get sworn in for the latest job I don't want to do."

"Checking on Malcolm."

"There's no change," White told me gently. "Magdalena and Tito spent the night in the infirmary, but Mister Buchanan is still non-responsive."

"I don't care. I'm going to see him before we leave."

"Let's eat, shower, and dress first," Jeff said. "Breakfast is ready."

"How come you never make breakfast?" Amy asked Christopher as we headed for the dining room.

"Because I don't need anyone's votes."

"I heard that," Jeff called from the kitchen. "It's really because you're worse in the kitchen than Kitty is. No offense, baby."

"Absolutely none taken. But I appreciate having yet more dirt on Christopher to use against him when he least expects it."

"As if my not being a good cook is something to be embarrassed about?"

"It is when your wife thinks your cousin's cooler because he can and does cook."

"I make my wife happy in other ways."

"Yes, you do," Amy said as we all sat down. "But sometimes a girl likes the little extra gestures that Jeff does."

Christopher gave Jeff Patented Glare #1 as he served us plates of beautifully cooked and perfectly arranged food. "You cooked all this while somehow talking with all of us at the same time?"

Jeff grinned. "I don't give away political secrets, sorry."

CHAPTER 48

CHRISTOPHER, AMY, and White headed out right after eating so they could get going. I called Raj and told him what the plan was.

"I think that's wise. I'll get Henry and Yuri up and running, Ambassador."

"Thanks, Raj. Any thoughts on all of this before we part ways today?"

"Yes, and a question. The question relates to the thoughts. What are you planning to do with Vance? As in, do you want to leave him alone in the Embassy complex, take him with you, or send him on his way? He doesn't belong with the group going to the Gaultier facility."

Considered before I replied. "What do you think I should do with him?"

"I think you should bring him with you. In part so he can fill you in on what was discovered last night." Raj sounded tense. Meaning he either was tense or wanted me to think he was tense, meaning he wanted me to think.

There was only one thing done last night for which I didn't know the outcome. "Vance's theory has merit?"

"I believe it does. Please ensure that you take Len and Kyle with you, especially since Mister Buchanan is out. I personally feel that when your most efficient bodyguard is the person attacked, extra caution should be applied toward everything."

"Gotcha. Could you wake up the boys and Vance along with Henry and Yuri?"

"Will do. And Ambassador? Please be careful. I realize we're focused now on Vance's theory, but the assassins are very real, and out there, along with everything else."

"I will do, Raj. You be careful, too."

We hung up, and I went back to Jeff and Reader. "Raj is on it. We'll be taking Vance along with us."

"Why?" Jeff asked flatly.

"Yeah, why?" Reader asked, in the same tone.

"Wow. I am totally and completely touched that the two of you are so jealous of my sort of budding relationship with Vance. We're taking him along to get the intel from last night regarding his theory. Raj thinks he's on to something."

"It could send the wrong message, that he's with us at the swearing-in," Reader pointed out.

"Maybe." An old fact surfaced. "Isn't the official swearing-in date like the third of January or something?"

Reader and Jeff both stared at me. "You can't remember important things like our political status within the United States, but that random piece of information you can toss right up?" Jeff sounded shocked. Had no idea why. Coming up with this kind of random information was one of my go-to moves.

I shrugged. "Sometimes high school and college come back to me in odd ways and at odd times."

"You're right," Reader said. "However, because this is an appointment, and an emergency appointment at that, Jeff needs to be sworn in immediately."

"Works for me. We can always leave Vance in Santiago's office, too, if we have to. Besides, it'll be interesting to see how the rest of the Cabal of Evil acts if Vance is hanging this tight with us."

Reader nodded slowly. "Actually, that's a good point."

"I like the Brewers," Jeff said. "I don't think they're evil. I've never gotten anything negative from Ed toward any of us, and if we take the assumption that these empathic blockers and overlays didn't exist several months ago, then they aren't our enemies. I get why you don't like most of the rest of them, baby, but I really think the Brewers are okay."

"What about Vance?" Reader asked.

Jeff shrugged. "He's excited to be helping, frightened of being killed, and willing to sleep with any and every member of our household."

"Sounds like Vance."

Reader chuckled. "Okay, so where do we meet up? Jeff has to be seen leaving, so we can drive or we can walk, but we can't take a gate."

"What's the best impression to make?" Jeff asked. "I don't know that we want to walk the entire way to the Capitol complex, especially since it's still raining."

"Raj wants us to keep Len and Kyle with us, so limo sounds like the right choice."

"Wouldn't want the jocks to miss any of the fun," Jeff said, sarcasm knob only at around a six.

"I'll meet you two in the garage, then."

"Remember we're stopping to see Malcolm first."

"Fine. Don't take too long having sex," Reader said as he headed for the door. "Or I'll make you hoof it."

Jeff grinned as the door closed. "I'll take that risk."

I loved showering with Jeff. Since becoming parents, our showers together had been more infrequent, because amazing soundproofing in the Embassy or no, bathrooms really helped get a reverberating echo going and I'd woken Jamie up a couple of times.

But with her still safely at the Pontifex's Residence, we had free run.

Jeff and I were definitely on the same wavelength. We got out of our nightclothes as fast as possible and were in the shower in record time.

The shower was limiting in terms of positions, but Jeff having me up against a wall with my legs around his waist was, as had been proven many times since we'd first met and again last night, one of my all-time favorites.

In deference to Reader and the others waiting for us and the busy day ahead, we only did it a couple times, with me howling like a happy cat in heat. A couple times with Jeff, of course, didn't mean just a couple orgasms. I was a very satisfied girl by the time we actually cleaned up and dried off.

Jeff finished up in the bathroom and zipped out while I used the blow dryer. Most days I didn't bother, but since it was wet outside, there was no sense in courting a cold, or worse, so I put forth the effort.

Jeff was tying his tie when, hair dried, I went to the closet. The Elves had a nice white dress waiting for me. It did have slits up both sides, so apparently the Elves felt I should look sophisticated yet sexy today. Doubted this was the standard look for the Representatives' Wives Club, but apparently we did it differently at American Centaurion.

Sadly, this meant I had to wear heels. The Elves had left a black pair sitting under the dress. Wearing heels in the rain was not my favorite thing to do, but such was life in a place with actual weather. Still wasn't a big fan of weather, but kept that to myself.

Today I also had a trench coat with a hood hanging up. Clearly it wasn't cold enough for my long winter coat with the fur-lined hood, which was a pity, because I really loved that coat. I also wasn't sure that the Elves were right about the weather, but perhaps we had some rule about always wearing a trench in the rain. Decided not to ask lest Jeff again point out that I didn't remember the important things.

Jeff had left his trench and fedora in the closet. I brought them out with me. He shook his head. "It's not raining that badly and we're driving over."

"You're going to be sworn in. Let's keep you dry. Put the hat and coat on now."

He grinned and gave me a quick kiss. "No. People are waiting for us. But, I'll make you happy and wear them when we go out, okay?"

"Super." Maybe, even within all the intrigue that was going on, we could fit in a quickie somewhere along the way.

Jeff laughed as I grabbed my purse and coat. "Glad to see you're still focused on the priorities, baby."

CHAPTER 49

AS I'D SAID, we went to the infirmary first. Tito and Nurse Carter looked exhausted and worried.

"No change," Tito shared morosely. "I wanted to move him to Dulce, but they said they don't know what's going on with him, either, and feel it's safer if he's not moved, just in case."

"Is he in a coma?"

"No, his reactions aren't coma-like. It's more like he's in the deepest sleep possible. But nothing we do rouses him. I'm not sure if I should have him under quarantine," Tito said as he led us to where Buchanan was, for lack of a better word, sleeping.

The Embassy infirmary was nice. Not as complex as the hospital section of the Science Center, but impressive for an in-house medical facility. Under most circumstances, it was perfect for our needs, because under most circumstances, if we had a truly bad medical situation, we took the patient to Dulce. Sadly, the current circumstances were ensuring that our infirmary, like the rest of us, was falling a little short.

Buchanan was in a room that Tito could indeed quarantine if needed. It was modeled after many of the hospital rooms at the Science Center, in that it was like a fishbowl. Buchanan was a very big, unmoving fish.

I'd never seen him asleep; I'd only seen him in action. It was unsettling. I wanted to run in there and shake him, get him up, tell him what was going on, find out who'd hurt him.

I also wanted to pull all the tubes and needles out of his body.

"Maybe you shouldn't go in, baby," Jeff said quietly.

"No. I know part of you is jealous of my relationship with Malcolm. But he's saved my life, and Jamie's life, more than once. I'm going in, regardless of whatever risk there is or isn't. I don't leave my friends like this without at least trying to help."

"I'll wait with Tito," Jeff said. "And not because I'm jealous."

"Liar."

Jeff chuckled. "Okay, a little jealous. Your reactions are really strong."

"Many times Malcolm reminds me of you. Right now, he reminds me of when you're in isolation."

"Ah." Jeff hugged me gently.

"He can't feel any of this right now, Kitty," Tito said.

"And isolation saves lives, baby."

"Right. That makes it less freaky and scary for me how?"

"Good point. Head in. I'll let James know you'll be a few minutes. And yes, feel free to draw the curtains if you want."

Went in and did draw the curtains, mostly because I didn't want to feel like I was being watched as opposed to my planning to ravage Buchanan while he was unconscious.

Buchanan was lying still on the bed. He looked peaceful, as if he was indeed merely having a very deep sleep. "Malcolm?" No response, and I hadn't expected one. I took his hand in mine. "Malcolm, if you can hear me wherever you are, I'm going to find out what was done to you and fix it, I promise."

Thought about the other times someone I cared about had been down. About when Reader had almost died. I'd had ACE to talk to then. Couldn't bear to try to talk to him in my mind and not have him answer. Couldn't bear to act like ACE wasn't there, either.

"ACE, I know I can't ask you to intervene. And I wouldn't want you to take focus away from whatever's going on with you. But if you have the ability, can you please watch over Malcolm? He hasn't been in space, but he's my friend and he's saved my life, a lot. He's kind of like you, ACE. He has his mysterious ways, and I don't know where he goes or what he does when he's not with me. But he's always there when I need him, like you've always been. He's not an astronaut, but he's still an important penguin."

There was no answer, but as I looked at Buchanan and thought about ACE, I remembered something important. Maybe I remembered it on my own, maybe ACE was around and strong enough to give me a little nudge.

"Thanks, ACE. Malcolm, I'll be back, hopefully with the cure." I squeezed his hand. "Don't leave me yet, okay? I need to get the rest of the Justice League and the X-Men rolling on this."

Trotted out of the room. "How's Buchanan doing?" Jeff asked. "Is he awake?"

"No, why would you think that?"

"You're excited and focused, versus worried and sad."

"Well, yeah, but that's because something dawned on me. Doctor Strange is probably on the astral plane and we need to bring him back."

"That's not exactly a help, Kitty," Tito said.

"This will be. You need to contact Serene, and probably Jeff's dad."

"My dad? Why?"

"Because over the past couple of years, we've forgotten a few key things. Surcenthumain became the Superman drug. But it's original purpose was to put human and A-C astronauts into a deep sleep so that they could travel to distant stars without dying and, I think, aging. That drug was created by Gaultier Enterprises."

Had to say this, Tito and Jeff weren't slow or stupid. Tito was on his phone calling Dulce, while Jeff called Alfred. Meanwhile, I sent Amy and Raj a text, telling them to focus their search on the space exploration section, or whatever it was, at Gaultier, particularly any offshoots of the Surcenthumain project.

We all finished about the same time. "Serene and Brian are on their way," Tito said. "They just have to drop Patrick off with the other kids at the Pontifex's Residence."

"My dad's coming, too. He's going to swing by NASA Base and pick up some files first."

"Be sure he's under guard."

Jeff nodded. "Already handled. I sent a text to James."

"Great. Tito, Magdalena, right now we probably need to

do whatever it is NASA would do for an astronaut in suspended animation."

Nurse Carter was at one of the computers. "I have it here. We're already doing much of it, but we can add certain fluids to the mix of what he's getting. And if you're wrong, they shouldn't harm him."

"Tito, while you're at it, do we have the autopsy results back on Santiago yet?"

"It hasn't happened yet. We left a team from Dulce at the hospital with his body and Melanie and Emily are going to be there when the autopsy is performed. I was going to go over today, too, and help, but I don't want to leave my patient now. Why?"

"Have them run toxicology on what killed him. I know we all think it was arsenic, and I'm betting it was mostly arsenic. But I'd like to know if there was something more in that mix. Have them run it at the Science Center, because we need fast results. If we need to throw around our political weight to make that happen, feel free to share that, husband in the House or no, the American Centaurion Ambassador is ready to knock some heads."

Medical assignments handed out, Jeff and I headed for our underground garage. He put his coat and hat on as we started downstairs. I laughed.

"What's so funny?"

"I think it's cute that you're worried I might think Malcolm was better than you."

"Who says I think that?"

I settled the fedora on his head just so. "Oh, nothing." Leaned up and kissed him. "To quote today's go-to music, I'm forever your girl."

Jeff put his arm around me. "Good. And let's have different go-to music, if that's okay with you."

"If you insist."

"I do."

"Boy bands or divas?"

"With that as my choice," Jeff said as we reached the garage, "I pick Aerosmith."

"I knew I married well."

CHAPTER 50

LEN AND READER WERE already inside one of our standard-issue gray limos. Kyle was waiting to open the door for us, chatting with Vance, who was dressed like every other man associated with Centaurion Division.

"Have to say that you have the best valet service in the world," Vance shared as we reached them. "I was told my clothes would be ready by the time we got back."

Didn't share that this meant that the Elves, for whatever reason, wanted Vance to look like he was one of us, because I knew they could have gotten his clothes back to him two seconds after he'd taken them off.

"Yeah, it's a great perk. You ready, Kyle?"

He nodded. "Raj said we needed to be on high alert."

"We always need to be on high alert."

Kyle grinned. "That's what Len said."

"Glad to see our paranoia levels are at DEFCON High. So, you know, routine."

He laughed, opened the door, and helped me into the car.

I took the seat that had my back to the driver and Jeff sat next to me. Vance sat in the back seat, next to Reader.

Len turned around. "You realize we're getting to the Capitol hours before the swearing-in ceremony."

"We're on a mission. From God."

"Whatever you say, Kitty. Music?"

"Does a duck swim? Does a bear poop in the woods? Is the Pope presumed Catholic?"

"Gotcha," Kyle said. "Random or selected? Or do you want *The Blues Brothers* soundtrack?"

"While I'd be all for Jake and Elwood, the newest representative for the great state of New Mexico has requested Aerosmith."

"Over boy bands or divas," Jeff added.

"Nothing wrong with either," Vance said.

"Yes there is," Len and Kyle said in unison.

The music started and the intro to "The Other Side" hit my ears. I relaxed as Steven, Joe, and the rest of my boys rocked on.

My phone rang. Dug it out of my purse. It was Nathalie Brewer. "Hey, what's up?"

"Kitty, we were wondering if you wanted to go over with us for today's ceremony. It can be a little overwhelming, even with others there. When it's just you alone, it can be daunting."

Jeff had faced down more scary things in his lifetime than the Brewers could imagine. Standing in a hall getting sworn in wasn't going to daunt him. However, it was easy to guess that the Brewers wanted to cement their relationship with the Presidential Appointee.

"Going over as a group today?" Looked at Reader. He shook his head. "I don't know if we can. We have some things we need to take care of prior to the ceremony."

"I just meant with me and Edmund. We live so close to you, it seemed like it would be convenient." Nathalie sounded disappointed. Out of all the Cabal left, I liked her the most. Jeff liked Brewer and had been gently urging me to give both of them another chance, even before the party. And Vance was going to go over with us.

"Well, maybe. Can I call you back? If we're done in time, it'd be fun."

"That would be wonderful." Nathalie sounded a lot happier. "Let me know if you have time for us to do lunch. You want to have a good meal before the ceremony, because there are a lot of pictures taken and I'm sure there will be reporters."

Reporters. Knew I'd forgotten something. "Gotcha. I'll call you in a while." Hung up from Nathalie and dialed. He answered quickly. "MJO, how's my favorite reporter?"

"Quite well, Ambassador. Hoping to see you later in the day. If I can get into the Capitol."

"Oh, you'll definitely be getting in. We're coming to get you," I tossed over my shoulder. Len nodded, and turned down the next cross street. "Leave the parrot at home."

"He doesn't have to," Jeff said.

"Oh, yes, he does, he definitely does."

"Miss Bellie will remain safely at home. I'll hurry up, Ambassador."

We hung up and a thought occurred to me. We were heading out into dangerous territory, and my Royal Guardians were nowhere around.

No sooner did I think this than I realized that there was something on the seat next to Reader. I stared and a yellow eye opened, looked at me, winked, then closed. So Bruno was in Stealth Mode. Didn't know if that meant Vance was untrustworthy, or Bruno felt playing it cool was the word of the day. Figured we'd find out.

Opened my purse to drop my phone back in and discovered Harlie, Poofikins, Gatita, who was Reader's Poof, as well as a variety of other Poofs in there. Good.

We collected Oliver. He sat next to Reader, so technically on Bruno. Casually put my hand onto the seat next to me. Sure enough, I felt feathers. Gave him a hopefully unobtrusive pat and put my hand back in my lap.

Vance was clearly happy to be with his idol again. "I just wanted to say that last week's edition of your "Get to Know Your Aliens" series was amazing. Each one has been so informative, but your in-depth analysis of how many people have been saved from superbeing attacks over the course of time was mind-blowing." Oliver had been doing regular articles to explain how great the A-Cs were. None of us would have called them mind-blowing, but they were good, and very pro-alien, of course.

"Thank you," Oliver said, looking both flattered and embarrassed. "I must confess, I'm not used to having fans. Well, sane fans."

Vance shook his head. "You have a lot of fans now. You're a celebrity."

"Ah." Oliver winked at me. "It's always nice to be popular."

Reyes' office was in the Rayburn House Office Building, which was the biggest and most modern of the buildings that housed the representatives. It went up four stories, had two stories underground, and three levels of underground parking. Resisted the urge to ask if the A-Cs had helped build it.

Modern in D.C., of course, didn't mean the twenty-first century. It was a big, sturdy, stone and marble set of buildings architects said was in an H design. If it was an H, it was the most humongous H ever. As we drove around to get to the right entrance to the parking garage, I got the two huge city blocks full view. This one building made our Embassy and Zoo setup seem small and ordinary.

The less said about the security stops and checks to get into the Capitol complex and down into the bowels of the Rayburn House the better. They were there for a reason, but more than once the desire to park the car elsewhere and use hyperspeed to get inside was almost overwhelming.

"This is taking forever." Okay, I'd ruled out hyperspeed, but not whining.

"It's because so many things are different now," Oliver said.

"It's a lot to do just because people now know there are aliens living on Earth."

"It's not just that," Oliver explained patiently. "Most Congressmen don't spend all their time in Washington. They're here the days Congress is in session, perhaps for special events, and a few other days besides. The rest of the time, they're home, in their districts."

"I won't be doing that," Jeff said. "I live here now."

"Yes, you do, and I'm sure that's understood. You also, ah, have a very easy way of getting back to New Mexico quickly if necessary."

"I can't wait to see a gate," Vance said. "Do they really look like airport metal detectors?"

Unlike the rest of us, we'd managed to keep the gates classified. There was no way Vance was cleared for that information. Then again, he hung with the Cabal, and he read Oliver's column. Meaning Vance was likely well-informed.

"You won't be seeing one today," Reader said. "You're not authorized."

"He is," Vance said, indicating Oliver.

"Oh no, I'm not. I've never seen one." Oliver smiled. "However, I was explaining something to the ambassador. Normally there are always some Congressmen who choose to live out of their offices. Not most, you understand, but a few."

"Like Santiago was?" Chose not to thank Oliver for the smooth conversational shift. Presumably us taking him along was thanks enough.

"Yes. Some Congressmen see no reason to spend the money on alternate housing here, since they're not here all that much. Some rent apartments or houses. A few stay in hotels. Normally. But these past many months haven't been normal. There are now far more Congressmen housing in the Capitol complex than ever before."

"They can't all be doing that."

"No," Vance said. "Plenty have a home here, too. Nathalie and Edmund, for example, because they can afford it, easily. Eugene and Lydia have a home here, too. So do the Armstrongs. That's one of the reasons we all know each other."

"What do you mean?" Jeff asked.

"Not everyone stays here year round. Guy and I do, and so do Lillian and Abner. But most of the politicians aren't here all the time. So, the ones whose company we enjoyed who also have homes here, we went out of our way to get to know. Soon we all started visiting back and forth."

"Senator McMillan has a home here, too," Reader said.

"He doesn't like Guy or Lillian," Vance said with a shrug. "So he's not part of our group."

Refrained from comment about that, mostly because I didn't like Gadoire or Joker Jaws either. Plus I wanted to ask about something else. Or rather, someone else. "You know, Vance, Jack and Pia Ryan used to be part of your group, didn't they?"

"Yeah. Poor Pia. She's never really recovered. They had that huge fight and she slept somewhere else the night he killed himself."

Jeff nudged me and Reader gave me the "shut up" look. Not that I was going to share that Vance had this detail wrong. "Is Pia still hanging out with you guys?"

Vance shook his head. "I think she saw Eugene a few times, but that was it. He reached out, I guess." Vance's eyes widened. "You think he was going to try to kill Pia next? Or that he wanted her in his harem?"

"Anything's possible." What I was thinking was that I'd forgotten to share a really key piece of information with anyone else, namely that Eugene had said his "orders" had come to him via Pia. I didn't want to share this in front of Vance, however. Time to get us off this subject. "So, MJO, all that still doesn't explain why we're going through so many checkpoints just to have the thrill of parking."

"Well, what I described is how it was in the olden days. More Congressmen lived here more of the time. Once air travel became relatively inexpensive, that changed." He sighed. "Altered the political landscape in a way, though I'm sure most would prefer their Congressmen to be in their home states. At any rate, with the new changes brought about due to the invasion, Congress is being required to remain in session almost nonstop. So there are more people at the Capitol complex, all the time, both living here and coming here. It's affected security, which is why we're going through so many checkpoints."

All this Congress Chat had passed the time and we were finally allowed to park. Only there wasn't a spot big enough for the limo. "We should have walked it," Jeff said as we headed up and outside.

"I'll drop you and park the car," Len said.

"No. Take the car back to the Embassy and just meet us outside Santiago's office."

"Can I go with him?" Vance asked. "So I can take the gate back, too?"

"No. You're supposed to be telling us about how you and Hacker International have determined that every person in the building we're about to go into is in danger."

"Oh, right." Vance slumped in his seat.

"Keep Kyle with you," Jeff told Len. "I don't want anyone wandering solo right now."

The boys didn't look happy. "We're supposed to stay with you," Kyle argued.

"We're going into an office building. Just get the car back home and get over to us. By the time we get through security, you'll probably already be back."

Jeff had a point, and it was hard to believe that anyone was going to attack us between the car and the entrance.

Len pulled up into the loading zone in front of said entrance and Kyle helped us out of the car. I was sure I saw Bruno get out, though I didn't think anyone else had spotted him. It was still raining, so I flipped my hood on.

"You're sure we should go?" Kyle asked me. "Len's driven alone before, you know."

"Yeah, we'll be okay. Just don't take too long."

Vance and Oliver went ahead to get out of the rain as Kyle got back in the car. The boys waited for the rest of us to go inside. Which we would have done immediately, only there was a gust of wind. My hood flipped back, and Jeff's hat flew off. He caught it quickly and had it back on his head in just a moment.

However, that's why I was looking up and so saw someone on the roof of the building. Someone I was pretty sure was holding a sniper rifle.

CHAPTER 51

I DIDN'T THINK ABOUT IT. I just grabbed Jeff and Reader and ran up the stairs and for the entrance at hyperspeed.

Managed to stop before we slammed into Vance and through the doors. Let go and spun around. There were no bullets hitting the ground, nor were any hitting the limo. Kyle gave me a "you so crazy" look, and the limo drove off.

"What was that about?" Jeff asked quietly.

"I thought I saw—" Who knew what I'd really seen, four stories up and in the rain? Bruno hadn't freaked out, so I was probably mistaken.

"You thought you saw what?" Vance asked.

"Donuts." As replies went, this had to be in the running for Most Lame Reply Ever, but it was all that came to me.

"Okay," Reader said slowly. "We'll get you a snack once we've gotten checked through, okay, Kitty?"

The others seemed to accept this, but Oliver gave me a look that said he didn't buy it. However, we shortly had other issues to worry about.

Apparently, even though Jeff was going to be sworn in today and had been pointedly told he was inheriting Reyes' office, no one had told anyone here so no one was prepared for us to arrive. It got better. The police had cordoned off Reyes' office, so we weren't going to be allowed in it anyway.

When asked why the police had closed off an office where no crime had happened, the only answer was that the Rayburn House prided itself on always working with the fine policemen and -women of Washington, D.C. That was the party line, verbatim, because we heard it from at least six different people.

No one seemed moved at all by the fact that Reyes' dying wish had been for me to clean out his desk. Apparently precedent said that if a representative died, then whoever wanted a look at his stuff could wait until someone "in authority" gave the go-ahead. The boys rejoined us long before that happened.

Irene, the woman who helped us the most, as in the one who stayed with us throughout the ordeal, insinuated that Jeff had been assigned a much better office than Reyes had been given, and as soon as clearances were authorized, we'd be allowed to see it.

Time was wasting, we had no idea what Vance's theory had turned up, and no way to get into Reyes' office to do anything, let alone hunt for clues. It didn't help that Jeff's office was going to be on the fourth floor, and Reyes' had been on the third, either.

"We just have so many offices being cleared out these past few days," Irene said mournfully, as we once again waited for another someone to tell us that, no, sorry, not authorized yet.

"Ah, yes," Oliver said. "The three other representatives who passed away earlier this week. It must be putting quite a somber tone on the holiday season."

Irene nodded. "Two were so young. And Representative Holmes was always so full of life, even at his advanced age." Her lower lip quivered. "I can't believe I'm never going to see any of them again."

"Are their offices all near each other?" I asked.

"Yes, most of the committee members liked to stay nearby."

"Which committee?" Jeff asked.

"The House Committee on Foreign Affairs," Irene replied. She shook her head. "It's such a shame, we've lost so many good people this past year."

"All from that one committee?" Because if so, then I had to question why Chuckie or Oliver or others who lived for conspiracy theories hadn't noticed.

"Oh, no. It's been a very bad year for us overall. But the Foreign Affairs committee has lost four people."

Vance caught my eye and nodded. Took this to mean that his research had shown that this committee had popped.

"Santiago wasn't on that committee, was he?" I asked.

"I don't think he'd found his place yet," Irene said sadly. "But Representative Bowers had been on the committee for years before he passed." She smiled at Jeff. "So perhaps you'll be able to follow in his footsteps."

"I hope not," I said under my breath.

"Excuse me?" Irene said.

"Just wishing we had some donuts."

"Oh, I'm sure we could get you a snack if you're hungry."

"Thanks, I'm sure I'll be fine." Chose not to mention that "donut" and "snack" weren't necessarily the same thing. Clearly to Irene and Reader, they were. Or else I was the only donut-lover in attendance.

Would have liked to have had something to do other than fret, though. We now needed to get in and search not only Reyes' office but the other offices belonging to reps who'd died. We needed help. Not to search but to just get past the lobby because we hadn't made it out of this area. Oh, we'd tried, and had made it up to the second floor once, before we were told we weren't authorized to go anywhere yet.

Had a variety of people I could call, but, based on Jeff's opinion, decided to go for the Inside Man. Dug my phone out from under the Poofs and called Nathalie back.

"You're ready for lunch already?" Nathalie asked with a laugh.

"No. We need help." Explained the situation. "We foolishly thought this was all handled somehow, based on how fast everything else has happened. Any suggestions for what we can do?"

"Hang on. Edmund and I will be there shortly. He'll handle it."

Had no idea if Brewer could really help in this situation or not, but it was probably better to have another rep come by as opposed to asking Mom or Chuckie to assist. I wasn't clear on how well-liked the C.I.A. or P.T.C.U. were on Capitol Hill, but figured betting on "not well" was closer to right.

I was bored, so I went and looked out the doors to watch for the Brewers. A cab pulled up and a man who

was clearly an elected official of some kind got out. This
was something to occupy my mind, so I watched him. He
paid the taxi driver, turned toward the steps, briefcase in
hand, and jerked his head as he put his free hand up to his
neck.

As the taxi pulled away out of the loading area and onto
the street, the briefcase dropped out of the man's hand. He
fell to his knees, clutching his chest. Then he fell flat on his
face.

It happened so quickly that I didn't have time to scream.
But that was okay. Irene had come over to join me, perhaps
to share news of donuts or snacks, and had seen some of
this, and she was covering the screaming part.

Jeff and Reader didn't hesitate. They ran outside. The
boys ran after them.

I ran after all of them. "Check his neck," I said as they
picked the man up and got him out of the rain and into the
building. I looked up and around. I was certain someone
was on the roof. But they hadn't been shooting at me or Jeff.
So, was it the Dingo and Surly Vic, Raul, or someone else?

Decided there was only one way to find out and it was
stupid to stay standing out in the rain, so I went inside.

The man was on his back and Reader was doing CPR. It
didn't seem to be helping. Irene was on the phone, crying,
getting help of some kind, and Vance was doing his best to
comfort her. Len and Kyle were watching for other attacks.
Oliver was on his phone.

Jeff pulled me aside. "There was a small mark on his
neck, like a bug bite."

"I think the shooter was on the roof."

"You think he was shot?"

"Yeah, I do, though obviously not with a bullet. You
know, Jeff, we're here with another dead guy. That can't be
good for the press. They're already calling us the Embassy
of Death."

"It's just a coincidence."

Thought about this. "Is it?"

"What do you mean?"

"You're rushed into accepting a position, and told that
you have to be sworn in *the next day*, when, frankly, January
third isn't all that far away. And yet, here we are, all ready
to get going, and we've been kept in the lobby the entire

time. Convenient we were here, or Irene would have had to drag that man inside all by herself."

"I don't get anything dangerous from her, but right now, that means nothing."

"Yeah. I don't know that I'm accusing Irene. She's not the one who hasn't authorized us to go in. And she's also not the one who asked the police to cordon off the dead representatives' offices."

"You said the shooter's on the roof. Should we check it out?"

"No. I don't want them shooting you."

"I'm not a target."

"Yeah? I'm firmly one with Vance's theory right now."

"There's a reason. If people are really being murdered on this scale, there's a reason for it."

"Either there's a reason or there's a serial killer. Either way, Vance is right—you're a target."

"I was out there twice and no one shot me."

"True." I hugged him. "Superbeings were so much easier."

Len came to us. "Representative Brewer and his wife just arrived in a taxi. Kyle and I are going to escort them in." With that the boys ran outside. As they got out of the taxi, Len grabbed Nathalie, Kyle grabbed Brewer, and they moved them in like they were Secret Service and the Brewers were the President and First Lady.

Didn't take a lot to bring the Brewers up to speed. We also now had enough people to play a decent game of volleyball. It was going to be harder than hell to search anywhere. But we needed to.

Trotted over to Irene, who was off the phone but still crying. "I need to find a restroom, but I don't want to go without my husband."

She nodded. "I understand." She handed me a piece of paper and a key. "That's the information for your husband's office. I can't imagine that it's going to matter that you went up a little early, not with this." She pointed to the man on the floor.

"Who is that?"

"Representative Juvonic."

"What committee was he on?"

"Homeland security. Does it matter?"

"I hope not." I squeezed her hand. "Thanks, we'll be back as soon as possible." Gave Vance a look that I hoped he understood meant "stay here and keep Irene distracted." He seemed to get it because he started talking to her about Juvonic.

Rejoined the others. Brewer was on his phone, making angry calls. "I need to throw up. Seriously. Nathalie, can you manage things here? Because I need Jeff with me."

"Of course, Kitty. I'll call you if you're needed before you're back."

"Thanks." Grabbed Jeff and headed for the stairs.

"Are you actually sick?" he asked, sounding worried.

"No. But girls visit the bathroom together if all we're doing is peeing, and experience says Nathalie is totally a group-goer. However, no one wants to help you vomit. And no one wants to barge in on that, either."

"So, where to first?"

"We find your official office, so if someone needs to find me puking we can get back there. And then we find the office with police tape and search it. We'll worry about the others once we get that done."

"I married the smartest, and sneakiest, girl in the galaxy."

"Let's hope."

CHAPTER 52

AS SOON AS WE were out of sight, Jeff took us to the fast hyperspeed. Even though there were people on the stairs, they didn't see us, and Jeff ensured we never touched them.

It was a little confusing to find Jeff's office, but hyperspeed made things go faster. Irene was right—he had a window and a nice view and newer furniture.

"It's going to take us a while to find Santiago's office," Jeff said. "This place is huge."

"Nope." I pulled out my phone and dialed.

"Hello?" Stryker sounded tired, but conscious. Good.

"Eddy! Nice to see you're up and about."

"Like we had a choice? What's going on, Kitty?"

"Need you to give me the names and, more importantly, office numbers for every dead representative that Vance had you identify last night. And, unfortunately, you need to add in Representative Juvonic."

"Someone else died?"

"Just died. Show some respect for the dead and get me his office number so we can go through it for clues."

"Okay. Most of them are in one building, but not all."

"I hope it's Rayburn House because that's where we are."

"Yeah, it is. It won't take long; Raj already had us compiling this list. Just need to determine office numbers."

"I need Santiago's office number first."

"Thirty-ten."

"You rock, Eddy. Text the rest to me and Jeff, okay? Oh

and make sure, once you do that, that we get a full listing of what committees each dead rep was on. And make that snappy, I think it's relevant."

"Oh, yes, ma'am." Stryker's sarcasm knob was definitely hitting nine.

"That's the spirit!"

"You want the update from Gaultier?"

"Sure. Have they found anything yet?"

"Yes, they've found Eugene Montgomery's workspace. Not a lot there, but Henry downloaded everything on Montgomery's laptop over to us. The laptop's Gaultier property so we can't remove it without making a scene."

"Okay, did they find papers?"

"Yeah, about a briefcase's worth. Raj has them. Henry's using the laptop to hack into the rest of the Gaultier system, but he's hitting blocks that the laptop can't get around. They need to get to the main servers, and that'll take a little time."

"Well, at least they're moving forward. Keep me updated."

"Absolutely, madam." Stryker had turned the sarcasm up to eleven. "Is there anything else I, your humble servant, can do for you?"

"Dude, I'm going to remember to hurt you when I get back."

"I'll risk it."

"Alfred never talks this way to Batman."

"I'm not Alfred and you're not Batman. I can talk however I want to Wolverine with Boobs."

"Oh, you did *not* go there, bub. Never forget, I'm the best there is at what I do."

"Now *that's* true. Just don't ask me what I think you do best."

"Remember that what I do isn't nice."

"Despite wanting to make a joke that would make you blush and me snicker, I'm going to stop now, because I think Chuck has my cell phone tapped and if I say anything else he'll make my head explode."

"Or Jeff'll crush your skull with his bare hands."

"Same difference."

Comics jokes only Hacker International, Chuckie, Reader, or a few others would get done with, we hung up. Texts from Stryker started coming in almost immediately.

"Should we get moving?" Jeff asked. "Or should I go home and crush the squatter's head with my bare hands?"

"No, we still need him. We should get going . . . wait. Hey, one of reps who was killed had this office before. Stryker sent the info over based on timeline of death, most recent first. The rep who was in here died a few months ago."

"Why haven't they put anyone else in here?"

"No idea, maybe their replacement hasn't been elected yet. But let's see if there's anything worth spotting."

An A-C using hyperspeed can search an entire house in less than five minutes. So searching one smallish set of rooms didn't take Jeff long. He even lifted any furniture that wasn't bolted down.

While he was busy, sent a text to Stryker, asking him to verify which reps had been replaced and which hadn't, and also to see if replacement reps were given the same offices as their dead predecessor or not.

Jeff put a small pile of papers on the desk. "This is it."

"Not a lot to go on." We dug through it. Most of it was trash. Anything with writing or print on it we saved. "Can't tell if any of this means anything yet." Jeff put the few pieces of paper we were saving into his coat pocket. "Wait, let's see if there's an envelope or something we can put all that in."

"There is." He went to the filing cabinet and pulled out a box of legal envelopes while I checked the desk for a pen. "Should we take these along?" he asked as he transferred the papers in his pocket into an envelope.

Took the envelope from him and marked it with the office number. "Yeah, grab a dozen, that should be plenty."

"I have them, so let's see what we can find elsewhere."

"This floor or Santiago's office?"

"How long do we have before we have to go back downstairs?"

"You're asking me? I'm not the super-empath. But I can pretend to be sick for hours if necessary. All I have to do is think about when I was pregnant with Jamie. I can pull those memories back easily."

"Don't remind me. And, I've checked, everyone's still dealing with the drama, so I don't think we're missed yet. In which case, let's do this floor and work down."

Counting Jeff's office and with the unfortunate addition

of Juvonic, we had twelve offices to check out here in Rayburn House. Per Stryker's texts, there were four to check in the Cannon House, and five in the Longworth House.

There was no way Jeff and I were going to get to check out the other locations today. And I knew time was of the essence. So, while Jeff searched the other two offices on the fourth floor, I contacted Tim.

He agreed that it sounded like a job for A-Cs, but we needed a human along to ensure that everything would be checked. I'd dealt with A-C versus human searching during Operation Confusion, and, as I reminded Tim, if we'd relied on the A-Cs to find and especially to interpret the clues he'd left me, Tim and a lot of others would be dead.

Duly convinced, Tim compromised and assigned Lorraine and Joe to Cannon and Claudia and Randy to Longworth. They each had two Field teams with them as well, and were advised to be on the lookout for people on roofs holding guns.

Scraps of papers that seemed to mean nothing put into envelopes worked great, but I found myself wishing we'd brought along a briefcase or bag, because there were more than scraps in some of the offices. I was carrying because Jeff was searching, and my arms were getting full.

We'd saved Reyes' office for our last stop on the third floor. Not out of any meaningful reason, it was just the farthest from where we'd entered that floor from the fourth and we had five offices to check on this level. It was easy to spot, though—yellow police tape crisscrossed on the door stood out.

Once inside, I wondered if we'd been intelligent about not starting here first. Reyes had truly been living here, and that meant that there was stuff everywhere. On the plus side, there was also a briefcase, and it wasn't locked.

Decided Reyes wouldn't mind my borrowing it, especially since he'd wanted me to clean out his desk. I dumped our other findings in, taking the time to put the larger papers into bigger envelopes he had available and marking them. No one was going to accuse me of not paying attention to detail in regard to this hunt for a tiny needle in a really huge haystack.

Since Reyes had been specific in his last request, I did

the desk while Jeff did everything else. "There's not much here. Just some bills I think Santiago was reading."

"Maybe what he bought has something to do with whatever's going on," Jeff said from inside the bathroom.

"No, not that kind of bill. Bills like those that go through Congress. Passages of laws and such. You know, the 'light reading' you'll be getting to enjoy starting, I guess, today." Reyes certainly had a lot of them in his desk drawer. Took them all, put them in the briefcase. Hoped he had another case somewhere—the bills took up a lot of space.

"Oh." Jeff came out. "Kitty, I have no idea what I'm doing in this job. I don't even know how long my term is supposed to be. I'm unfamiliar with the terminology. And I've already been told that lobbyists are going to be my best friends from here on in."

"In normal times, which I know we are not living in, every representative is elected to a two-year term, and the elections are every even numbered year. This was supposed to be an election year, but due to all the many decrees, everyone's held over, which is why Santiago had to go through a special election to get here. Congress officially starts the first week of January, so technically you could expect to get out of this job after the next election—you know, two years from now."

"How do you know that?"

"Some from memory." I held up a booklet I'd found. "Some from this: 'A New Representative's Guide to the House.'" Tossed it into the briefcase. "I'd assume you'll get one, but we'll take Santiago's so you have it to read sooner as opposed to later. As for lobbyists, technically, we've been functioning as such since we took over the Diplomatic Corps, and while I don't love and adore them, at least we know Guy Gadoire and Lillian Culver. It's not much, but it's a start."

"Why are you so calm about all of this?"

I shrugged as I went back to digging through the desk. "I know you can handle anything, Jeff."

He came over, pulled me to him, and gave me a deep kiss. "Thanks, baby," he said softly as he pulled away. "I needed that."

"Any time, as long as you thank me like you just did."

We continued to toss Reyes' office, but there wasn't anything meaningful we could spot. I took his calendar and anything else that I felt I could get away with out of his desk. There'd be a problem if the police had already looked in here, but we'd cross that bridge when forced.

There wasn't a lot of ornamentation in here, but there was a small stuffed animal, a bald eagle, in one of the drawers. It had a card tied to it: *To Mister Reyes, the best man for the job, from everyone at Oasis of the Desert Middle School.*

"What did Santiago do, before he was elected, do you know?"

"I think he was a teacher."

Put the eagle into my purse so it wouldn't get squished in the briefcase. While I did my best not to tear up, I searched for more personal things like that, but there weren't any, at least not in the desk.

My phone beeped. "Len says we need to hurry up." Replied back that I was still busy being sick and please stall.

We had to be cautious leaving Reyes' office because we didn't want to disturb the tape and therefore had a bigger risk of being seen. However, the halls weren't really hopping, so we only had to wait for a couple people to get to their offices and then we were off and on to the second floor.

The three offices down here didn't take too long. It was the same as the others—nothing much but trash left. Trash which I dutifully bagged and tagged and put into Reyes' now bulging briefcase. At least it was soft-sided.

Reyes' office had taken us the longest, fifteen minutes easily, so with the others, we'd been gone about thirty minutes.

We had only Juvonic's office left to do, but as we reached it Bruno appeared before us, wings spread impressively. He didn't make a sound, but his expression said to stop running, right now.

CHAPTER 53

WE STOPPED RUNNING.

"What the *hell* is that bird doing here?" Jeff managed to keep his voice down, for which I was proud. I hadn't screamed when Bruno appeared out of thin air. I was proud of that, too.

"Guarding."

"How did he get here?"

"He came with us in the car."

"Really. Then why didn't I see him?"

"He doesn't trust Vance?" Bruno did a head bob, wing flap, scratched with his foot, then stared at me. "Ah, no, that's not it. Vance seems okay. Bruno didn't want you freaking out about him coming along, he knows the game is afoot and therefore needs to be with us at all times, and he feels that it'll be easier for us, you in particular, if he's incognito."

Bruno nudged against me to share that I was indeed the most insightful of chicks, then disappeared.

"I'm never getting used to that. I'm just telling you now."

"Hence why Bruno's in Stealth Mode. He wants us being really cautious here, and quiet, and going very slowly."

We walked by Juvonic's office and Bruno's concerns were explained—there were people in there. People who were about to have a shock, I was pretty sure, but not as big a one as me and Jeff appearing inside their offices out of nowhere would have been.

We walked on at human speeds down the rest of this

hallway. We were passed by someone who I took to be a page—he was young, had an upset expression, and he was walking fast. I turned to watch him—yep, he went into Juvonic's office.

After we passed the Bearer of Bad News we weren't that far from the lobby. I ensured I leaned on Jeff and he had his arm around me and had the briefcase in his free hand. We definitely had the "not feeling awesome" look going. The issue was whether Irene would remember that Jeff hadn't come in carrying anything or not.

There were paramedics here now, though not the ones from last night, so we had that going for us. There were also police, and not the K-9 squad. The people from Juvonic's office came running in behind us. Which was nice, because they caused a small amount of chaos, which made it simple for Jeff to hand Reader the briefcase and ask him to hold it.

Reader having possession meant that as the Head of Field, he didn't actually have to surrender anything to the police. He could if he wanted to play nicely, but if he didn't so want to do, he didn't so have to do.

Our absence was explained and the police were quite sympathetic to my reaction to seeing a man die in front of me. We were witnesses and Jeff was one of the people who'd brought the body inside, so the police wanted our statements, since they already had Reader's and the boys'. We didn't have a lot of information to give, and we were done quickly. No one mentioned the briefcase.

Irene was still basically a mess. I went to her and gave her a hug. "Thank you so much. We cleaned up, so I don't think anyone will know I was upstairs barfing my guts out. Well, other than the police. But you know what I mean."

She nodded. "Your clearance arrived. After the police," she added. "I'm so sorry you had to witness this. If your husband's clearances had been done right away, you all would have been upstairs."

"That's true." I hugged her again. "But then you'd have had to go through that alone, so, even though I got sick, I'm glad we were here to help you."

"You're so sweet, thank you. Your young men have been so helpful, especially Vance." Vance was with the Brewers and the boys. She gave him a little wave. He waved back and blew her a kiss.

Irene was younger than Mom but older than me for sure. I didn't call her as Vance's type. And she didn't seem to be taking this sexually. True to his own hype, there appeared to be more to Vance than met the eye.

The paramedics declared the death a heart attack. No one mentioned anything about marks on the victim's neck. The police told us all we were free to go. Which was good. Because I wanted to go. But I had one last question for Irene.

"Who finally cleared us to go up?"

"Oh, Representative Brewer solved it. He called someone in Homeland Security and they basically had a fit that you'd been waiting so long."

"Cliff Goodman?"

"Yes! He was outraged you'd been kept waiting. I believe he's going to be investigating what happened."

"That's nice." It was. It hadn't even occurred to me to call Cliff to see if he could help with this. Well, at least Brewer had had the foresight.

My phone rang. "Excuse me." Pulled it out. "Hello?"

"Kitty, it's Cliff. Are you and Jeff alright?"

"Yeah. Thanks for clearing us to get into our offices."

"No problem, that was unreal, bureaucracy in action, but that's not why I'm calling. Ed said that someone had been hurt."

"No, someone's dead. Representative Juvonic."

"I don't really know him, but that's awful news."

"We don't know him either, and now we never will. The paramedics say he had a heart attack."

Filled Cliff in on what had happened before I'd gotten "sick," leaving out any mention of a potential sniper, me seeing Juvonic touch his neck right before he went down, my suspicions that Juvonic had been murdered, or the fact that Jeff and I had just rifled through a lot of other people's offices. Chuckie trusted Cliff so I trusted Cliff, but there was no reason to bring anyone else into my theories right now, especially someone who might not like the idea that we'd gone through those offices without any official sanction.

However, the rest of it, including the number of times we were told we couldn't go to Jeff's office, I gave him in Technicolor detail. "So, now I don't know what we should do."

"You know, you have a couple hours before Jeff gets

sworn in. Why don't you guys just go somewhere and relax? The work can wait, and it's not like Jeff's going to get caught up today anyway. You've had a hell of a couple of days, Kitty. Take a break and get a breather."

"The Brewers did want to go to lunch."

"See? Do it."

"You want to join us?"

"I'd love to. Unfortunately, I can't. But I'll see you at the ceremony."

"Sounds good. And, Cliff, thanks. We'll worry about Jeff's office later."

"Good plan."

We hung up and I joined the others. "Cliff says we should stop trying to be responsible and just have lunch and hang out before the swearing-in ceremony."

Nathalie nodded. "Just think, if I'd convinced you to play hooky earlier, you'd have missed all this."

"We'll never say no again," Jeff said with a short laugh.

"We need somewhere we can seat a lot of people," I added.

"Not to worry," Nathalie said as she linked her arm through mine. "I know a perfect place."

CHAPTER 54

OLIVER CHOSE TO STAY at Rayburn to get all the details for his now front-page story. Everyone else decided getting out of here was a great plan.

Despite my being almost pathologically against the idea of walking outside, unprotected in the streets, the Brewers were all for it. So it was either go along or tell them why I wanted to remain safely inside.

We went along, Len in the lead, Kyle bringing up the rear, with me trying to surreptitiously look up and keep an eye out for snipers on roofs, potentially carrying blowguns armed with tiny, killer darts. After I tripped three times, had to stop that.

The third trip meant that Jeff took me away from Nathalie, under the quite accurate assessment that someone needed to keep me from falling flat on my face, and he was probably the best person to do that.

Which was fine, because I not only got to walk with my husband, but I got to walk with my husband while he was wearing the trench and fedora. "I love this look."

Jeff shook his head with a laugh. "Whatever makes you happy, baby, I'm all for."

Jeff taking me away from Nathalie also mixed up who was walking where. So Brewer had gone up with Len, presumably because he knew where we were going, Vance was in the rear, talking with Kyle, and Reader was walking ahead of us with Nathalie. They were chatting up a storm.

Could understand why the Brewers wanted to walk—

the place we were going to wasn't that far away from where we'd been. There was a little row of cute restaurants near the Capitol South Metro station. Brewer led us into one.

"The Teetotaler? Really?"

Nathalie heard me and laughed. "It's new," she said as we went in. "The owners started it after they found out that there was a whole new group of people on Earth who couldn't drink. It's an alcohol-free restaurant, and it specializes in a wide variety of teas, as well."

"Plus the owners like golf," Brewer added. "So it's a joke on at least three levels. Oh, and don't worry, gentlemen— they serve food that can handle male appetites here, not just dainty sandwiches for the girls."

"Thank God, because after spending a half an hour upstairs, I'm hungry." Well, I was hungry from the searching. And I figured everyone would appreciate my not actually sharing that I'd supposedly been throwing up, the other patrons and the restaurant's owners for certain. "But how did you guys find this?"

Brewer shrugged. "Despite owning one of the most successful wineries in Northern California, we don't drink with every meal, and we enjoy finding new restaurants first."

This didn't surprise me all that much. What did surprise me was that Reader sat next to Nathalie and they were still in animated conversation.

We were early for lunch, which was good, because a table for eight in here filled up a good third of the restaurant. The owners were beside themselves with excitement to be serving their first A-C in the form of Jeff. Apparently no one had told them that the majority of A-Cs ate at their Base commissaries or at home. Then again, they hadn't asked, either.

Jeff was good-naturedly embarrassed by all the fuss, but thankfully we liked tea so there was happiness all around. The owners, Rosemarie and Douglas, asked if they could take a picture for their wall. Jeff shot me the "help me" look. I took off his hat and fixed his hair. Hey, I was a good wife that way.

Picture taken and Jeff thoroughly embarrassed, we ordered. While waiting for our orders and enjoying the tea, I finally had to ask. "James, I didn't know you and Nathalie knew each other."

He grinned. "We do, but from way back."

Nathalie nodded. "We modeled together, oh, years ago now. In Milan and Paris."

"And other places," Reader added, which sent the two of them into gales of laughter.

They were both former international models, so this didn't surprise me all that much. What did was that Reader had never mentioned it. "Why didn't you say something? Before today, I mean?"

Reader shrugged. "We haven't seen each other in years. And I didn't make the connection."

"I did, the moment I saw James last night," Nathalie said. "But then he's still as beautiful today as he was when we were teenagers. Possibly more beautiful. However, last night was not a good time to renew an old acquaintance."

This earned her the cover boy grin. "Nathalie still looks as gorgeous as ever, but I knew her by her maiden name."

"No, no," she said with another laugh. "You knew me by my *working* name. Kitty and everyone else here know me by Gagnon-Brewer, but my working name was Nathalie Belle. I don't share that with many people here."

"I knew you were a model."

"Yes, but you didn't need to know more." She looked down at her tea. "It's not as if I was going to drag you to my home and make you look at my portfolio," she said with a little laugh.

The way she said this made me look at Brewer out of the corner of my eye. He didn't look annoyed or angry or bored; his expression was a sort of sad resignation, as though he expected the conversation to move on, right now.

I was many things, but despite much of the evidence, stupid wasn't one of them. "You still have your portfolio? I'd love to see it sometime."

Nathalie looked up, clearly shocked and incredibly pleased. Brewer looked surprised and also pleased. Yep, I'd called that one right. The group they were running in liked having a former model in their company, but they didn't actually *care* about what she'd done as a model. She was a nice addition, not as good as an actress, less worrisome than a rock star, but not a politician.

"Be flattered," Reader said. "She's never asked to see mine."

"Oh, I had your best shot up in my room for a long time, James."

Jeff groaned. "Not the Calvin Klein ad again. Every time I think she's forgotten about that, it comes right back up."

The group laughed and our food arrived. True to the Brewers' promises, it was tasty and filling. While we ate, Brewer engaged Jeff and the boys talking about sports, and Nathalie talked fashion with me, Reader, and Vance. Turned out that Vance had seen her portfolio. Also turned out that he was, out of all her friends in town, the only one who had. It shocked me that Gadoire hadn't gone for it, too, in hopes of dragging Nathalie into their Bed of Love, but perhaps he was clear that he wasn't ever going to be her type.

Realized I was enjoying spending time with the Brewers and really reassessing Vance and how deep his waters might be running.

Also realized that the Brewers were ensuring that we didn't discuss the events from earlier in the day or the prior evening. Wasn't sure why, but put it down to them wanting this to be a fun, relaxing, really-get-to-know-you lunch. Even though we were in the middle of trying to figure out what was going on, having a couple hours without stress worked for me.

We finished up and Rosemarie and Douglas asked for another picture, this one a group shot. We obliged. Brewer insisted on paying for lunch for all of us, which Jeff strenuously opposed, but Brewer won on the basis of Jeff's being sworn in later.

Douglas then presented each of us with nice, rectangular, stainless steel tins stuffed with an exclusive, and tightly packed, special tea that they blended themselves. He refused to allow any of us to pay for them.

Hugs all around, we all left. Checked the prices as we left the restaurant – the tea we'd been gifted was very pricey. Opened my purse to put our tins in it and realized I had too many Poofs. And tea this expensive should be taken care of. "Jeff, I need to go back and get a bag. My purse is too full to hold these, and so is the briefcase."

"Nah, don't bother them. This coat's loaded with pockets." He took the tins from me and put them into an inner left pocket.

"Wow, I can't even see much of an extra bulge. Or maybe

I'm just used to your pecs bulging under normal circumstances."

"Hilarious." But he looked pleased.

We strolled back toward the Capitol. The rain had stopped while we were inside so the streets were wet but it wasn't so bad. Managed to avoid any big puddles so my shoes didn't get wrecked.

Still kept an eye out for rooftop snipers, but saw none. Didn't feel better—just assumed they'd moved down to street level.

It was a longer walk back to the Capitol building than it had been to get to the Teetotaler. Hoped my feet weren't going to be killing me by the time we got there—in the heels vs. Converse battle, comfy Converse won any round where a lot of walking was required.

"Need me to get a cab or want to take the subway the rest of the way?" Jeff asked, as we neared the Metro station. We were on the opposite side of the street from the station and its big parking lot. Seemed like more work to get over there, go down, get tickets, and wait than just walk on. Same with hailing a cab.

"Wow, picked up my internal whining, huh?"

"It's an easy guess. I'd be happy to carry you, but I think people would talk."

"Haters gonna hate, true enough."

As I said this, a car horn went off near us and a gray limo pulled up alongside the curb. The front window rolled down. "Hey baby, want a ride?" Jerry called from the passenger's seat. Tim, who was driving, waved.

Now the back window rolled down. "Is there a reason the eight of you are walking?" Chuckie asked. "The Pontifex and I are just curious."

"We wanted to get good and sweaty before Jeff's sworn in. It's a nice-ish day."

Chuckie and Gower laughed. "Would you like a lift?" Gower asked.

"Like you wouldn't believe."

The others joined us. "There's not enough room for all of us in there," Brewer pointed out.

Jeff shrugged. "Let's put the girls in, I'm sure they'll appreciate it."

"James, too," I said. Wanted the briefcase in our complete control. "And Vance," I added mostly because he looked like his feelings were about to be hurt.

"We'll stay with the Congressmen," Len said when Reader hesitated.

Nathalie gave Brewer a quick kiss and got in. Had Vance go in after her. Reader handed the briefcase to Chuckie as I kissed Jeff. "Be careful."

"Always, baby. You too."

"I think I can manage a three block car ride."

Jeff grinned. "You never can tell."

Started to get in, then something dawned on me. "Oh, hey, do you want to give me the tea tins since I'm driving now?" I asked as I turned back.

Jeff, who'd bent to help me, straightened up so my head didn't knock into his. He opened his mouth to answer, but was interrupted by two things.

Bruno appeared, screaming, to slam in between us. He spread his wings, hard, and shoved us both aside. As he did, I heard a shot ring out.

Jeff slammed back against the limo, then fell to the ground.

CHAPTER 55

"DOWN!" I shouted as I flung myself on top of Jeff. His eyes were closed and he didn't move.

Heard the boys hustle Brewer inside, heard Nathalie screaming and Len telling her and Brewer to stay down and stay quiet, as Chuckie and Reader got out, amidst the screams of passersby. Heard a bird's scream. It wasn't from pain—Bruno was going after the shooter.

A car peeled out somewhere nearby. But I wasn't paying much attention to all of this. I was looking at Jeff. Specifically at his chest.

His coat was a mess—ripped up and shredded, with pieces of metal strewn all over. Brown and red flecks were slathered everywhere across his chest. "Oh my God, Jeff," I whispered, as I put my hands over the hole to stop the bleeding.

Only there was no blood.

Jeff's eyes opened, then he blinked. "What the hell?"

"Stay down," Chuckie said, as he knelt next to us. He wasn't looking at Jeff. His gun was drawn and he was scanning the area. "Don't talk. Jerry's got an ambulance coming and Doctor Hernandez will be here soon."

"Why?" Jeff asked.

"You were shot." Could tell my voice was shaking. "There's metal and . . . stuff everywhere."

"I don't feel shot. I feel hit, but not shot. I want to get off the street."

"No." Chuckie looked at him. "What the . . . ?" He holstered his gun and ripped Jeff's jacket and shirt open. There was a huge bruise forming over Jeff's left pec, but no blood. "I'm willing to call this miraculous."

Looked at my hands and realized what the miracle had been. "It's the tea."

"What?" Chuckie sounded confused and shaken. I could relate.

"The owners where we ate lunch gave us tins of tea as a gift. They were heavy and in stainless steel, and Jeff had them in the pocket over his hearts. I didn't realize they could stop a bullet."

Chuckie flipped Jeff's clothes over and examined the damage. "It's because the shooter used a hollow-point."

"How can you tell?" Jeff asked. "And can I get up?"

"Not yet. Area's not secure."

"The limo would be," Jeff pointed out.

"No," Chuckie said sternly.

"How do you know it was a hollow-point?" I asked Chuckie. He hadn't answered and I wanted this information.

"The pattern. Hollow-points are designed to cause more damage when they hit. They have less velocity than a non-hollow bullet, though. So the tins of tea were able to deflect the bullet, versus just be the first things it passed through."

"A regular bullet might have gone through Jeff, or through you and Jeff," Reader said, voice tight, as he knelt down next to us. "But if the hollow-point had gone in, it would have expanded and probably splintered, sending bits through the body, bouncing off bone, and so on."

"So they specifically wanted to kill Jeff."

"Want to explain that?" Chuckie asked. "The Peregrine knocked you out of the way, Kitty."

Thought about it. "No, he knocked both of us, and if he hadn't, then the bullet would have hit Jeff's head." Felt sick to my stomach, and a little dizzy. "They were aiming for Jeff. The bullet's the proof. You can hit me with a regular bullet and I'm likely to die. But A-Cs heal fast, and Jeff's survived worse than one bullet. However, it sounds like even an A-C would have trouble with a hollow-point."

"Maybe," Chuckie said. "I'm not convinced."

"I'm not either," Reader said. "Though I can agree that,

based on the bullet, the shooter only wanted to hit one of you."

"Or he wanted to hit them both and the bird knocked the second target out of the way," Chuckie said tightly.

"Can the first target get the hell out of the street?" Jeff asked. "I'm not hurt. Well, I hit my head on the car or the concrete or something, and my chest hurts, but neither is life-threatening."

"It's clear," Kyle said, coming over. "We can't find anyone. Field teams are spreading out. Ambulance will be here in less than five minutes, Doctor Hernandez in less than one."

"Cancel the ambulance," Jeff said. "And tell Tito to stay home. We're heading there right now anyway."

Kyle nodded and stepped away to make the calls. Tim joined us. "I have another limo coming. We have too many people to get out of here."

"Floater gate would work," I suggested.

"Not in the middle of the street," Chuckie said. "It's bad enough that we have a crowd forming."

Looked around. Sure enough, we had a lot of people in a ring around us. Len, Jerry, and Vance were officially keeping them back.

"I want up off the street or I'm going to bust some heads," Jeff growled.

Chuckie sighed, but he nodded. He and Reader helped Jeff up, while I retrieved his fedora. Jeff bent down and helped me up. "It's okay, baby," he said softly.

That did it. I clutched the fedora and burst into tears. Jeff pulled me to him, held me, patted my back, and kissed the top of my head. To applause.

He wasn't really hurt, the danger seemed past, and my face was nestled between his awesome pecs, rubbing against the hair on his chest. My libido helped me get over my crying jag relatively quickly.

Heard another car pull up and doors open. Hughes and Walker had arrived. I knew this because I could hear them politely giving orders to the crowd. Got the impression they were in their Navy uniforms, because people appeared to be obeying.

Decided I should take one for the team and pull my face out of Jeff's chest. Did so unwillingly. "You okay now, baby?" Jeff asked.

"For the time being. I hope the Elves can whip up new clothes pronto."

"I'm sure they can. Which car do you want us in?" he asked Chuckie.

"You go with the new one," Chuckie said. "Reader, get in with the Pontifex and get him to the Embassy pronto."

"Oh, yes, sir," Reader said. "Sorry about this, Jeff."

"It's not your fault," Jeff said. "It's not anyone's fault. It's just part of what's going on. Let's talk about it at home."

"What's going on?" Chuckie asked, eyes narrowed.

Reader sighed. "We were going to bring you up to speed after Jeff was sworn in. We'll do it on the way."

Chuckie looked at me. My turn to sigh. "Yes, yes, I know what's going on and yes, I'll tell you in the car. I just don't want a lecture, and to ensure there won't be one, trust me when I say that, right now, I can start crying again at the drop of a hat."

"She did it once," Jeff said with a laugh, as he took the crumpled fedora out of my hands. "So I believe she could do it again."

Chuckie shook his head as he got us, Hughes, Walker, Len, and Kyle into the car, while Reader got Vance into his. "Everyone's a comedian."

"What about the police?" Jeff asked.

"What about them? I'd rather be home."

Chuckie nodded. "Let's get to the Embassy, and while we're headed there, why don't you two tell me exactly what's going on?"

CHAPTER 56

IT TOOK LESS TIME to catch Chuckie up than anyone else so far, in part because he didn't interrupt me with questions, and in other part because I was so emotionally freaked out I was talking at close to hyperspeed.

"I'm not sure if I can buy the murder mystery theory," he said as we pulled into the garage behind Tim's limo. "At least not based on this last incident."

"Raul is out there."

"So, apparently, is the Dingo. Nice of you to be protecting him." Chuckie's sarcasm knob was at eleven. Twelve loomed on the horizon.

"He's protecting me, and I believe that."

"Maybe. But one or both of you would be dead if not for your Peregrine. They may be animals, but they're more trustworthy than any human. Particularly assassins. And men who may or may not be a missing and presumed dead traitor."

"Presumed traitor. If we really met the human, living Colonel Hamlin, he's not the traitor."

"You think. We have Buchanan in the infirmary, and that tells me that Hamlin wasn't our friend."

"You're just mad because you were on the suspects list."

Chuckie snorted as we got out of the car and he motioned the other guys to go on ahead. "Kitty, if you hadn't had me on the suspects list I'd say you were an idiot. Of course I should have been there. Your mother, too. I agree with every reason you all had for taking us off the list, just as I can understand why Cliff's still on it. But unless you're looking at all possibilities, you can't hope to find the truth."

"Your feelings aren't hurt?"

He shrugged. "A little. But only because I know I'm not the Mastermind, if there really is one."

"There could be," Jeff said as we started slowly for the stairs.

"I'm a lot more worried about emotional blockers and overlays that our scanners can't find," Chuckie said. "To me, that's the biggest issue we have."

"Just means we need to learn to counter it," Jeff said.

"No," Chuckie said patiently. "It means that someone understands your strengths. And your weaknesses. And if they can block the empaths, then it's only a matter of time before they can block the imageers. And if you have no empathic or imageering skills, then what, exactly, do you think the A-Cs bring to the table in terms of their usefulness to the United States in particular and the world in general?"

I looked at Jeff's chest. The bruise was already starting to fade. "They're strong, fast, smart, hard to kill soldiers. And if you give them Surcenthumain, they're even better."

"There are other options," Jeff said. "We do them already. Math, science, space, medicine."

"The majority of people doing your brainwork are women," Chuckie said. "Kitty's being realistic. You need to be, too."

"Why is it always the War Division?" I asked nobody in particular.

"Because we're all warlike," Vance said. Hadn't realized he was waiting for us. We stopped walking. "The others went on upstairs already. But I just wanted to ask if you believe my theory now. Maybe with the C.I.A.'s help we can stop whatever's going on."

Chuckie rubbed the back of his neck. "No. I mean, I don't. Kitty does. But I don't disbelieve it, either. We don't have enough proof, of anything yet."

"Okay, so, Vance isn't wrong about a lot of representatives being dead. Why hasn't that popped to you, of all people, in some way? I'd expect the Conspiracy King to be taking an interest."

Chuckie heaved a sigh. "Really? Fine. We had a huge

interstellar invasion, and since I'm the head of the E-T Division, I'm on the line for anything related to that. We've had every A-C on the planet outed—guess who's in charge of everything relating to that? Right, me. I'm trying to get married and have world governments involved in those plans, complicating them in the extreme."

"Okay, I know you've been really busy, but this is your 'thing.' I'm just surprised you're not even sort of aware."

Chuckie rolled his eyes. "I realize this is coming as a shock to you, but I don't have time or interest in anything that isn't relating to aliens right now. You want to ask someone at the F.B.I. why they're not paying attention? Go for it, it's their bailiwick. Let me be around to hear what they say, though."

"Fine, fine, calm down, Secret Agent Man. Not meaning to diss the skills."

"Whatever. Basically, Vance could be right, but since I haven't seen any of his evidence, and, from what you said, neither have you, I can't make a determination."

"Then let's go visit Hacker International."

"We can't," Vance reminded me. "Jeff has to be sworn in."

There was a clatter of feet on the stairs before anyone could remark on my ability to forget something that big. Len came down, looking stressed. "Kitty, you need to get up here, right away." He turned and ran back up.

"Okay, that was different." I started forward.

Chuckie held me back. "Me first." He drew his gun and started up. I went after him.

Jeff held me back. "No. You come after me." He followed Chuckie.

Looked at Vance. He shrugged. "I'm great with you going ahead of me."

"Hiding behind the girl?"

"Protecting your rear." Vance added a leer in case I'd missed the double entendre.

"Don't let Jeff hear you say that, particularly in the way you just said it."

"I'm a lot of things, Kitty, but as stupid as I appear actually isn't one of them."

"Vance, this actually could be the beginning of a beautiful friendship."

CHAPTER 57

VANCE AND I HEADED upstairs. No one was waiting for us. Under the circumstances, this boded.

"Com on," I whispered.

"Yes, Chief?" Walter whispered back.

"Wow. You're good. What's going on? Where is everyone?"

"Everyone is in the Ballroom, Chief. And I'm not sure what's going on. However, we have visitors, and neither Pierre, nor I, nor anyone else let them in the Embassy. And the shields are up and active, I've verified."

"Gotcha." I headed for the stairs. Vance stayed close to me.

We trotted up as quietly as we could. Reached the second floor. No one was on it. Figured Walter had really meant *in* the Ballroom. No worries. We'd had, and won, a standoff here before.

Slunk around, keeping our backs to the wall. "We look ridiculous," Vance whispered.

"Yeah? You feel free to just saunter on in then, Mister I've Got Your Rear."

"Oh, no, I'm happy following you."

Considered options. I could pull out my Glock and activate my Poofs, but that could be overkill. Then again, all the men who'd been with us weren't around. How to tell what to do?

"New plan, Vance. You go in, and if things are scary, you scream."

"No way."

"I'll come in and save you."

"You'll save me last, after you save everyone else. I know where I fall on your particular totem pole."

Hard to argue with the truth. "Fine. Coward."

"You know it."

Decided we needed to get closer anyway. Got to where I could see into the ballroom but they'd only see me if they were looking through the door at a certain angle. No one seemed to be doing much other than standing around.

Of course, that was reminiscent of the last standoff in our Ballroom. Sighed.

Jeff stuck his head out. "Stop playing around and get in here," he said quietly, but with a lot of emphasis. "They're here for you. I think."

"What do you mean, 'you think'?"

"They won't let us talk and they have ways of ensuring we don't. My head hurts enough. I can read them, I think, and they don't like any of us other than Nathalie. And they are waiting for a woman, and I think it's you. Now get inside."

Well, that seemed clear. Resisted the impulse to make a joke in a fake Nazi voice and instead entered as requested. Everyone who'd been in the two limos was in here, as was Pierre. Pierre was wringing his hands, probably because he was afraid we were going to have a fight and destroy all his birthday party decorations.

But it wasn't just them in here. They were all standing around looking at two women, who weren't really looking at any of them. No one was speaking.

One woman was taller than the other, and both were taller than me. The taller one, who I was also sure was older, looked like she'd stepped off the *Mad Men* set and into our Embassy. She was dressed in a very 1960s business suit, hair pulled back.

The younger one had just left a revival of *Dynasty*. She was sporting a suit with some serious shoulder pads and big jewelry. Her hair was big, too.

"It's a costume party. Who are you and why are you here?"

The taller woman looked at me. "Our message is for the leader of the American Centaurion people and her alone." She clearly hadn't gotten the joke, nor had she taken it as an insult. The shorter woman hadn't either. They seemed blithely clueless—and not at all intimidated to be surrounded by all these men, most of whom were pretty big, all of whom weren't looking friendly.

Vance scurried over toward Nathalie, who was off in a corner of the room behind our two costumed chicks. Well, he tried. He made it near the women and was flung back. Most of the men I could see winced, and it was a "been there, done that" kind of wincing.

Gower caught Vance before he slammed into a wall. Whatever Vance had hit had been invisible, but I got the feeling that it was around Nathalie, too, because she wasn't moving much.

Studied our "guests" a little more closely. They weren't wearing anything that matched, specifically no matching jewelry. Nothing was obviously wrong about them, other than their clothing. Perhaps I was going out on a limb, or perhaps my brain was working at warp speed, but I didn't think they were from around here. Of course, it took television and radio waves a long time to reach the Alpha Centauri system. Or maybe they, like Jeff, just preferred to watch the older shows.

"Look, the last time a couple of gals from your planet showed up without an appointment, they tried to kill everyone. So, share your secrets or launch your attack, but you're not hanging out with me alone."

The women's eyes widened but they didn't do anything.

"Oh, for God's sake. I'm Ambassador Katt-Martini. What can I do for you? But first, name, rank, and planetary number, pronto. Or I'm going to go through your Girls-Only force field and kick some serious Amazonian butt."

The younger one shook her head. "This is not for ... them, the others." She indicated all the men. Shocker.

"In my opinion, it is. So, guys, what I think we have here are either two women who haven't gone out of the house or looked at a fashion magazine for decades. Or we have two Free Women from Beta Twelve, what we might now call the Planet of Possibly Not As Pissed Off As They Were Before Amazons. I'm betting on the latter, but that's because I hate to take the long shots."

The women stared and the younger one gaped. "How—what do you mean?" she asked.

I rolled my eyes. "Look, girls, really, I have no idea why you're here, but I do know it takes a lot of effort to *get* you here. So either you're about to try to kill us or something, or you need our help. No one changes solar systems just to hang out. Oh, and drop the disguises, will you? You both look ridiculous."

The taller one seemed to reach a decision. "Fine. Your guardians may remain. We were told about what happened . . . before. I can understand your hesitation."

"Are you sure—" the younger one hissed.

"Yes. You are along to learn. And not question." She sounded annoyed.

"I can question." The younger one sounded petulant. I revised my guess as to their relationship.

"Look, can you two have the sibling squabble after we know what you really look like and what your names are?"

Now they both gaped at me. "How—" The older one collected herself. "Our mother said you were wise beyond your years. I see she was, as always, right."

Their mother. I'd only met one Amazonian who we hadn't had to kill. I ensured I was standing up straight. The men with me noticed and did the same.

I gave them a short bow. "I hope your coming doesn't indicate that Queen Renata is unwell."

"We're disguised!" the younger one said, while the older one looked ready to strangle her.

"Not really. Not to anyone who's met the Planetary Council, anyway. Seriously, change into whatever you really look like and how you really dress, and, once you pass along whatever your message is, I'll explain why you look wrong."

The taller one nodded and they shifted. Both of them had short, spiky hair. The taller one was a brunette, the shorter one was a blonde. They were both very muscular in an attractive way, though, and, as with the other Free Women I'd met, their limbs were elongated just a bit so that they looked out of proportion compared to a human or anyone from Alpha Four. Their eyes were just like their mother's, and also like the other Free Women's—larger, more elongated, and a dark purple.

They also looked younger than they had when they were disguised. Lifespans were different in the Alpha Centauri system than those of Earth, but I put them in their early 20s in terms of human years. All the Free Women resembled each other, but these two were clearly sisters—the only differences I could see were height and hair color.

And, as per how the rest of the Free Women dressed, they were both in *Xena: Warrior Princess* wear, complete with boots and weapons. Clearly no one on Beta Twelve really liked to branch out and try a new look, ever.

The taller one bowed at the waist. "Greetings to the great warrior, Kitty Katt, from the Royal Family of Beta Twelve." She straightened up.

The shorter one now bowed at the waist. "Our mother, Queen Renata of the Free Women, sends her regards."

"I am Princess Rahmi," the taller one said when the shorter one had straightened up. "And this is my younger sister, Princess Rhee. We are here to help you celebrate the first annual of the future ruler's birth."

CHAPTER 58

THAT SAT ON THE AIR FOR A BIT. "Wow. Today's just full of fun surprises. So, before we go down this rabbit hole, let me ask something—is this your mother's idea of a joke?"

The princesses looked shocked. "No!" Rahmi said. "We are here on business of state."

"Uh huh." Thought fast and furiously. "Um, Chuckie? I need you to clear out anyone who doesn't have the highest security clearances."

"That would be me and Nathalie," Vance said. "And trust me, we know what's going on." Nathalie nodded. She looked worried.

"Okey dokey. Girls, first off, you are scaring the nice lady you think you're 'protecting.' Let her out of your force field so she can be with her husband. Do it now. I will consider noncompliance to be an act of war."

Rahmi shrugged. Nathalie ran to Brewer, who hugged her. "Thank you, Kitty," she said. "They wouldn't listen to me."

"No, I'd imagine they wouldn't. You're not a warrior." Heaved a sigh. We needed this like Jeff needed a hole in his chest. "Thanks, girls. Now, I want the two of you to listen very, very carefully to my words. If you hurt anyone in here, men especially, I'm going to break both your necks."

They looked shocked and both mouths opened.

I put up my hand. "Every man here is someone I care about. We have a lot of male operatives and every damn one of them had better be treated nicely by you, and with

respect, my husband in more than particular. You are tres-
passing in my home, and if you ever slam someone I don't
want you to slam again, my husband in particular, as I said,
necks will equal broken. Got it?"

"Yes," Rahmi muttered.

"Yes," Rhee said, sounding hurt.

"Now, that that is out of the way, let's get onto the next
fun facts. Your mother knows I'm married, who I'm married
to, and that I'm not the one 'in charge.'"

"She said you would say that," Rhee replied. "She said
that you were modest."

Heard Chuckie, Reader, Tim, and the flyboys making
coughing sounds behind me. Clearly they were crazed with
the new power of not getting smashed. Ignored them.

"No, what I think your mother actually believes is that
I'm smart. I know your mother's smart. And I also know
that she didn't send you here for the reasons you've told me.
They may be the reasons she told *you*, but that's not why
you're here."

The princesses looked confused. "Would you explain?"
Rahmi asked slowly. "We have told you why we were
sent."

"Yes, yes, and my daughter's birthday is coming right
up." Considered a bit more. "Who else knows you're coming
for a visit?"

"The Planetary Council, and the rulership of Alpha
Four," Rahmi answered promptly.

"Why are you the only representatives coming? If this is
such a big deal?"

"Oh," Rhee said with confidence. "I understand. You're
offended that the others are not here." She stepped closer
and handed me a letter. "This is from Councilor Leonidas,
extending everyone's well wishes and explaining why they
are unable to attend in person."

Took the letter, didn't even look at it, just held it out.
"Chuckie, this is for you. Have a read, I'll want to know
contents in a bit."

"No, it's for—" Rhee started.

"No, it's not. You are not here for the reasons you two
think you are. Tell me, do you have Rite of Passage tests and
such on your planet? Things that prove that you're able to
rule?"

Rahmi nodded. "Yes. We have both passed all of them with flying colors. Mother is pleased with our progress."

"But neither one of you is able to represent your mother and your planet on the Planetary Council yet, are you?"

They both looked just slightly ashamed. "No," Rhee admitted. "We are not experienced enough yet in the ways of diplomacy."

"Oh, are you kidding me?" Jeff muttered. "This is their damn training mission? Tell me I'm wrong."

"Nope, I think you got it in one. Chuckie?"

"Oh, it's all that and *more*. I could read the whole letter, but it's very long. Very complimentary, very babbling, very unimportant sounding."

"So, read the code portion, if you'd be so kind."

He cleared his throat. "Have lost regular contact with Earth. Fear sabotage from enemies on your side. Civil and solar system unrest prevents our sending any support. Sending best warriors in system under the only viable option. Mother says they need training you can provide, also says their helping you is payment for training."

"I'm never wrong. Note, girls, that that was not a modest statement. So, okay, per that note, you're here to help and do what you're told. There are a variety of people here who will have the right to tell you what to do. I'm going to say their names, they're going to raise their hands, and you're going to remember who the hell they are."

They both looked lost and concerned, but they also both nodded.

"Jeff, Chuckie, James, Tim, Paul. Get that girls?" More nods. "Great. The next group are the ones who you'd damn well better listen to and if they sound like what they're asking is urgent, you will do what they say, too. Jerry, Matt, Chip, Pierre, Len, Kyle. Got that?"

The princesses could not have looked more forlorn, but they nodded again. "Now, everyone else you see in this room are people you have to be incredibly civil, polite, and helpful to. You may question their motives and requests with me, or one of the men I just told you to listen to and obey, but you will not treat them badly unless we give you that order. Got that?"

More forlorn nodding. This mission was *not* what they'd been expecting. Sucked to be them. "Last but not least,

there are going to be many other people you're going to
meet. Some of them will fall into the 'obey as you would me'
category, some will fall under the 'damn well listen and help
and even obey' category, and most of the rest will fall under
the 'treat with the utmost respect' category. Failure to treat
any of these people in the way you've been told will be
considered a black mark and I will report it back to your
mother. In stunning, Technicolor detail. And if you really
piss me off, I'll be telling her that while I send your dead,
mangled body back in a small bag marked Return To
Sender, Merchandise Sucked. Now, can I get a 'yes, ma'am,
we understand,' please?"

"Yes, ma'am," they said together, joined in unwilling and
unhappy confirmation of the worst news in the world. "We
understand."

"Good job. So, next up, it surely sounds like the plan is
for you to be with us for a while. Pierre?"

"I'll prepare two visitor suites for our royal guests." He
was practically vibrating with excitement. It wasn't every
day we entertained royalty, if you ignored the fact that Jeff
and Christopher were technically royal. They both did their
best to ignore it, of course, and so did everyone else.

"They fall on the more austere side of the house, Pierre."
Rahmi nodded. Rhee looked disappointed. She'd been
disguised as a *Dynasty* extra, after all.

"Well, I'll prepare as we would for any other royal dignitary and then our two lovely princesses can tell me what
isn't pleasing in their sight." With that, Pierre dashed off,
presumably to completely redecorate two rooms, if not the
entire Embassy. At least it was something positive for him
to focus on.

"You've made Pierre's day. Good job and look at that, a
ticky mark in the 'well done' category. It's your first, so treasure it. Now, next up, you get to shape-shift back into looking
human, but you're going to dress like you're from this decade.
Nathalie, please help them look appropriate. Jeff and I need
to change clothes. Girls, while I'm gone you're not hitting
anyone in this room unless they are actively trying to kill
someone else, and 'actively' does not mean 'looking at' or
'daring to be a man speaking.'"

"You need to change quickly," Brewer said, proving either his bravado or how well he'd thought I'd impressed the

new reality upon the princesses. "Jeff's due on the floor of the House in less than thirty minutes."

Jeff nodded, took my hand, and we zipped off and up to our apartment. "You sure it's safe to leave them down there?" he asked as we raced into the bedroom and, most importantly, the closet.

"Yeah." Let out a sigh of relief. The Elves had come through again. Full outfits for both of us. I even had a new pair of shoes, and Jeff had another trench and fedora.

Jeff started to get undressed. I helped him. Not to go for Sexy Time—we had a ton of people waiting for us and were about to be late to a huge political event—but because I wanted to be really, seriously, completely sure he wasn't badly hurt.

"I'm fine, baby," he said softly as I dumped the trench, suit jacket, shirt, and tie onto the floor. "My head and chest both hurt a little, but it's fading."

Ran my hands softly over the bruise. "This shot would have killed you, Jeff. It was perfectly aimed to hit your hearts, both of them."

Jeff took my hands in one of his and pulled me closer with the other. "I don't care about this appointment, Kitty, so if you need to take time to relax, then I'll be happy to explain that we were late because my wife was shaken after someone tried to assassinate me and if they don't like it, they can appoint someone else to this position."

Leaned my head on his chest, but not on the bruised part. "James was right. There's still all these other things going on and we have to pay attention to them, too."

Jeff was quiet a moment. "You don't think this had anything to do with the murders Vance is worried about?"

"I think it might, but I think it's also got the potential to be Raul."

"Raul could be here for a job, not just a vendetta."

"True enough." Slid my hands out of his and around his back so I could hold him tightly.

Jeff hugged me back. "Kitty, we've had close calls before."

"I thought you were dead. Really and truly dead. The shot was so accurate. Bruno knocked you away and everything, but you were still hit."

"Yeah." Jeff sounded thoughtful.

"What?"

"Well, you said it yourself earlier—if the bird hadn't knocked me out of the way, the bullet would have gone into my head. Instead it went to the one place where, based on random occurrences, I had something in my pocket that deflected the bullet."

"You think Bruno knew?"

"I think the bird was invisible to us almost the entire day. He'd never have been allowed in the restaurant, but that doesn't mean he wasn't there."

"I'll ask him when he gets back."

"He's not back?"

"He went after the shooter."

"Hope he's careful. I don't want to end up having to avenge a Peregrine, and I know you, so I know if someone hurts one of your pets you're going to want to avenge them."

"Yeah, but Bruno can probably take care of himself." I hoped. Sent what I hoped was a message that Bruno shouldn't take any risks.

Jeff rocked me for a little bit. "If you're okay to go, we do need to get dressed and back with the others, baby."

Heaved another sigh. "You're right."

Jeff grinned as we pulled apart. "Love to hear you say that. So, onto our latest situation. What are we going to do with Renata's kids?"

"We're going to do exactly what she expects—bring them into things and force them to learn how situations, wartime and diplomatic situations in particular, don't always go according to plan."

"You think that's Renata's goal?"

"Yeah, I do. Clearly there's trouble in the Alpha Centauri system. They can't reach us, figure, rightly, that we're in trouble, too. So they sent the only help they could—the kind that doesn't attract a lot of undue attention."

"Two warrior princesses being sent to Earth wouldn't attract attention?"

"No, not if their cover was that they were coming to ensure that no one on Earth got pissed off because no one from the Alpha Centauri system bothered to attend Jamie's birthday party."

"Oh, yes," Jeff said, sarcasm knob firmly at eleven.

"They'll fit right in for that. Maybe Pierre can find them a couple of Disney Princess gowns. By the way, want to give me the excuse for why the birds and Poofs didn't do anything when those two slammed all of us against the walls?" Jeff asked as we finished getting undressed and redressed.

"You weren't in actual danger. They must have slammed carefully, nothing looked messed up."

"Yeah, that's only because Pierre had managed to scream out that the décor was for Jamie while he was flying through the air."

"Whatever, it worked and everyone's fine. And that force field of theirs is going to come in handy."

"I'm having a vision of the future. You're going to take them with us to the Capitol Building, aren't you?"

"You got it. Enjoy your new personal bodyguards."

Jeff groaned. "Can it get any worse?"

"Oh, I'm sure it can. Just give it some time."

CHAPTER 59

WE HEADED BACK DOWNSTAIRS. Everyone was still in the ballroom, it remained unscathed, and Rahmi and Rhee looked like they'd been dressed by a former international model. In other words, they looked hot.

None of the men in the room were giving them any kinds of looks other than suspicious, truculent, angry, terrified, or, in the case of Chuckie, thoughtful. Even Gower's normal calm and cool appeared to be affected.

"Looking good, girls. Great work, Nathalie. Guys, why so serious? And Chuckie, what's going on in my favorite conspiratorial mind?"

He looked at the others. "We need a minute. Representative Brewer, would you be in a position to advise the Speaker of the House that there's been an attack on Representative Martini, and that we may be coming a little later than planned?"

"Yes, absolutely." Brewer pulled his phone out and started dialing.

"Jeff's not really a representative yet, is he?" I asked.

"Technically he is, because he's a presidential and gubernatorial appointee, so he assumed office the moment they appointed and he said yes," Chuckie said. "However, it's a little gray until he's sworn in, which is why they wanted that to happen so quickly."

"So I can still get out of it?" Jeff asked hopefully.

"You wish." Chuckie jerked his head at Reader, who nodded. Reader still had Reyes' stuffed briefcase and was also holding a folder he hadn't had when Jeff and I left the room.

Chuckie moved us out of the ballroom. Reader, Gower, and Tim followed. We went down the hall to one of the unused music salons. Chuckie looked around and sighed. "I hate to ask this, Paul, but would you mind—"

"Checking for bugs?" Gower asked with a grin. "Not a problem." He zipped through the room and was back in a flash. "We're clean. And thanks for getting us out of the room. I still remember fighting the women of Beta Twelve, and other than Renata herself, not that fondly."

"Sorry about the flashbacks, but I think they'll be helpful." I did. At least, I figured they'd be helpful to me, and if they could put that force field around Jeff and keep him safe, then they could move in permanently.

"Love your optimism," Tim said.

"I don't want to talk about Renata's daughters," Chuckie said. "They've been trained to follow the head female, and ours just laid down the law to them. I also happen to agree with Kitty—I think they'll be useful. However, Kitty, to answer your question—I'm wondering about who shot your husband."

"Raul the Revengeful Assassin. At least, that's my assumption."

Chuckie shook his head. "The shot didn't come from the rooftops. I'm not saying that every assassin works from the roofs, but in the daylight, with a lot of people around, it's the smartest place to be. The inside of a car that's moving is also a smart spot. You do the drive-by, floor it, and are out of there before anyone's registered anything."

"So maybe he's getting frustrated."

"I watched everything that happened to the two of you and I've been replaying it in my mind. The shot came more from the side than from above. And based on the way you were positioned at the curb, it came from nearer than I think any of us realized at the time."

"I heard a car peel out."

"Yeah, but that might not have been the shooter's getaway car. If most people see and hear someone being shot, their first instinct is to get far away fast." The other men nodded their agreement.

"Okay, so what are you thinking?"

Reader had that file, and he waved it at me. "He's think-ing about the information regarding Vance's theory."

"Oh, so that's not from the briefcase, you got it from Stryker?"

Reader nodded. "There are a lot of representatives dead, I'll give you that. But they all look legitimate. Heart attacks, illnesses, accidents. Santiago and the thankfully unsuccess-ful attack on Jeff are the only ones that stand out as not being normal."

Chuckie rubbed the back of his neck. "Is there anything you've forgotten to tell me, or held back for some reason? Anything at all? It could be small."

"Tito asked me the same thing, about Santiago. And, I did remember something that helped. So to speak. I haven't withheld anything, but there's a good chance I've forgotten something. Hang on, lemme ponder."

"Take your time," Jeff said. "The longer we wait, the more chance I have of being told I'm not representative material."

"Jeff, we've been through this," Gower said patiently. "You don't have a choice."

The rest of them started in with the "no option" reminders, while I begged my memory to do us all a solid and toss up whatever it was we needed. Chuckie was right—there was something I was pretty sure I'd forgotten. Remembered I'd forgotten to tell Reader something, which meant I'd certainly forgotten to tell Chuckie, because when I'd caught him up I hadn't added the statement explaining that I'd forgotten to share.

Sat in a chair while the men verbally wrangled and closed my eyes. Had to think back to when I'd remembered I'd forgotten something. Where had we been? It had been today that I'd remembered my forgetfulness, meaning it was something I'd learned yesterday sometime.

"...don't know where Oliver's gotten to." Jeff's voice pulled me back. "We left him at Rayburn House before we went to lunch. Don't know why we bothered to pick him up and get a civics lesson if he's not coming with us to the swearing-in to actually provide a useful service."

"That's it!" Jumped up. "I remembered what I'd forgot-ten when we were driving to Rayburn House. I was going to call James but we were stuck in that bureaucratic nightmare it took Cliff to get us out of, and then Representative Juvonic dropped dead in front of us from that supposed heart attack I still don't believe was real, and I completely forgot."

The men all looked at me. "Do you remember now?" Chuckie asked finally, with hope in his tone.

"Yes, and you're not going to like it. Eugene said that Pia Ryan—the widow of the late Jack Ryan, and another fine member of the C.I.A.—is the person who passed the information to him. Eugene said that Pia told him the envelope, which was addressed to Eugene, was sent to her and that she didn't know who had sent it or what it contained. She said she'd figured someone had sent it to her because they knew she knew Eugene."

"And he was actually gullible enough to believe that?" Tim asked.

"Yeah, he said she seemed to be telling the truth, and that she gave it to him at a party, in front of the rest of the Cabal of Evil. It was an envelope with a packet inside, all sealed. That's what Christopher and his team are over at Gaultier searching for. Well, part of what they're searching for."

"Unless they need us, I don't want to know," Chuckie said. "But I need to see that information immediately, if they've found it or even part of it."

"Why?" Reader asked. "I mean, why so urgently?"

Chuckie looked grim. "I think I recognize a pattern. An old pattern."

"A pattern?" I asked. "As in, you've seen something like this before?"

"Seen? No. I'm too young. Everyone in this room is too young. However, I've read about it. The Church Committee."

"You're sensing a pattering about religious institutions?"

Chuckie sighed. "No. It's the nickname for the Senate committee that investigated the C.I.A. after Watergate. It identified an encyclopedia's worth of C.I.A. violations, including the murder of a host of people. And that's when the 'Heart Attack Gun' was discovered."

"The C.I.A. has a gun that gives people heart attacks?" Jeff asked.

"Yeah." Chuckie didn't look happy about it.

"You have the best job in the world."

"Your mother recruited me for it. In part so the C.I.A. wouldn't decide to shoot me with the Heart Attack Gun because I was too close to figuring out everything they were doing when we were in school. And I'm mentioning that again, now, to all of you, because I know Angela also recruited me to stay on the legal side of the C.I.A.'s laws."

"And to stop the bad ones, we know, Secret Agent Man. No one's going to tell you that you can't marry their sister or cousin, I promise. Because if they do, I have a couple of girls who really aren't too clear on much about Earth other than that they get to follow my commands."

Chuckie managed a grin. "Yeah, thanks. The thing is, if this is a C.I.A. plot, there's no rhyme or reason to it. Most of what the Church Committee found related to the overthrow of other countries, the Kennedy assassination, Watergate, and the like. But there were always reasons. Right now, I see no reasons for why anyone's been killed, other than Santiago, who we believe was an accident, or Jeff, who could have been attacked by one of your myriad enemies."

Tim jerked. "Distraction."

Everyone else stared at him. I, however, knew that my replacement had learned to think like me, at least somewhat. "Oh, Megalomaniac Lad, I'm so glad you're here."

"I can pass on that nickname, Kitty."

"You mean you can hope I'll forget it, but I won't."

"Why distract anyone from anything?" Chuckie asked. "Vance put this together. He thinks we have a serial killer, right? So why make two murders stand out so much from the others?"

"Right now, we have only one murder and one attempted murder," Jeff pointed out. "There's no proof that anyone else died unnaturally or because of malice aforethought."

Reader nodded. "The only thing that's suspicious is the number of people doing the same specific job who are dead. Otherwise, nothing in the file says foul play."

"Unless you know that the C.I.A. has a Heart Attack Gun," I pointed out.

"Which we now do," Tim agreed. "I'm with Megalomaniac Girl who is, in fact, actually agreeing with me. Showing her brilliance and insight."

"See? Wasn't so hard to embrace your superhero role, was it?"

"You have me as the sidekick, and I know it."

"Blah, blah, blah. Think of yourself as Nightwing to my Batman. Sort of thing."

"You two want to stop bantering and share?" Jeff asked.

"Oh, if you insist. What Megalomaniac Lad meant was that Eugene killing Santiago—or Brewer, if he'd been successful in his mind—and someone trying to kill you is a great way to make anyone who might be linking these deaths together start thinking that maybe we don't really have a serial killer or a massive murder plot going."

"How would those events alter thinking?" Gower asked.

"Because they're so obviously *not* part of a conspiracy. Murder someone in a really elaborate way that also ensures the killer will be caught red-handed. Shoot another one in broad daylight. Because, no worries, there are obvious, legitimate reasons for them to both be victims. Everyone focuses on other problems."

"Like a declaration of war," Gower said.

"We can't declare any more," Jeff reminded him. "Because I've taken this assignment."

"You're not sworn in yet . . ." Stopped talking as Chuckie and I looked at each other. "Meaning he's in that gray area you mentioned. But if Jeff was dead, then what would I do?"

"What would you do if you thought he was dead because he was now a representative, might be the better question," Reader said. "Because we need to know if Vance is right, or if Vance is playing us."

CHAPTER 60

"I THINK HE'S RIGHT," Tim said. "What does Megalomaniac Girl think?"

"I'm with you, Megalomaniac Lad. I don't care how 'natural' those deaths look, we now have over twenty representatives dead in what seems like a very condensed time period and that cannot be considered normal. I also don't think Vance would have brought this to my attention if he was trying to play me, and while he's clearly smarter than he acts, I'm not feeling Mastermind potential."

"I'm still not sold on the murder mystery theory, girlfriend," Reader said. "As Reynolds says, there's no point to it."

The answer was there, at the edge of my mind. I could feel it tickling, but it wasn't coming to me. In order to think well, running my mouth was my go-to move. So I went to it. "Okay, let's take Jeff's attack out of the equation for a minute, because it could be related to 'us' instead of the Mystery of Who is Killing the House of Representatives. So, let me ask this—is Eugene's damage part of the plot, or is he part of something else?"

"You mean, if Eugene was telling you the truth, right?" Reader asked. "As in, if Eugene being told Brewer was a robot, was that part of the overall kill-the-representatives plan?"

"Yeah."

"Let's assume he was," Chuckie said. "Because he named the person who gave him the file and then was shot in the head. We all think that the shot was meant for Kitty, but the shooter wasn't using a hollow-point so the bullet could have killed both of them."

"The Dingo said it was Raul."

"I say again that Raul could be here on a job instead of revenge," Chuckie said patiently. "Or else he could be getting a double out of it. But let's go with it and say that Eugene is part of this conspiracy to kill off the House. Why choose him?"

"Perfect patsy?" Jeff asked. "He was caught and killed already."

"But that makes no sense, other than as a distraction from the real plot, because the only murder that can be pinned on Eugene is Santiago's. Let's say Eugene had succeeded and killed Brewer as he intended. We'd still have caught him red-handed. So, what would be the point of having him be a patsy? What would you gain?"

"I have an idea," Christopher said, as he, White, and Raj joined us. "But first, did I see and hear correctly that we have Queen Renata's daughters here?"

"Yes. Where're Amy and Henry?"

"At the Zoo with the other hackers. We need to get over there, too."

"I'm supposed to be at the Capitol," Jeff said. As the words left his mouth, my phone rang.

Dug it out of my purse. My purse had far fewer Poofs in it than it had earlier, but still contained Reyes' stuffed eagle. Belayed worry about the Poofs for the moment. History showed that the Poofs were pretty darned good at staying safe.

"Hello?"

"Kitty, it's Ed. I spoke with the Speaker of the House, and he called the President." He sounded annoyed. "I told them what had happened, and after reassuring them that Jeff's alive and well and basically unhurt, asked if they could move the swearing-in to another day, perhaps January third, with the rest of the new appointees. I mentioned that you were both shaken and also had some very foreign dignitaries that just arrived for your daughter's birthday celebration, which is an important cultural event in the Alpha Centauri system."

"I'm guessing from your tone that they said not just no, but hell no?"

"Not in so many words, but yes. Under the circumstances, they said that they're thankful Jeff and everyone else are okay, and for you two to take some time to pull yourselves together while the House does some other business, but then to please join everyone as planned. By which they mean you have probably about an hour, and then get over to the Capitol."

"Do they want you over there now?"

"Yes, but we're not voting on anything and I told them I wasn't going over until I went with you and Jeff. I can't believe they're being so callous. Jeff could have died."

"True, but the President, for sure, knows what we used to do for a living. And, much as I'd like to take the time to relax and hide, and much as Jeff would like to put this off as long as he can, we both know we can't."

"I suppose. They could have at least let it wait a couple of days."

"Maybe, but since he was appointed last night and they want him sworn in today, it's clearly a big deal."

"That's standard for any special election or appointment in Congress. You're sworn in the day after you win."

"As always, I learn something new every day. By the way, what did you mean, about the others who were appointed? I thought representatives were never appointed and Jeff was just stuck being special."

"Technically, you're right. However, there are a lot of bills going through the House right now. There's talk that we're going to end up filibustered or worse, since we have so many empty seats. Because the President and New Mexico's governor have now set the precedent, the President felt okay about asking the other states' governors to appoint replacement representatives as well. So, for any district that hasn't held its special election, the governor is picking from either the candidates or the available political pool and making an appointment."

"How many positions is that, do you know?"

"A couple dozen, give or take. I know that doesn't sound like a lot of people, but when the votes come down to the wire, I've learned that two dozen votes can mean the difference between a bill's passage or defeat. By the way, has anyone ever told you it's strange to be on the phone with someone who's just a few rooms away in the same house as you are?"

"Yeah, but you get used to it. So the other replacements are getting sworn in on the third along with the rest of Congress?"

"No, as it turns out. They're getting sworn in the day after Christmas."

"This is moving very fast."

"Those bills are important, they need to be voted on pretty much as soon as we officially convene for next year, meaning the first week of January, and I don't think the President wants any suggestions of unfairness or foul play. He's taken a lot of heat for suspending elections—this allows him to bring in new blood and ensure that Congress is completely filled."

There was a lot of foul play going on, regardless of the President's desires, and things were hot and getting hotter, but now wasn't the time to share all that with Brewer.

"Makes sense. We'll be joining you guys soon. Need to let Jeff know the good news that we get to relax for a little bit." I also had to tell everyone else the very interesting news.

"Not to worry, Pierre's going to escort everyone out of the ballroom and get us settled in one of the salons downstairs while we wait for you. Still wish you could drink wine—I could use a glass by now."

"Dude, I could use a whole bottle by now. But such is life in the big A-C city."

Brewer laughed. "So I'm coming to learn."

Hung up. "Boys, we have bad news and we have interesting news." Shared what Brewer had told me. "So, we get to put off the swearing-in for a whole additional hour. But we don't get to stop worrying during that time, because I think Edmund just told us what's going on."

"How so?" Gower asked. "It just sounds like the President wants to make sure that no one can complain that the bills that did or didn't pass didn't have a quorum."

"I think Kitty's right," Christopher said. "We need to go over what we found at Gaultier, and we need to do it now."

CHAPTER 61

WE DECIDED TO TAKE the time Brewer had bought us to do what Christopher wanted. We all raced off for the Zoo. I stayed with the humans while Jeff went on ahead with the A-Cs, so he and Gower could speak at hyperspeed to catch Christopher, White, and Raj up on what we'd learned.

"What's in the briefcase?" Chuckie asked as we humans or mostly-humans headed for the walkway.

"All the papers and such Jeff and I found in the various offices we searched earlier today, Santiago's included. Probably nothing but trash, but we figured it was better to take what we could find and throw it away here than to miss something important."

"I'm finding it hard to believe that all of this is going on because of a few bills going through the House," Reader said.

"It would depend on what's in the bills," Chuckie said. "But while there are a lot of bills relating to the A-Cs circulating, none of them are up for a vote yet, at least as far as I know."

"Some of the reps killed were from the Foreign Affairs and Homeland Security committees. Per Irene at Rayburn House, Foreign Affairs has lost four members."

"Could be related to what those committees are working on," Chuckie said. "But the research shows that we have reps dead from a wide variety of committees. Transportation lost several, too. Over twenty dead means a lot of committees are down members."

"I'm having a harder time figuring out how that Vance guy is the only one who's put this thing together," Tim said.

"Yeah, I know, but he's claiming that he's been hiding his smarts because they're not as appreciated as political sway."

"That's true enough," Chuckie said. "But Tim brings up the relevant point—why Vance, versus Oliver, who looks for things like this?"

"Maybe he's not handling his sudden fame well," Reader said thoughtfully.

"What do you mean?" Chuckie asked.

Reader shrugged. "When we were all outed, Jeff brought Oliver along with him and Alexander to the big summit meeting where Alexander laid down the law, remember?" Chuckie nodded. "Well, that sent a statement. Oliver's still with the *World Weekly News*, which went from being 'the world's biggest rag' to 'the only paper telling the truth' overnight. He's become something of a celebrity."

"Vance said as much in the limo earlier today," I added.

"And Oliver was embarrassed by Vance's fawning," Reader said.

"True. So, okay, MJO has probably been focused on handling his new popularity and fielding questions about us, versus looking for new conspiracies. But then, why was he snooping around the Embassy last night?"

"That was still all about us," Tim said. "I think James is right. So the two people most likely to pay attention to these deaths have been incredibly distracted."

"The first death was right after we were outed," Reader confirmed, looking at the file. "Huh. That's interesting."

"The first one was the guy Santiago replaced, wasn't it?" I asked as we waited for the elevator and my mind spun the facts around.

"Yeah. I know that expression, girlfriend. What are you thinking?"

"I'm thinking that Megalomaniac Lad is right again. I think we do have distraction going on, and I'm willing to say that the Mastermind, or at least this Operation's Mastermind, waited until he or she had the perfect storm of distractions going on to launch. If over twenty Reps had died like this two years ago, both Chuckie and MJO would have been on top of it."

"If your timeline's right, then the Mastermind also

waited until the President suspended this year's elections," Tim said. "Whether that's because they expected some of those now dead to lose their elections, another reason, or just convenient coincidence we don't know."

"And who knows if we'll find out," Reader added.

"I can buy all that," Chuckie said slowly. "But we still don't have a lot to go on."

"Well, I also think we have a couple of key points, one of which is that whoever's in charge likely knows you and Oliver, or at least your underground reputations, so to speak, because, elections suspended or no, I think they chose this plot's start time specifically to stay off your radars. And the other is this—why did whoever try to kill Jeff before he was sworn in?" The elevator arrived.

"Convenience, accessibility, guard was down," Chuckie ticked off. He motioned for me to go in the elevator.

"Stupid placement and timing, random location, and guard wasn't down since we'd had three people die around us in less than twenty-four hours," I shared as I stayed put. Wanted us to think this through ourselves, because I felt we were getting somewhere. The others would add in soon enough.

Chuckie sighed as the elevator doors closed. "In your own time, Kitty."

"As it should be."

"I'll play," Tim said. "What if the entire point of all of this is to ensure that the person representing our district in New Mexico isn't pro-alien? The former rep is killed and a really anti-alien guy runs for the position. Santiago was a teacher and wasn't expected to even come close, let alone win in a landslide. So, maybe our Mastermind isn't happy that he's elected. Maybe Eugene lied and was always after Santiago."

"I'd say there's a high probability that at least part of the point is to ensure an anti-alien rep is in place. But I think we have more going on—you wouldn't want to kill as many people as have died, because fewer would make it all seem less suspect. And, if everyone thought the former rep died of natural causes, Eugene killing Santiago doesn't scream 'conspiracy.'"

"But the poison was put into Brewer's glass," Reader reminded us. "And the only reason Santiago drank it was that he'd almost choked to death, which is not something anyone could have predicted."

A thought occurred. "Hang on." Conveniently my phone was still in my hand. Dialed. This wasn't a discussion I wanted to have over the intercom system.

"Yes, Kitty darling? How may I be of service?"

"Pierre, who was in charge of the drinks portion of our Dinner Party of Death? Specifically, who was in charge of making sure the water glasses were kept filled?"

"Hmmm . . . let me verify. Ah, here it is. Annette Dier. She was part of Chef's Beverage Team. Why?"

That sounded familiar. "Spell that last name please, Pierre." He did. Memory shared that this matched the name of the SWAT guy I'd spoken to when I was going to interview Eugene. "Did Chef vet his choices for safety within our Embassy?"

"Oh, yes, absolutely. Everyone had to go through a screening."

"Was she in charge, or just the water girl?"

"Just one of the beverage staff, but she was assigned to your portion of the room for water refills during dinner."

"I'd like to see her screening results, Pierre. In the most extreme, 'we will accuse you of trying to murder our people and destroy our party' way if Chef is unwilling to provide confidential information. In fact, if Chef doesn't come across with this info immediately, please call Chuckie and have him take Chef into custody. In the meantime, we need this Annette Dier's info pronto. Send it to the Computer Lab."

"On it in less than a second." We hung up.

"What was that all about?" Reader asked.

"You know, what are the odds that we would have two people randomly at our Embassy, doing very different jobs that let them in or around it without their being invited guests, both named Dier? With the oddest spelling of that name I've ever seen?"

"Low with an odd name," Chuckie said. "Who were they?"

"One was a guy in a SWAT uniform. Until right now I'd have said he was with the SWAT team, but I don't remember seeing him once Eugene was shot. The other was the girl who was in charge of filling up the water in our section of the dining room." My brain suggested I play the same name game I had during Operation Assassination. "You know what Dier is spelled backward? Or rather, spelled what I'm going to bet is the right way?"

"Reid," Chuckie growled. He pulled out his phone and dialed. "I want all the information in our file on Leventhal Reid, most specifically on known associates and next of kin. Yes. Yes, faster than that. Because I'm going to be there in less than a minute and I want that information waiting for me the minute I walk into the room, Stryker." He hung up. "I hate where this is going."

"Not as much as I do. How did this slip past us? I know we ran extensive security and background on everyone."

"I'm betting we find that the water girl was a late addition," Reader said. "I'm more concerned with the guy who was with the SWAT team."

"I'll ask Officer Melville about him. I'm betting he just showed up and blended in."

"For all we know, he's the guy who shot Eugene," Tim said. "Sure the Dingo thought it was Raul, but it's not like they were standing next to the shooter."

"No, the Dingo and Surly Vic were definitely on different roofs from whoever shot Eugene. And, you know, Dier the Fake SWAT guy could also be doubling as Raul the Pissed Off Assassin."

"This is all bad and indicates a larger conspiracy, or maybe even a different conspiracy, but I still don't see how you could know that anyone other than Brewer would be drinking that water," Chuckie said. "And much of the theory we're all talking about hinges on that fact."

"Maybe whoever put Eugene in motion and ensured Annette Dier was on water duty knew Brewer well enough to know that the man doesn't care for water all that much and would rather drink just about anything else, preferably wine. Somewhere along the way, someone was going to ask for a water refill, she wasn't going to be around to do it, and Brewer was going to offer his glass."

"It's a stretch to assume that drinker would be Santiago," Tim said.

"Not really. Santiago comes from a desert region. We all drink water like crazy in Arizona and New Mexico because it's so dry. And Santiago was a teetotaler, meaning he was going to drink his water down because that's what he drinks all the time. With the guarantee that Brewer wasn't going to drink his."

"It's still a stretch to think that Santiago would be the one killed," Chuckie said.

"Him, Brewer, me . . . I think if any one of us had died the Mastermind would have counted it as a big mark in the win column. Anyone else dies, well, still probably a win."

"Does the man really not drink water?" Reader asked.

"Not really. He drinks wine. Or tea. He likes tea . . ."

"What?" Chuckie asked.

"The only reason Jeff's alive is that we called the Brewers for help at Rayburn House, and Edmund called Cliff, which was the only reason we got into Jeff's office. Juvonic was killed while we were waiting for the Brewers. Then we went to The Teetotaler, which was a place the Brewers have just discovered, and the owner was so thrilled to have us he gave us all gifts. Those gifts were in Jeff's coat pocket. But if you knew us, you'd assume they'd be in my purse."

"Why weren't they?" Reader asked.

"I have too much stuff in my purse, because Jeff and I searched every empty office at Rayburn House and took anything that wasn't nailed down. But no one would know we'd done that, because we used hyperspeed and I know we weren't spotted by anyone. So there was no way in the world to know what we'd be doing or where we'd be going. Unless, frankly, you were following the Brewers."

"You think they're involved?"

"No. I think we need to put guards on Edmund Brewer. I think he's going to be the next one targeted."

CHAPTER 62

WE GOT INTO THE ELEVATOR NOW. While we went up to the fifth floor I sent Officer Melville a text asking about any officer named Dier. Requested he keep the search confidential, just in case Dier was a legit dude and it was simply a common name around these parts. Also asked for a list of any officers named Reid, just in case.

Exited the elevator to find all of Hacker International present and accounted for, along with Amy, Jeff, and the others who'd been with us at the Embassy.

"Took you long enough," Christopher said.

"We were figuring out what's going on."

For this statement I received Patented Glare #4. "I told you we'd found out what's going on over at Gaultier already."

"Right. Where are the Barones?"

"Sent them on an errand," Jeff said. "And I've explained to everyone here that, even if they're engaged to one of them, this is confidential in the extreme."

"I won't tell Jennifer anything," Ravi said. "But she's completely trustworthy."

"Other than in her taste in men," Amy said under her breath.

Stryker handed Chuckie a thick folder. "Here you go, my lord and master. Be happy American Centaurion bought us better equipment than we had at Andrews, because you'd still be waiting for the printouts otherwise."

"Whine later," Chuckie said. "Expect to work right now. Henry, you seem happy."

He did. It was probably safe to consider that Dr. Wu looked close to giddy. Point of fact, I'd never seen him looking this cheerful, and that included the few times he thought he'd found a girl willing to go to bed with him. He'd been wrong those times, so I was cautiously optimistic about his joy being something ultimately useful.

"Proximity equals access, Chuck," Henry said. "And a twenty-petabyte external hard drive, courtesy of the Dulce Science Center, means we now possess every bit of information Gaultier Enterprises has."

"Nice work. What's a petabyte?"

Henry shot me a withering look. "It's a term for data storage capacity."

"Dude, I guessed that, based on the fact that I know what a terabyte, a gigabyte, a megabyte, and a kilobyte are. I know what an octet is, too—it's the smallest, the thing that makes up a byte. So we can stop with the idea that Kitty Cannot Grasp Our Genius Speak. However, I thought terabytes were the biggest things going."

"They are for regular use," Omega Red said. "But a petabyte is made up of a thousand terabytes."

"It's the next inevitable phase," Big George added.

"Works for me. So, Doctor Condescending Wu, what did you find? We know you found Eugene's laptop."

Henry took a deep breath and Christopher put his hand up. "The highlights. We're on a schedule now."

Henry shot Christopher his own glare, though he had a long way to go to even hope to touch the hem of Christopher's Glaring Garment. "Fine. I was able to use the laptop to access the entire system. We're running the data right now to identify anything related to deep space suspended animation."

"What are everyone's initial thoughts—are we going to be able to help Malcolm?" Prayed the answer would be yes.

"Yes," Stryker said. "I believe we have enough in here to be able to figure out what he was hit with and, therefore, what to do to bring him out. We're sending relevant information to Dulce and Doctor Hernandez."

Allowed myself to feel cautiously optimistic again. Everything going on was making it easy to focus on something other than worrying about Buchanan, but now that we were talking about him, all the worry showed up to kick cautious optimism to the curb while sharing that there was no proof Stryker was right or that we'd find a cure. Or that Buchanan would ever wake up again.

Jeff came over and put his arm around me. Clearly I was broadcasting the worry. Did my best to pull myself together—I wasn't going to help Buchanan with worry.

"What else did you find?" Reader asked.

"There are three hidden floors in the building," Amy said. "I've been there before and didn't know about them, but Henry found them on the schematics."

"Did you explore them?" Chuckie asked.

She shook her head. "We couldn't get in, at least not on this trip."

"We have the building blueprints," Henry said. "All of them."

"All of them?" Jeff asked.

"There are five different sets," Henry replied. "They're doing a lot of shady stuff over there. Anyway, I think we'll be able to identify what's going on with Gaultier."

"I'm also sure that Henry found the information on the emotional blockers and overlays," Ravi said. "However, the encryption on those files is some of the toughest we've ever seen. It's going to take a while to break."

"Be sure to include my dad in whatever you're doing with that."

Stryker opened his mouth. "Do it," Chuckie snapped.

"I was *going* to say that we already hooked him in. Geez, Chuck, you're as quick on the trigger as Kitty."

"We have a lot of dead people, Eddy, and not a lot of answers about what's going on. And who the hell are you calling quick on the trigger anyway?"

"Not you, Missus Martini," White said with a smile. "However, what our young men here haven't mentioned is, under the circumstances, disappointing. Other than within the late Mister Montgomery's personal temporary office space, we've found no indication of anything to do with any representative, other than the usual military contracts and the like."

"So Gaultier is likely a dead end there. Which sucks."

"Gaultier is a dead end, but Eugene wasn't." Christopher handed me a bunch of papers. "We took everything of his from the facility, other than his laptop. No one seemed to care, other than the accounting manager who was in charge of his work, and he was more upset about having hired a lunatic murderer to help cover the load while he has three of his staff out on maternity leave than anything else."

"Pregnancy leaves confirmed and legitimate," Amy added. "And Eugene wasn't working on anything that seems too interesting, but we're going to run all his information through everything, because if there's one thing I've learned it's that my father and his ilk are willing to be really intricately crazy."

"So true, Ames, so true. So, is it safe to assume that no one at Gaultier either knew about Eugene's belief about hidden robots or was giving him the orders?"

"Unless they read through his stuff, and it didn't seem like anyone cared. For whatever reason, no one at Gaultier knew Eugene had killed anyone or was dead until we told them." Christopher shook his head. "I'm happy the story's been suppressed, but we weren't the ones who did it, I've already checked with Serene."

"So the police didn't release any information," Chuckie said thoughtfully. "That was probably because Kitty brought in the K-9 squad. Have you heard back from them yet?"

"Nope. What does Eugene's mystery package say?"

Reader sighed and took it from my hands. "Give me a minute."

"Your unwillingness to read anything other than comics is still with you, I see, Kitty," Stryker said. "I don't know how you got through college."

Chuckie and I exchanged a glance. He raised his eyebrow. I shrugged. While I appreciated his willingness to defend my intelligence honor with Hacker International, there was no point at this time. I'd make Stryker pay for that comment later.

"Dude, ability and desire are not the same things. So, James, what do we have? I ask because Christopher, who's read the file and could have shared already, seems reluctant to hog the information spotlight."

"I just thought you'd like to read the file," Christopher snapped, gracing me with Patented Glare #1. "The rest of us already have."

"I haven't," Chuckie said.

"Me, either," Tim added. "Some of us don't get to read at hyperspeed no matter how many times we ask."

"It's pretty much what Kitty said Eugene told her," Reader said. "Lots of buttering up of the operative, though. 'Your intelligence and dedication to country' and all that jazz. I can understand how someone could believe the robot theory, though. There's full schematics in here."

"Are we lucky enough that they match what we know of the androids?" I asked, fully expecting that we wouldn't be lucky.

"No," Ravi said. I was currently batting a thousand on my expectations, go me. "We've already run this information against what we have on the androids, and the super-soldiers. If these things are real, and with the way things go, I'd never suggest we assume they aren't, they're a different breed."

"Better, worse, or just different?"

"Can't tell without a full structural analysis, which we haven't had time to do yet," Omega Red said. "Not sure that they're real, though, Kitty."

"But you'll keep at it, right, Yuri?"

"Right, because I know that tone of voice of yours, and I don't like being kicked."

"Yuri, you are so much smarter than Eddy."

"I've been telling you that for years."

"Better looking, too." Take that, Stryker.

"*Anyway*," Reader said, "I can see how someone with no real background in espionage, science, or the military could believe this. What's still hard to swallow is the way he got this information."

"I think it's time to visit Pia Ryan. Chuckie, your thoughts?"

"I want to investigate her and her department again, first. I investigated them when you were in Florida. But we were treading on Internal Affairs' territory, so I had to be careful."

"Don't you still?" Jeff asked.

Chuckie looked around the room. "Not nearly as much, no."

"Hacker International now work for us, Jeff. Therefore, they're hacking into the C.I.A. illegally, but it's not authorized by the military or by Chuckie. It's going to be authorized by me."

"Why you?" Stryker asked.

"Because I'm the ambassador now, no co-anything. So,

make it so or make your reservations at the nearest Best Western."

"She's even meaner than she used to be," Henry muttered under his breath.

"And my hearing's better, too. But don't worry; you did well, so you get to stay. For the moment."

"You know she's not going to kick us out," Ravi said quietly. "We're too useful."

"I'd kick you out in a heartbeat," Jeff said. "And I wouldn't lose any sleep over it. The ambassador's the only reason you're all still here. So, do what she wants or I have another location in mind for you, and it's called the Oak Hill Cemetery."

I looked up at Jeff. "Funny you should mention that place. That's the cemetery where I lost Clarence but found the Dingo."

"Really?" Chuckie asked. "That's interesting."

"Why?"

"Because there are a couple of infamous Confederate Civil War spies who are buried there." He turned to Big George. "Pull a map of the cemetery up."

"Does he actually know everything?" Jeff asked me quietly.

"Pretty much, yeah."

Big George indicated the map was live. "Kitty, can you tell me where you were when Clarence disappeared?" Chuckie asked.

"I think so." Ran everything back through my mind. "About here. Keeping in mind that this map is a drawing, and I was running after Clarence at hyperspeed."

"That's near one of the spy's graves," Big George said.

"That needs checking," Chuckie said. "It could be a long shot, but if someone's got a sense of humor, I could believe they have a hideout around there."

"Clarence doesn't have a sense of humor," Jeff said.

"At all," Christopher added.

"Does this solve our problem?" Amy asked. Everyone looked at her. She shrugged. "Look, I get it, Clarence is somehow alive and well and running around trying to blow us up. We think. But how does that relate to everything else? And if we rush off to the cemetery, does whatever we find there fix our problems?"

"We don't know," I said before anyone else could. "Last night, we were thinking we had the usual three, maybe even five plans, going. Now, I don't know."

"They sure don't feel cohesive," Tim said. "At all."

"Am I right in believing you've told everyone all the details, Ambassador?" Raj asked. Realized he'd been silent this entire time.

"Yes, everyone in the room with us is presumed to be totally trustworthy."

"Good. Then I'd like to ask an important question."

"Go ahead."

"Where is Colonel Hamlin and what are we doing to find him?"

CHAPTER 63

"GOOD QUESTION." It was. "We left Malcolm alone with the good colonel and now Malcolm isn't waking up."

Raj shook his head. "We don't know that Colonel Hamlin is the one who injured Mister Buchanan. Based on the information we have, it was Mister Buchanan who moved the colonel out of the Embassy."

"Right, so, what?" Jeff asked. "You think Buchanan is a traitor?"

"No. I think we haven't asked a very important question — why did Mister Buchanan feel it was safer to have Colonel Hamlin in the tunnels than in the Embassy? Or, to put it another way, who was Mister Buchanan trying to protect? The colonel, himself, or you, Ambassador?"

"Why me?"

"Because your safety is his sole and entire job," Chuckie answered. "Your mother put her best and most highly trained operative onto you, Kitty. She gave me the full details once he was exposed to us as P.T.C.U. He's worked all over the world. He's more skilled than I am. So, while anyone can lose concentration and anyone can slip up, Buchanan's about the last one out of all of us to do either."

"You make him sound like he walks on water," Jeff said.

Chuckie shot Jeff a look I could only think of as a combination of long-suffering and fed up. "Feel free to check your jealousy at the door on this one. We're talking about someone who is expected to be the last man standing, and he's expected to be standing in front of your wife and child. He's down, without a mark on him, and Raj is right. We've been so distracted by everything else, we're not asking what the hell happened to the person he was last with."

"We've reviewed all the feeds from the tunnels," Omega Red said. "No signs of anyone in them, at any time. And before anyone makes a comment, I have ways of seeing things, I just see them differently than any of you."

"No one's trying to pick on the blind guy, Yuri, cool your jets. So, we have no visuals of Malcolm or Colonel Hamlin in the tunnels at all?"

"None," Big George said. "We didn't expect to catch any of Christopher, because he was moving at hyperspeed. However, we should have seen Mister Buchanan, even though he was hidden from the camera feeds where Christopher found him. But to get him there, someone would have had to pass one of the cameras."

"Someone disabled all the camera feeds?"

"No. They're all working."

"Have you checked for tampering?" Chuckie asked. "Because that seems impossible. Even if we say that Clarence showed up and overpowered Buchanan and Hamlin, which we know he could, they should have been on the feeds when they left the Embassy's basement elevator."

"Unless . . . I told Hamlin to tell Malcolm everything. Let's say he did. Immediately after that, Malcolm now wants to get Hamlin out of the Embassy. Why? Either Hamlin's a threat to us, or there's a threat to Hamlin here, and Malcolm believes Hamlin needs to be protected."

"Okay, all that makes sense," Chuckie said. "He told Walter they were going into the tunnels."

"Right. Why? Why tell Walter that? He didn't ask Walter to let me know they were going into the tunnels. In fact, he made Walter think that I already knew."

"To have Walter undo the shielding?" Raj suggested.

"Maybe. If it was on at the time."

"It was."

"Okay, but we have nothing that shows that anyone left the elevator. The cameras aren't focused on the elevator; they're focused on the tunnels. Because we know who's coming out of the elevator and that's someone with access to our Embassy."

"Where are you going with this?" Jeff asked.

"I'm trying to think like Malcolm." Stryker snorted. "Eddy, I'm just saying, I'm going to kick you *so* hard, when you least expect it. Anyway, Malcolm has Doctor Strange powers. If he doesn't want you to see him, you don't see him. He comes and goes like the wind. And yet, he told Walter where he was going."

"Why are you so shocked by that?" Reader asked.

"Dude, think. We've been all over the Embassy and the Zoo. Have we checked in with Walter? Has even one of us told Walter where we were? No. We assume that Walter is monitoring and will alert us if necessary and unless we need him, we leave him alone to do his job."

"You think Walter's the traitor?" Jeff asked, sounding like he was hoping I was going to say no.

"No. I think that Walter is very dedicated and that he was focused pretty much a hundred percent on the party. And I'm sure Malcolm knew he would be. However, Walter could stop worrying about the basement if Malcolm's told him that he's leaving it and going out the tunnels. Walter can turn all his attention to the Zoo, which is where everyone *other* than Malcolm and Hamlin are."

Raj looked at me. "You don't think they ever went into the tunnels, do you?"

"No, I don't. I think Malcolm told Walter they were going into the tunnels so that Walter's attention would go back onto everyone else. Then I think they walked out of the basement. The question is, did they walk out the front door, or did they go over to the Zoo?"

"Why would they do either?" Jeff asked.

"Front door would be to get Hamlin away from us or to a safe house. Zoo would be to have Hamlin identify someone Malcolm felt was at the party. Richard, does the shielding keep us in or just others out?"

"Others out. Our shields are set up to allow anyone inside to exit, so the shields can't be used to trap. And they've always been that way, but Gladys had a very focused team improve them after Operation Confusion."

"I love you, Richard, I just have to say."

"Again," Jeff said. "Why does it make you so happy that he uses those names?"

"Because I'm the only one," White replied. He winked at me. "I like to support my partner."

"Why would Buchanan risk it?" Tim asked, presumably to get us back on track. "Especially with Clarence and the assassins around?"

It had to be said. I didn't want to, but I had to. "I never told Malcolm about the Dingo, and he didn't believe that Clarence was back from the dead. As far as Malcolm knew, our only issue of the day was the appearance of Colonel Hamlin."

"So the question is, where did Mister Buchanan actually go?" Raj asked. "I agree with the ambassador—it seems unlikely he went into the tunnels."

"Well, Christopher found him in the tunnels under the Gaultier Research facility," Amy said. "I'd say it's a good bet he went there."

"How?" Christopher asked. "It's miles away."

"We have these newfangled things called cars, and Malcolm has one. He got into his car and drove. So, the question is—did he drive Hamlin somewhere first, or did he take Hamlin with him?"

"Why does that matter?" Christopher asked.

"It matters because if he took Hamlin somewhere first, then we have a chance of finding Hamlin alive and well. And if he took Hamlin with him, we have a good chance of never finding Colonel Marvin Hamlin alive again."

CHAPTER 64

"ALL THAT'S GREAT," Jeff said. "But we've used up most of our free time, and I still have no idea what was going on with Eugene, and I read the materials. And who but a moron would believe that someone who works for the C.I.A. would 'accidentally' receive a package addressed to someone who has no connection to the C.I.A. other than knowing a couple people who work there?"

"Chuckie, I've never met Pia Ryan. Is she pretty?"

He shrugged. "She's attractive enough." He jerked. "Oh. Yeah, I could see it."

"See what?" Jeff asked.

"Eugene lost his mistress when Nathalie confessed to Edmund, remember? So, maybe he was looking for another one."

"I can't believe that guy was a player," Gower said. "My brother, I get it. But I've met Eugene. He's not exactly what I think you, or anyone else, would consider hot, Kitty."

"He wasn't," Amy confirmed. "He wasn't hideous, but he wasn't going to have to worry about making *People*'s Sexiest Man Alive spread. Ever."

"No, but Nathalie told me he was more man than Edmund. I'm betting that means Eugene was either hung or he'd learned some moves to make up for his lack of external appeal. At any rate, women talk, and I'm just betting that Nathalie slipped up and told someone, Marcia Kramer, probably, who she'd been doing the deed with. Once it was over, I mean. And that means Pia probably knows, because I doubt Marcia could keep something that juicy to herself."

"I can buy him looking for another mistress," Amy agreed. "Just because you're a loser doesn't mean you don't think you're awesome on a stick."

"And maybe he found one," Reader said. "Because I can buy that a lot more easily. But why lie to you about it?"

"Because Kitty's never forgiven him for using her as his cover for adultery," Jeff answered. "I've caught up," he added to me with a grin. "There is no way in the world Eugene was going to tell Kitty that he got this information from Pia because they were sleeping together."

Reader nodded. "Makes sense. He'd just murdered someone in front of her; telling her that he was cheating on Lydia again would have only made her angrier, and he was trying to convince her that he was doing this for God and Country."

"Okay, so Pia recruited Eugene using one of the oldest recruitment techniques in the book. Meaning, Chuckie, that it might be time to call Internal Affairs."

"Not yet. I want a full workup done on her and her department, as far back as you can go," he told Stryker. "Do it in a way it can't be traced. And before you whine, I realize that will take longer. I also realize it won't take as long as you want to pretend it will."

"You know, I'm late on my deadline," Stryker muttered as he started typing furiously.

"Look at it as getting new plot ideas, Eddy."

"Just kick me after I turn in my next manuscript, okay, Kitty?"

"I make no promises. I'm going to have Raj read your manuscript before you send it in, just in case you've decided to add a female character and make her an unflattering version of me."

"Focus," Tim said. "Jeff's right. We have only a few more minutes before we have to head to the Capitol, and I know you're going to have to drill those two Amazons on how to behave, and I guarantee that'll take more than a minute."

"Oh, yes, sir. So, what do we focus on? We're kind of spoilt for choice."

"I want teams assigned," Jeff said. "We have enough people who are all capable." He looked at Reader. "If that's okay with you, James."

Reader grinned. "You're allowed to make decisions,

Representative Martini. And I agree. However, regardless of anything else, our biggest concern is protecting you. You've already been attacked with intent to kill. If Vance's theory is correct, then you're a target just by being in the House. If Kitty's 'assassin's revenge' theory is correct, you're a target there, too."

"Yeah," Tim said slowly. "Because Kitty killed that guy's wife, right? So maybe he wants to kill her husband to make her suffer."

"Maybe he does, but let me remind all of you of a very important point—I didn't kill Bernie. Malcolm did."

"But he's not dead," Chuckie pointed out. "So I have to lean on the side that says Buchanan was hit by someone other than the assassins."

"So who goes where?" I asked.

"Paul and I have to be with you," Reader said. "Reynolds, too. So, Tim, that's going to put you and Airborne on one of the other teams. Christopher, you'll head the other one. Who wants to hunt assassins and who wants to determine if Buchanan stashed Colonel Hamlin somewhere?"

"Put Christopher and a team of A-Cs on the search for the assassins," I said, before the others could reply. "We're safer with people who can move at hyperspeed going after them, because while I don't think the Dingo intends to harm anyone I like, if he feels threatened, I'm sure that concern will go out the window. And Raul has no such compunctions."

"I can agree with that," Christopher said. "So, who's with me? Dad? Raj?"

They both nodded. "Take the Barones, too," Chuckie said. "That gives you a fully trained Field team along."

"Amy stays with us or works a different angle," Jeff said. "Only A-Cs for this." Christopher nodded.

"I'll stay here and keep these guys working on the Pia angle and anything else you have them working on," Amy said. "I want to dig deeper into what's going on inside the company I'm trying to reclaim, and that way, you have me here as point."

"Be sure to be looking for other potential patsies," Reader said. "The information you found indicates that Eugene might not have been the only one contacted." He handed the file to Chuckie, who started speed-reading it.

My phone beeped. "Officer Melville's checked in. He says that he couldn't find anyone named Dier on the rosters, and he checked not only D.C. but all the surrounding counties, he says that's why it took him so long to reply. There are a couple of officers named Reid out there, and he's running backgrounds on them now."

"Does Airborne search for Hamlin or search for the Dier-Reid people?" Tim asked.

"Melville just offered to start a full search. Impersonating an officer is a big offense. So, I've told him to coordinate with you, Tim, if I'm not available. Amy, make sure that Hacker International here stays on the Leventhal Reid angles, too, in their research."

"We're in the room, Kitty," Stryker said.

"I'm fully aware, Eddy. Okay, Tim, that leaves Airborne with the hunt for Colonel Hamlin."

Tim nodded. "I'll call your mother and Kevin and see if they have any idea where Buchanan lives, if he has safe houses, and, if so, where they are. Can we ask for help with any of this? Because if your mother and Kevin have no idea, or those are dead ends, all I can come up with is going door-to-door."

Looked at Chuckie. "The Middle Eastern Contingent and/or Romania's New KGB?"

Chuckie heaved a sigh. "They fall under the 'not sure we can trust them' category. Do we want to take the time to revise that now?"

"Ask my mom," I told Tim. "If she thinks they're okay, add them in."

"I see we do." Chuckie's sarcasm knob was at eleven.

"Dude, you're trustworthy and Mom is trustworthy. Let's just assume that you both know what you're talking about when it comes to who to trust and who to figure is a lying sack of excrement."

"Time's up," Gower said. "We have about ten minutes to get everyone over to the Capitol and get Jeff sworn in."

"Let's roll, people," Jeff said.

Reader and I looked at each other. "He sounds so street when he says that," Reader said with a grin.

"Yeah. Let's all go keep it gangsta and be sure we shoot the other guys before they shoot us."

CHAPTER 65

THE OTHERS HEADED DOWNSTAIRS. I left the brief-case from Reader with Amy and the hackers, but told them not to go through it until I was back. For whatever reason, I wanted to be there when we went through everything. It was a gut thing, so I didn't argue with myself.

Headed to our rooms to grab Jeff's new trench and fedora and my coat. Took a moment while I gathered these to relax and try to center myself. This wasn't one of my go-to skills. When it came to focusing on the Inner Me, I was best with doing so in order to rev up to kick butt.

Opened my purse to make sure my Glock and a few clips were in it and saw the stuffed eagle from Reyes' office. Decided it had seen enough action and put it with the brief-case. As I did I noted that it was a stuffed hand puppet. "I'm going to keep this, if it's okay with you, Santiago," I said softly. "I can play with it with Jamie and that way we have something of you with us always."

Eagle out, extra clips in, no Poofs at all. "Poofies? Any Poofies?" Nary a mew or a whiff of a bundle of cuteness. Hoped this wasn't indicating bad news. "Peregrines able to report, please assemble."

Harold appeared. And only Harold.

"Bruno's not back?"

Got some cawing, ground scratching, and head shaking. Bruno was still on the case, being supported by a lot of Poofs. The rest of the Poofs, along with all the female Peregrines, were guarding Jamie and the kids. The male Peregrines were stationed strategically throughout the complex. Harold, however, was going to come along and fill in for Bruno, in case someone again tried to kill Jeff or me.

"You'll be in stealth mode?" I asked as I gave him a nice scritchy-scratch between his wings.

Affirmative. Harold disappeared from view. I only knew he was there because I was touching him.

"Super. Going to do my best to forget you're there. I'm getting the impression that's how all of you prefer it."

Harold squawked his approval about me being totally on board with Peregrine Thought Patterns. Thusly armed and accompanied, I headed downstairs. Time was of the essence, so I used hyperspeed.

Checked the first floor, but found no one, which wasn't too surprising. Was all kinds of proud of how well I was doing with the control, as I headed down to the basement.

Fortunately Jeff was waiting at the bottom of the stairs and he caught and stopped me from barreling right through him and into everyone else and the wall. Clearly I'd self-congratulated a little prematurely.

Jeff chuckled. "I'm not wearing the hat and coat right now, we're going via gate."

"I still want them along."

"Whatever makes you happy, baby."

Everyone leaving the Embassy was going via the gate, so pretty much everyone in the Embassy was down here. "Doreen and Irving are meeting you there," Christopher said. "She just called me. Naomi and Abigail are staying with the kids at the Pontifex's Residence." He grimaced. "Naomi's using the time to figure out which kids will be doing what at her wedding."

"Good use of time. I guess. Is Kevin still there, too?"

He nodded. "And Michael's there now, also. Caroline's feeling better and she had to work. Gladys is there, too, as is your father."

"Works for me."

White was manning the gate controls, while Gower explained how gate transferences worked in layman's terms and how they should be considered highly classified information in strictest terms. Vance was vibrating with excitement, Nathalie and Brewer looked concerned but game to try, and Rahmi and Rhee seemed relieved to see me. Pulled them aside.

"Okay, girls, you two are visiting dignitaries. You can identify as princesses, but that's it. No sharing what planet you're from, who your mother is, and so on. You are coming along to be seen but not heard." They both nodded. "Good. You're also coming along to put that force field of yours around Jeff. Someone's already tried to kill my husband today and I don't want anyone else to try or, worse, succeed."

Rahmi nodded. "Our mother said you protected the men. We will follow your lead."

"But where is the Great Tito?" Rhee asked without any form of guile, as Reader took the lead and stepped through the gate.

"Excuse me?"

"We expected that the Great Tito would be going to protect you and your . . . husband," Rahmi said, trying out the word as if she'd never heard it before. Maybe she hadn't.

"Was the Great Tito killed in battle?" Rhee asked politely, radiating sympathy.

"Ah, no. The Great Tito is a doctor. Our doctor. On staff. He still kicks butt when needed, though." The princesses looked shocked and sort of horrified. "He's a great doctor."

"I'm sure he is." Rahmi looked incredibly disappointed. Rhee looked as if she might burst into tears. Clearly meeting Tito had been top of their list of Awesome Things To Do On Earth.

"He's, ah, guarding one of our warriors who was felled in battle. You two can meet him later, when we're back. Would you, ah, like that?"

Both princesses brightened up immeasurably. "Oh, yes, please!" Rhee said. Rahmi nudged her, no doubt due to her excessive enthusiasm.

"If it would please the Great Tito to meet *us*," Rahmi said, "we would be incredibly honored."

"I'm sure it'll make his day." Tito would probably prefer that someone get him enough information to be able to cure Buchanan, but that didn't seem diplomatic to share right now.

Vance and the Brewers were through. We sent Rahmi, then Gower, then Rhee, so the princesses could flank him, so to speak, with stern admonitions from me that Gower was also to be protected. Chuckie was next, then Len. Jeff and I were next, with Kyle bringing up the rear.

"Uncle Richard, alter for two, please," Jeff said as he swung me up into his arms.

"It's not exactly a professional look," Christopher shared.

"Don't care. I don't want this job, my wife had to watch me be gunned down in the street in front of her, and we're going through like this or we're not going."

"What Jeff said. Double. Good luck to everyone else and please be careful. Christopher, your dad's a better agent than you are, which is not actually an insult, so I'd listen to him while your team's out on Assassin Patrol. Mister White, call if you need me."

With that I buried my face in Jeff's neck and prepared to get sick to my stomach.

CHAPTER 66

SINCE DAY ONE with Centaurion Division, gates had been the bane of my existence. Getting A-C powers hadn't changed that, either. The gates could move you thousands of miles in seconds. And it felt like it.

As Jeff stepped us through, time both sped up and slowed down, and the two met in my stomach. It was lucky that gate transfers were over fast, though they never felt fast to me, because too much time in this state meant what we'd be doing was watching me barf for real, probably on the nearest congressman.

But the horror stopped and I pulled my head out of Jeff's neck. We were in a bathroom. Always the way.

"Seriously, we got let out in a bathroom? Here?"

"Easier to explain," Jeff said as he put me down and we walked out of the stall. Len was still here, waiting, and Kyle came out right after us.

"We're going to be explaining why I had a foursome with all of you in here, that's what we're going to be explaining."

Luck was on our side, and the rest of our group had congregated near enough that they were blocking the bathroom door from view. I credited Reader with that move.

"That was interesting," Brewer said. "We have about three minutes to get to the floor of the House."

"Do we all go?" I asked as we all scurried off, Brewer in the lead. I wasn't sure at this point.

"You do, for certain. I'd assume your Pontifex should be there, too. The others?" Brewer shrugged. "You can get away with a lot by claiming that it's your alien ways."

Rahmi caught up to me. "We can guard from a distance," she said in my ear. "So if we are not to be nearby, we can still assist."

"Awesome, thanks. Take the rear with Kyle right now, then, please, and thank you. Only attack if someone is pointing a gun or another projectile weapon at anyone in our group. And be sure it's really a weapon."

The Capitol was a beautiful building, but as with so many beautiful buildings I got to visit, my focus wasn't on getting to enjoy the architecture or the artwork—my focus was on keeping me and my team alive.

"Chuckie, who goes down on the floor besides Jeff, me, and Paul?"

"I think, under the circumstances, Representative Brewer and his wife should."

Looked at Chuckie's expression. His poker face was on. Now wasn't the time to ask if he wanted Brewer down there for a political reason or because I thought Brewer was a target and therefore would take a bullet intended for Jeff.

Brewer looked incredibly pleased. "Only if you and Jeff think it's appropriate."

"If Chuck says it's alright, then it's great with me," Jeff said pleasantly.

Managed not to swallow my tongue with the shock of Jeff being totally reasonable and not arguing with what Chuckie suggested. Figured Jeff was either picking up Chuckie's emotions or didn't want to have a fight with anyone right now. Or both.

"Who else?" I managed to ask without sounding shocked out of my mind.

"Reader is the Pontifex's husband, so he makes sense. I don't, so I'm going to stay with the others. We'll be spread out. Vance will stay with us," Chuckie added as Vance opened his mouth. "His husband isn't a representative nor a religious leader."

"What about Doreen and Irving?"

Doreen shook her head. "This isn't a diplomatic thing. We're here to witness and show support, but I think we should be with Chuck and the others."

Irving nodded. "We'll have a better view of the room, too. Just in case."

"In case?"

Doreen and Irving exchanged a look. "You are aware that we know that someone tried to kill Jeff earlier today, aren't you?" Doreen asked carefully.

"How did you know? I'm not asking because I wanted to hide the information, but how you found out might be key."

Doreen shrugged. "We saw it on the news. Thankfully the kids were in the other room, because I think Jamie would have comprehended what we saw."

"Huh. So, no one announced that Eugene murdered Santiago and then was shot to death inside a SWAT van, but an unsuccessful assassination attempt made the news. Interesting."

"There's a lot more going on, isn't there?" Irving asked quietly.

"Yeah, there is. We just haven't had time to fill you guys in." Or time to determine if they were totally trustworthy.

Doreen gave me a long look. She stepped close to me. "I don't blame you for wondering," she said in a very low voice.

"Wondering?"

"If you can trust me. They were my parents, I was an only child, I could resent what happened to them. But I don't. Just like Amy doesn't. We talk about it a lot, when she and I can get away and be alone, or when one of us wonders why we got stuck with such terrible parents. But when you see your parent for the evil being they truly are, it becomes hard to continue to love them."

"I know. I'm still sorry about it." I wasn't sorry we'd killed the Colemans. I was sorry that Doreen lost her parents.

Doreen hugged me. "Don't be. My parents made their choices. I made mine. I chose you, Kitty, and what you believe in and stand for. And I chose you a long time ago. If you don't feel safe filling us in on what's going on, I won't be hurt. But if you want or need to, I promise you, you can trust us to do whatever you need."

"You're the best, Doreen, thanks," I said as I hugged her back.

"We need to move," Brewer said as Doreen and I broke apart. Len took our coats and Jeff's fedora, then the others went up to the balcony area.

"Onward?" Jeff asked. He sounded a little nervous.

"Yes." Brewer smiled as he opened the door. "It's showtime, Representative Martini. Enjoy the moment."

CHAPTER 67

OUR MUCH SMALLER group of six entered the big auditorium that was the Floor of the House of Representatives. It reminded me a lot of the giant classrooms I'd
been in in college, if they'd had incredibly cushy seats and
been covered in nice carpet, wood paneling, and pictures of
former U.S. politicians and heroes.

We headed down to what Brewer said was called the
Well of the House, which was in front of the Speaker and
other bigwigs' seats, with the main body of the House sitting
in a semicircle going up.

The place was packed, though there were a few empty
seats here and there. Presumed they were the seats of the
dead representatives, because it looked like anyone else
with a pulse was in attendance.

Brewer and Nathalie led the way. "The Senate's here," he
said quietly as they stepped past us. "That's why the balcony
is so packed. No wonder they wouldn't let Jeff put this off."

Took Jeff's arm as we followed them, Reader and Gower
behind us. "I'm getting stage fright."

Jeff chuckled, though it sounded forced. "All you have to
do is stand there and look supportive, sexy, and gorgeous,
baby. You've got the last two covered with ease."

"Flattery will get *you* everywhere. I think all you do is
have to stand there and look presidential and commanding.
You're good at commanding, should be a piece of cake." He
was especially good at commanding in the bedroom, but this
probably wasn't the appropriate time or place to share that.

"Love how you think," Jeff murmured. "And before you ask, all my blocks are up, on the highest levels. I just read the expression on your face. Thanks for focusing us back onto the priorities, baby."

Looked up and around as we strolled on down the aisle. Was fairly sure I spotted Senators Armstrong and McMillan in the balcony audience. They weren't sitting with Senator Kramer. In fact, as I looked around the room and spotted some of the Cabal of Evil in the balcony areas, Armstrong was nowhere near the rest of them. Interesting.

We reached the Well and the Speaker of the House came down from his chair to Put Us At Our Ease. It was clear he was going out of his way to be personable and jolly. I didn't think he came by jolly naturally, but it was nice of him to make the effort.

There were photographers. Noticed them because they started snapping as soon as the Speaker joined us. Realized this was a great way for an enemy to get close.

Examined them as well as I could. Most of them had their cameras up and were flashing pictures. One of them smiled at me and, when I caught his eye, winked. Oliver was here, and I felt oddly better. Not like any of us were safe simply because Mister Joel Oliver was in attendance, but at least someone else on the Floor was on our side.

Things were explained, more to Jeff than to me. I wasn't paying a lot of attention, mostly because I was too busy scanning the room. We'd avoided a lot of security checks by taking the gate, but the assassins I knew or knew of could circumvent those easily. And sure, Rahmi and Rhee felt they could handle the force field, but I hadn't had time to ask them how it really worked. Maybe it couldn't stop projectiles.

"Don't be nervous," Nathalie whispered to me.

"Why are there so many reporters? I thought all the photo ops happened after this, in the Speaker's office or something."

"This is an incredibly historic moment," Nathalie said. "Enjoy it. Your life will change forever, but at the same time, your husband is doing something greater than just paying attention to his own interests."

I nodded. Wasn't the time or place to mention that my husband had spent his entire life doing something greater than just things that would benefit his own interests. Maybe that's why the President had felt it was an easy choice to ask Jeff to take this position. Perhaps the President was right.

There was some discussion about what book Jeff should swear on. Gower said that the Judeo-Christian Bible was a-okay with the A-Cs. This didn't fly for the Speaker, however, seeing as Jeff had to swear or affirm on something he believed and agreed with, at least as near as I could tell.

"Dammit," Reader said under his breath.

"What?"

"Our A-Cs don't have a specific book like we do. They have a set of beliefs they follow that they hand down orally. This shouldn't be a big deal, but I think everyone's jumpy because Jeff's an A-C."

There were a lot of things I could have done. And probably standing back and keeping my mouth shut would have been what Mrs. Darcy Lockwood of The Washington Wife class would have recommended, especially because there were reporters and cameramen in the room and Nathalie had said this was a historic moment, and I knew she was right.

But if that's what Lockwood would have suggested, then I was going to do the exact opposite. And historic events could turn into historic disasters if allowed. Besides, I had two Amazonian Princesses in the audience somewhere to continue to impress. Time to cowgirl up and channel Mom.

Stood up straight and stepped up next to Jeff. "Excuse me, I can't help but note that we're fretting about what book Jeff swears on?"

"Ah, yes, Missus Martini," the Speaker said, seeming shocked that I was speaking. Well, no time like the present for him to learn.

"That's Ambassador Martini, Mister Speaker. I'll thank you to remember that in the future, we're a little touchy about titles. However, we're not nearly as touchy about religious texts. I happen to be a Jewish-Catholic mix and since Representative Martini is my husband, and also since our Supreme Pontifex, the religious leader of every A-C on Earth, has said the Bible is just fine by us, use the Bible. Now. Or you can explain to the President why you've given me another reason to get touchy about how the U.S. government is treating my husband and people."

The Speaker stared at me. Everyone was quiet for a moment. Then he nodded. "Well put, Ambassador, thank you."

I nodded and stepped back into my Good Wifely Place. The Speaker went on with his explanations to Jeff of what was going to happen.

"I love watching you work," Reader said out of the side of his mouth.

"Dude, stay quiet," I replied in the same way. "If I release the Inner Hyena I think it'll ruin the effect."

The Speaker nodded to Jeff and held the Bible in his hand. Jeff put his left hand on the Bible and raised his right. Gower stood between them, a little back, giving his blessing by overseeing this event, as was the A-C requirement for this kind of thing. He looked solemn, but also proud.

Jeff looked over at Gower, who smiled and nodded. I'd seen White do the same when he was Pontifex. Jeff nodded and when he turned back to the Speaker, he looked confident, resolved, and also proud.

And all of a sudden this went from being something that we were worried about and an inconvenience to a moment in time I knew I would always remember because my husband was about to take a position of very public importance.

Jeff looked the part, too. He was a natural leader, of course, and he radiated the same confidence he had when he was the Head of Field. The way the lights hit him made him almost glow.

Slid my arm through Reader's. He patted my hand. Found myself wishing that we hadn't sent Christopher and White and all the others elsewhere—this was a moment they wouldn't have with us, with Jeff. I suddenly realized why everyone's families came to a swearing-in like this in full force.

The cameras snapped like crazy. Jeff was going to make the front page of every paper in the world that had anyone who wasn't totally blind in charge. Because he looked almost breathtakingly beautiful, solemn, and inspiring—like you want your elected officials to look but they so rarely did.

The Speaker cleared his throat. "Do you, Jeffrey Stuart Martini, accept this position representing the great state of New Mexico's Second District and do you understand that which you are accepting?"

Jeff nodded. "I do solemnly swear that I will support and defend the Constitution of the United States against all enemies, foreign and domestic; that I will bear true faith and allegiance to the same; that I take this obligation freely, without any mental reservation or purpose of evasion; and that I will well and faithfully discharge the duties of the office on which I am about to enter: So help me God."

Jeff lowered his hand and the Speaker shook it, while they both smiled and Jeff got a standing ovation. I clapped too—it helped me focus on something besides blinking back tears.

CHAPTER 68

NOTHING MUCH OF importance happened once the ceremony was over. We were all taken to the Speaker's office and a tonnage of pictures were taken.

Oliver joined us here, of course. "You look a little, oh, disappointed," he said to me while Jeff took yet another couple hundred pictures with various politicians.

"Long story, but some of Jeff's closest family weren't here. I hadn't realized that they should have been, either."

"Not to worry. I took video of the entire event. I also had three other *World Weekly News* cameramen with me, so if one video didn't come out right, the others will."

"MJO, you rock the awesomeness. It won't make up for no pictures of them with Jeff, though."

"We all have sacrifices to make. Speaking of which, pictures and sacrifices both, I believe you're up." Oliver escorted me to Jeff and the next round of Picture Frenzy started. After fifteen minutes I hoped my smile didn't look too fake or plastered on. After another fifteen minutes I didn't care if it looked fake—I was far more worried that I'd never be able to close my mouth again.

But finally it ended. The Speaker gave Jeff a stack of bills, with instructions to read them all, because they were going to be going to vote in the first week of January.

"Should have brought a briefcase," Jeff said as we and our ever-growing entourage left the Speaker's office.

"I left it at home, sorry."

Chuckie joined us, Cliff in tow. "Nicely done."

"Went well," Cliff agreed. "So, how are you guys getting home? You can't go the same way you came."

This was true. We had a lot of people with us now, and more than that, we had a lot of reporters around.

"We'll call for the limos." Of course, our drivers were here with us or out hunting for Colonel Hamlin. "Or, you know, maybe not."

Jeff took my coat from Len and helped me into it. "We'll take a cab. Well, a fleet of cabs," he added with a laugh as he put his coat and hat on.

Managed not to say that he should have worn the hat and trench while being sworn in, too. This look didn't need to be shared with the world—this look belonged to *me*, and I was going to be both extravagant in its use and miserly in who else got to enjoy it. "I'm a little nervous about being outside, Jeff."

"Who can blame you?" Cliff asked. "I drove over here. Why don't I drop at least the two of you and Chuck at the Embassy?" He grinned. "Besides, I just got a new car and I really want to show it off."

"Well, how can we refuse an offer like that?" Jeff asked. "But what about everyone else?"

Chuckie shrugged. "If you leave," he said quietly, "the interesting person leaves, the rest can go home by more mundane means."

Oliver was near us and he nodded. "I and the rest will follow the four of you. Guaranteed."

"Then that's the plan," Cliff said. "If that's okay with you, Congressman."

Jeff shook his head. "Jeff, unless we have to be formal for some reason now."

"Nope, just teasing you. You ready to go?"

"Let me tell the others what we're doing first." Extracted myself and went to Gower, who was the closest. Explained the plan. "So, once we're gone, you can get everyone else home."

"Sounds like a good plan, Kitty." He hugged me. "Thanks for handling the situation on the Floor."

"Oh, I figured you'd win eventually, but why waste everyone's time and your patience? Are you going to the Embassy or to your Residence?"

"Residence. I want to make sure everyone's fine there."

He grinned. "And Uncles Paul and James want a little Jamie-Katt time."

"You had her last night."

"Not really. By the time we got home, all the kids were in bed and had been for hours. I'd offer to keep her overnight with us again, but I'd imagine you two would like to see your daughter."

"Yeah. Should we have had her here?"

"No," Reader said as he joined us. "Unless you were desperate for a photo op."

"We absolutely were not. I'm just feeling guilty about us not having everyone here."

Gower shook his head. "Everyone for us means *everyone*. We care about that for weddings much more than for appointments like this."

"Okay, I'll trust you on that one. What are we going to do about Vance and the Brewers?"

"Escort them home, unless you want them back at the Embassy," Reader said.

"I don't know. Jeff just got assigned homework by the Speaker of the House and I'm feeling tired from the last couple of days. But I think we need to have guards on them, Edmund Brewer in particular."

"We'll handle it," Reader said. "You get going, your ride looks impatient."

Cliff didn't actually look impatient, but I could tell that he, Chuckie, and Jeff were ready to go. I hurried over to Vance and the Brewers. "I think Jeff and I are hitching a ride with Cliff. Hopefully that means the paparazzi will clear off and leave you guys alone."

Nathalie laughed. "It makes me nostalgic. But do you want us to go back to your Embassy, or would you like to just go home and collapse?"

"Honestly? I'd like to collapse. But I want you guys to be careful. There's been a lot of bad and weird going on."

Brewer nodded. "Let's all get a good night's sleep and we can regroup tomorrow. I'll be happy to help Jeff with the bills. Not that I don't think that he can manage them all on his own, but I had help when I came on and it really does make it easier if you have someone to show you the ropes."

"Absolutely. You know, you've been over to our place,

why don't we go over to yours tomorrow? That way Nathalie can show me her portfolio while you and Jeff work?"

They both beamed at me. Clearly this was a suggestion they liked. I knew without asking that Jeff would like it, too. After all, he'd been trying to have us become friends with this couple for months now.

"It's a date," Nathalie said. "Brunch at our place? Bring your daughter, too, if you want. We don't have children yet but that doesn't mean we don't like them."

"We'll see how she's behaving." Jamie was always pretty darned well-behaved but I wasn't sure how good an idea it was to have her exposed right now. There were assassins and Clarence and probably bears, oh my. "She's had a fun couple of days and may just want to stay home."

"See you around eleven, then?" Brewer asked.

"It's a date. I'll call you if something changes, but otherwise, we'll see you tomorrow." Gave them both hugs, which got photographed, and then trotted back to Jeff.

"I've told the jocks what's going on," he said. "They'll gather anyone else who matters and get them home. They already have the princesses in tow. And the mountain of bills I have to read and form an opinion of in a week."

Had a moment's worry about leaving Rahmi and Rhee unattended and in the care of males, but decided that they'd behaved well so far and there was no time like the present for them to get used to how things here worked.

Cliff led us out of the Capitol building. True to expectations, all the media followed us. It was raining, so I put up my hood. "How far are you?" Chuckie asked.

"I parked on Southwest Drive," Cliff said. "No worries, we're not too far. Can't wait for you to see it, it's great. I haven't been this excited about a car in years."

"So, what kind did you get?" I asked as we walked quickly through the wet. Chuckie didn't care that much about cars and since A-Cs had reflexes that were so good they actually weren't able to safely drive, I was the only other "car person" here.

Cliff grinned. "Toyota RAV Four EV. All electric. It's great. Wanted it in red, but they only make it in white and blue, so I got the blue. Tricked it out with everything extra I could, too."

Spotted a blue car in the near distance. "Is that it?"

"Yeah. And, don't worry about being cold, Kitty. It has the remote engine starter. I can have it running and warm inside before we ever get there."

"I'm not worried about being cold, but if your car can do something about the wet, that'd be great."

He laughed. "Well, I'll get her started and the heat on. That'll help."

As Cliff pulled out his key fob and clicked the button I felt something with feathers slam into me.

So when Cliff's car exploded, I wasn't nearly as surprised as I could have been.

CHAPTER 69

OF COURSE, this didn't mean I wasn't surprised. And I wasn't the only one.

We were close enough to the car that the blast threw all of us back. Sure, I'd had help from Harold, but the men flew backward, too.

We were lucky—because of the angle of the blast in terms of where we were, we were thrown onto grass instead of concrete. This was good in that we were unlikely to be hurt because of the fall. However, it meant we were all covered with mud. The less said about the state of my nice white dress the better.

There were scattered screams and a lot of yelling from the paparazzi. Jeff rolled to and then on top of me. "Kitty, are you okay?"

"Yeah. Harold knocked me back. Are you alright?"

"Yeah, I felt something hit me right before the blast. I'm assuming it was a Peregrine, since it didn't hurt me. We need to get out of here, baby."

"Well, that bomb was intended for Cliff, not us. I think we need to get Cliff out of here."

Chuckie was helping Cliff up. Cliff seemed to be in shock. "I just got that car . . . that's my dream car . . . it does everything and it's good for the environment . . ."

As Jeff helped me up I realized the blast had knocked a lot of the press on their butts, too. "Wow, that was one hell of an explosion. Chuckie, let's get Cliff to the Embassy."

Chuckie nodded and put his arm around Cliff's shoulders. "Come on, buddy. Let's get you out of the rain."

"I have stuff in the car," Cliff said, rather piteously. "I need my stuff."

Looked at the wreckage. "Unless it's fire, fireproof, or improved by being blown up, you don't need it. Let's move, guys."

But we'd been too slow. The press were back on their feet and we were surrounded, fast, with a lot of people shouting questions at us.

In the good old days, we would have just used hyperspeed to get out of this. But we couldn't, because the press wasn't surrounding four random people—they were surrounding four public figures.

They were also shoving in closer and closer. Claustrophobia was going to become an issue, and if anyone shoved me, I had a feeling Jeff's first official act as a representative was going to be to punch someone in the face.

"That's enough!" a man bellowed. The bellower wasn't Jeff; it was Oliver. He didn't bellow as well as Jeff did—no one could match Jeff's bellowing abilities—but he sounded furious and very much in charge. Remembered that Oliver had covered war zones. "You will stop acting like a pack of wild dogs!"

Looked back at the car. Explosions were one of the Dingo's calling cards. Clearly he wasn't aware that we liked Cliff, or else he had a contract that said he didn't care.

The paparazzi started to quiet, but there was still grumbling. "What's wrong with all of you?" Oliver snarled. His voice was projecting, however. "These people need help. At least let them get the hell out of the rain before you barrage them with questions for which we all *know* they have no answers."

"We just want to know who the target was," a woman shouted from the back. Couldn't see her face, but I was pretty sure she was blonde.

"Do you?" Oliver asked. "Perhaps you're all too stupid to put two and two together. I, however, am not stupid, and neither are these people. And we'd all like to get out of the rain."

With that, Oliver reached his hand to me. I took it and grabbed Jeff with my other hand. Jeff grabbed Chuckie, who already had a hold of Cliff. Oliver shoved through the throng and we followed, staying connected.

"The moment the five of us are out of sight, it would be a brilliant choice on the part of Representative Martini to take us to the fastest hyperspeed possible. I'm sure Mister Goodman will vomit the moment we stop, but I believe he's going to do that anyway."

Risked a look behind me. Yeah, Cliff looked kind of green. "MJO, as always, you're the man with the plan. Jeff, did you catch that?"

"Yep. It's going to be hard, because there are a lot of people heading toward us and it's a long way to anything that will provide a legitimate excuse for how we disappeared."

"Jeff's right." Contemplated our options. "We're basically across the street from Rayburn House."

"I like that plan," Jeff said, as he turned to his left and pulled the rest of us along. "I want you all at a run," he said with authority.

Contemplated the options again. I liked these heels. Then again, the Elves seemed to have unlimited access to Armani, Aerosole, and, for all I knew, Converse and Levis. Therefore, I could play Cinderella. Kicked my heels off.

Most sprinters like to run in shoes, but there were a few who preferred to run barefoot. I didn't normally fall into the latter camp, but under the circumstances, I had less chance of slipping or falling behind. And I didn't want to fall behind, because the moment the press had realized we were running, they gave chase.

"Is this really a good idea?" Chuckie shouted as we all ran along. He was keeping Cliff moving, and the shock of the explosion seemed to be wearing off, potentially because Cliff was a really smart guy and it didn't take genius to figure out that someone wanted him dead and that someone could still be around.

"We're running because we're afraid one of the press is the mad bomber," I shouted back. "Trust me, I can spin this."

"You can spin anything," Chuckie agreed. "I just don't know if we can outrun them believably."

"Sure we can," Jeff said, as he headed us directly into the street. Independence Avenue wasn't exactly a side street, and there were plenty of cars. However, there were also sirens. And the screeching of tires as drivers slammed on their brakes to avoid hitting us.

I could feel Jeff using just a little bit of hyperspeed. Not enough to make us go so fast that a human would notice that we were blurry or suddenly disappeared, but enough to maneuver us safely across the street while ensuring no car had to brake so hard and fast that it would be in a wreck.

Safely across, we ran like hell for the doors. Made it inside and into the lobby area. Irene wasn't around. A small favor, because I didn't really want to explain this to anyone. "Let's get to Jeff's office."

Now we went to hyperspeed, the really fast kind. We were inside Jeff's office, with the door locked, in about five seconds.

Took stock while Cliff retched into the toilet. "Wow, we look like refugees. Why is that always somehow our go-to look?"

"No idea," Jeff said as he put his hat onto the filing cabinet and pulled out his phone. "But I'm sick of it. James. Yeah. No, that was really us. Yeah, on TV again so soon, we're just that kind of lucky. No, everyone's okay, but only because Cliff has, well, had some remote starter he was showing off. Yeah. Yeah. You're kidding, really? Fine." He sighed and handed the phone to me. "Coordinate the story with James, will you?"

Took the phone. "This wasn't my fault."

"It's never your fault, girlfriend. Our phones are going to light up like a Christmas tree. What's the official spin?"

"The vehicle belonging to the Head of Special Immigration Services for Homeland Security was blown up right before he, the head of the C.I.A.'s E-T Division, Representative Martini, and Ambassador Katt-Martini could enter it."

"Wow, you're living it up with the titles."

"They matter. The press seemed very antagonistic, we were worried that the bomber was still around or might be disguised as press and egging them on to violence, we saw an opening, and we ran to the safety of Rayburn House. That's the story, and we all need to stick to it."

"It sounds true."

"It is true, which is helpful. So, can you send a car for us?"

"No, that's what I was telling Jeff. The streets are officially closed off due to the car bomb. You're not leaving Rayburn House in a vehicle, at least not any time soon. And if you leave it using hyperspeed, then the press surrounding the building are going to wonder how you disappeared. Aliens are one thing. Aliens who can perform at comic book superhero levels are another. I'd love to keep a few of our secrets actually still secret from the general public."

Heaved a sigh. "Fine. I have other options. Besides, we need to give our statements to the police anyway."

"Keep your eyes open for that suspicious SWAT member, girlfriend. Cliff may have been targeted for something unrelated to us, but I doubt it."

"Same here, since his job is us. Did everyone else get home safely?"

"Yes, we all used a floater gate to the Embassy, then sent those who don't live here home by limo. Len and Kyle got back just as the news lit up with your latest exploits."

"I say again—"

"I know. It wasn't your fault. Keep me posted, going to try to handle things. Oh, and I'm going to assume Jamie's spending the night again."

"I miss my daughter."

"We have Field agents keeping the press away from the Pontifex's residence. I doubt the Embassy is going to be that lucky."

"You and Paul just want to hog her."

"Dang. I was too obvious."

"Yes, you were. We'll discuss it when we see what time we get home."

"I'll ensure she's in bed before then."

"So it's a race. Got it. Get someone to install a gate in the bathroom of Jeff's office here, will you?"

"Oh, yes, ma'am, I'll get right on that. But for now, you stay put and we'll figure out a very normal way to get you all home."

"You take the fun out of everything these days, did you know that?"

"Yeah. There's a whole manual about how to do it, too. I'll read it to you sometime."

We hung up and I contemplated who to call. Officer Melville seemed like a logical choice, and yet there was going to be a lot of police bureaucracy to get through. Decided we had a lot of important people in the room, and dialed a different number. She answered on the first ring.

"Kitten, are you and Jeff okay?"

"Yeah, Mom, we are. Look, someone blew up Cliff's car right before he could give us and Chuckie a ride. And it just dawned on me that you and Dad weren't at Jeff's swearing-in ceremony and I'm sure that's because I didn't tell you about it or ask you to be there, and I'm sorry."

Mom sighed. "We were there, kitten. So was the President. So were Alfred and Lucinda, who are back home now. We weren't visible from the Floor, but we were all there. Nice fix on the whole religious text issue, by the way. But that's not why you called. You called because, if my television is correct, Cliff's car blew up, you were all surrounded by paparazzi, and for some reason, the four of you, assisted by your personal reporter, decided to make a run for it."

"We're in Jeff's office at Rayburn House and the press isn't. I'm calling that a win. However, James says he can't get cars to us, and using a floater gate doesn't seem like a good idea. I had to lose my shoes, we're all wet and muddy, Cliff's out his brand-new car, and we're all exhausted. I want to go home. I don't care which home that might be, by the way, but I want to go to a place I have, at least at one time in my life, called home."

"Despite your strong hint, Tim and Alicia don't need you barging into our house."

"That wasn't what I was going for, though it'd be an acceptable option. James said the police have the streets blocked off, and the press are at the gates, so to speak. I'd really like someone, anyone, my mother for preference, to come get us out of this."

"I'm sure you would, kitten."

There was something in Mom's tone that made me think for a moment. She'd been with the President at the Capitol building, watching Jeff get sworn in. That event hadn't been all that long ago. Meaning she was with the President right now. Meaning that she couldn't do much to help her daughter out of a jam. However, these days, I was more than her daughter. And Mom had mentioned the religious fix for a reason, at least, that was my guess.

However, she was going to need proof that she wasn't pulling strings merely to get her daughter's fat out of the fire one more time. Not a problem, I was good with public speaking.

"Mom, you may want to put me on speaker. I'm putting you on speaker over here."

"Do I really?"

"You do. You really do."

"Okay, I hope you're right." There was a short pause, then Mom's voice came back with a really impressive echo behind it. "You're live with me, the President, and the Joint Chiefs of Staff."

Oh. Good. As Reyes would have said, dinner *and* a show.

CHAPTER 70

THREE OF THE FOUR men in the room looked at me with various degrees of horror in their expressions. But since we were on speaker, none of them could speak, or at least they all had the good sense to remain silent.

Oliver turned on his pocket tape recorder with the look of a man who has been shown what Santa has for him in the sack of goodies and is reveling in the proof that, this year, he was a very, *very* good boy indeed.

Cleared my throat. Time for the official spin. "Mister President, I apologize for interrupting your meeting. However, I'd appreciate some assistance from the P.T.C.U."

"Why is that?" The President had a smooth baritone. Now probably wasn't the time to offer a compliment, though.

"Because I feel that we have, yet again, been the focus of a terrorist attack."

There was a lot of noise in the background. Heard my mother point-blank tell everyone to shut the hell up. Which they all did. My opinion of my mother's pull, which was pretty damned high already, ratcheted up. Either that or she was about to be fired. Went with the rosier outlook.

"Why is that, Ambassador?" Mom asked in her All-Business voice.

"Because the vehicle belonging to Clifford Goodman, the Head of Special Immigration Services for Homeland Security, was blown up right before he, the Head of the C.I.A.'s E-T Division, newly sworn in Representative Martini, and I could enter it. Fortunately for all of us, Mister Goodman chose to show us his brand-new car's remote start function, which is the only reason the four of us are alive at this time."

The murmuring started again, and again Mom shut it down.

"Why did you flee the scene?" Mom asked.

I snorted. Loudly. "The press were incredibly antagonistic, we were worried that the bomber was still around or might be disguised as press and egging them on to violence, we saw an opening, and we ran to the safety of Rayburn House. We now feel unsafe to leave, but if I'm forced to remain in Rayburn House, I'm going to have to assume that the U.S. government actually wanted us herded here for some reason. And, if that's the case, I'm going to have to be offended on behalf of every A-C on the planet. And for those not on the planet as well."

"We are, of course, horrified to hear of this attack, and relieved that all of you seem unharmed," the President said. "However, the United States government had no hand in the car bombing."

Chuckie scribbled something down and handed it to me.

"That's nice to hear. However, until the bombing is investigated—by the F.B.I., I presume, though I would prefer that the P.T.C.U. be the investigating agency, and that is an official, diplomatic request—there's no proof of that, is there? And it's going to take them more than five minutes to examine the remains of the car. In the meantime, we are literally trapped in Rayburn House. I'm requesting assistance to get us safely home to our Embassy."

"We can request a police escort," a different, somewhat familiar voice said. Chuckie scribbled again. Aha, Langston Whitmore, the Secretary of Transportation, was the speaker.

"Secretary Whitmore, terrorists are not the police department's bailiwick. They belong to the C.I.A., but even more so, they belong to the Presidential Terrorism Control Unit. Now, let me be very clear. At this moment, I have two royal emissaries from the most warlike planet in the Alpha Centauri system waiting at the American Centaurion Embassy. They are not overly clear on much, other than that the one person on this planet they are to obey without question happens to be me. Now, I'd like someone there to,

perhaps, brief you on just what one woman from Beta
Twelve is capable of. We'll wait."

"Hello Ambassador Katt-Martini, it's Colonel Franklin."

I liked Franklin a lot, and I wanted to be very sure that
everyone else in the room knew I liked Franklin a lot. "Arthur, how are you? It's been too long since we've had a
visit."

Chuckie grinned and nodded.

"I'm well, and concerned for your safety. I can assure the
rest of those present that just one Beta Twelve warrior
would be capable of destroying a battalion, particularly if
armed with a battle staff."

"They never go out without them." Had no clue if Rahmi
and Rhee were packing battle staffs or not, but that wasn't
important now.

"Two of them, therefore, would present a very real threat
to U.S. security," Franklin said.

Chuckie looked at me sharply. Not to worry, I knew
where this was going.

"Oh, did I give the impression the two princesses were
here for any kind of military action? I'm so sorry, Arthur,
but not to worry. They're here to help celebrate my daughter's first birthday. It's a huge event in the Alpha Centauri
system, particularly for Alpha Four and Beta Twelve. In order to keep a low profile, only the princesses have come. At
this time.

"However, as I'm sure you can understand, I have very
royal guests who are, by now, concerned about my welfare.
They're young, and headstrong, and probably aren't nearly
as well-trained in diplomacy as their mother, the queen,
would like. It wouldn't surprise me if they felt it was incumbent upon them to come and rescue me from this situation,
perhaps to show how dedicated they and the other Alpha
Centauri planets are to those from that system who live on
Earth. And that would be bad for relations, don't you
agree?"

"Absolutely," Franklin said. "And I'm assuming you're
requesting the assistance of the P.T.C.U. because a military
escort could give the wrong impression?"

Changed my mind. I didn't like Franklin; I loved him.
"Exactly, Arthur. But we do want to give our statements to
someone who can actually act on them. Again, we all know

it's unlikely to be the police. And all of us were thrown by the blast—we all need to be examined by our Embassy Physician. The sooner the better."

"Ambassador," Whitmore said, "are you sure you're not requesting the P.T.C.U. simply because you want your mother to come and fix everything for you?"

The jaws of all the men in the room dropped. Yeah, I was also impressed with Whitmore's balls or lunacy, take your pick. Unfortunately for him, I knew a lot about him, potentially more than he realized, and I got this kind of crap from Hacker International all the time.

"Secretary Whitmore, while I'm fully aware that you have a host of unresolved and subjugated Mommy Issues, I'm not pretending to be anything I'm not. That my mother happens to be the most competent woman—and potentially the most competent staff member, period—that the President has working for him is something I'm quite proud of. That you're clearly intimidated by strong women says much more about your character, or lack thereof, than anything about either me or my mother."

"I beg your pardon—" Whitmore started angrily.

"My pardon for your insult is not given, Secretary Whitmore. In fact, I expect an apology, immediately. Or I'm afraid I'm going to have to take your insinuations as an unfriendly act."

Jeff was grinning. Chuckie looked amused in the way he always did when I was doing exactly what he expected and wanted me to do. Cliff looked impressed. Hoped Mom shared their opinions. Oliver, of course, looked like he was holding a winning lottery ticket.

"Apologize. Now." The President didn't sound like he was asking.

"I apologize, Ambassador, for my careless and thoughtless remarks." Whitmore sounded like his teeth were clenched. Figured they probably were.

"We'll have a full team from the P.T.C.U. over to you in just a few minutes, Ambassador," the President said. "Including the Head of the Unit. Again, we want to stress that the United States government neither ordered nor condones any attacks on anyone attached to American Centaurion or Centaurion Division or those who work closely with Centaurion."

"We feel confident that you, Mister President, along with Colonel Franklin and the P.T.C.U., are working for and with us. And thank you for your support."

"We'll be to you shortly, Ambassador," Mom said.

"We'll be waiting."

We both hung up.

Jeff was still grinning. "I told you you'd be great at this job."

"It's growing on me, I have to admit."

"Well," Cliff said. "That was . . . the most high-powered call I've ever been a part of. I really hope I have a job tomorrow."

"You will. Or else I'll get that Unfriendly Act Feeling again."

Cliff shook his head. "I'm amazed Secretary Whitmore was that aggressive with you, especially in that setting. You handled it really well."

I shrugged. "As Wolverine would say, 'These claws? They're adamantium, bub. I only pull 'em out for show. Or, you know, to stick 'em in someone who bothers me.' And Whitmore bothers me."

Chuckie laughed. "And the lesson is, as it always is—never, ever piss off the comics-geek girl."

CHAPTER 71

WE SENT SOME TEXTS and made some calls, so everyone who needed to know was aware of where we were and who we were waiting for.

"How'd you know this was Jeff's office?" Cliff asked once we were all done and still sitting around, waiting for Mom and her team to get here. "I thought you hadn't gone into it earlier today."

Cliff's car had been blown to bits, which meant he was probably out of contention for being the Mastermind, but was definitely in contention for being yet another person in deadly danger. I looked at Chuckie, who shrugged and looked at Jeff, who concentrated. He shrugged. "I think it's okay."

"What's okay?" Cliff asked.

"To tell you what we think is going on," I said.

Cliff put up his hand. "Don't."

"Huh? Why not? You're obviously in danger."

"Yes, and I'm not saying don't protect me. But everything Chuck's told me about how you guys operate means that you're going to be doing things that are, let's be honest, not always within the confines of the law."

Cliff had a point. Jeff and I had searched every office of every dead representative earlier in the day. That was definitely not within the confines of the law. "Maybe. So?"

He shook his head. "So, my job is to keep you guys safe and in line. If you tell me, for example, that you broke into another Embassy to search it for clues, that's a great thing if it saves the day. But it's an illegal thing in every other way. And I'm duty-bound to report that, because that's one of the tenets of my job. Sure I could lie, but I'm not a great liar in the first place, and I don't want to have to lie in the second place."

"Chuckie, um, lies. When he has to."

Cliff laughed and gave Chuckie a gentle, friendly punch in the arm. "Chuck's C.I.A. They're *supposed* to lie. It's pretty much a job requirement."

"Oh, we occasionally tell the truth," Chuckie said.

"Just to keep the rest of us guessing," Cliff replied with a grin. Then he turned back to me. "So, do *not* tell me what you're doing, what you're thinking, and what you're going to do. That way, I have complete deniability, can pass a lie detector test without worry, and you get to keep your positions and hopefully save the day. Everybody wins."

"You're sure? You don't even want to know the high-level theories?"

"Not a one. I trust you guys. Because I know Chuck, and I trust his judgment, and he trusts all of you. I know you're always going to do the right things for the right reasons. I don't want the responsibility of knowing specifics or even generalities, though, unless I'm the last resort. So, until I'm the last resort, keep me out of it, so I can say with complete honesty that, as far as I know, you're being the best boys and girls in the world and not even thinking about putting one little toe out of line."

"Okay, you got it," I said as there was a knock at the door.

Chuckie put his hand up as Jeff moved to get it. "My job." He stood, pulled his gun, and opened the door carefully. "Hi, Angela," he said as he opened the door and holstered his weapon. "Good to see you."

"Good to be seen." Mom strode in. She was alone.

"Where's the rest of your team?"

"Arresting the press. You're going to suffer some nasty attacks for that, by the way."

I shrugged. "And yet, I'll find the will to go on. Besides, Mister Joel Oliver here has the exclusive of exclusives. They'll hate him more."

"Too true," Oliver said.

Mom heaved a sigh. "You were in the room while that

conversation was going on?" Oliver nodded. Mom looked at me. She didn't look pleased. "And you didn't say anything?"

Hoped I wasn't going to get grounded. I was almost thirty, married, with my own child, and an ambassador, but my mother could probably still ground me if she really wanted to. "Nope."

Mom grinned. "That's my girl." She hugged me and it was her breath-stopping bear hug. "Glad you're okay, kitten."

"Me too, Mom. Thanks for coming. Whitmore was right—I did want my mother to come and make things better."

She kissed my cheek. "He's a prick. And he's now your enemy. Remember that."

"I've never actually thought he was my friend."

"But your allegiances are already shifting," Mom reminded me. "And they'll continue to do so the longer you and Jeff are working in D.C. However, no matter what he does or says, that man is your enemy for life now. You humiliated him and threatened to out him to the entire Cabinet and the President and you did it in such a way that *he* had to apologize to *you*. He will never forget or forgive that, so you need to always remember that he's not on your side."

"Got it, I won't forget. You want our statements?"

"At the Embassy. I want to get all of you out of here." She looked around. "Nice office, Jeff. Get a gate in here pronto."

"Already asked James for that, Mom, we're actually ahead of you. Not far ahead, I'm sure, but still, a half-step at least."

Mom rolled her eyes, but didn't say anything. She just ushered us out and down the hall. We took the stairs, Mom going first, Chuckie at the rear.

Exited to find a set of big, black Escalades with tinted windows waiting for us. The six of us got into one, Mom driving, Chuckie taking shotgun. The cars in front and behind ours pulled out when Mom did and they drove in formation all the way to the Embassy.

No one shot at us and, as near as I could tell, no one followed us, either. "Cliff, are you coming back to the Embassy with us?"

"I don't know. Angela, what do you think?"

"I think I want you in some form of protective custody. We can assign operatives to you, as can Centaurion Division, if you'd prefer to stay at home."

"I think I would," Cliff said. He looked at me. "You know why." I nodded; he'd made his position clear.

"I'm going to take them home first," Mom said. "Then we'll get a team assigned to you at the Embassy."

Jeff had his phone out. "I've sent a text to James. He'll have two Field teams waiting to go with your team and escort Cliff home."

"Thanks," Cliff said. "I'd say I don't want to be a bother, but I'm glad to have the protection. I just don't understand why someone wanted to blow up my car, presumably with me in it."

I patted his hand. "That, I promise, we're going to find out."

CHAPTER 72

CHRISTMAS WAS IN TWO DAYS, meaning Jamie's birthday was in two days. I wanted to get this entire Operation, whatever it was, put to bed before then. Just wasn't sure we were going to manage it.

Once Cliff was bundled off, those of us who were muddy changed clothes, the men into yet another version of the Armani Fatigues, even Oliver. The Elves provided me with a black velour sweatsuit. Chose not to argue and hoped they'd learned their lesson about putting me into white.

Then we had a quick meeting, because Reader had re-called our other teams immediately once Cliff's car had exploded. Unfortunately, no one had anything good to report, other than the fact that Dulce was confident they were going to be able to figure out what would cure Buchanan before the year was over.

"I think we all just need to rest," Gower said once everyone's reports of the nothing they'd found were complete. "We've been on edge and running for the past few days, and it's taking its toll."

"I agree," Jeff said. "Reynolds, I want you staying in the Embassy."

"Why?" Chuckie asked.

"Because if someone's after Cliff, then there's a good chance that same someone will be after you," I replied. "Let's keep as many of our people in A-C shielded facilities as we can."

Chuckie shrugged. "Fine. I'll have Kevin bring everyone back."

Dad and Jamie came to the Embassy along with everyone else who'd been over at the Pontifex's Residence. "I'm going to stay in your guest room, if that's okay," Dad said after Jeff and I got our hugs and kisses from our little girl and Reader and Gower gave up suggesting that she was safer at their home.

"That's good with us, Dad." Hey, the rooms were very soundproofed here. "Where is Mom going to be?"

"Working. The President is taking that car bomb very seriously. So, if she's able to come back to sleep, she'll come here, but I wouldn't count on it, kitten."

"No problem, Dad. We're heading to full house territory, and who knows how many more unexpected guests we'll have before this is all through."

Speaking of our most unexpected guests, Rahmi and Rhee were thrilled to meet Jamie, happy to meet Denise and the Gower girls, pleasant enough to the other children, polite and stately to "the husband of the triumphant warrior who shaped the Great Kitty Katt" and, unsurprisingly, rude to Kevin.

Kevin, however, took it in stride. He gave the princesses a formal bow. "Your Highnesses, I'm Kevin Lewis, the Defense Attaché for the American Centaurion Embassy."

Whatever the official title was for Our Guy In Charge of Fighting, those who made fighting their way of life always seemed able to recognize it. Both girls gave Kevin more attention than they'd given any man they'd met yet. Sure, he was tall, very dark, and even more handsome, but I doubted either Rahmi or Rhee was looking to make Denise's marriage rocky. So far as their mother, the other Planetary Council members, and the A-Cs had told me, the Free Women had pretty much done away with men. I was fairly sure they procreated by way of a cloning process of some kind.

Rahmi inclined her head. "You are the one who vanquished the Leader of the Resistance? We had understood it was the Great Tito's victory."

We all stared at her. I recovered quickest. "Ah, no. My husband, Jeff, was the one who, ah, vanquished Kyrellis. I vanquished Moira."

Rhee shook her head. "My sister means he who destroyed the would-be usurper to the Alpha Four throne."

Had to take a couple moments to figure this one out. "Oh. You mean Gregory from Alpha Four?"

"Yes." Rahmi looked at Kevin. "You did not vanquish the Leader?"

"No, your Highness, I did not. That was indeed the, ah, Great Tito's doing."

"Then why did the Great Tito allow you the position of Defense Attaché?" Rhee asked Kevin politely.

"Ah . . ." Kevin looked at me, clearly asking for diplomatic help.

"What did your mother tell you about my mother?" I asked the girls.

"Mother said that your mother trained you and molded you into the triumphant warrior you are," Rahmi said with enthusiasm. "She said your mother was worthy to be a leader of the Free Women. And you as well," she added quickly.

I doubted Renata had felt I had real Amazonian Leadership Potential, but I decided not to question Rahmi's honesty, since she was doing her best to look innocent, and no one I'd ever met from the Alpha Centaurion system could lie very well to humans.

"Well, my mother recommended Kevin for the position he holds within our Embassy. She molded and trained him, too."

"Oh!" both princesses chorused. They also both looked at Kevin with much more interest and admiration than they had before. He wasn't getting full-on hero worship from them, but at least he was no longer a loser to be tolerated. Chose to put that into the win column.

It was past dinnertime, but most of us hadn't eaten. Pierre and the Elves whipped up a nice, easy dinner while we all headed to the group dining room on the second floor. Tito and Nurse Carter, however, requested to have food sent down—neither one of them was willing to leave Buchanan unattended.

When Rahmi and Rhee offered to take the food to the Great Tito, though, I knew something had to be done. Looked at White, who smiled at me and nodded. "I'll take the food down to the infirmary, Missus Martini. And I'll keep Magda-

lena company and send the Great Tito up to have dinner with
all of you."

This offer earned White looks of appreciation from the
princesses. He took trays down as Pierre started to get food
onto the table, with Denise, Abigail, and Amy's help, and
the rest of us milled around and tried to stay out of their
way.

Naomi did this by being on her phone talking to people
about her wedding—from her attitude and tone of voice, I
presumed she was talking to those who helped create weddings, as opposed to guests. At least I hoped she wasn't
snarling at guests and telling them she didn't care about
difficulty levels, money was no object, and to do what she
wanted or suffer the consequences. Wasn't sure whose
money she meant, but A-C tradition said that the groom's
side paid for pretty much everything. Also wasn't sure I
liked her spending Chuckie's money without care, but had
to figure he'd told her to do it.

Tito arrived right after Naomi hung up on someone I
particularly felt for in terms of her snarling attitude. I was
happy for the distraction. Tito was wearing a suit. I knew
he hadn't been wearing one in the infirmary, so White had
clearly impressed upon him that he had the most rabid of
fans in the dining room. Because he lived in an A-C facility, this meant he was in the typical Armani Fatigues.

"You wanted me to join all of you for dinner, Kitty?"
Tito sounded tired and just a tad annoyed. Hoped he
wouldn't follow Naomi's lead and turn nasty because I
didn't think I was up to it.

"Yes. We have visitors from Beta Twelve, Queen Renata's daughters, Princesses Rahmi and Rhee," I indicated
which was which. "They wanted very much to meet you.
Princesses, may I present the Great Tito."

Tito shot me the "you so crazy" look. So maybe White
had only told Tito he was needed and to dress up. Which,
knowing White's sense of humor, was likely. "It's an honor
to meet you, Your Highnesses," he said, putting out his
hand.

Rahmi grabbed it and shook it vigorously. I got the impression hand shaking wasn't something normally done on
Beta Twelve and that she'd learned how to do this from the
same source she'd used to pick her "disguise."

"I am so honored to meet you," she said breathlessly.

Rhee shoved in and literally grabbed Tito's hand out of her sister's so she could shake it as well. "Me too! I'm at least as honored as Rahmi. Maybe more."

Tito looked confused but he rallied as he carefully extracted his hand. "I'm honored to meet the two of you as well. I hope your mother's well?"

"Oh, yes," Rahmi said. "Mother's fine. Would you do us the honor of sitting with us for this meal?"

Tito looked around the room. "Seriously, you guys, this is a bad time to pull a practical joke, don't you think?"

Every man in the room, my dad included, shook their heads vigorously. Jeff, Chuckie, and Christopher, who were all standing behind the princesses, each made his own version of the Stop/Cut/Shut Up/Kill Gesture.

Rahmi and Rhee looked crushed. "We didn't mean to offend," Rhee said in a whisper.

"Girls, the Great Tito did *not* mean it that way," I said quickly. "We try not to put one warrior above the others here, and the Great Tito is very modest and humble. He's not offended by your total and complete hero worship that has clearly been encouraged by your mother. He actually *is* modest, unlike me, so he's a little embarrassed and is thinking we've asked you to tell him he's great as a way of friendly, teasing camaraderie."

The princesses didn't look convinced, but Tito again proved that his main go-to move was being smart, capable, and fast in a danger situation. He turned back to the princesses and gave them a beaming smile. "Really? You'd do me the honor of letting me sit with not one but two of the finest warriors in the Alpha Centauri system?"

The girls perked up. "You can recognize that we're great warriors?" Rahmi asked timidly.

"Absolutely. I met your mother, and there's no way her daughters would be anything less than stellar. That she sent you here, alone, just proves that you're the best of the best." Tito walked to the dining table, stood in front of one chair, and pulled out the two on either side of it. "If you'd allow me the honor."

The princesses rushed over and allowed Tito to help them into their chairs, Rahmi first and then Rhee, and push them in. The collective tension in the air ratcheted down to normal. Made a mental note to hurt White later, but realized that I'd never follow through on it. In the retelling, this was going to be hilarious.

As the princesses happily talked fighting with the Great Tito, the rest of us sat down and ate. The meal itself was uneventful, with the kids prattling about what they'd done on their extended sleepover, the couples getting to actually relax together, and everyone else talking about Jeff's appointment.

Oliver had his Poof, Button, along for the ride, but he was concerned about Bellie, who was alone in his apartment. Reader sent a Field team to pick her up. Sadly, they were remarkably fast and efficient. Bellie was happily settled on the perch Jeff had refused to get rid of within fifteen minutes. Jeff, Oliver, and Vance were making much over her and giving her tons of bird treats less than a minute later.

"Bellie loves Mister! Bellie loves Jeff! Bellie loves Vance!"

"Nice of you to share, Bellie."

"I like the bird," Vance said. "She appears to have good taste. And she learned my name so quickly, too, so she's clearly smart."

Jeff and Oliver both started sharing the wonder that was Bellie with Vance, presumably so that he'd know all the details when they initiated him into the Bellie the Parrot Fan Club.

"I don't get why Jeff loves that bird so much," Christopher muttered. "At least the Peregrines do some actual work."

"Dude, it's like you read my mind."

CHAPTER 73

DINNER OVER, everyone went to bed, either in their own rooms or assigned guest rooms, or, in Tito's case, back to the infirmary. Jeff tried to get Bellie to stay with us, but I put the ambassadorial foot down and she and her perch went along with Oliver to his room over at the Zoo.

We got Dad settled into his room in our apartment and then got Jamie ready for bed. "What's this?" Jeff asked as he picked up the stuffed eagle.

"I found it in Santiago's office. I want to keep it. To have something to remember him by."

Jeff kissed my forehead. "Fine with me, baby. Again, his death isn't your fault."

"No, but finding out who really caused him to be killed is my responsibility. And I don't feel any closer to doing that than we were before."

"We'll figure it out," Jeff said confidently. "But for now, let's get our little Jamie-Kat into bed."

After bath time, Jeff and I still sang songs to Jamie. Decided to work the eagle into the act, so I slid it onto my hand mid-song. My fingernails brushed against something in the head. It didn't feel like a bug or anything dangerous, so I waited until the song was over to see what was in there.

Retrieved a piece of paper that had been folded many times over. Figured it was a note from one of the kids from Reyes' old school. I'd look at it later—now was Jamie Time. Dad came in for the second half of our songfest and Jamie went to bed a very happy little girl.

"You two look exhausted," Dad said after we closed the door to the nursery. "Get some sleep. I'm going to do the same." After hugs and kisses, Dad trotted down the hall.

Tossed the paper I'd found inside the eagle onto our dresser, which was where the all the bills Jeff had to go over were sitting. Decided all of that crap could wait.

"We're having brunch with the Brewers tomorrow," I told Jeff as we got undressed and into the standard-issue pajamas.

"Great. See? They're not as bad as they used to be, are they?"

"No. They seem genuinely interested in being our friends."

"Yeah. I didn't pick up any guile or fake interest. I mean, they could have been wearing an emotional overlay, but if they weren't, they feel just like they always have to me — that they're interested in us as people."

"That's nice. Edmund said he'd help you with the bills if you want."

"Yeah, I think I will. Is that part of tomorrow's plan?"

"Uh huh. You two will do that while Nathalie and I, or Nathalie, Jamie, and I, look at her portfolio." We snuggled into bed.

"Do we want to bring Jamie along?" Jeff sounded worried.

"Well, Nathalie said they love kids, but I'm sure it's not them you're concerned about."

"No. There's a lot of dangerous things going on right now. I think I'd prefer to keep Jamie safe in the Embassy or at the Pontifex's Residence. Unless you think that much time away from us is going to be bad for her or hurt her feelings."

"You'd be the one who could tell that for surc. But I think she'll be okay with it." Had a thought. "Can Jamie be affected by the emotional blockers and such? Or are the blocks you put in strong enough that she won't notice?"

Jeff sighed. "I don't know. The blocks Christopher and I put into Jamie should mean that she couldn't pick up anything, any more than a regular, non-talented child could. But she obviously can pick up things, and I think it's more than her, as you put it, baby animal senses. Whether that means she's learned how to manipulate the blocks like

Christopher and I do, or if they just aren't as strong as her powers, I don't know. And I'm honestly afraid to ask."

"Yeah, I know what you mean. She's going to be okay, though, right?"

He hugged me. "I'm sure she is, baby. She's our daughter. She's got guts and gumption and common sense from you. Jamie will be able to handle anything. Not that I want to find out what she can handle just yet."

"Me either." Snuggled closer. "So, you tired?"

Jeff chuckled. "Not too tired to make you happy, baby."

"Oh, I like where the Distinguished Gentleman from New Mexico's head's at."

We weren't too tired to do the deed, but we were both too tired to get fancy about it. Of course, Jeff's version of nothing fancy meant I had a nice selection of orgasms before we finished up and fell asleep, wrapped around each other.

Woke up in the middle of the night, my face buried in between Jeff's pecs. This was a great position to wake up in, but I could tell he was still fast asleep.

As with the night before, tried to figure out if I was up for any significant reason. Didn't hear anything other than the baby sleep sounds Jamie made coming from the baby monitor. So I either had to go back to sleep or move out of one of my favorite positions.

Under the circumstances, figured I should take one for the team and be sure that all was well. Moved carefully so I wouldn't wake Jeff up, and rolled out of bed. Nothing seemed amiss in our room. The entire Poof Contingent had returned with Jamie, as had all the cats and dogs. The dogs were happily snoozing in the guest room with my father. The cats and Poofs were asleep in their condos.

Put my nightclothes back on, got into my slippers and robe, and checked on Jamie. She was asleep, Mous-Mous snuggled in her arms, a variety of other Poofs in the crib with them. Harlie was one of them. Harlie opened its eyes, mewed quietly, and closed its eyes again. All was well in Jamie Land.

By now, I was awake. Mister Clock shared that it was 2 a.m. No wonder I was tired—I kept on waking up at these ridiculous hours for no good reason whatsoever.

Figured it was time for some hot cocoa and maybe I'd

get sleepy again. Also figured that nothing was going to
bore me faster than reading a bunch of bills. Gathered up
all the stuff on our dresser, including the folded piece of
paper that had been in the eagle puppet, and headed out of
the room.

Dumped the stuff on the couch, turned on the table
lamp, closed the bedroom door quietly, and went to the
kitchen. "A big cup of hot chocolate with a lot of whipped
cream, please, and thank you," I said to the pantry. Opened
the door, and there it was, complete with a tonnage of
whipped cream. "You guys just totally rock."

As I'd said to Stryker and the rest of Hacker International only a few hours prior, ability and desire were not the
same things. I had the ability to read and comprehend
pretty much anything that wasn't the highest-level science
or mathematics. And despite appearances, if I'd really
wanted to, I could have learned them, too, and not only
because Chuckie would have helped me.

What everyone tended to forget was that I was in every
class but one language class with Chuckie all through high
school and most of college. He took German, I took French.
That was our entire deviation. Meaning I was in honors
classes. Idiots didn't score the honors track, at least not at
our high school, and not at ASU, either.

However, in school, being the brain was never a fast
track to popularity, which Chuckie's school career as the
Bully Magnet proved. I had no ego attached to proving I
was as smart as anyone, and since my best friend was the
smartest guy in the entire school district, there seemed to
be little point in competing with anyone else, anyway.

So I didn't worry about what anyone thought, including
whether or not they thought I was smart or an airhead.
Chuckie called this protective coloration—that I could give
the impression that I was a fun party girl while at the same
time getting straight As in honors classes all through school.
He'd never mastered this skill, at least not as a kid.

Once out of college, though, I'd learned another really
important lesson—in marketing, you didn't have to read every, single, minute, boring detail in order to know how to sell
something well and accurately. You only needed the high-
level, pertinent facts, features, benefits, and so on. Turned
out, that was true for a lot of the world. I'd proved that every

single day since my first superbeing had appeared on the streets of Pueblo Caliente.

But despite my desire to avoid the dull and boring reading, I had the ability to read these bills and understand exactly what they were trying to achieve, both the stated purpose, the real purpose, and the hidden purpose. That each bill had all three of these was something my father had taught me at a young age.

Took my cocoa and settled in for some dull reading. Only, it wasn't all that dull.

The bills were a variety—some from each of the major committees. And there were a lot of them. Clearly Congress felt that the way to look supremely busy to the aliens outside our solar system was to pass a lot of legislation. Or at least ask to pass a lot of legislation.

The first one I decided to read was a Transportation bill focused on the travel of "undocumented aliens" between states. I read it carefully, and was rewarded with the certain knowledge that Jeff should fight this bill with his last breath.

There were too many clauses and lines about "aliens not naturally from Earth" which was not the same as "naturalized citizens" or "illegal aliens" or "illegal human aliens". There were a lot of negatives about all of these in the bill that I was sure was supported by the Ku Klux Klan and neo-Nazi lobbies, but far more about the aliens not naturally from Earth.

Decided I wasn't going to enjoy the rest of my cocoa if I read another bill, so I checked out the piece of paper I'd found in Reyes' stuffed eagle.

Unfolded the paper with one hand while I held my cocoa with the other. There was nothing on the paper. Turned it over. Blank on that side, too.

"What the hell?" Put my cocoa down and held the paper up to the light. Nothing, nada, zip.

"What are you doing, kitten?" Dad asked sleepily as he came into the room.

"Reading stuff. Why are you up?"

He shrugged. "I'm not used to the dogs in the room with us any more. Their snoring woke me up and I couldn't get back to sleep. Figured I'd make some cocoa and see if it helped."

"Sit, Dad, I'll get it. Is this a whipped cream or marsh-mallows night?"

"Marshmallows, please, kitten."

Went to the kitchen and retrieved another cocoa from Elf Delivery. Came back to find Dad looking at the blank piece of paper.

"What's this?" he asked as I put his cocoa down.

"No idea. I found that in something of Santiago's. I thought it was going to be a note from a student or some-thing, because I don't know why else he'd have folded it up and shoved it into the head of a stuffed hand puppet. But there's nothing there."

"Hmmm." Dad stood up. "Give me a moment." He headed for the kitchen. I followed him. He turned on the oven and put the paper into it.

"Really? We're going all *National Treasure*?"

"We lose nothing by trying it, kitten," Dad said. He turned the oven light on. "And, I see that it was worth the effort." Dad opened the oven and pulled out the paper. It had writing all over it.

We took it back into the living room. "What's it say?"

"It's written in Spanish," Dad said. "I don't read Spanish very well. But I can guarantee this wasn't written by a child. The handwriting is an adult's, and so are the words that I can translate."

Took the paper from him and turned it over. "Wow, invisible-no-longer writing on both sides. There's a lot here. And I'm just betting we need to know what this says." Contemplated all my options. Decided that the easiest answer was in the Embassy.

Went to the com switch. "Walter, are you up?"

"Yes, Chief," he said. He sounded drowsy, but as near as I could tell, the Security team functioned on almost no sleep. "Are you alright?"

"Yes. I need you to calmly wake up Tito and Magdalena. Please ask them to come up here quickly and quietly. This is not a medical emergency. I need people who can read and translate Spanish."

"Yes, Chief." The com turned off.

"Why wake up both of them?" Dad asked.

"Because all language is regional. Magdalena is from Paraguay. Her slang will be different from Santiago's. But

Nevada and New Mexico aren't that far apart, so Tito should be able to translate the slang."

"Makes sense. What about the rest of these things?" Dad indicated the bills.

"I'm trying to figure out what's going on, and why we have so many representatives dead." Dad cocked his head at me, and I remembered we hadn't really told him what was going on. Did a fast recap and was done by the time Tito and Nurse Carter arrived.

Explained the situation as they examined the paper. "This is going to take a little while," Nurse Carter said. "The handwriting is cramped—I think the writer was trying to get a lot on the page. Also, since he was writing with invisible ink, some of the lines are running together."

"He didn't write this all at one time," Tito said. "You can tell by where some lines start, and the older 'ink' is lighter."

"Do you need to translate in the infirmary?"

"No," Nurse Carter said. "Richard is with Mister Buchanan while we're up here." She looked a little guilty. "Oh, and Kitty? Richard filled me and Tito in on everything that was going on. He said to tell you that he made the executive decision because he felt the team needed our perspectives and he wanted to be sure we both had all the information."

"Wise man chooses his allies carefully. I'm okay with it."

She looked relieved. "He said you'd appreciate him saving you the time."

"True enough." Would have liked to have pulled White up here, but if Tito didn't want Buchanan left alone, then Buchanan would not be left alone.

Tito and Nurse Carter went into the kitchen to do their translations. Dad picked up one of the bills. "Let's get these read while they're working. So, you want to log the offering committee, the general gist of the bill, and anything that stands out as wrong or something being snuck in, right?"

"Right."

Dad and I didn't read as fast as the A-Cs or even Chuckie could, but we were both pretty fast in our own rights. After the first couple, though, we both started skimming. Because we'd both found a similar sentence in all the bills and were now just looking for it and other lines like it.

Dad finished his half of the stack before I did. "Kitty, I found the same line, sometimes worded a little differently, but with the legal gist and thrust intact, in every one of these bills."

"I did, too."

The bedroom door opened and Jeff came out, yawning. "You want to tell me what's going on?"

"Sorry we woke you up, but we've made a lot of progress." Waved the last bill at him. "Let me finish this and we'll catch you up."

Jeff sighed. "I was having a nice dream. We were in Cabo and absolutely nothing interesting was going on."

"Well, we're in D.C. and absolutely a lot of scary interesting is going on."

"Oh, good," Jeff said. "Routine."

CHAPTER 74

JEFF SIGHED as he sat down next to me. "Lay it on me."

"Okay, Dad and I just finished reading all these bills, every one of the bills the Speaker gave you to go over, the ones that will go to vote in the first week of January."

Jeff nodded. "Yeah, I know. I don't know why you two read them. That's my job. Now, I mean."

"Let's make sure we're on the same page. Bills are legislation going through the House or the Senate." *Schoolhouse Rock* was coming back to me with a vengeance. "A congressman introduces a bill, for whatever reason. Many times the reasons are good, like to give teachers and schools more money."

"But many times, they're not," Dad said. "Some bills are restrictive in their nature, such as bills about illegal immigration."

Jeff nodded. "Right. Bills go to committee. This got explained to me when they shoved the job on me and then again earlier today. The different committees take the bills, research them, and make their recommendations. Sometimes they table the bill, which means they get rid of it, sometimes the committee favors the bill and sends it up for a vote. And all bills get debated somewhere along the way."

"They also get amended along the way, which is where many politicians, lobbyists, and special interest groups come in to try to use their influence to affect the bill," Dad said.

"Right," I added. "The former Diplomatic Corps used their influence to, supposedly, ensure that bills and other actions going through Congress were doing things to help, versus harm, the A-Cs."

"Okay, so someone wants to affect the bill. So the committee says no."

"The committee doesn't always say, no, Jeff," Dad said. "Sometimes the committee agrees with what the lobbyist wants. And then they amend the bill. Sometimes they amend or change a bill about, say, protecting butterflies, with a single line forbidding the sale of alcohol in every state in the union."

"Why is that allowed?" Jeff sounded worried now.

"Because that's the way things work. Think about the Cabal of Evil. Lillian Culver represents a lot of big defense contractors. Let's say you're on the Defense Committee. She's going to want to wine and dine you, so to speak, in order to influence your putting in something in the bill that suggests that you must use one of her clients. No biggie, right? I mean, they're established defense contractors, buy American, sort of thing."

"Okay, but that's obvious, and there would be opposing sides on every committee. Someone would catch it and stop it."

"Love your faith in the political system. And maybe that would happen. But let's say that you're on the Education Committee. Lillian still wines and dines you, and convinces you that her clients will give money to the schools if you'll just get this one line in requiring that all schools have to have, say, Titan Security instead of local police providing protection. You agree, and either slip it in or passionately argue the case for the committee, and the committee buys in and puts the line in willingly."

"I can see how that would be dangerous, but even if the committee went for it, so what? These things get debated in session. That's where something like what Sol just described could be stopped."

"Only if everyone's read it or someone brings up the line about forbidding alcohol in every state or having Titan Security in every school." I held up one of the bills. "These things are humongous by the time they're done and go to the Floor of the House or the Senate for a vote. And not everyone reads them. Many rely on the committees to make their recommendations and then they vote accordingly."

Jeff nodded slowly. "And many who vote will think they're voting for the obvious parts of the bill, not the sneaky stuff. So, every bill needs to be read carefully. That's the job, isn't it? At least a big part of it, I mean. To read every bill that comes your way?"

I dropped the stack of bills in his lap. "You're an A-C. You can read at hyperspeed. I don't believe every single representative is going to read every word, let alone find the line that Dad and I found, over and over again, in a plethora of legislative bills that have almost nothing to do with each other, and also almost nothing to do with the line being snuck in."

"I'd agree with that in general," Tito said, as he and Nurse Carter joined us. "But not for one in particular. We can guarantee that Santiago Reyes read every bill that he was given. And I'd bet he found the same things you did."

"What did you all find?" Jeff asked. "I'm obviously the only one not clued in."

I held up the last bill, which I still had in my hand. "This bill is supposedly about making the nation's schools better. But get a load of this particular sentence—and really pay attention, because Dad and I found this or close to it in every one of the bills now sitting in your lap."

"Edge of our seats," Jeff said, sarcasm knob only at a sleepy six on the scale.

"*You* will be. I think Tito and Magdalena are already aware. From the middle of a paragraph describing school bus specifications in extremely boring detail, we have this gem: No aliens not naturally from Earth shall be allowed to overrule any U.S. state or federal government law, mandate, or directive, now or in perpetuity."

We were all quiet for a few long moments. Tito cleared his throat. "That's what Santiago was doing. He had a listing of every bill and the specific anti-alien lines from them. He had the ones about human illegals called out, too. This shouldn't surprise anyone in the room, but there were a lot less of those than the ones clearly put in to cover the A-Cs both of Earth and elsewhere."

"I understand why this is bad, but what does it all mean?" Nurse Carter asked.

Seemed obvious to me. "It means we know why all the representatives are being killed."

CHAPTER 75

"HOW DO THESE lines correlate to the murder or suspected murder of over twenty people?" Jeff asked.

"Edmund Brewer told me that he'd been amazed to discover that two dozen people could mean the difference between a bill's passage or failure. He also said that they were worried about filibusters and that this legislation is considered important."

"So?" Jeff asked.

"So somebody has influenced every single one of the committees that worked on these bills. That's a lot of influence. And yet, other than Club Fifty-One and similar crackpot groups we've discovered in the recent months, there is no functioning Anti-A-C lobby out there. So who got this line or its close cousin into every single one of these bills?"

"An enemy, I get it," Jeff said. "But why does that equal murder?"

"I'm with Jeff," Tito said. "I'm not seeing how these bills are related to anyone dying."

Resisted the impulse to heave a sigh. Also resisted the impulse to wake Chuckie up and have him come in here so I'd have some help with my conspiracy theory. I was here, I was up, time to go it alone. Always the way.

"Ah," Nurse Carter said. "There was something else. One line, near the bottom of what we think is the second page. 'There is more going on than just this. Must find out what.' We think it's the last thing he wrote."

"See?"

"Still not seeing anything other than Santiago being suspicious about how those lines got into every bill," Tito said. "It makes sense he'd think more was going on."

"Santiago died at our dinner party and the President asked New Mexico's governor to appoint Jeff. That's pretty much never been done before."

"Everything that's happened this year has pretty much never been done before, Kitty," Tito said. "Appointing a representative is a lot less touchy than halting all general elections and everything else governments, ours and everyone else's, have done since the invasion."

"But I thought we'd decided my appointment was done to prevent an anti-alien faction from taking over," Jeff said.

"Yes, and I'm sure that's the excuse the President gave the governor. It's a great excuse. But I think if Eugene had succeeded and killed Brewer instead, the President would have done the same thing, only asking California's governor to choose an appointee. He needed precedent to be set."

"You're saying the President is behind all the killings?" Dad asked, sounding shocked and worried.

"No. I think the President has noted the many missing seats in the House and is trying to forestall bad legislation passing or good legislation failing. But more than that, I think he's trying to avoid having legislation pass with the House down significantly so that no one can say anything shady happened. One less thing to protest, in that sense. In part because one of these bills, the one from Transportation, is openly anti-alien in the extreme, and I'm sure the President knows of its existence."

"Okay," Tito said. "Let's say you're right. Why does killing people help whoever's behind this?"

"Because the Mastermind, whoever he or she is, knows that this bill is around, and therefore knows that the President is going to want to do whatever he can to ensure that this one bill fails. We're sitting precariously, as far as anyone in government knows, because the entire Alpha Centauri system, minimum, is watching. So if anti-alien legislation passes, it had damn well better pass with everyone's consent. Only, it won't. But this anti-alien bill is not the problem."

"It's the other bills," Jeff said. "Right? We're about to have twenty new reps sworn in the day after Christmas.

They'll have one week to read these bills before they vote on them. Some of them will read them fully, but some won't, per the civics lesson you two gave me."

"The House will normally have something of an even split for bills like these," Dad said. "Not a hundred percent of the time, but bills pass or fail in part because of all that political maneuvering we talked about. It has to be worth it for a rep to vote yea or nay, and what's worth it to one isn't the same as another. Some will support a party-endorsed bill no matter what. Some will always vote no when a bill from, say, the Foreign Affairs committee comes through. So those two dozen votes can make the difference."

"And it's safe to assume they'll be making the difference coming up, or else all those people wouldn't be dead."

"We still have no proof that anyone other than Santiago was murdered," Jeff said. "And besides, so what if they pass through the House? They have to pass through the Senate, too, right?"

"Right. So, what if the President knows or has a good guess that the Senate's already going to be on board with these bills, at least some of them? The government wants to control the A-Cs. These bills are giving them carte blanche to do it." Sent a text to Caroline, asking her if I could get five minutes with McMillan on the phone and, if I couldn't, if I could get those five minutes with her.

"I still don't see how anyone could know the President would start appointing people," Jeff said. Tito nodded. Nurse Carter and Dad didn't seem convinced one way or the other.

"I can see it because I believe Colonel Hamlin was right—we have a Mastermind. And a Mastermind is going to be thinking of all of these things like a chess game. In chess you anticipate your opponent's moves, and you do it based on the first move. The better the player, the more potential moves you can see."

"It's always a chess game, at least according to you and Reynolds," Jeff said.

"It always is," Nurse Carter agreed. "Chess is a game based on war, on strategy, and on politics." She looked at me. "I can see how the President's actions could be expected, if they were based on long-term observations of his character and earlier decisions." Dad nodded.

"And I'm sure they were. If we have a Mastermind, not just for what's going on right now but for literally everything that's gone on, then that person has been around a long time and knows everyone."

"Maybe." Tito looked thoughtful.

"What do you mean?" Jeff asked.

"Maybe there's more than one. I know Colonel Hamlin told you he thought there was one person involved, but what if he's wrong? He didn't have a lot of time to research before he had to run, right? So what if it's a small group, just a handful of people?"

"The more people you have, the more people who can betray you," Nurse Carter said.

"Good point. Look at the Cabal of Evil. They're shifting their allegiances right now. Armstrong, Vance, the Brewers—they're all suddenly much more aligned with us than with the others. And that means that they can give away each other's secrets."

"Yes," Nurse Carter agreed. "So I wouldn't think the Mastermind would want a lot of people. You always need someone to be your interface, at least if you're going to hide in shadow, but you don't necessarily need a lot of people."

"Yeah, your underling could be the head of the crime syndicate, but he'd be the only one who knew who you were."

"It seems farfetched to me," Jeff said.

"So do aliens living on Earth and yet here you are."

My phone received an automated text from Caroline: "In a locked-door meeting, will respond when able. Happy Holidays!" So much for getting answers from that source. Bit the bullet and sent a text to Armstrong.

The com came on. "Excuse me, Chief," Walter said. "But Mister Dane has asked me if you're awake. Are you? Awake to him, I mean."

"Yeah, Walt, patch him through here."

"Kitty?"

"Hey, Stryker, what's up?"

"We've found some things I think you're going to want to know about right away. Walter said he was going to patch Chuck in, too."

"Okay. You guys are still up?"

"The slave driver won't let us rest," Stryker said bitterly.

"I heard that," Chuckie said over the com. "So whatever you woke us up for had better be good."

"Oh, it's good. Okay, first off, Dulce just let us know that they're confident they've identified what Mister Buchanan was hit with and they'll have the cure ready in a couple of hours."

"That's great news!"

"It comes with a couple downsides, Kitty. The waking up process is slow, which is for the safety of the 'sleeper,' so it'll take about twenty-four hours for Buchanan to come back to full consciousness. But that's not a side effect, that's just the way the cure has been designed."

"Okay, that's not the end of the world."

"This will be, in that sense. Per everyone at Dulce, and based on what we've found in the information from Gaultier, the drug has one major side effect."

My throat felt tight. "What is it?"

"Short-term memory loss. We'll get him awake and he'll be fine, but he's not going to remember anything that happened to him from about thirty minutes before the drug hit him."

"Fabulous," Chuckie said. "So Buchanan won't be able to tell us who attacked him, where he was when he was attacked, or anything else related to the incident, including who he was or wasn't with."

"Nope. It was considered a worthwhile side effect, since the idea was that all the recipient would be forgetting was going to sleep on a long-range spaceship."

"Why does it affect memory?" I asked.

"Near as they can tell, it's because it slows the aging process, and that affects the brain as well as the body. That's the best we have, so focus on the happy that your guy will be back among the conscious by Christmas. We hope."

"Yeah, okay, I'll take the loss of intel to have Malcolm back alive and hopefully well. I'm sure, in the long run, he'd rather lose those thirty minutes than the rest of his life and all his training."

"Anything else?" Chuckie asked.

"Yeah. We've hacked into all the police departments that work D.C. and the surrounding areas. We've also hacked into the F.B.I."

Was suddenly incredibly glad Cliff had chosen the Hear No Evil, See No Evil, Don't Have To Tattle About Evil plan.

"And?" Chuckie asked, sounding tired and impatient. Couldn't blame him.

"There was a body in the car that exploded today. They've managed to make a DNA match."

"That's awfully fast," Chuckie said.

"Yeah, well, that's because the dead woman's in the system. Because she worked for the C.I.A."

Jeff and I looked at each other. "Well," I said. "So much for us getting to interview Pia Ryan."

CHAPTER 76

"HOW'D YOU KNOW?" Stryker asked.

"Our luck runs no other way, Eddy. So, do they think Pia was the one who set the bomb or do they think she was dead before the bomb went off?"

"They don't have enough to be able to guess. They're lucky they can identify the body at all. The blast was huge and burned hot. She had some weird dental work, which was all that was left of her."

"Dental records can be faked," Chuckie said.

"We've done her background check, Chuck. Unless someone altered all of it in advance of this, that was her in the car."

"Now what?" Jeff asked.

"Now we all go back to bed," Chuckie said. "Though I should probably ask why you two sound so wide awake."

"There are five of us here, actually, and we're all terribly alert because we've been working. I'm now convinced we have a Mastermind and I know why all the representatives have been killed."

"Can I get this in a very high level right now?"

"Yes. We have a Sith Lord trying to control the Imperial Senate, and I think he, or she, is out their Apprentice. Meaning that there are others in line to be the next Sith and we need to figure they've been helping in anticipation of a move up the Sith Corporate Ladder."

There was a pause while everyone in the room stared at me, each one giving me their version of the "you so crazy" look. I ignored them. The person I'd tailored my answer for wasn't confused, I was sure. He was just processing.

"You think Pia was the Apprentice?" Chuckie asked finally.

"Yeah. I think she either blew something when she was supposed to kill Cliff, or she was tossed into his car already dead so she could blow up with him, probably being punished for failure, possibly for the fact that Eugene passed along her name to me and I'm still alive."

"That theory would explain the long-running nature of the conspiracies," Stryker said. "The Sith Lord who started it all could be dead and his Apprentice, or the Apprentice's Apprentice, could be in charge now."

"That makes a lot of sense," Chuckie agreed. "Especially since the indications were that the Mastermind had been around for decades."

"What in God's name are you all talking about?" Jeff asked. A-Cs avoided science fiction shows and movies, presumably because they looked at them as being inaccurate or boring documentaries about stuff they already knew.

"*Star Wars* movies."

"Seriously?" Tito asked, clearly speaking for Jeff and my dad, too.

"Yeah. Lucas based a lot of that on how he saw politics working, or not working."

"I agree," Nurse Carter said. "Not that they're going to show up with lightsabers or something, but that a setup like the Sith makes sense for a shadowy Mastermind situation."

"Moriarty had a few lieutenants," Dad said, coming around to my side of the explanation house. "But most didn't know who he really was. And it took a lot of work for Sherlock Holmes to determine who he was and then to stop him."

"Yep. So, Chuckie, that's my theory. Our Professor Moriarty is a Sith Lord. So, go get 'em, Sherlock Skywalker."

"I'm going to get a migraine. Thanks for the theory. I don't know what's worse, that you've offered up a Sith Lord Theory or that I'm actually considering it as a viable explanation. Stryker, I know you've bought in. What's the vote from the rest of you in the Computer Lab, who I know are listening in?"

"We figured you'd want them in the loop," Stryker said

quickly. "Guys, show of hands, who's in for the Sith? Yeah, it's unanimous, Chuck."

Chuckie sighed. "Oh, good. Okay, I'd like to get more sleep before I have to figure out how we find a Sith Lord in Washington."

"No ideas here, but that would be a great title for a comic."

"Good night, Kitty."

"Mister Reynolds is off the com, Chief," Walter said. "Would you like to remain on with Mister Dane?"

"Eddy, anything else for me?"

"Just that, under the circumstances, I'd like to suggest that you go for the Princess Leia in the bronze bikini look again sometime. You can still carry it off."

"My husband is sitting right here, Eddy, and I think he's going to go for killing you with his bare hands."

"Oh, no," Jeff said pleasantly. "I'm focused on the words 'again' and 'still.'"

"She wore it at a few Halloween parties," Stryker shared. "I'm sure I can find the pictures pretty easily. Stryker out."

"Mister Dane's com is off now, Chief."

"Thanks, Walt. Go back to bed."

"Yes, Chief." The com turned off.

"I don't want to witness the argument," Dad said.

Jeff shrugged. "I'm not going to go into a jealous rage over the fact that Kitty wore a sexy costume when she was younger. And, let's be honest—the squatters aren't exactly people I need to worry about from a romantic perspective, are they?"

I snorted. "No. Not at all."

Jeff grinned. "Then I'll be sure to make the Head Squatter give me all the negatives."

CHAPTER 77

THE FIVE OF US WENT BACK TO BED. Jeff and I snuggled together but we both fell asleep before we could consider having sexy times or not.

The morning that came with sunlight arrived far too early, but we got up anyway. My phone shared another automated text reply: "In a locked-door meeting, will respond when able. If this is urgent, contact my secretary." Armstrong hadn't left the secretary's name or number, meaning, I figured, that he only wanted to be disturbed by someone who knew said name and number. Meaning he didn't want to be disturbed by me. Always the way.

Reader had teams working on the hunt for Colonel Hamlin and the retracing of Buchanan's steps, half of Hacker International was doing a full workup on Pia Ryan and anyone she'd ever interacted with from birth through death while the other half worked with Amy on a full Gaultier breakdown, and Christopher and the Barones were still searching for the Assassination Squad.

Because we were going to brunch with a politician and former international model, I broke down and wore a dress and heels. The Elves had another nice number, this one in black, with slits up the side. Apparently this was a big look with Armani this season. Jeff, of course, was in the Armani Fatigues.

Mom came to the Embassy looking like she hadn't slept in days, so all we got was a quick set of hugs and kisses and then she went to sleep. The cats and dogs went with her, and she didn't object when half the Poofs joined them, either.

We discussed it, and Dad insisted he'd keep Jamie and stay with her and Mom in our apartment. Jamie was all for spending extra special time with her Papa Sol, so we left them having fun, which meant Dad reading history books to her and Jamie paying rapt attention. Shoved aside the worry about how an almost-one-year-old could even hope to comprehend what she was hearing, in part because I had a strong suspicion she was comprehending every word.

Jeff and I retrieved the briefcase filled with what we'd stolen at Rayburn House from Amy and took it downstairs to the kitchen. White and Raj were there, and we all started sorting through the trash, while Pierre brought us drinks and kibitzed. White had brought Pierre, and Walter, up to speed as well.

"Anyone you've missed sharing this with, Uncle Richard?" Jeff asked, as White explained that Pierre was on the same page as the rest of us.

"Not that I can recall, Jeffrey. We're not making progress, and, as Missus Martini is well aware, we work best with our entire team involved. And we did establish that it was unlikely that Pierre or the others were the Mastermind or working against our interests."

"Jeff's just being cautious," Pierre said loyally. "But never fear, as with every other secret or mission, I shall take the confidential to my grave and offer assistance as needed."

"Doreen reassured me yesterday that, whatever was going on, she was on our side."

White nodded. "She spoke with me about it as well. She fears that whatever it is, her parents were involved somehow."

"Maybe they were, but so far, unless they're maneuvering things from beyond the graves they don't have, it doesn't seem likely that they have much to do with what's going on in terms of the deaths of all the representatives."

Gower joined us. "What are you doing here, Paul?" Jeff asked. "Not that it's not nice to see you."

Gower shrugged. "James is working, I was told I wasn't allowed to do any Field work on the grounds that we have assassins and mad bombers everywhere and I'm so very important. I'm bored, because being important has a lot of boring moments, and Jamie is here, meaning I have no cute little girl to babysit. So, I figured I'd come to see what you have going and if you need any help, while I ask Richard what he did to stay sane when he was locked up for his own safety."

"I became quite good at card games," White offered.

"You know, we could use help." Figured I should say that before White and Gower went off into a Pontifex Standup Routine. "We need to sort this stuff, and we also need a listing of what committees every dead representative was on, or going on, and exact dates and supposed causes of death."

"I'll get the information from the Computer Lab, you sit," Raj said to Gower. He zipped off and was back in a very short time. "Fresh off the printer," he said, flashing the troubadour smile. "I made copies for each of us."

We ended up with three piles of stuff from Rayburn: calendars and planners, of which we had very few; Post-It Notes and other scraps of paper with writing; and things that were either trash or such obscure clues we'd never figure them out. This third pile every one of us looked at, Pierre included, and then we set it aside for Chuckie to enjoy at his leisure, with the assumption that if there was something in them, he'd be the only one with a prayer of finding it.

This focused us back onto the pieces of paper and the calendars and planners. Gower and I took the pieces of paper, Raj and White took the planners, Jeff had the calendars. I explained my Sith Lord Theory while we searched. Everyone other than Jeff thought it made sense.

"I believe I've found something, Ambassador," Raj said after a while.

"Dude, what happened to Kitty?"

He grinned. "Just testing. At any rate, there are some consistent entries in all the calendars. They aren't much to go on, but every one of these has some meeting with 'L' in them. Most are within a month of death."

"So, our killer's name begins with the letter L."

"Maybe." Jeff didn't sound convinced. "But that's quite a leap, baby."

"Is it? We know three people who could be or are involved whose names start with that letter."

"We do?" Gower asked.

"Lillian Culver, Langston Whitmore, Lydia Montgomery. And that's just off the top of my head. I'm sure there are more."

"I'm sure there are more, too," Jeff agreed. "That's my point. There are a lot of people whose first or last names start with L. That doesn't mean they're the same person in each calendar entry, or the murderer. A lot of people abbreviate their appointments."

"Do you have anything else?"

Jeff sighed. "No, not yet. And before you ask, yes, I see some L appointments."

"If the Mastermind is as thorough as he seems, why would he leave this information for us to find?" White asked.

"Why in the world do you think the Mastermind would do office cleanup?" Pierre asked, sounding just slightly offended.

"What do you mean?" I asked.

He shrugged. "Darling, do *you* clean this Embassy? No, you absolutely do not. You are the ambassador, and the Embassy is cleaned *for* you. Does the President pick up his own dry cleaning? I sincerely doubt it, and if he does, he and I need to have a serious talk about what a personal assistant is and why the most powerful man in the world should be using one. And so on. If the Mastermind is as everyone says, then he's not going to be doing something so mundane as cleaning out the offices of his victims. That's what one has staff for, darlings."

"Pierre makes an excellent point," White said. "And if we go with the Sith theory, then one of the Apprentices or aspiring Apprentices would have done that work."

"It could explain why you found less in some offices and more in others, too," Raj added. "Different Apprentices doing the work at different times."

The com turned on. "Excuse me, Chief, but we've been contacted about the late Mister Reyes' things. Apparently he left no forwarding address and they can't determine next of kin. The lady at Rayburn House is asking if we can take possession of whatever was left in his office."

"Yes, Walt, tell her we will. Please tell her we'll also be sending over some people to do the packing and such."

"Will do."

Gower was already on his phone. "Great, thanks." He hung up. "James is sending over some Field Teams to do the packing."

Raj looked at me. "Would you like me to oversee that, Kitty?"

"Dude, it's like you read my mind. Please, and thank you."

Raj handed his pile of stuff to White, then he zipped off. Gower sent a text. "James is aware and has advised his teams. Raj will handle any confusion, I'm sure."

"Me too." Looked at my watch. "We've got to get moving. Jeff and I are supposed to be at the Brewers' place in a few minutes."

"They live close, at least as far as they said at lunch yesterday," Jeff said. "Should we walk, take a gate, or take a car?"

"I'm freaked out about walking. You're such an easy target if we're on the street."

"So are you." Jeff shook his head. "We didn't live in fear when we were with Centaurion Division. I don't want to live in fear now, either."

"Sorry, Jeff," Gower said. "But under the circumstances, you're not allowed to walk around with a target on your chest. You're taking a limo. Com on!"

"Yes, Pontifex Gower?"

"Please have Len and Kyle get a car ready. They need to drop the ambassador and Representative Martini off."

Jeff grumbled but he didn't argue. I raced upstairs to grab my purse, our coats, and my hat. Got a few more hugs and kisses from Jamie as well as a discussion of Ancient Babylonia. "Take Harlie and Poofikins, Mommy," she said as I was finally heading to the door.

"Why?" Opened my purse. No Poofs. "I don't know that Harlie and Poofikins want to leave Jamie today." As soon as I said their names, the Poofs appeared, though.

"They just want to be sure you want them, Mommy," Jamie said. "Don't worry, they still love you best."

"Mous-Mous loves you best, right, Jamie-Kat?"

"Right!" Her Poof was on her head, purring. Confirmed this meant that it was agreeing as well.

Poofs on board were never an issue. Gave Dad and Jamie one more kiss each and trotted back downstairs. The boys were in the kitchen, discussing my Sith and Dial L for Murder theories.

"I'm with Kitty," Kyle said. "The Sith idea makes total sense, and I think the L is suspicious in the extreme."

"I'm kind of with Jeff," Len said. "It seems like a stretch."

Kyle shot me a long-suffering look. "He's not into the comics like we are."

"Oh, we'll bring him around. Richard, Paul, are you guys okay here?"

"We'll call you if we discover anything or make any new connections," White said. "Go actually have a little fun."

"I'll ensure you're contacted with any news, Kitty darling," Pierre added. "Now, off you go."

We headed down and got into a limo. "You know, have you listened to any tunes recently?" Kyle asked.

"Actually, no, I haven't."

"Well, we can't have that." He fiddled with something. "I made you a playlist," he said a little shyly.

"Really? That's so awesome, Kyle, thanks."

He beamed. "I went for songs I think will help you think." He hit the button and the sounds of "Live and Let Die" by Paul McCartney and Wings hit my personal airwaves.

"I love you, Kyle."

"How is this song a help?" Jeff asked.

"Just channel your inner James Bond and let's let the good times roll, boys."

CHAPTER 78

THE BREWERS TRULY didn't live that far from us. They were in the Dupont Circle area, at the Cairo, which was a really cool, tall, older building.

We had enough time for "I'm Still Here" by the Goo Goo Dolls and "Some Might Say" by Oasis. Len pulled us up in front of the Cairo in the middle of Pink's "Bad Influence."

I felt a hell of a lot better as we got out and went up the stone steps. The foyer was all glass with marble floors and Egyptians columns, along with a nice lounge that was doubling as the lobby. Happily, no one shot at us or the boys as we waited for Brewer to come down and collect us.

Living up to its name, the Cairo was a U-shaped building with an Egyptian theme. It also had gargoyles above the front entrance, griffins high up on the cornices, and then some. One wall of the lobby had a big mirror surrounded by photographs of the building's construction and other photoworthy Cairo events. There were two reddish-orange square columns in front of two elevators. Double glass doors between them showed a stairway leading down to a stone central courtyard that was in the center of the U. We were admiring these when Brewer joined us.

"It's very Zen, isn't it?" he asked after we'd shaken hands, indicating the courtyard.

"If you say so. It's all pretty as far as I'm concerned. This is a great building."

He beamed. "We love it. It's just so full of character. The

first floor has elephant heads, looking left and right from
the stone windowsills of the front windows. Their trunks
interlock at the corners of the entrance arch."

"Wow."

"And the fourth floor has dragon and dwarf crosses.
There are carved stone façades all over, too." There were
two wide staircases made of marble and wrought iron.
Brewer pointed them out, too. "They span the height of the
building. But we'll take the elevator, unless you'd rather
walk all the way up."

"You're at the top?"

"Oh, hell, no. Though the Cairo rooftop has a fabulous
view. You can see the entire northwest skyline, including
the Capitol building and the Washington Monument. But
no, we live on the sixth floor. And that's high enough, believe me."

Remembered Brewer had said he was afraid of heights.
I could understand not living up too high if you were acro-
phobic.

Their apartment had a marble orb for a door handle.
Apparently, that was a standard Cairo feature. So were the
exposed red brick walls inside. By the time Nathalie had
given us a tour, I was having serious apartment envy. Sure,
theirs was smaller than ours, but theirs was normal and cool
and quirky. Ours had the Elves, though, and Pierre, so I decided not to whine to Jeff about how we needed to move
into this building.

Brunch was very nice. By mutual consent, we didn't talk
about anything bad that had gone on over the past few days.
As Nathalie had put it, we just wanted to relax and make
the rest of the world go away for a little while.

Once we finished, the men went into Brewer's study to
talk about the bills, and Nathalie and I looked at her portfolio. "You've got some amazing shots," I said as we finished. "Why did you stop modeling?"

She shrugged. "It got boring. I wanted to do more. And
I met Edmund." She smiled. "He went out of his way to win
me, and I was dating several actors at the time. He was just
the right one for me."

"I'm glad you guys worked out your problems."

"I as well. Eugene reminded me of how Edmund had
been at the start. But after you found us, well . . ." She

looked down. "I saw how you looked at me, how horrified you were, and how disappointed in both of us you seemed. We weren't close then, at all, I know, but you were the only one who told me the truth."

"I don't remember saying anything."

"Your expression was enough. Eugene told me how you wouldn't speak to him any more. I realized you were right—what we were doing was wrong. Especially because I hadn't told Edmund that I was unhappy." She took my hand. "So thank you for your moral objection. It saved my marriage."

"No." I hugged her. "You and Edmund saved your marriage, not me."

Girl bonding moment over, we were now both closer and feeling a little awkward. "Would you like to see the view?" Nathalie asked. "I can almost never get Edmund up there, but it would be a shame for you to miss it. And since we have no rain right now, it would be a good time."

"Sure. Edmund said the view was great."

We went up to the top, and I could see for myself that the Brewers hadn't misrepresented the view. It was spectacular. "There are storm clouds coming."

"Maybe we'll have a white Christmas," Nathalie said.

"Or just more rain."

We laughed and headed down. Beautiful view or not, it was cold at the top.

Jeff and Brewer were waiting for us when we got back. "You want the scenic tour, too?" Brewer asked him.

"Nah," Jeff said with a grin. "I'll save it for next time."

"And don't you worry about those bills," Brewer said. "Like I told you, I've already spotted the problems. They won't be passing as long as I'm around." He grimaced. "Too bad Wendell's gone. We were working together to be sure to get these shot down."

"You told me that it only took a few to cause a bill to pass or fail. And there are some strong anti-alien lobbies out there now. Should we be worried?"

"No," Brewer said. "This kind of thing happens all the time, Kitty. As long as there are enough of us with pull around to ensure the undecided sway to our side of things it'll be fine. Now, you two need to get going."

"We do?"

"Yeah," Jeff said. "Raj called me. We're needed back home. The jocks are on their way to collect us."

I sighed. "Well, at least we had a couple of hours off."

Hugs all around and the promise to do this again soon made, Brewer escorted us down to the lobby. There were several people waiting for the elevator when we got down. Brewer walked us to the front doors. "I'm glad we took the time to really get to know each other," he said as the boys pulled up at the sidewalk.

"Us too," Jeff said. "See you tomorrow?"

"Yes, we'll be glad to attend the birthday party." Brewer winked. "The photo ops should be great, and I'm sure you'll appreciate more bodies there to block your daughter from the press."

"Like you wouldn't believe," I confirmed.

"You going up?" a man called from the second elevator. He seemed to be holding it for Brewer.

"Great tenants here, too," Brewer said to us. "Coming," he called to the man in the elevator. "See you both tomorrow," he said over his shoulder as he headed toward the elevator.

I turned to watch him and felt like something nudged into me and I teetered. Assumed I'd just lost my balance on the slick marble as Jeff steadied me. Diplomat or not, I wasn't used to wearing heels every day. Brewer waved to us, and we waved back, as the elevator doors closed.

We stepped outside and I realized something. "Crap, you left your hat. And coat."

Jeff sighed. "We can ask them to bring them tomorrow, baby."

Felt a pout coming on. I was becoming addicted to Jeff in the trench and hat look. "I guess."

He rolled his eyes. "Or I can inconvenience our hosts and ask them if I can run back up and get them."

"Oh, look, it's a moot point."

Nathalie came out, carrying Jeff's things. "You forgot these," she said with a laugh.

"Thanks, you've made Kitty's day," Jeff said as he took them and put them on.

"Where's Edmund?" Nathalie asked.

"He went back up already."

"Oh, we must have passed each other in the elevators."

She pulled out her phone. "He tends to worry if I'm not where he thinks I should be." She dialed. Her brow wrinkled. "That's strange. He's not answering."

My Megalomaniac Girl early warning signal started to act up. "I think we need to find Edmund, right now, Jeff. Boys, out of the car."

As they got out Len looked up. "Is that part of the building?" He pointed.

We all looked up. So we were all able to see the man teetering at the edge of the rooftop.

CHAPTER 79

TIME MOVED SLOWLY. Nathalie was screaming, the boys were trying to get to her and me, I was trying to tell the Poofs to activate and do something.

Jeff, however, had been the Head of Field for a lot longer than he'd been anything else. He took off into the building.

But using the fastest hyperspeed available or not, I saw the man fall just as Jeff got there. Jeff grabbed for him and almost fell off the roof himself, though he managed to stay on. But he wasn't Mister Fantastic, and he'd have needed elongating rubber arms to catch the falling man.

Time might have been moving slowly, but gravity was on the case. The man hit the sidewalk with a sickening thud, cut off mid-scream. He was on his back, so identification was easy. Nathalie screaming even more and having to be held back by both boys made the confirmation. Brewer was on the sidewalk.

No one was holding me, and I ran to him. "Ed, Ed, are you okay?" He'd fallen twelve stories; I knew he wasn't okay. However, I asked anyway, hoping against hope that he'd fallen onto the soft concrete.

His eyes were open and glassy. I touched his neck. Felt no pulse. My phone rang. I managed to get it out of my purse. "I almost had him," Jeff said. "Is he . . ."

"He's very dead. And there's no way in the world he went up there willingly."

"He was alone up here. There's no way a human could have gotten to the elevator and past me, not at the speed I was moving at. And someone had to have forced him up there, because I had to jump up onto the ledge to try to catch him."

"Don't touch anything and get back down here. Fast."

Jeff was with me by the time I'd hung up. "Why did you want me down?"

"Because if a human couldn't get past you, that means there's only one logical explanation. I thought I'd lost my balance when we were in the foyer, but now I think someone brushed past me at the super-fast hyperspeed."

"Clarence," Jeff growled.

"Yes. So he ran into the elevator before the doors closed and forced Brewer up to the roof. He ran down the other staircase, or he ran past you and you didn't notice." A thought nudged. "I told everyone to get security on Brewer. Why weren't they on the case?"

"No idea. I'll call James."

"No. Let me. You need to help the boys with Nathalie." I dialed. But not Reader.

"Yes, Missus Martini?"

"Mister White, I need you at the Cairo five minutes ago."

"On my way."

Hung up and now I called Reader.

"Kitty, what's up?" Reader asked.

"Edmund Brewer just fell to his death. There is no way this wasn't foul play. Jeff tried to save him but he was just a moment too late. There are no guards anywhere and it just occurred to me to look around for them. Did you assign teams to guard the Brewers?"

Jeff was holding Nathalie and he helped her over to Brewer's body. I moved out of the way as she sobbed and Jeff held her.

"Yes, I assigned four agents." Reader's voice was tight. "I'll call you back."

White appeared. Raj was with him. "I see we're too late," White said quietly.

"Yes, but I called you after. . . . I think Clarence was or is here. James said he had four agents assigned to protect the Brewers but I haven't seen any sign of them."

"Rajnish and I will do a search," White said. "Keep the young men with you and on guard." White and Raj disappeared.

My phone rang. "The agents aren't responding to any calls," Reader said. "Sending more teams over."

"Richard and Raj are already here and searching. I need you to call the police and advise Chuckie. And whoever else needs to know. My mom. She needs to know. Probably."

"I'll handle it. Kitty, are you okay?"

"No. I'm numb with shock and horror so I expect to be really freaked out later. And right after that I'm going to be enraged. But right now, I'm just trying not to believe this has happened. I'm also officially more than done with people dying near me, especially people I know and like."

"We'll find who's doing this and stop them. I promise."

We hung up and I dropped my phone back into my purse. The Poofs weren't there. Jamie had pointedly told me to bring them and now they weren't around. Tried not to be upset with them and reminded myself that they tended to do their own thing, for their own reasons, all of which had worked out for the best in the past. Decided to trust them now, too, and sent a mental "be careful" message to them.

What was in my purse, however, were the burner phones. Pulled out the one that was supposedly my new hotline to the Dingo and dialed. "Yes, Miss Katt?"

"I need the truth, the whole truth, and nothing but the truth. Have you or your cousin killed a C.I.A. operative named Pia Ryan, put her and/or a car bomb into Clifford Goodman's car, or shoved or caused Representative Edmund Brewer to fall off the top of the Cairo building?"

"No. To all of those."

"I mean it. I *need* to know the truth. Frankly, if you've done all that, my life will be less complex, confusing, and stressful. So I want a truly honest answer."

"I am not lying to you. We have not harmed or interacted with any of those people."

"How about Representative Juvonic? Did you hit him with a blowgun dart tipped with the heart attack drug serum? Or something like that?"

"What? Who? No. What's going on?" The Dingo sounded genuinely confused.

"Raul the assassin—is Raul his real name, or is it his assassin's name? Like I know your parents didn't call you the Dingo when you were growing up."

"That is his name in the business, yes."

"Do you know his real name? I know yours, at least, what the government assumes your last name to be — Kasperoff."

"Correct. But no, I don't know his real name. I do know that he comes from Florida. Originally."

Leventhal Reid was from Florida. Time to make another leap. "Does he ever use the alias of Dier, or Reid?"

"Dier, yes. I haven't heard of him using Reid."

"Okay, so, when you said that Raul was around the Embassy the other night, he was disguised as a SWAT cop, wasn't he?"

"Yes."

"Why didn't you tell Amy and Caroline that?"

"I am not here to help you arrest Raul for impersonating an officer of the law. I am here to protect you from him."

"Because he's broken the rules, I know. What about his sister? Is she an assassin, too?"

"I am not acquainted with any of his relatives, other than the late Bernice, who was indeed his wife."

"Are you planning on killing Raul, or are you merely planning to show him the error of his ways and appeal to his reason and sense of assassin's honor?"

"The former, why?"

"Because I have a feeling that Raul is combining business with pleasure. I think he's under contract, and that his sister's in on the deal, too. Who normally hires him?"

"The Central Intelligence Agency."

CHAPTER 80

"IT SO FIGURES."
Heard someone talking in the background. "My cousin says that the police are on their way to a potential suicide. Are they headed to wherever you are?"

"Yes, and it wasn't suicide. It was murder."

"So you said. Murder and assassination are not the same. The end result is the same, but the motivations are normally very different."

"Yeah, I know. Need the truth again—have you or your cousin been killing off members of the House of Representatives in ways that look natural or like accidents?"

"No. We have been working outside of the United States for the past many months. Because of your good advice."

"Okay. Good." Logic said the Dingo could be lying outrageously. But I knew he wasn't. The only reason I could give for why was that ACE always said that I thought right, and my thoughts confirmed that the Dingo wasn't willing to sully himself by lying to me, whether out of honor or pride or a combination of both.

Of course, thinking of this meant I was thinking of ACE. But there was no answering "think" in my mind. I missed ACE. A lot. And not only because if ACE were around I could ask him what was going on and get a clue. "I don't know what to do to stop this."

The Dingo was quiet for a few moments. "If you look at the facts, and when you have eliminated the impossible, whatever remains, however improbable, must be the truth."

"Sherlock Holmes said that."

"Yes."

"You're a fan?"

"Very much so, yes. You don't believe people in my business read for pleasure?" He sounded amused.

"No, I'm just sort of thrilled at the moment. Because I need help. And despite what every single person I know would tell me to do, I need to meet with you and tell you what's going on."

"Why?"

"Because I think I need Sherlock Holmes. Chuckie's the Conspiracy King. I'm Megalomaniac Girl. We know there's a conspiracy at work, and we know the person behind it is a megalomaniac. I think we even know the why it's all happening, or at least a lot of the why. But the who is escaping us, and we're running out of time."

Speaking of which, sirens were in the distance and coming closer. I was going to need to get off the phone soon.

"Ah, I hear that you have company coming."

"You're good. Or you're close by."

"I am both."

"Did you see who shoved Edmund Brewer off the rooftop?"

"Perhaps. Meet me in the cemetery, where we met before. Ten o'clock tonight. Don't be late. Come alone."

"You know no one's going to let me sneak out by myself, especially not now. And, let's be honest, it's sort of a stupid move to meet the two best assassins in the business in a cemetery at any time, let alone late at night."

"I do not wish to have someone attempt heroics."

"Noted. I'll ensure that whoever I bring with me is in agreement that we're coming to you for help, not to make an arrest. Deal?"

He was quiet for another few moments. The sirens got a lot louder. "I should not trust you, but I do. I accept your terms. I will see you tonight, Miss Katt." He hung up and I dropped the burner back into my purse and closed it up.

So, the Dingo and I were in agreement that we shouldn't trust each other but did. Couldn't wait to share that with the people I was going to take to the cemetery with me tonight. They weren't going to be my husband or either of my best guy friends, so I had a hope that they wouldn't yell at me.

White and Raj returned. They beat the police cars by seconds, but by enough that the officers wouldn't realize they'd just come back from an excursion.

"We found them," Raj said in a low voice, while White went to greet the police and Len and Kyle went to help Jeff and Nathalie up off the ground. "They were all in some big trash cans nearby." His voice shook. "All dead. Necks broken."

"It's official—Clarence Valentino is alive and somehow well and he is here."

"I agree. So does Former Pontifex White."

"We all prefer first names, Raj."

"Right now, I prefer titles, Ambassador," he said as the cops approached us. "Please allow me to do the talking."

"Why?"

"Because, in this case, I'm going to be better at it."

CHAPTER 81

RAJ WAS BETTER at handling the police because he played the Diplomatic Immunity card within a minute of speaking to the officers.

White had a quick word with the boys, and I did with Jeff, so we were all on the same page. We all gave short statements to the police that left out Jeff running to the top of the building in less than two seconds and the fact that we'd had A-C Field agents here who were now dead.

Nathalie was far too much of an emotional wreck to say much of anything and the police were understanding. When a woman sees her husband fall to his death, apparently her being incoherent is a given.

There was no way in the world that we were going to leave Nathalie alone, though, police around or not. Raj gave the police our Embassy's number and, once they'd gotten our statements and hers, we bundled Nathalie into the limo. Jeff hadn't been able to let her go—the one time he'd tried she'd practically collapsed.

Len drove slowly back to the Embassy, in part because we didn't want to attract any more police attention. I tried calling Caroline, Senator McMillan, and Senator Armstrong. None of them picked up, all had the same locked-door meeting message going. Sent a text to Kelly McMillan.

"They're investigating it as a suicide," Raj said. "And we're going to let them, at least for now."

"There's no way that's true," Jeff said.

"I know. However, Congressman, we need to have you

and the ambassador as removed from the situation as possible." Raj stressed the titles.

Jeff sighed. "Point made." He looked at Nathalie then back at me. "What are we going to do?"

"We're going to figure out who's behind this and stop them. Permanently."

Of course, this was a hell of a lot easier said than done. I'd hoped to glean some insights from Caroline or either senator we were close to, but Kelly's text explained why they hadn't been available—they were all in a very high-level meeting regarding Armstrong's presidential run. The presidential election was two years away, but was, like everything else, being affected by the government's moratorium on elections this year.

She said she could reach them if it was vital, but it had to *be* vital for her to do it. Passed along the news of Brewer's death, but chose not to use Kelly's access at this moment. Mostly because I figured I might need it at another time.

We got back and got Nathalie into Tito and Nurse Carter's care. She had to go to the infirmary because Tito had to give her a sedative to calm her down, and, as with Buchanan, he wanted her watched.

The others were already back, so the rest of our team met up with them in the Computer Lab. Thankfully it was big. What it wasn't, though, was full of answers.

"Serene's checked in," Gower told us. "She hasn't gotten much from the emotional overlay device. Once she had all she could get, she tried to open it."

"Is she okay?"

"Oh, yes, she used robotic arms within a blast-proof container. Unfortunately, it was a good thing she took the precaution."

"Blew to bits?" This was an easy guess.

"Yeah, so we have nothing, other than what we'll get from what we took from Gaultier Research."

"It's going to take us weeks to go through everything from Gaultier," Amy said. "It's giving me great ammunition for my case to take over the company, but otherwise, it's a morass of data and information, and it's going to require detailed attention and a lot more time before we have a hope of knowing what all's going on."

"So, we say we got what we needed out of Gaultier,

which is Malcolm hopefully back with us soon, and we say they're a dead end for now."

"What if the Mastermind is at Gaultier?" Amy asked.

"Then we don't find him or her right now. Look, I go back to what I said to James yesterday, I think it was—we need to solve these murders, first. If that leads us to our Professor Moriarty, great. If it only leads us to the Sith Apprentice, then at least we stop that person."

"If Clarence is back, where's he hiding out?" Jeff asked.

"I'm more interested in who he's working with. Because I'm going to bet money that Clarence is who hit Malcolm with the suspended animation drug. He's about the only one who could."

"Clarence isn't the brains of the operation," Christopher said. "There's no way."

"There's no way he's the Sith Apprentice, either. I'm sure he's being used as really effective and apparently quite loyal muscle."

White shook his head. "Loyalties shift. I'm sure Clarence is loyal to whoever helped him recover after the invasion. That may not be anyone he's known before."

"Sith Lord or Sith Apprentice," Stryker suggested. The rest of Hacker International nodded their agreement.

"Chief," Walter said over the com, "Mister Beaumont is here."

"Send him in and up, Walt. Scan him first, if you're able."

"Yes, Chief."

"Did you invite him?" Reader asked.

"No. I'm assuming he's heard about Edmund's death."

Vance arrived. "Now do you people believe me?" he asked by way of saying hello and proving me right. He had an overnight bag with him.

"I've been with you for a while, but yeah, I think we have more converts to the theory. What's with the bag?"

"Lydia's still at our place. I'm hoping to spend the night here again. Potentially for weeks or until she removes herself."

"Fine with me, we can fit you in I'm sure. And I don't think we want to let Nathalie go home alone so if she insists, you can go with her."

"I'm agreeable. My husband's consoling one new widow, I'll be happy to console the much better-looking new widow. Have you figured out who's killing everyone?"

"Not yet," I admitted.

"Have you at least figured out why?"

"Sort of. It's political."

"In this town, that's like saying water is wet."

"We have assassins here," Jeff pointed out. "Why are we assuming they aren't involved?"

"Well, one of them is, for sure. And, I'm going to say something and I want everyone to let me finish before they yell at me or forbid me to do something."

"Can't wait for this," Jeff growled under his breath.

"I called the Dingo. He insists he and Surly Vic are not the assassins we're looking for. However, he also confirmed that Raul is a professional name, kind of like Madonna. Raul also uses the alias Dier, though he's never used Reid to the Dingo's knowledge."

Chuckie cursed quietly and looked at Mom. "This has never popped, not once."

"No," Mom agreed. "It hasn't." She looked seriously pissed.

"So, it's safe to assume that Leventhal Reid still has friends in high as well as low places. However, the various Reps' murders were not carried out by Club Fifty-One—they just don't possess the skills."

"Could Reid have been the Sith Lord?" Reader asked.

"He was too young when he died to have been involved as far back as the Mastermind theory takes us," Mom said.

"Not if he was the Apprentice to the first Sith," Stryker said. "I'm looking at timelines here, and I'd say it would have been very easy. He was a career politician, he went to George Washington University, and did all his internships on the Hill."

"And Reid was a sick, twisted bastard. And that means he'd have been attractive to whoever was running their Overlord Campaign."

"It's all pure conjecture," Mom said. "We have no facts and less proof."

"That matters for you, Mom, and Chuckie, but it doesn't matter for us. I've spent the past three years working with no facts and less proof, and I always end up being right, because the Force is strong on my Megalomaniac Girl skills. By the way, you all interrupted me before I was done."

"Oh, *beg* pardon," Mom said, sarcasm knob firmly at eleven. "Do go on."

"I will. I made a date with the Dingo."

A lot of people started talking, loudly. "Quiet down!" It wasn't Jeff bellowing—it was Raj. And he wasn't bellowing, just speaking strongly. But everyone shut the heck up. "Thank you. The ambassador has more to say. Let's allow her to say it."

"Thanks, Raj, I officially like having a troubadour around. Okay, the Dingo knows more than he wants to tell me. I think I can get it out of him in a face-to-face meeting. However, he won't show if I come with anyone who might have the idea of arresting him, and that includes Mom, Chuckie, Kevin, all of Alpha Team, all of Airborne, and Jeff and Christopher, too."

"Then you're sure as hell not going," Jeff said.

"No, I'm going. I told him I wasn't going alone. And I won't."

"Just who do you plan to take to a meeting with the best assassins in the world?" Mom snapped.

"I plan to take Richard, Raj, and the two best warriors currently on planet Earth."

CHAPTER 82

"**NO,**" Jeff said flatly. "You are not going to this without me along."

"Sorry, you're not invited. *You* are the target, not me. Besides, I'm sure Rahmi and Rhee will be thrilled to be given a mission by the Great Tito, and I'm equally sure they'll kill any man I tell them to and not even think about asking questions later. They can move at hyperspeed, they're stronger than A-Cs, and they have an even faster ability to heal."

"Take your Glock," Mom said. She looked at Jeff. "Kitty's right, she's going, you're not. I'll have Charles knock you out if you argue. Because, what none of you know is that the President wants Jeff in the severest form of protective custody."

"Does he think Jeff killed Brewer or anyone else?"

"No. He, like you and Vance and, frankly, me, thinks that Jeff is a target. Now that I've brought the number of dead representatives to his attention, the President is also worried that we have a conspiracy or serial killer on our hands. And the absolute last representative the President wants killed is our first A-C congressman."

"I don't care, Kitty's not going to this meeting without me. I don't want her going at all, but if she's going, then she's taking me, period. And that's an order."

White cleared his throat. "Ah, Jeffrey, I hate to say this to you, but you're actually not in a position to give anyone in the Embassy orders any more. You're now a congressman.

Missus Martini is the ambassador and, as such, her word is law in here."

"James," Jeff said. "You can overrule her."

"I can, but I don't think we want me to. We have nothing to go on. The leads we have are all going on a fast path to nowhere. We think it's Clarence, but we don't know. We think Raul the assassin is Leventhal Reid's relative, but we don't know. People are dropping dead all over and we have no handle on why or how. You were shot, and it's only by a miracle of a string of coincidences that you're alive at all. If we have a chance to get some clarity, even a little, then I say we go for it."

"I'm not going to allow my wife to have a midnight meeting with assassins," Jeff growled. "And that's final."

"Then I have no choice but to arrest you," Mom said. "For your own good."

Jeff's jaw dropped. "You can't be serious."

"I can and I am. I'm not talking as your mother-in-law. I'm speaking as the Head of the P.T.C.U."

"It's Mom's turn to use me for bait, Jeff. And, just like way back when, I approve and endorse being the bait."

"Jamie's birthday is tomorrow," Jeff said quietly, but with a catch in his voice.

Went to him and hugged him. "I know. And I'll be there for it. I'm not going alone. I'll be with four others, and we all have hyperspeed. Richard and I know what we're doing, we really do. The princesses will protect us. And Raj will find what Christopher couldn't."

"What is *that* supposed to mean?" Christopher asked, as I received a nice blast of Patented Glare #5.

"You've been searching for where the assassins are holed up. Chuckie thought that they might be using someplace in the cemetery as a base. The Dingo asked me to meet there, so I think the likelihood just went up. But you don't think like a sneaky human—and that's a compliment—so you're not going to spot where a really sneaky human would be hiding. Chuckie would be best for this, but he can't go. So Raj will have to do."

"What makes you think Raj will be better at this than me? He has no Field training at all."

"I'm happy to arrest you, too, Christopher," Mom said.

"I don't want to go. I mean, I would if Kitty wanted me,

but clearly she prefers my dad. But at least they've worked together before. What does Raj have that I don't have?"

"Troubadour talent and an actual awareness of popular culture," I answered without missing a beat. "He's also seen all the evidence we found. And the only reason Raj has no Field training is that you wouldn't let him have any. I'm not prejudiced against troubadours like you are. So he's coming with me."

"I agree," Mom said, voice icy and completely in charge. "And I want to make sure that every person in this room understands that the person with the most authority *in* this room is me."

Jeff and Christopher glowered, but they both shut up. Everyone else other than Kevin and Chuckie had I'm A Good Boy or Girl expressions on their faces. Kevin and Chuckie merely looked like they were enjoying that Mom was laying down the law to someone other than themselves.

"I'm approving this, but I want all five of you in Kevlar. I don't want to hear any whining about it being heavy or itching or anything like that. You're in Kevlar or you're not leaving any more than Jeff is."

"No problem, Mom. I'm all for not getting shot."

Reader made a call. "We'll have something for all five of them before they go."

"Good, thank you, James. Kitty, when is your meeting?"

"Ten at night."

"Fine. Go brief your strike force, then relax until it's time to get ready to go. Jeff, if you put one toe out of the Embassy Complex I will shoot it off, is that clear?"

"Yes," he said with a sigh. "Fine. I'm neutered, you don't have to put the plastic collar on me, too."

Hugged him again. "It's not being neutered. It's being protected. Because I don't want to experience what Nathalie is going through right now, ever."

He hugged me back. "I don't, either, which is why I don't want you to go."

"If you two are going to start, do you mind taking it to your room?" Tim asked. "Some of us have spouses who are elsewhere and we're a little bitter."

"Happy to," Jeff said, a little too eagerly.

Mom rolled her eyes again. "Kevin, Charles, you're assigned to Representative Martini. I'd assign Christopher as well, but he tends to be as much of a problem."

Michael, Abigail, and Naomi Gower came in. "You wanted us, Amy?" Michael asked.

"Yeah. Kitty's about to do her usual, and Jeff and Christopher are confined to the Embassy. Chuck and Kevin are on guard duty, but I think it'll be a good idea to have some A-Cs along who can keep them in line." She looked at Mom. "If that's okay with you, Angela."

"Works for me," Mom said tiredly. "As long as Lorraine and Claudia are at Dulce."

"All of Airborne is at the Science Center," Tim confirmed.

"Bummer," Vance said quietly.

"Do you want them brought out?" Tim asked Mom.

"No, but have them stay ready."

"Kitty's a bad influence on you," Christopher said to Amy, who just laughed.

"We're happy to help," Abigail said. Michael nodded.

"What can we do?" Naomi asked with more than a little disinterest in her tone. "I mean, me and Abby. Any more."

"Can you help keep Jeff and Christopher in the Embassy Complex?" Amy asked. "If yes, then we need you to help. Because we can't trust them to behave like adults right now."

"*Fine,*" Jeff said. "I'll be a good little boy and let my wife run headlong into danger. Again."

Reader shrugged. "It's her specialty, Jeff, and you know it."

"You can come with me to tell Tito about the fun orders he gets to hand out to Rahmi and Rhee."

"So, that would be me, Christopher, Reynolds, Kevin, Michael, Naomi, and Abigail included in this field trip?"

"Yeah. It's a party. Vance can come, too, so he can see Nathalie, if she's conscious."

"We have hours to kill before you leave," Reader said as we headed for the elevator. "So make sure the 'party' focuses on what little solid intelligence we have. If we can figure out who's behind what's going on, Kitty and her team won't need to go on their group date."

CHAPTER 83

TITO HAD NO ISSUE giving Rahmi and Rhee their special orders. As expected, the princesses were beside themselves with the excitement of being sent on this top secret and vital mission. They raced off to work out and prepare in our exercise room, which was where they spent most of their free time anyway.

That took far less than an hour. Nathalie was still sleeping, so we all went up to the kitchen to look one more time at what Jeff and I had brought back from Rayburn House. One by one and in small groups, the rest of the team other than Hacker International wandered into the kitchen to join us.

We hadn't had the findings from the Cannon or Longworth Houses before. Reader brought those and we added them in.

Unfortunately, extra trash, planners, calendars, scraps of paper, and brainpower or not, we weren't getting much more than we'd had, and that included Chuckie. "I'm not seeing anything other than the letter L connection, and while it might mean something, it might not as well."

"It's on at least a third of the calendars or planners we found," Raj pointed out. "I think it has significance."

"It might." Chuckie shook his head. "But if it does, one letter, with nothing else added in, isn't enough to go on."

"My Conspiracy King is letting me down? I'm crushed." I looked around. "Hey, where's Mister Joel Oliver? I thought he slept here last night."

"He did," Reader said. "I have no idea where he is, though. He was supposed to tell me if he left."

Looked around. Oliver wasn't the only one missing. "Com on! Walter, are Mister Joel Oliver, Len, or Kyle within the Embassy complex?"

"No, Chief. Len asked me to tell you, when you noticed that they were gone, that he and Kyle were meeting Mister Joel Oliver at the Romanian Embassy. Mister Joel Oliver left right after you and Representative Martini went to have brunch. Len and Kyle left shortly after you all returned."

"Super, thanks." Pulled out my phone and dialed.

"Ambassador, I was wondering when you'd notice the young men and I were missing."

"Tell me you're over there extracting useful information from Olga, MJO."

"We are indeed. We'll be back shortly to share what we've learned. It was a hard fought lesson."

"If it was hard for you, I'm thankful I missed it. I'm a little too stressed to indulge Olga's sense of humor right now."

"Which she's quite aware of. You'll be pleased to know that your young men gave a good showing."

"Awesome. Hurry back. The rest of us are very lead-frustrated."

Tim's phone beeped. "Interesting. Kitty, Oren from the Israeli mission asked me to tell you and Chuck that Pia Ryan was a double agent for, and you're going to love this, France. She was considered a benign mole, by the way, just someone passing along low-level intelligence."

"There's no such thing as a benign mole in espionage," Chuckie said. "So, why did Mossad wait this long to tell us?"

"I'd assume because it wasn't relevant until now," Tim said. "They're trying to help us by running their own intel on anyone who could be involved."

"And I didn't have a relationship with them during Operation Assassination, which was when Pia's husband 'killed himself.' You know, if she was still alive, I'd suggest that she was the one who shoved Edmund Brewer off his roof, or at least the one who orchestrated it."

"Why couldn't she have been?" Jeff asked. We all looked at him. "What? We plan ahead, and we know our enemies do so all the time. Why couldn't she have orchestrated Ed's murder? She wasn't the one who pulled it off, but that's what Clarence was for, right?"

"There are times when I forget why you were the Head of Field," Chuckie said. "Tim, please ask Oren if they can help us trace Pia's movements for the past week. We have her prior history, but the last few days are key and for them our intelligence isn't as good."

"Oh. I just remembered something I forgot to tell you all," I said as Tim texted away.

"You're doing that a lot," Chuckie said. He looked mildly worried.

"There's a lot going on and I haven't been sleeping well. At least I remembered sooner this time. Anyway, the Dingo said that he and Surly Vic haven't taken a job in the U.S. since Operation Assassination. But good old Raul's number one client is, wait for it, the C.I.A. So, we know how he got out of jail."

"Tim—" Chuckie started.

"On it, on it, I can only text so fast and I have to pussy-foot the wording for them so there's nothing concrete to be traced."

Mom put her head into her hands. "Really? You can quote every single song on every single Aerosmith album, but the fact that you've been told a top assassin is getting his assignments from the C.I.A. you forget?"

"Been busy watching people die in front of me for the past three days, Mom. For whatever reason, and my total lack of getting enough sleep, I've been forgetting stuff. I've remembered it all now." Contemplated asking Walter to play some Aerosmith. Decided Mom would ground me.

"You're sure? You haven't forgotten some vital piece of intel like the name of the person who's behind all this?"

"Sadly, no."

"Speaking of forgetting," Raj said, "I forgot to tell you that we brought Representative Reyes' things back here. Representative Brewer's death wiped that out of my mind, too."

"See? It's not just me. Should we go through his stuff?"

"Yes," Mom said. "Your father told me about the paper you found in that stuffed animal. It indicates more than just the fact that Santiago found what you did, that there's some dangerous wording in all those bills. It shows he was afraid he was being spied on."

"And that he thought there was more going on. Per his last line and all."

Raj and Pierre went to get Reyes' things. We now had more stuff to go through.

"We'll never finish this," Amy said. "Com on! Walter, I need the hackers down here, pronto, other than Yuri, he can stay up there and keep things going in the Lab. They'll whine about it. Tell them that Kitty and I will kick their asses if they're not here in two minutes."

"Yes, ma'am."

"You want the extra hands or just to make them suffer?"

Amy laughed. "Both. Besides, spotting anomalies is supposedly one of the many things they're good at. Let's see if that's so."

"Check inside innocuous things," I suggested as we all started to sort through Santiago's stuff. Well, everyone other than Tim, who was texting like he was a teenager talking to his newest crush. "Santiago hid that paper in a pretty odd spot."

"That's why he wanted you to clean out his desk," Reader said. "Because he figured you'd find it."

"We took everything, including the trash," Raj said. "Just in case."

Four-fifths of Hacker International arrived, all looking annoyed, at the same time as Oliver and the boys returned. Amy told them what to look for—anything that might help—and everyone started pawing through and sorting Reyes' stuff.

"Before you tell them where we're at," Tim said, nodding to our new arrivals, "let me give you the latest from Mossad. Leventhal Reid had no siblings, at least as far as the information shows. However, he 'adopted' a younger boy when he was home from college. It's a heartwarming story, really. Supplemented his parents' incomes so they could house and raise the kid, sent him to school, everything."

"That seems far nicer than I'd ever have thought Reid could be."

"Well, here's where the story starts to sound like the man we knew and loathed. Reid's parents weren't rich, but they had good investments and really good life insurance. They died in a car accident. The police found it suspicious but couldn't prove anything. Reid inherited a small fortune, just in time for his first major political campaign. And the 'brother' fell off the radar."

"So, Raul's first assignment was to kill off the people who'd helped raise him?"

"Leventhal Reid was a psychopath," Chuckie said. "If he found a kid he wanted to raise and train as his own, the smart money is on him finding another psychopath."

"And, going along with Chuck's theory, it sounds like Reid paid his parents to care for the kid," Kevin said. "So the kid probably had no love or loyalty for them."

Tim nodded. "Mossad agrees with Chuck, and I agree with Kevin. They also found records, records that have been sealed and hidden, that show the kid took the legal name of Lars Reid, changed from Raul Diaz. Which is nice and close to Dier, isn't it?"

"I guess Raul's getting a double out of that. So how is Mossad finding all this?"

"Remember Leah? She was at the dinner party?" We all nodded. "She's in Florida, digging through old court records."

"How did they know to go down there, let alone what to look for?"

Tim shrugged. "Per Oren, Mossad has a strong interest in Raul, because he's killed a variety of their operatives over the years. We told them he was one of our main suspects, they did the math."

"Strong interest means they want to kill him," Chuckie said.

"That's nice. So do we."

"No," Gower said. "Actually, we don't."

CHAPTER 84

"W E DON'T WANT TO kill the assassin?" Jeff asked. "Why not?"

"Because right now the person who's most likely able to identify who the Mastermind is would be Raul," Gower explained.

We enjoyed a long moment of silence. "I'll let Mossad know," Tim said as he went back to his texting frenzy.

"Good catch, Paul. No killing Raul until we get who took over for Reid out of him. Okay, so Mossad's confirmed what we suspected there. What about a girl? There was a female Dier serving, or not serving, water at our party, too."

"There's no female relative that they can find, for either Reid or Raul, other than the mother who's dead," Tim reported. "And Bernie, who Buchanan killed."

"So was she legit and just has a weird spelling of the name?" Christopher asked.

"That seems like too much of a coinkydink to me."

Vance shrugged. "What's hard about this? Dude's found a new woman."

Chuckie nodded. "Sound theory and it makes sense. He was used to working with his wife."

Tim continued to text. "They'll look into new known female associates. Raul's not on radar a lot. If he was, he'd be dead. He was released from custody a lot sooner than any of us knew, by the way, and right before Mossad could take him out."

"Well, we know the Mastermind has a ton of pull. So, can we prove that Raul killed all the reps?"

"Doubtful," Oliver said. "In part because I doubt that he killed all of them."

The entire room stared at Oliver. Tim even stopped texting for a few seconds again. "Excuse me?" Jeff asked finally.

Oliver shrugged. "Raul the Assassin probably did not kill all of the people whose deaths we're investigating. I'm sure he killed his fair share, mind you. He killed Eugene Montgomery, of course, but I believe we already knew that."

"Right, he was disguised as SWAT. But what about Edmund Brewer? We think it was Clarence, but he could have had help."

As I thought about it, the man who'd pointedly held the elevator for Brewer could have been Raul. I'd only seen him once, when he was in SWAT gear, and I'd been very distracted at that time. And I hadn't really paid any attention to the people at the Cairo.

"That death may be attributable, but we have no confirmation yet. Madame Olga has a theory. However, until Representative Reyes was killed, and then Eugene Montgomery was killed immediately thereafter, she'd no more put things together than anyone else."

"I had," Vance mentioned.

"Yes, I shared that with her. She said that you might be allowed inside the Romanian Embassy as a welcomed guest in the future."

"I feel so honored."

"You should." Chose not to mention that the invitation probably didn't include Gadoire. "So, what did Olga deign to share?"

"Well, I must say that until the young gentlemen came back with their sad news, I believe Olga was as in the dark as the rest of us," Oliver said. "But Representative Brewer's death triggered her feeling that Eugene Montgomery is the key."

"And she thinks that we're not paying attention to the important things," Kyle added. "And she realizes we have over twenty Congressmen dead but she means besides them."

Mouths opened, mine included. "Olga knows Eugene wasn't a politician," Len said quickly. Mouths closed. "And she's not discounting those deaths, just thinks they're not telling us what we need to know. She also likes your Sith Lord idea."

"But she's not wild about the L name theory," Kyle said.

"I believe her exact words were 'even if those appointments were all with the same person, you have no proof that person is the one you seek,'" Oliver shared. "We're taking that to mean Olga feels we could better use our time elsewhere."

"By figuring out who the Sith Lord is," Kyle said.

"It's not Eugene," Len added. "But, as Mister Joel Oliver said, he's the key."

"Why?" Mom asked.

"Because he doesn't fit the pattern," Amy answered. The hackers all nodded, but didn't speak. Got the impression they were at least as afraid of Amy as they were of me, possibly more.

"What do you mean?" Chuckie asked her.

"Every other death looks like it's natural or an accident, right?" The room gave its general consensus. "But Eugene killed Santiago very publicly."

"And in such a way he was caught immediately," Michael added. Abigail nodded, nudged Naomi, who was alternating between looking lovingly at Chuckie and glancing at her cell phone. Naomi nodded, too. Clearly we had at least three-quarters of Team Gower in agreement with Amy, if I pretended Naomi was paying attention.

"He was trying to kill Edmund Brewer," I said. As the words left my mouth I could practically see Olga give me her Encouraging the Slow of Wit look. "Hang on. What're our thoughts about the whole robot theory thing? As in, do we think others got the same packet and sales pitch, or was that for Eugene, only?"

"Show of hands for who'd believe that if they'd been approached," Amy said. Every hand in the room went up. "Okay, right, but we know more than the average person."

"A good number of the representatives are in the know, too," Mom said.

"Half the country would believe," Stryker said. "Especially if you showed them the packet we saw."

"So, anyone approached was likely to believe it, but good try, Ames. But, the next question is, would you, the bad guys at Gaultier who are working on the next level of robotic manipulations, share this randomly with a bunch of politicians? And if you did, why? It would potentially expose that you had androids out there already that were really good at passing for human."

"You'd show to recruit," Chuckie said. "But why would you want to? And recruit for what? If you've created robots who are passing as representatives, you don't show your next victims so they know you're going to kill and replace them."

"You also don't take specific, detailed, accurate technical information and toss it around randomly," Ravi said. "I'm not joking—I believe we can build a working robot from that information, and by 'we' I don't mean Dulce. I mean we like Amy and Kitty."

"I think I should resent that somehow."

"Oh, I do resent that, no somehow," Amy said.

"Point made," Chuckie said, presumably to keep Ravi alive. "And I don't believe Pia was really trying to stop the robot makers, either."

"Mossad agrees with you," Tim said. "No way she was trying to stop these particular bad guys. My bet, and they'll research it, is that she was connected to Antony Marling in some way. And because we're all tense, I'm not going to make a French Connection joke."

"Your self-restraint is impressive, Megalomaniac Lad."

"Okay, so what was Eugene doing with the full packet of schematics?" Amy asked. "Do you think he stole it from Gaultier? He wasn't working on that project, we've confirmed that both with his supervisor and our own research."

"Why did he take the job at Gaultier?" I asked. "He was freelancing. Maybe he was trying to find information for Pia."

"Or confirm the information she gave him," Naomi said, proving she was at least listening with one ear.

"I'd want confirmation," Abigail added. "You know, before I tried to murder someone and all."

"Maybe, but I don't know that we'll ever know," Reader said. "And if we do figure it out, I don't think it'll be today, because Eugene and Pia are both dead."

"If we're disregarding the letter L theory," Raj said, "then perhaps we should also assume that there is no group of Stop the Robot Representatives people forming, either."

"Raj . . . you complete me." Raj grinned while Jeff and Reader both glared. Felt all special for a minute.

"If we assume that Eugene was the only one shown the information by Pia, then that begs certain other questions," White said. "To Olga's point, why Eugene Montgomery?"

"Can I ask a question or two before we try to answer that?" Michael asked.

"Certainly," White said with a smile. "We're all on the same team."

"Okay. I understand the Master and Apprentice thing, at least I think that's what you mean by the Sith Lord theory, right?"

"Yes," Henry said. He looked like he was going to keep going, but Amy shot him a glare almost worthy of her husband and he shut up.

"Okay. But why do we think there's only one Apprentice?" Michael asked.

"Because that's how it is in the movies," Stryker and I said in unison. We looked at each other. "Eddy, does that reply seem as totally lame to you, now that we said it out loud, as it does to me?"

Stryker grimaced. "Yeah. Sort of."

"Totally, dude. Totally. And, come to think of it, before we went to brunch, Raj had already posited the idea of more than one. Sorry, Chuckie and Mom, I forgot."

"Me too," Raj said quickly.

"And he's a loyal suck-up, too. I love that in Embassy staff."

Tim snorted. "You like that in everyone."

"What's your point? Anyway, sorry, where are you going with this, Michael?"

He shrugged. "I get why you'd only have a few people in the know, but when we're choosing who gets to go into space and who doesn't we start with a select group and we whittle them down via a variety of trials. Sometimes you don't go for a simple reason—you caught the flu. Sometimes you don't go for a more complex reason—you underperformed in key stress tests and scenarios. That's done so that the team that does go into space is the very best it can be, and that includes being able to complement each other's strengths and weaknesses."

"You firmly believe there's more than one Apprentice, don't you?"

"Yeah, I do. Let's face it, twenty people is a lot. Sure, we have a professional assassin out there who's working for the C.I.A. But I can't think of a better way to make someone prove loyalty to me than to have them kill someone on my order."

"The Mob's been using that philosophy for decades," Chuckie said. "And it's been working for them for decades, too. So, you think Eugene was trying to be an Apprentice?"

Michael's example made things seem so much clearer that I could answer this question. "No, not Eugene. Pia. Pia was in training to be an Apprentice. She has all the aspects you'd want—security clearance, job with the C.I.A., already a double agent."

"She's dead," Christopher pointed out.

"Because she failed," Jeff said. "She had Eugene set up to kill Ed Brewer. But he killed Santiago instead. And he told Kitty about her and the robotics packet she'd given him."

"So, either someone at Gaultier killed her for leaking that, or the Master killed her." Wasn't sure if I preferred Master versus Mastermind versus Sith Lord. Decided I could worry about this later. "But if we take Michael's theory to the farthest reaches, I think that begs two important questions."

"Who are the others vying to be the next Sith Apprentice?" Reader suggested.

"That's one. And the other is this—why is there competition for this slot in the first place? Or, phrased another way, which Apprentice, or Master, did we take out during Operation Destruction?"

CHAPTER 85

"WELL, my bitch of a stepmother's dead," Amy said. "So was it her?"

"No, and Ronaldo al Dejahl is out, too, and before you all tell me he's dead I point to Clarence Valentino and say that there's a good chance al Dejahl also got better. However, they were out of this part of the galaxy for too long. And I don't see either one of them as willing to be an Apprentice to anyone other than good ol' Mephistopheles."

Chuckie jerked. "That's the original Mastermind, Yates, or the Yates-Mephistopheles superbeing combination."

"That makes so much sense it makes me sick to think about it," Jeff said. "But does it work from a timeline perspective?"

Stryker nodded. "Yeah, definitely. Chuck's had us research all we could on Ronald Yates. He was old, but he was active all the way through until his death."

"And he's influenced every plan already, and we know that, too." Looked at White. "Richard, what do you think?"

"I'm in complete agreement with Jeffrey, including the nausea."

"How about Reid fitting into that scenario?"

"Works for sure," Big George said. "He received several campaign donations from different divisions of Yates Enterprises."

"Did you memorize the file?" Abigail asked. She didn't sound appalled—she sounded impressed.

"No, but I could have," Big George said, flexing his mind

muscle for the pretty girl. "We've been spending a lot of time on Leventhal Reid."

"Flirt later, we have other questions that need answering. Can we all agree that Reid was the Apprentice to Mephistopheles?" Everyone nodded. "Super. Then let's get back to the question of who the Apprentice was we got rid of during Operation Destruction."

"All the options are dead or not Apprentice material," Christopher said.

"Well, if Clarence and al Dejahl are still alive, what about that heinous bitch?" Amy asked.

"LaRue's definitely dead, I watched Esteban Cantu shoot her in the head instead of me. Oh. Wow. Chuckie?"

"Yes, it would fit. He was involved in everything and it took catching him trying to kill you while the world was being invaded for us to be able to arrest him."

"So, does that make him the Master or the Apprentice?"

"It makes him someone we need to question again," Mom said.

"Do we have time for that?" I still had time before I had to go meet the Dingo, but probably not enough to question Cantu unless he was close and we used hyperspeed.

"Maybe. He's not that far away."

"In some hole in the ground type of not far away or in some official prison not far away? I'm asking because if he's accessible he could be the Mastermind."

"Yes to both. He's not accessible. Other than to me and a handful of other people. And if one of them is the Mastermind or the Apprentice we're all screwed anyway."

Heaved a sigh. "Thanks for that, Mom. So let's presume Cantu was the eager Apprentice. And he got caught, and so the New Mastermind is having an open recruitment period. Start by killing off a few congressmen."

"But why?" Abigail asked. "It makes no sense."

"Well, we know the why—they have all these bills with anti-alien stuff hidden in them about to go through the House."

"Bills get shot down all the time," Vance said. "Why kill people over something like that?"

Jeff straightened up. "I need to see a list of the dead representatives."

"It's upstairs," Raj said. "I'll get it." He zipped off and was back quickly. He handed a sheet to Jeff.

"What is it?" I asked, speaking for the whole room based on everyone's confused expressions.

"When Ed and I were working after brunch, I told him about what we'd found, the anti-alien lines in the bills. He said he was already planning to fight them. And that Wendell had been planning to help him. He meant Wendell Holmes. Who died in the hospital from pneumonia right before our party."

Chuckie went and looked at the list along with Jeff. "There are only a few staunchly pro-alien supporters on this list. And a few staunch anti-alien supporters, too. Both definitely cross party lines and the pro and anti factions tend to be nonpartisan."

"Ed said that as long as he was around to sway the undecided voters, none of these would pass," Jeff said. "And now he's not around. Wendell Holmes isn't around. Some others aren't around. And we have two dozen new reps getting sworn in two days from now and voting on these bills in just over a week from now."

"I'm still not seeing the point," Mom said. "And we need to see the point of all these murders in order to stop whatever's going on."

"The Mastermind moves in murky ways." Hey, it was all I had at the moment.

Len cleared his throat. "I think we're forgetting something. And that's what Olga wanted us to focus on—Eugene Montgomery. We're not sure if she wanted us focused on his incompetence in killing the wrong target or something else, by the way."

"Wait . . . no one say anything for a minute." It was there, right there. The answer was simple—it was us who were making it complex. "Eugene was supposed to kill Edmund Brewer, right?"

"Can I speak?" Tim said. "Because if I can, the answer is 'right.'"

"Okay . . . let's ask ourselves this question: What would have happened if he'd succeeded?"

"Well, Ed's dead, so does it matter?" Jeff asked with more than a trace of bitterness.

"Yes, it matters. What would we have done?"

Chuckie closed his eyes. "I think the better question is, what would *you* have done, Kitty? You drove every reaction we had."

It was easy to extrapolate. "I wouldn't have gone down to the bathroom with Edmund, Nathalie would have. And while she might have come for help, we would have reacted differently. Slower, maybe." After all I hadn't liked them all that much until after Reyes was killed. "And if Nathalie had reacted the same as she did today, which I'm sure she would have, we'd have been taking care of her."

Shoved aside the wish that I'd listened to Jeff months ago and had let the Brewers in sooner. Now I'd never have the chance to really get to know Brewer, any more than I would Reyes.

"There's no way anyone could have expected Eugene Montgomery to murder anyone at that party and get away," Mom said. "Maybe Kitty would have been too busy handling Nathalie Brewer's reaction to question Eugene. But I locked us down the moment we knew something was very wrong, and the police absolutely would have found what Charles and the dog found. It might have taken them *longer*, but they'd have found the incriminating evidence."

"So Eugene was supposed to be caught."

"Let's say you're on the right track with this," Chuckie said. "Why?"

"Because they wanted Edmund Brewer dead, not Santiago Reyes."

"Santiago wasn't hiding that paper for no reason," Mom reminded me.

"Then let's rephrase as they wanted Edmund Brewer publicly murdered by Eugene," Amy said. "And they wanted Eugene caught for it. But why?"

"Good question, Ames. Let's go back to our very early theory from when Vance first tossed out the whole Serial Killer of Representatives idea. Somewhere along the line, someone was going to wake up and notice that all these people were dead. Because Eugene screwed up, we're all really aware of it now. But let's say he hadn't screwed up. He kills Edmund. He's caught. He tells the police about robots. They put him in a padded cell. Then they put the whole mistress thing together, in about an hour, tops, and Eugene's on death row without a problem. No one's going to believe him because no one will find the paperwork."

"He had it at his desk at work," Amy said. "Not exactly hidden."

"He didn't have it at his house or real office. And I'd bet he told Pia he'd destroyed it."

"I still go back to why," Mom said. "And I also still go back to the fact that Santiago was worried that he was being spied on, and as near as we can tell, it was because he'd found those anti-alien lines in the bills. His last line about there being more going on isn't enough for us to extrapolate anything."

"Wait," Chuckie said, and I could see his Conspiracy Wheels turning. "Hang on one moment. If we take Jeff's view, that Pia orchestrated Brewer's murder today, then they were trying again, right?" Everyone nodded. "So they definitely wanted Brewer killed. She was allowed to set up the second attempt, and this time they used Clarence."

"And I think they may have used Raul."

"How?" Jeff asked.

"Man who held the elevator for Edmund, did you look at him?"

Jeff cursed. "No. And that makes sense. Have Clarence do it, because you needed someone strong to get Ed up onto that ledge. But have your professional oversee, just in case things go badly this time."

"Logical and efficient, and a good follow up," Mom said. "However, still more public than any of the others."

"The police are investigating as a suicide. I don't think it'll hold up, but Nathalie is with us. If Raul was in the building, and I'm now really sure he was, then he's already broken into their home and planted proof of Edmund's hidden despair."

"Wow, Kitty, are you psychic?" Tim asked. "Because Mossad just confirmed police have found a suicide note."

"Thank God we took Nathalie with us," Jeff said. "Or it might have been a murder-suicide the police think they're investigating."

"Oh, Jeff, like, in that sense, where your head's at. And Tim, since when did you become best friends forever with the Mossad team at the Israeli Embassy?" Tim, Reader, and Mom all contrived to look innocent. "Oh, great. It's classified. Well, at least we all like them. Anyway, the Conspiracy King has more for us."

Chuckie nodded slowly. "I think we need to answer this question. Why is Pia Ryan dead?"

CHAPTER 86

"BECAUSE SHE SCREWED UP," Michael suggested. "She was in the running, her plan backfired."

"Maybe." Chuckie's eyes were closed. "Santiago Reyes is dead, yes. But Raul was there, and he was there with SWAT, meaning the plan was always expected to be exposed, police were always expected to be called, and Eugene was always expected to be arrested."

"Meaning Raul was in place to cover as backup, in all cases," Raj said. "Especially if we believe there are other aspiring Apprentices, at least one of them was likely at the dinner party, too. If it were me, I'd want to be sure I had someone I could trust to clean up if one or more of them blew it. And our intel shows that Raul has the strongest connection to someone we all feel was a Mastermind, so I say he's following the current Mastermind's orders."

Chuckie nodded. "Logical. Everyone going for the 'job' would have to be politically connected in some way. And that makes the most sense for his presence in town, too."

"So Raul was there to kill Eugene before he could blab, and he's around to take care of whatever else is needed while Apprentice Tryouts are going on. Getting to have the chance to kill me and Jeff is probably just part of his Christmas bonus."

"Right." Chuckie closed his eyes again. "We agree that Brewer's 'suicide' is Pia's M.O. But she was dead before it was carried out. So I ask again, why was she killed? She adapted and got her target. Why kill her before you see if she can get Brewer on the second try?"

"Well, there's always the possibility that she was in Cliff's car when he turned it on and just had bad timing," Jeff said.

"It's possible, but why would you put the car bomb in so late?" Chuckie shook his head. "I can't buy that. Cliff had to park and go inside the Capitol building, for a specific event. There was no way to judge how long it would be before he left the event to return to his car. Thirty minutes would be your best guess for the fastest he'd be back, and you always work assuming worst-case scenario. So, you wouldn't wait to set up the bomb until the last moment. You'd set it and be far, far away, confirming your alibi."

"And car bombs aren't the same as supposed suicides," Christopher said.

White nodded. "Those are more of a terrorist's or an assassin's tool. At least in our experience."

"The Dingo swears that Cliff's car wasn't set up by him. But Raul and Bernie used explosives, too, even more than the Dingo and Surly Vic do. So, Raul was told that Pia wasn't getting the job and he took her out and dumped her in Cliff's car when he rigged it to blow. Just think of the confusion when both Cliff and Pia were discovered to be together."

"We'd spend a lot of time trying to figure out the connection," Reader agreed.

"Well, Chuckie and I would, for sure."

"And you're a pit bull," Vance said.

"I beg your pardon?"

"Don't mean it as an insult. You're just someone who gets her teeth on a bone and won't let go. Metaphorically speaking."

"Metaphorically speaking, find a better metaphor next time." I loved my pit bull, Duchess, but didn't really want to be compared to her if at all possible.

"Vance is right," Chuckie said. "And that's it. That's why Pia was killed. She wasn't killed for failure. She was killed because her failure got you, and therefore the rest of us, investigating. The only reason you listened to Vance was because Santiago was dead and you'd questioned Eugene and he'd spilled his guts. That's the failure, and that's why she's dead."

"I agree," Mom said. "But we still haven't answered my question, which is why kill all those people?"

"I think the Dingo knows, or suspects. And now I have more to give him in return, or confirm for him in return. He's a lot like Olga."

"They trained in the same arena," Mom said. "So glad she's keeping you on your toes, because while you think you can trust the Dingo, I'm not nearly as convinced."

"Mossad wants to know if you want them along when you go on your cemetery sleepover," Tim said. "I haven't told them where you're going, by the way."

"Tell them thank you but no and do *not* tell them where the meet is. We need whatever intel we can get out of the Dingo and he's sure as hell not going to show if Mossad is hanging around. I'm sure they want to take him and Surly Vic out as much as they want to take Raul out, too."

"Gotcha. I'll give them another location if they seem like they're going to try to follow you anyway."

"Good plan," Mom said. "I think it's time for me to get going to question Esteban Cantu and see if he can shed any light on the subject. And I want Jeff and Christopher going with me."

"Seriously, we'll behave," Jeff said.

"Are you going to handcuff us, too?" Christopher snarked.

Mom rolled her eyes. "Really? I want the strongest empath and imageer in the world to help me question the only person we all think can tell us what's going on and who's behind it. I can take you there in handcuffs if you'd like, but I'd prefer to not have to explain why I'm bringing prisoners in and then right back out again, if it's all the same to you two."

They both had the grace to look embarrassed. "Sorry," Christopher muttered.

"Ready whenever you want to go, Angela," Jeff said, giving her his best You're the Greatest Mother-In-Law in the WORLD smile.

Mom shook her head. "Sometimes I truly understand why Kitty's so enthusiastic about working with Richard."

"You want me and Chuck along?" Kevin asked. "Or do you want us here?"

"Will Cantu talk more if they're along?" Jeff asked. "Or less?"

"He hates Chuckie. I say take Chuckie and Kevin, too, Mom. Keep Jeff and Christopher hidden, have Chuckie in there to bait Cantu. He may give something away while he's gloating about Chuckie needing his help."

Mom shot me the "really?" look. "Thank goodness you're here, because none of that would have ever occurred to me." Yes, Mom's sarcasm knob went well above eleven. "Yes, Kevin, to answer your question, I want both you and Charles along. I'd like Michael Gower along as well."

Michael looked surprised. "I'm flattered. Why?"

"I want another A-C with us. One who I can trust not to try to run off to handle someone else's part of the operation."

Michael grinned. "I'm your man."

"Good. We'll be leaving within the hour, so all of you need to be ready." Mom nodded to Kevin, then went out of the room, presumably to make high-security-level calls to secret underground strongholds.

"Uh oh," Tim said as soon as Mom was out of range. "I think we have an issue with Mossad. They know you, Kitty, so they assume you're heading into danger. They also don't seem to understand why we're not hiding in the shadows to protect you, regardless of what the Dingo thinks."

"In other words, if they go wherever you're telling them, and you're not there, Mossad's going to get suspicious, right?"

Tim nodded. "They're good. They'll find you."

"And screw up the meet," Amy said. "I think Kitty's crazy, too, but I'm also clear that you don't tell the nice assassin you're coming with people who aren't going to try to take him down, and then show up with people trying to take him down."

"Maybe Mossad is right," Abigail said. "They have more information on Raul than we do. They might have more on the Dingo, too."

"Look, I know I'm right on this one."

"Paul," Naomi said. "What does ACE think?"

Every head swiveled toward Gower. And there were three of us who were really wondering what in the world he was going to say.

CHAPTER 87

GOWER GOT THE LOOK on his face that I was familiar with, the one where he was listening to someone in his head.

He looked back at all of us. "ACE says Kitty thinks right."

"That means ACE is all for my plans, both the one we know about and the one I'm about to tell you," I said as quickly as possible.

"Okay," Tim said doubtfully. "That's all ACE said?"

"Look, time's going to be of the essence for what we'll need to do with Mossad. I'm sure ACE, more than any of us, is aware of that."

Gower nodded. "You need to tell the others what you're thinking, Kitty."

"Right. Okay, if Mossad is going to shove in and try to be all protective, let's give them something to do."

"Who needs protection?" Jeff asked. "Those of us with Angela? There's only so many she can take, right, Chuck?"

Chuckie nodded. "Right, so you can't use us to distract Mossad, Kitty."

Clearly these two were as aware as I was that ACE hadn't suddenly returned. Also as clearly they didn't think I had an actual plan in place and was just bluffing until I came up with something. Chose to be offended later.

"We need a variety of people found. I'd love to send Mossad on the Hunt for Colonel Hamlin, but then we'd have to tell them what's going on with Malcolm and probably everything else and I think we'd rather not."

"We'd definitely rather not," Chuckie said emphatically.

"Okay, so before I roll my plan idea, where's Camilla? She showed up because we had a tip that something was going down, right?"

"Right," Chuckie said. "And something did. Now I think we were tipped so that Eugene would absolutely be caught."

"I agree. Okay, so, nice dodge and all, but what is Camilla working on? I need to know so I don't duplicate effort in the wrong way."

He sighed. "She's inserting into Gaultier. Based on what happened with Buchanan, what was found there, and some other intel we have, it's the best place for her right now."

"Super, so no one's going to be on her turf. Tim and James, you guys need to get Mossad looking for Clarence. He's more dangerous than the Dingo, by far, and we need him captured. Just like Raul can tell us who took over for Reid, Clarence likely can as well. Or else he's now Raul's BFF and that means he can tell us where Raul is. Bottom line, we need him found and neutralized, but not killed. Not yet, anyway."

"What other intel, Chuck?" Amy asked. "And don't try lying to me."

"No, I can tell you. Now. We think some of the former human employees for the former Diplomatic Corps got jobs with Gaultier. We know some went to work for Titan, but they've moved on since that company's been under investigation. Camilla's been tracking them for almost as long as Jamie's been alive. They're hiding well, which means they have help and protection."

Amy nodded. "Once I take over, whatever you need, you let me know."

"This is touching," Christopher said. "But I haven't heard anyone say where they actually think Clarence is. I've been searching, and before someone insults my abilities again, I'm the fastest person here. And I've searched most of this damn town. He's nowhere, and there's no sign of him."

"I'm worried that he's in the cemetery Kitty's going to," Big George said. "That's where he ran when you chased him, right?"

"He ran in, yes, but if he kept on going, I think I have a guess as to where he went. Clarence was running all over the place when I was after him. He was trying to lose me. He gave that up finally and pretty much made a beeline for the cem-

etery. But while I think the Dingo's there because he has a
sense of humor, Clarence would never have the American
history background to find hiding out where a Civil War traitor is buried funny, and we've established that he also has no
sense of humor anyone's aware of."

"So, where is he, if he's not in the cemetery?" Christopher asked.

"I think he's somewhere he can sleep and get food without
anyone paying much attention. I think he's at Georgetown
University somewhere. He can go into a student's room and
sleep—they're not monitored and they're on winter break.
He can steal food easily, either on campus or at the Medical
Center, which is there if he gets hurt."

"That's brilliant," Reader said.

"If he's there," Christopher pointed out. "But before
anyone asks, no, I didn't search the colleges, other than the
grounds."

"So, get Mossad over there on whatever pretext you like,
then tell them why Clarence is a bigger danger than the
Dingo."

"We'll work it out." Reader looked at Gower. "You're
not coming along."

Gower rolled his eyes. "I know. I get to be bored. You
need Airborne, though. Because if Mossad says 'screw you,
we're after the Dingo,' you're going to need help."

"Yep," Reader said as Mom came back in.

"We're cleared to go, so my team, let's move. Say your
good-byes, we leave in five." Got a hug and kiss from Mom,
then she went to say good-bye to Dad and Jamie. Kevin
followed her to go say good-bye to Denise and their kids.

Jeff held me tightly then gave me his usual slow, sensu-
ous, and great kiss. "Be careful, baby," he said as we pulled
apart.

"You too. Remember to keep your head low."

"We're going to a prison facility. I'll be fine. You're having a romantic meeting with an assassin. It's you I'm worried about."

"Unless I'm there with you and no one's trying to kill us,
I don't find cemeteries to be romantic. So you can keep your
jealousy in check."

He grinned, gave me another quick kiss, and followed
after my mother to say good-bye to Jamie. Christopher and

Amy and Chuckie and Naomi were having similar good-byes. Michael looked kind of down.

"You okay?" I asked him.

He shrugged. "My girl's not here, and I don't want to call her because I'm sure I'm not supposed to be telling anyone where we're going." Chose not to share that he probably couldn't reach her anyway. Wondered how long locked-door meetings went. Too long when I needed to talk to my Washington Insiders was my feeling.

"The player's missing his girl?" Put my hand to his fore-head. "No fever."

He looked embarrassed. "Caroline's just . . . special."

"Yeah, she is. She likes you too, don't worry."

"There's liking and then there's *liking*, you know? I'm not sure she's in the *liking* category."

"Wow, are you feeling well? I've never seen you this un-confident about a woman."

Abigail came over. "Someone's in lo-ove."

Michael looked more embarrassed. "Wouldn't tell you if I was."

Abigail snorted. "Because I can tell." She sighed. "Well, not in the usual way. But I can tell by how you're acting."

"Michael, we need to go," Christopher said. "Angela doesn't like to be kept waiting."

"Later," Michael said as he trailed after Christopher and Chuckie.

"You think Caroline feels the same about Michael?" Abigail asked worriedly.

"I haven't talked to her about it." Or anything else since the party. "But I do know that they've been going out exclu-sively for longer than she ever has with anyone else."

"That's good then."

Naomi, who had been at least somewhat alert and in-volved, seemed to lose all interest the moment Chuckie walked out. She was looking at her phone, but a quick glance told me she was looking at wedding cakes.

"Okay," Tim said. "I have Mossad set up. They want to get into position early, because they're really anal."

"Or just that good."

"Yeah? Then why are we leading them on this wild goose chase? Oh, that's right. So you can meet up with as-sassins you think are your friends now."

"They are. Anyway, how are you going to search if they stake out?"

"Now, see, that's where my special genius comes in. I told them you wouldn't tell us exactly where you were meeting the Dingo. So we're going to search the area first, which because most of us are human, will take a while. James, Airborne just landed in the Georgetown Student Center bathroom. We'd better get moving. Won't look good if Mossad beats us there because they don't get to use a gate."

"Okay, girlfriend, if it goes bad, which I fully expect it to, don't play hero and call us right away. We'll use a floater and get to you."

"Will do, James, I promise."

Reader hugged and kissed Gower good-bye, then he and Tim took off. The room, which had seemed incredibly full just a few minutes ago, now felt empty, despite the fact that we still had a lot of people in here.

"What do the rest of us do?" Naomi asked, looking at her phone instead of any of us. "Sit here and wait around?" Abigail rolled her eyes and shot me a "sorry" look.

"No. Let's see if we can figure out who the mysterious L is and if there's a deeper reason for why all the reps have been killed."

"But why?" Henry asked. "Everyone's said that there's no point."

"There's still a point. We need to know if Santiago was killed only by accident or if he was on the hit list, too. Mimi, Abby, I want you two in charge of that."

"Why us?" Naomi asked, still looking at her phone. "Abby and I don't have our powers working. And I have wedding things I need to focus on," she added in a tone I could only think of as whiney and petulant.

Maybe it was because I was tired. Maybe it was because she was whining and I wasn't used to hearing any Gower whine, let alone Naomi. And maybe it was because I knew that she and Abigail felt they were handicapped now and I was tired of pretending that this was an okay attitude for them to have. Or maybe it was because she wanted to screw around with wedding stuff while everyone else tried to stop the bad guys.

I snapped.

"Oh, cry me a river."

"What?" Naomi looked and sounded shocked. Well, at least she wasn't looking at her phone for the moment.

"That means stop whining and acting like your life is all suck and no happy. Look, I get it. You have no talents any more. I'm sure that's tough. But you still have all five senses, and you've still got your minds. Why are you refusing to use them?"

"We can't function like we used to," Naomi said defensively.

"I know, believe me. Everyone knows. You've been having a humongous pity party for the past several months and I guess no one feels up to telling you the truth. But I will, because we have a lot of dead people and they'd all trade losing one sense over losing their lives, I can guarantee it. So here's the truth. You've taken the bravest, most important thing the two of you ever did and turned it into your excuse to never do anything ever again. And I personally think that sucks and you're both better than that."

"Whoa," Henry said quietly. "That's kind of harsh."

"What Kitty means," Amy said quickly, "is that we need your help, even if it's not all the help you could have given in the past."

Naomi's eyes were narrowed. "No, that's not what she means at all."

"True enough, but thanks for the attempted diplomatic save, Ames. Yes, it's harsh and yes, I mean it. I have two Cultural Attachés who haven't done squat for this Mission or their people since Operation Destruction. All you've done, Naomi, is plan a huge freaking wedding that your fiancé would rather die than attend. He'll attend it because he loves you, but he won't enjoy it."

"What?" Naomi looked seriously pissed. "How dare you! You got the huge royal wedding. You're the only one who's good enough to get one, is that what you mean?"

I snorted. "Hardly. I didn't *want* the huge royal wedding. Jeff and I had no choice. And I'd like to remind you that we were fighting for our lives, and the lives of everyone on this planet, up to around ten minutes before we trotted down the aisle, around the ballroom, and through the woods."

"I didn't want the big to-do, and neither did Christopher," Amy said quickly. "It's not the end of the world to have a small wedding."

"Chuck is *happy* to have this wedding," Naomi insisted. And then she went for one of the Standard Girl Arguments. "You're just jealous he's marrying me."

Amy cringed. Because she'd known me pretty much as long as Chuckie had, and she knew what was coming.

"Oh my God, really? Babe, let's be real. If I'd been more in love with Chuckie than I was with Jeff, *you* would not be in this picture. Happily for everyone, Chuckie's gotten over me and fallen in love with you, hurrah. But Chuckie's my best friend, and you're too busy feeling sorry for yourself and telling yourself that you 'deserve' the big wedding to pay attention to the fact that he's dreading the whole thing. He wanted to get married by a freaking Elvis impersonator in Vegas way back when. Buy a clue."

"He's never said anything like this to me! You're just making this all up!"

Abigail winced. "Sis, you might want to calm down," she said quietly.

Naomi ignored her. "You think you know Chuck better than me, but you're wrong. He'd tell me if he didn't want this wedding."

"He wants the wedding, you idiot. He just doesn't want the kind of wedding you're planning. And he hasn't said anything because he thinks you're happy. Or if he has, you've ignored it. You've turned into a raving bridal lunatic, and you know what? I was sympathetic. Right up until the moment you had the freaking nerve to act like all anyone wants you for is your talents at dream and memory reading or whatever and then to think your wedding is more important than saving people's lives. It's insulting to me, to Chuckie, to your brother, and to everyone else."

"I'm so sorry that you don't approve of my having issues with losing something that's been a part of me for my entire life," Naomi snarled.

"You want to keep on with your pity party? Go for it. But if that's your decision, here's mine—get the hell out of this Embassy and never, ever come back."

CHAPTER 88

THE ROOM WAS SILENT, to the point where someone honestly could have heard a pin drop.

Naomi huffed at me and spun on her heel. Abigail grabbed her and held her. "No," she said quietly. "I'm done. You don't get to leave."

"What? Why not? She's insulted us and told me to get out."

"No," Abigail said calmly. "She insulted *you*. By telling you the truth, what I should have had the guts to tell you months ago. And she only said to get out if you were refusing to stop feeling sorry for yourself."

Gower put his arm around Naomi. "You are not leaving."

"Are you getting rid of her, then?" Naomi asked.

"No," he said calmly. "Because Kitty's right. You've been acting like a spoiled, petulant child, and we can no longer afford to allow you that luxury."

"But she was mean to me!"

"Did you lose maturity when you lost your powers? I mean that seriously. I've never heard you this whiney and out of control, Naomi. Is it just the wedding crap, are you sick, or have you simply become the biggest whining pain in the ass ever?"

"How can you talk to me like this?" Naomi asked.

Amy rolled her eyes. "Oh, for God's sake. She's talking to you like this because she cares about you, and, more than that, she cares about Chuck. I'm with Kitty—why should we let him marry a whining loser? Or, to put it another way, who are you and what have you done with the Naomi we know and love?"

"Could she be an android? I'm sort of serious."

"You want to cut my head off to find out?" Naomi snarled. "Tito might be able to sew it back on."

"Tito. Good call." I grabbed her wrist and pulled. I was riding on waves of fury—there was no way Naomi was getting away from me. We headed out of the kitchen and for the stairs. Everyone else followed us. Dinner and a show. Though we hadn't had dinner, come to think of it.

"Let me go."

"Only when we get to the top so you can roll down the stairs."

"When did you become my enemy?"

"When did I become your romantic rival? You played that card, my friend, I didn't."

"You're pulling rank."

"Babe, I *have* the rank. Ergo, I get to pull it all I want." I'd been moving at the slower hyperspeed, so we reached the third floor quickly. I headed us into the infirmary.

Nurse Carter stared at us. "You two okay?"

"Major girl fight between me and Whiney Bridezilla here. Is Nathalie awake?"

"Yes. Doctor Hernandez is with her. I don't think it's a good idea for you to go in."

"No, probably not. But I think we need to." Went to the room Nathalie had been in. Knocked quietly and then opened the door.

Nathalie was crying. Less hysterically than before, but still, crying. I shoved Naomi into the room. "Her husband was just murdered in front of her, tossed off the top of the building where they lived and were happy. We don't know why. I wanted you in charge of trying to figure that out while the rest of us were off doing other things to try to figure out who killed him and why. We're fighting because of your response to that request. Think about someone other than yourself for the first time in what appears to be far too long a time."

I closed the door and held it shut.

"Kitty," Abigail said slowly, "I have to ask—is this a common human technique?"

"No, it's not."

"Ah. Because it seems like you and Naomi are really fighting."

"We are. She doesn't get her act together before I have to go hang with the Dingo, she's persona non grata in this Embassy."

"Um, she's marrying your best friend."

"Sucks to be her, then. He'll still have to come here all the time. She won't be allowed. Ever."

"I know you're angry with her attitude," Gower said. "We've all been dealing with it for months. But I don't understand why you're *so* angry, Kitty."

"Maybe you all don't. Here's the deal. I've seen a lot of people die in front of me over the past three days. Santiago died while I was holding his hand. Edmund Brewer fell to the ground pretty much at my feet. Representative Juvonic died on the floor of Rayburn House, in front of me. And Eugene Montgomery had his head blown off while I was standing next to him."

"I can understand why that's upsetting," Gower said soothingly.

"Yeah. And now my husband and yours are off on missions, and the rest of us are about to be. All of those missions have danger attached to them. And your sister made the unfortunate decision to whine about being asked to lead the team that gets to sit inside the Embassy, in our large yet cozy kitchen, and look for clues that we might be able to find in dead people's trash."

White cleared his throat and Gower and Abigail turned to look at him. "Yes, Uncle Richard?" Abigail said hopefully.

"If I may, Paul?"

Gower nodded. "Please."

"Katherine has not been allowed to grieve. At all. Whereas Naomi has been allowed to grieve perhaps a little too long. I believe there is a tiny bit of jealousy at the core of Katherine's reactions, though not about who's marrying whom. Katherine isn't allowed the luxury of wallowing in her loss."

"I can see how that would make you jealous," Abigail said. "Sis has gotten to plan a wedding, only, and we haven't done our jobs, when we can do them without talents. Maybe not as well, maybe just as well. But we don't know because we haven't tried. I'd be mad at us, too."

White came to me. "You're allowed to cry. And perhaps you should. Now. Before we go meet up with your 'uncle' the assassin."

"I don't need to." Felt far too angry to cry.

"I think you might," White said.

Looked at Amy. "How pissed off and crazy do I look?"

"I wish Jeff and Chuck were both here and I'm glad Jamie isn't."

"Ah. Gotcha." Looked back to White. "I'm too angry to cry."

He patted my shoulder. "That will pass."

There was a knock on the door I was holding. Decided to try to get back to normal, so I opened it.

Tito stepped out quickly. "I'd ask what's going on, and if I need to hand out sedatives to everyone, but I think I caught enough when you flung Naomi at my patient."

"Is Nathalie okay?"

Tito nodded. "I think what you wanted to have happen did." He opened the door and gently shoved me into the room. Naomi was holding Nathalie and rocking her while Nathalie cried and clung to Naomi.

Naomi looked at me and there were tears in her eyes. "I get it."

Someone came in and closed the door. It was Amy. She went over to Nathalie and took her from Naomi. "You two work it out," she said softly. "And do it quietly."

Naomi got up off the bed and stepped closer to me. "You really hurt my feelings."

"I know. You really disappointed me and pissed me off."

"I know. Did Chuck tell you he doesn't want the big wedding?"

"He had one guy for his side, James, who isn't his friend, in that sense, but is his fiancée's brother-in-law. Jeff had to suggest himself as best man. Chuckie didn't have to tell me, all I needed was to look at him and hear how friendless he feels. He'll do anything for you, but you need to do the same for him."

She nodded. "Do you really want me to leave and never come back?"

"No. Do you really want to keep wallowing in your loss?"

She looked over her shoulder. "No." She turned back. "I get what you meant. She'd give up a limb, her sight, her looks, if she could get him back. I lost something precious, but we don't even know if that's a permanent loss. But I haven't lost the most precious things. That's why you're mad at me, isn't it?"

"Pretty much, yeah. Well, that and you acting like your wedding is more important than saving someone's life or bringing a murderer to justice."

She sighed. "I was originally thinking a small wedding."

"I was originally thinking I'd get to enjoy my daughter's first birthday party."

"Yeah."

We were both quiet. My anger was ebbing fast. Which meant embarrassment for blowing up at Naomi in front of a lot of people was vying for my attention. "I'm glad Chuckie's marrying you, you know."

"I know. I've really been a horrible Bridezilla. I'm not asking, I'm saying. And you haven't even seen most of it."

"Everyone will forgive you if you go back to being you."

"Even you?"

"Especially me. You're marrying one of the five most important men in the world to me. I don't want to be angry with you or have you angry with me. I liked you before you and Chuckie got together. I want him to be happy. And you make him happy."

"I'm not sure he'd pick me over you."

"I am, but let's not force him to choose."

"Deal."

Amy sighed. "Kitty, you need to let it out. There's only us here, and Richard's right."

"Right about what?" Naomi asked.

"Right about the only thing Kitty's jealous of you over. You've gotten to wallow, and she hasn't even gotten to cry."

"I have. I cried when Santiago died. And even when Eugene died."

"But you just lost another friend," Naomi said softly.

"Yeah." I could feel tears wanting to come. I just didn't want to let them.

"Tell me about him, Nathalie's husband," Naomi said. "Please."

Could have said a lot of things about Brewer. But what came out of my mouth wasn't what I was thinking. "He was going to be Jeff's mentor, you know, the guy who helped him learn his job and was there to back him up. He was all excited about it, and it was like we were going to have friends, a couple, who we could do nice normal people things with, even though we're not normal people. Jeff's going to be all alone there now, with no one he likes or trusts to turn to. And I'm going to be all alone, too."

Naomi shook her head. "No, you won't. We're family, all of us. We fight, and we get mad, and we say angry words, but when it's over, we're still family. That's just how it is." She smiled. "And there's nothing you can do about that. You're stuck with us and we're stuck with you."

The tears chose this moment to decide they'd held off damn well long enough. I started to cry. Naomi hugged me and I hugged her back. Which of course meant that I was now doing the really big, body-wracking sobs.

"Sorry," I managed to get out, as I started slowing down.

"It's okay. I'm not crying because I used all my wallowing over stupid stuff. And don't worry. I promise, we'll work on what you wanted us to. And if there are clues there, we'll find them."

"I hate fighting with people I like."

She laughed. "Me too. So let's go fight with people we don't like."

"I want to help," Nathalie said. "It's my husband they killed."

Naomi and I pulled apart. "Are you sure?" Nathalie didn't look like she could walk, let alone focus on clues. Then again, I probably looked like a crazy person, so I was in no position to judge.

"Yes. Please, let me help."

"Absolutely," Amy said. "Let's get you and Kitty cleaned up, and then we'll get you a nice glass of warm milk and you can help us look for clues."

There was a sink in every infirmary room, thankfully. I did the cold water splash and then blew my nose for a while. Amy and Naomi helped Nathalie do the same. Reasonably presentable, we left the room.

Everyone was out there, waiting, looking worried or expectant, or both. "Everyone okay?" Gower asked.

"Yes," Naomi said. "Kitty and I are both sorry we had a fight in front of you, I was being a jerk, she's sorry she hurt my feelings by telling me the truth, and Nathalie wants to help us look for clues."

"I'm not sure that's a good idea," Tito said.

"Not a problem," Naomi said cheerfully. "You and Magdalena can come down with us to watch Nathalie and help dig through the trash."

Tito looked at me. "Seriously?"

"Yeah. I told you this job was going to be all you could ask for and more."

CHAPTER 89

MY FIGHT WITH NAOMI had taken up a nice chunk of time. We went downstairs, choked some food down, then the others got back to the business of searching for stuff. Oliver and the boys had brought Adriana over from the Romanian Embassy, possibly to help prevent me and Naomi from killing each other, but she was helping dig through our "clues" with good cheer.

Sent another text to Caroline, just out of pathetic optimism. Pathetic optimism was shown to be a sap as the automated response came back. Didn't they even go to the bathroom during these things?

Thusly foiled from getting any in-the-know answers yet again, trotted upstairs to say good-bye to Dad and Jamie. It was still obvious I'd been crying, but Dad didn't mention it and happily, neither did Jamie. She was ready for bed, so I sang her a song using the stuffed eagle, tucked her in, kissed her good night, then changed clothes.

It had been far too many days spent in heels and nice dresses. I was going to a late-night rendezvous and needed to be properly attired. Aerosmith thermal, jeans, and my Converse on, hair pulled back in a ponytail, Glock and clips in my purse along with all the rest of my usual paraphernalia, and I was just about ready to go.

"I need a shorter coat or jacket or whatever. The trench is great, but in case I need to run, I'd like to be able to do so while still staying warm," I said to the hamper. Backed out of the closet and closed the door. Opened the door and walked back in. There was a nice, shearling-lined, suede jacket—lining was white, suede was black. Maybe it was the Elves who drove the A-Cs' slavish devotion to white and black.

Chose not to ponder. Grabbed the jacket. "Thanks again, you guys rock."

Gave Dad another hug and kiss and then went back downstairs. My team was ready, White and Raj in their suits and trench coats, Rahmi and Rhee in all black, slacks and sweaters, but no coats. True to expectations and my threats, they both had battle staffs. Where they'd hidden them on arrival, I had no idea, but I was happy to see them tonight.

"You all can take your coats off," Gower said. "The Kevlar's here."

"Oh, right." Had forgotten we were all going decked out. Followed Gower into the salon where our body armor was waiting. "Paul, I count six vests, not five."

"You count correctly," he said as he took a vest. "I'm going with you."

"Um, James expressly told you to stay here."

"He did. But as the Pontifex, not only am I part of Alpha Team, but it's also my duty to watch over my people. You need me along, and I mean you, specifically, Kitty."

"Just because I got into a verbal chick fight with your sister doesn't mean you need to be at risk."

Gower shrugged. "I feel it's important I go, so I'm going."

Was tempted to ask him what ACE thought, but didn't think he deserved it. Gower wanted to kick butt, I was sure, but maybe he was right. I hadn't lost it like that with someone I liked in a very long time.

"Fine. But I'm in charge on this one."

Gower grinned. "Kitty, in all the time I've known you, when *haven't* you been in charge?"

"Good point."

We all went off, changed, and came back. It was hard to tell that anyone was wearing a bulletproof vest, which was the point. Quick discussion about how we were going to get there. Len and Kyle felt we should let them drive us over. Hacker International suggested we use a gate.

"We have more maneuverability if we run," Raj said. "We all have hyperspeed, so it shouldn't be an issue."

"Let's get going and get there, then. I don't want to be late."

"We have plenty of time," White said.

"Yeah, but I just feel like we need to get going."

"Maybe you're still upset," Gower said.

Considered this. "No, actually I feel a lot better. Naomi and I have made up, I had that cry you all wanted me to, I don't feel angry or upset or even tired anymore. I just feel like we urgently need to get to the cemetery, early or not."

"Then let's go," Rahmi said. "The leader sets the pace." Rhee nodded.

"Right, you two are going to flank our Pontifex and keep him safe. And, girls, please remember that you're not killing anyone unless they actively try to hurt one of us or I tell you to, okay? Or one of the men with us needs your help and all that. Got it?" They both nodded. "Good. Then let's go visit the dead."

Pierre opened the door for us, and we zipped out. White had my hand, but Raj led the way, with the princesses and Gower bringing up the rear. We stayed on the streets—no running over water for us. But it still didn't take very long to get there.

Once in the cemetery, I navigated us back to where I'd been when I'd seen the Dingo last. This took longer than I'd expected it to, but we were still in place well before ten. Raj and Rahmi went off to search for Hidden Assassin Caves and the like, while the rest of us hung around, waiting. Getting here early suddenly seemed really stupid.

Before I could mention that I was sorry we were all freezing our butts off, my phone rang. Dug it out. "Kit-Kat, I have a ton of missed calls and texts from you. What's going on?"

Wanted to ask questions, but figured being polite was probably a nicety we could afford. "Hey, Caro Syrup, how're you feeling?"

"I'm better, Michael took good care of me. But Kit-Kat, we just heard about Ed Brewer. Are you all okay? Is that why you've been trying to reach me?"

"Yeah, well, part of why. We were there. It was . . . pretty horrible, honestly."

"They're saying he killed himself. He never struck me as the type."

"He wasn't the type. But we'll let the police do their thing right now."

"How's his wife?"

"Nathalie's a mess. She's staying with us right now, though."

"Ah. Is Michael helping take care of her?"

"Um, what? No. He's doing something with and for my mom. Why?"

"Oh." She sounded relieved. "I've tried to call him a couple times and he hasn't picked up. I just . . ."

"You were just worried your man was hitting on the widow who happens to be a former international model?"

"Not at all!"

"Pull the other one."

"Oh, okay, fine. Yes, I was worried."

"Why? Has Michael been seeing other people?"

"No. Not at all. We see each other a lot, we're exclusive. It's just . . ."

"Caro, you're normally not this non-communicative."

"I really like him. I mean really. And I'm not sure I should. I mean, he's not ready to stop being a playboy."

"Um, Caro, all I can say is that you should stop worrying." Didn't want to give away what Michael had said, but I didn't want her worrying about this, either. "What does the senator think?"

"He thinks Michael's great. He wanted me to go out with him tonight instead of working. But since I can't reach Michael, I might as well work."

"What are you guys working on? It's Christmas Eve." Said the person hanging out in a cemetery with five other people, all wearing Kevlar. Yeah, I rocked the Christmas Eve spirit. "I mean, Kelly told me you were in meetings about Armstrong's presidential bid, but two days straight seems kind of excessive."

"Well, we have a lot going on. There are some bills the Senate's going to be voting on when the new session officially starts. The senator's got a lot of fighting and persuading still to do, and he and Senator Armstrong aren't certain they'll sway enough votes. And the outcome of the votes is going to affect Senator Armstrong's run."

Interesting new news. "What's on the line?"

"Lots of things to do with the A-Cs. The anti-alien groups have really shoved some crap into things."

"Why is Armstrong working on this with McMillan? I didn't think they were close. At all."

"Well, they're the two most pro-A-C senators on the Hill. Didn't you realize that's why they were sitting with you and Jeff at the dinner party?"

"No, I didn't. So why was Edmund Brewer seated with us?"

"For the same reason, just like Santiago Reyes. Representative Brewer was one of the most pro-alien reps out there. Santiago won on the pro-alien ticket."

Things started to click into place. What a pity I hadn't had this conversation with Caroline two days ago. Reminded myself that I'd tried to have said conversation. Mentioned to myself that I should have chosen to use Kelly's Batphone privileges and would not make that mistake again in the future. Should we have one. "Caro, who are the other pro-alien reps? The influential ones?"

"There are a few, but unfortunately, some of them have passed away in this last year." Almost asked her why she hadn't told me this before, but remembered that Caroline and Michael had missed Vance's big Reveal on the Rooftop, and Michael had only really gotten up to speed tonight. And Caroline had been paying attention to the senatorial side of this thing, where no one had yet to be killed.

"Name them. Please."

"Bowers, Holmes, Callahan, Porter, and Delarosa."

"So, does that mean we have no more pro-alien representatives in the House?"

"Well," Caroline said with a little laugh. "Jeff's in there now, so there's one for sure."

"I need to talk to Senator McMillan. Right now."

"Uh, okay. Hang on."

Covered the phone while Caroline spoke to McMillan. "Mister White, we need Raj and Rahmi back, pronto. The hell with the Dingo's hideout." White nodded and pulled out his phone.

"Hello, Ambassador? What can I do for you?"

"The bills you and Armstrong are worried about, there's a line in all of them that's basically saying that no alien can ever go against any U.S. law and such, correct?"

"Yes. How did you know?"

"Long story we have no time for. There are bills just like those going through the House."

"Yes. I heard Caroline's side of your conversation. She listed most of those in the House who were planning to use their influence to get those bills shot down or returned to committee."

"Right, they're all dead. Which of all of them was the most influential? Holmes?"

"Well, I'd say that Wendell was, yes. But Edmund Brewer was as well. He was a junior congressman, but he had a good ability to sway. And he was hugely pro-alien. You've lost a good friend in more ways than one today."

"Yeah, I'm picking that up. He didn't kill himself, by the way. So, Caroline didn't sound like you all think the Senate's going to shoot down those anti-alien bills."

"There are less of us, but not all constituents in all states feel comfortable with the new world order. There's quite a lot of clamor for restrictions, if you will."

"Those aren't restrictions, though. Those are laws that will force the A-Cs into slavery to the government."

"I agree. It's why I oppose them, as does Senator Armstrong."

"If they pass, the President could veto. What happens if he does?"

"If they pass in the first place, they'll probably pass again to overturn the veto. It would be very bad for the President, either way, honestly. If he doesn't veto, he's lost the trust and support of all of the A-Cs. If he does veto, he's going against the wishes of the majority of the country. At least that's how it'll be spun in the media."

"If they pass, the A-Cs will have to leave the U.S., if not the planet." Because I wouldn't let them stay, and neither would the rest of the leadership.

"Well, that's better than it could be, honestly."

"Really? What's a worse option than exile?"

McMillan was quiet for a moment. "War."

CHAPTER 90

"**SENATOR,** I need to ask you three questions."

"Go ahead."

"First off, the other representatives that are dead, are they all pro-alien in some way?"

"Honestly, no. At least as many virulently anti-alien representatives have passed away, and there were many undecided or neutral also who we've lost in this year."

"Interesting. Secondly, is there any one person who could influence enough of the House and Senate to ensure that these bills die without issue?"

"Lillian Culver. Her clients are incredibly influential, so her views hold great sway."

Awesome. My best option to save the day was Joker Jaws. Did it get any better than this? Sources said that it probably did. "Don't tell me, let me guess—Guy Gadoire would be number two on the sway list, wouldn't he?"

"Why do you think Senator Armstrong spends time with them?"

"You don't."

"I do when I need to make certain things happen." Well, at least I could comfort myself that precedent had been set in the arena of Making Pacts with the Devil.

"I'm just going to spitball it here and bet that Culver and Gadoire are being coy about using any influence on this issue, right?"

He sighed. "Right."

Of course right. They weren't idiots; they were really

damned good at their jobs. And that meant that what they wanted was for one of us—me, Jeff, Reader, Gower—to ask them for help.

"Okay, here's my third official question. Where is the nearby holding facility that no normal person knows about that's both underground, very secure, and where the P.T.C.U. and the C.I.A. and lord knows who else store their very special prisoners?"

"Why?"

"I need to find someone who's there, and it has no cell phone reception." Took the guess because Caroline had been calling Michael and he hadn't answered. "And I think I need to find them urgently."

"Well, your clearance could be high enough. I'd check but it's Christmas Eve so I'm going to assume it is and if I'm wrong, oh, dear."

"Works for me."

"The facility is in the Pentagon."

So much for the idea that I'd get a hold of Mom, Jeff, or anyone else on that team. I was willing to storm the castle if we had to, but the six of us breaking into the Pentagon's underground prisoner vault seemed wildly unwise. "Thank you. One more bonus round question, please."

"Go ahead."

"Do you know who's influenced the anti-alien wording in all these bills? Is it one person or a group or does everyone just really fear us this much?"

"There's no one specific group that's leading the charge, though of course there are always those who are more vocal. The Secretary of Transportation is very anti and he's barely hiding it. Because of his relationship with her Chief Aide, the Secretary of State is on the fence, but leaning toward getting the A-Cs under a firmer level of control."

"Wonderful. Anyone else?"

"Well, Senator Kramer isn't doing any of you any favors, and neither is Senator Montgomery. They aren't anti, per se, but whenever they're discussing the A-Cs, somehow you all come off sounding like loose cannons with absolutely no regard for the safety of those around you."

"I'm confused. All these people are friends with each other, and friends with the Armstrongs, and were friends with the Brewers. How is it that they can hang when they're diametrically opposed on a big issue? And don't give me the old 'politics makes strange bedfellows' answer. I got that enough from Armstrong."

"Before you were exposed as being here, you were a force to be manipulated, and everyone wanted in on that."

"Right. Everyone wants to control the X-Men or the Hulk."

"Correct. Now that you're outed, you're able to openly tip the balance of power, and that means that you yourselves have great power. Some, like Senator Armstrong and the late Representative Brewer, were excited by the possibilities of what could be achieved. Some, like the Secretary of Transportation, were worried about the power they could lose."

Two people appeared out of the shadows. "Okay, thank you, Senator. I have to go now, but I really appreciate you clearing things up for me. And thank you for fighting for us."

"I don't mind the fighting, but I do mind losing. I truly pray we don't lose this particular battle."

"Will do my best to ensure that we don't."

We hung up and I waved to the Dingo and Surly Vic. "Nice to see you. Need your help."

The Dingo looked around. "You have come with more than I expected." He didn't sound happy.

"It's a compliment because I know you two are just that good. Everyone, raise your hands so the Dingo can see you're not armed."

"They're holding staffs," Surly Vic pointed at Rahmi and Rhee.

"They are. You're both wearing high-powered semiautomatics. You just let me know the day staffs are faster than bullets and then I'll apologize for all of two of us having weapons. We're under attack, guys, and we can't really afford to be pussyfooting around with people we can supposedly trust not to harm us."

The Dingo nodded. "Fine. Let's ensure this meeting is swift."

"Absodamnlutely. Look, I have a ton of questions and you probably won't want to answer all of them, but we're running out of time and I honestly don't know what to do."

"Yes, you want me to be Sherlock Holmes."

"I do, I really do. Okay, gang, gather round, because I'm going to update our friends here on what I just learned and I want to avoid having to say it twice." My team came closer, though Rahmi and Rhee stood a little apart, keeping watch. "Someone's killing off people in the House of Representatives at the same time as there are a lot of anti-alien clauses that have been shoved into every bill going up for vote, in both the House and the Senate."

"The Senate, too?" Gower asked, sounding as worried as I felt.

"Yes, and Senator McMillan isn't feeling confident that the pro-alien faction is going to win the day on his side of Congress. He wasn't as worried about the House, because we used to have a lot of really strong supporters with a lot of influence there. As of today, they're all dead, other than my husband, and he's alive only by chance. He was shot in the middle of the street."

"We did not try to kill him," Surly Vic said.

"Neither did Raul," the Dingo added. "Word is that the shooter was a woman."

"Maybe that's why Pia was killed," Raj said to me. "She failed to kill two targets."

"I've got a better bet, and she's going by the name of Dier. Maybe she wasn't really serving the water at our dinner party to help or hinder Brewer's attempted murder and Santiago's real one. Maybe she was there so she'd know exactly what Jeff and I looked like."

"It's a common enough technique," the Dingo allowed. "And Bernice was very fond of getting close to her victims before killing them."

"Yeah, believe me, I remember. So Raul's found another chick with the same can-do, people person attitude."

"It is very likely," the Dingo said. "But I cannot believe this is why you wanted to meet with me."

"Nope, still just catching you up on the latest that is My So-Called Normal Life. Okay, so here's the thing—there are a lot more people dead in the House than just the six really pro-alien ones. We have almost two dozen dead and gone, including some very anti-alien representatives. Oh, and my team, based on my most recent phone call, I think Santiago was always on the kill list."

"You're sure?" Gower asked.

"We'll get the details for why later, Paul," White said. "For now, we'll assume Missus Martini is right. Please go on."

"Thanks. And, with this new information, I don't know that Jeff or I are really part of what's going on. I sincerely think Raul is combining business with pleasure."

"Again, we know he's here to kill you," the Dingo said. "He may have an assignment, but you are not that assignment."

"Gotcha, we are taking me and Jeff out of the equation for the moment then and just focusing on everyone who's actually dead. So, I get why our enemies would kill off the people who are pro-alien. They want some or all of these bills to pass, so legislation is put in place that forces us to become virtual slaves, leave, or declare war. What I don't understand is why you'd kill off the people who want to pass those bills."

The Dingo looked thoughtful. "Is that all?"

"No. I need to know why someone wanted Edmund Brewer killed so publicly. If, as said, we're removing me and Jeff from the picture, all the others were done so well they looked like natural deaths or legitimate accidents. And today, they set up Brewer's death to look like a suicide, complete with a note."

"Does he have family?" the Dingo asked.

"Yes, but we took his wife with us, so the murder-suicide option was removed from the Bad Guy Playbook. And that would have flown because, two days ago, they both publicly admitted that he knew she'd had an affair. So a very believable fight, a dead 'cheating' wife, a suicide of remorse."

Surly Vic looked kind of impressed. "That would be a good option to remove witnesses and ensure a message is sent."

"I think the message is 'I want a lot of people dead.' But the first attempt at murdering Edmund Brewer wasn't like any of these. Eugene Montgomery was trying to poison Brewer, and it seems like happenstance that Santiago Reyes died instead. Only, Raul and his female partner were on the scene. We've got a good guess now for why she was there. But why was Raul there? Was it just to get me? I don't think so, because Raul killed Eugene and we're pretty sure the shot was meant to take out both of us. He shot about a minute too late, though, after Eugene had given me some information I'm sure our enemies didn't want me to have."

"The delay was because of us," the Dingo said. "He was able to shoot because of your sister and your friend."

"So, he knows you're here?" Raj asked.

Surly Vic nodded. "Again, because of the two women."

"They're really sorry and won't do it again. So, do you have any guess, any guess at all, as to why Eugene was set up to kill Brewer at my dinner party, in front of tons of people, so that Eugene would be caught and convicted of the crime? Everything else that's going on makes some kind of logical sense, but that doesn't, any more than killing off your own supporters seems like a sane move."

"How varied were the causes of death?" the Dingo asked.

"We think there was probably more than one person doing the assassinations," Raj said quickly. Took that to mean he didn't want me to share the Master and Apprentice theory with our friends the assassins. Pity.

"We've been told there's one Mastermind out there who's cooked up almost every conspiracy and related theory since the nineteen sixties. We believe that this person has passed on their evil wisdom to an Apprentice, who becomes the Mastermind when the other dies."

"Like the Sith?" Surly Vic asked.

"Yes!" *Star Wars* was truly omnipresent worldwide.

"I could believe it," he said. "The C.I.A. is very involved in many bad things."

"Speaking of which, Esteban Cantu, Master or Apprentice?"

"If he was the Master then his Apprentice has taken over, because he is not accessible," the Dingo said calmly. "And believe me, we would like access to him, because the price on his head is quite high. He is an open assignment — whoever has Proof of Death will receive payment."

Tried not to worry about Mom and Jeff and the others going to visit the guy who had the Assassins' Open Season sign on his forehead. Failed.

"As for the others," the Dingo said, "if you are correct and there is competition for a slot, while at the same time there is the desire to ensure no one is aware you are killing specific people, then random selection would enter."

"Random selection?" Rhee asked. Apparently Amazons had great hearing.

The Dingo nodded. "You choose a set of victims for each contender. You put one or two of your truly desired candidates into each group."

"Ensuring, of course, that each candidate does not know your true identity," Surly Vic added. "Otherwise, you risk too much exposure."

"This method allows you to test your recruits' ability to follow orders while proving their loyalty to you. You are able to see if they are skilled enough to ensure the authorities consider the deaths accidental or natural, and if they are not successful here, they are the ones who the authorities arrest. And you remove your enemies at the same time." The Dingo said all of this like he was outlining how to best prep for the after-Christmas sales.

"They've killed almost two dozen people."

Surly Vic shrugged. "We have more than two dozen enemies. So do you. If the Mastermind is any good, so does he. So he used this test to remove many enemies at once, both for this plan and for others. If he *is* the Mastermind, then this plan makes much sense and becomes even more efficient."

"Your bigger issue is the public death, yes?" the Dingo asked.

"Yes. Because it seems out of character for the rest of what's going on."

"I agree. It was very ... showy, yes?"

"Yes," Raj said. "In a very horrible way."

"The question is why? Why kill Edmund Brewer in such a public way, when every other murder has been done so quietly?"

The Dingo shook his head. "That is not the right question. The correct question is this: Who had the most to gain from the situation?"

"The Mastermind," Gower said promptly.

The Dingo shook his head again. "No. The Mastermind wants the quiet deaths. His plan is insidious, yes, but it is a quiet plan. I would presume the Mastermind would have preferred no one notice that these deaths, any of them, were murders."

"One of those trying to become Apprentices," White suggested.

"Logical," the Dingo agreed. "However, which one had the most to gain?"

"We don't know who any of them are," White said.

"Find out who had the most to gain and you find your aspiring Apprentice."

"I would have said Pia had the most to gain," Raj said. "Only she was killed, and we think it was because this murder attracted too much of Kitty's attention."

"How was she killed?" Surly Vic asked.

"She blew up in a car bomb intended for the Head of Special Immigration Services for Homeland Security." Figured it was better to use Cliff's title—it could trigger something for my Assassin Agatha Christies. "We don't know, but presume, that she was dead before the bomb went off."

"Was the politician killed as well?" the Dingo asked.

"No, because he used his new remote starter function. The blast was unreal. My husband and I and one of our friends would have been in the car with him, too."

"Was that known?"

"No, it was pretty impromptu, so I don't think the three of us were the targets, just Cliff."

"So Raul was cleaning things up," Surly Vic said.

"You think that's his signature, too?" Because I sure did.

"Yes," the Dingo said. "As I told you, he has done much work for the C.I.A., and other government agencies. Another showy death, but presumably sending a different message than the other."

"You think it's not connected to all of this?"

He shrugged. "I have no way of knowing. However, it sounds separate, other than that your presumed aspiring Apprentice was in the car." He shook his head. "Determine who had the most to gain from the one man's death, or from the other man's capture."

The Dingo was going to say something else, when Rahmi shouted, "Down!"

So I wasn't too surprised when I heard gunfire.

CHAPTER 91

FORTUNATELY, A-Cs had really great reflexes. Despite Christopher's lack of faith in their abilities in a Field Situation, White tackled me and Gower, Raj tackled the two assassins, while Rahmi and Rhee moved so fast they were two blurs. So the bullets missed all of us. Barely, to be sure, but barely was darned well good enough.

The princesses were blurry, but I could still make them out. They were spinning their battle staffs while they ran in a sort of circle, creating a perimeter around us. As near as I could tell, the staffs were moving fast enough that they were deflecting bullets.

"Two attackers," Rhee called. "Both with projectiles."

"Girls, take out the projectiles if you can safely," I shouted. This earned another flurry of bullets. I couldn't see anyone, and that meant the probability of one of the attackers being Clarence was much higher. The princesses were still managing to deflect and avoid bullets.

The six of us were still on the ground, though now all of us were on our stomachs. The two assassins had gotten their guns into position before they'd hit the ground. We scooted and scrambled and got behind a couple of large headstones nearby. They weren't offering a lot of shelter, but something was better than nothing.

"Do you have a secret hideout nearby that we can get to?" I asked as I dug my Glock out of my purse and hooked said purse over my neck.

"We're blocked from it," the Dingo replied tersely.

"That's Raul shooting at us, isn't it?"

"Probably. He's anticipated us."

"And has likely discovered our hideout," Surly Vic added.

"Awesome. Think he's figured out you're trying to protect me?"

"Or that we're trying to stop him," the Dingo said. "Either way, either he or we die tonight."

"Super. Let's make sure that it's him. Richard, Raj, Paul, I think it's time for us to do something here."

"Raj, protect the Pontifex," White said. "Missus Martini, I believe I can see our shooters, and I meant the plural."

"Oh, good. Raul's new chick's along for the ride?"

"Presumably. Can you see where the shots are coming from? I can, but I want to make sure you can as well."

"They're in some trees. Dude loves to perch, doesn't he?" As I said this, it occurred to me that I had no idea where Bruno was. Or Harlie and Poofikins, for that matter. "So, do we run up into the trees or just shake them really hard?"

"You both stay down," the Dingo said, as he aimed and fired. The bullets didn't stop coming at us.

Something was wrong with all of this. It was like we were in an Old West shootout. We had the poorer ground—we were low, the enemy was high. And yet, the bullets weren't really coming near us. If we'd been standing up we'd likely be shot, but the shooters hadn't altered their aim. At all.

Meaning there wasn't anyone actually shooting.

"Richard, there's no one manning those guns. Can you get to them without being hit?"

"As long as the friendly fire ceases."

"Uncles Peter and Victor, please stop shooting. You're wasting ammo we're going to need."

They stopped and White took off. He had to run around Rahmi in order to not get hit by bullets or battle staffs, but he was up in one of the offending trees in just a couple of seconds. The shooting from that tree stopped. White climbed down the one tree and up the other. The gunfire stopped completely. The princesses stopped spinning their staffs.

"Why the elaborate charade?" Gower asked.

Been asking that myself. "My guess is that we need to turn around and be ready for an ambush."

"You do." The voice wasn't Clarence's. It was Doreen's. "Stand up, too, please."

Did as requested to see Doreen and Irving standing there. It was dark out but my eyes were adjusted and A-Cs had better night vision, which I'd also inherited, so it was easy to see that they were holding guns. Clarence was between them.

"Wow. Did not see this one coming." Though, as I thought about it, I hadn't seen Doreen and Irving all day or night.

She shrugged. "Clarence was my father's Chief Aide. He was like a second father to me. When you told me he was back, I used an old method I'd heard my father talk about to reach him."

"You nursed him back to health?"

"No," Clarence said. "That was my new friend who also hates you."

"Raul, or someone else?"

"I don't know," Doreen said. "I haven't cared enough to ask. We only connected yesterday."

There was something about the way Doreen was talking, her choices of words. And her tone of voice—she was Over-The-Top Evil Genius About To Twirl Mustache. And yet, there were three of us holding guns, and she hadn't told us to drop them. An idea nudged. "Is Raul here, too? Or is he killing Esteban Cantu?"

"I took care of that already," Clarence said with a grin. "And your mother and the two kings with her are dealing with the blame."

"Who tipped you off that they were going there?"

"Clarence says he has friends in high places," Doreen answered, sounding incredibly impressed. The idea solidified. Now, how to share it with the others?

"Like who? Langston Whitmore?"

"That idiot?" Clarence laughed. "He's not as important as he thinks he is." But since Clarence knew who he was, it was likely Whitmore was one of the Apprentice Wannabes.

"How did you get in? I mean, it's impossible. I wanted to go there, but realized there was no way any of us here could manage it."

Doreen snorted. "Especially since everyone with you is really untrained in any kind of Field work, let alone the skills needed to do what Clarence did." Hoped the others were catching the clue by now, but couldn't risk looking at their expressions.

"Don't buy it. Clarence has never struck me as that smart."

He smirked. "Your mommy had to call for clearance. We have the right people on our side, and they contacted Raul. It's hard to get into the Pentagon, sure, if you're a human," he sneered the word. "But I just waited around until they showed up and ran past them."

"Just like you did in order to kill Edmund Brewer earlier."

"Yeah, and you'd think your genius of a husband would have thought of that, but it didn't occur to him at all. So, once in, it was easy enough to move so fast no one could see me and get where I needed to go."

"Oh, I'm sure it wasn't easy," Doreen said. "Did you have to kill a lot of people?"

"No. That wasn't my part to play in this instance. Stole a keycard off of someone and used it to get down levels. Card stopped working? Grabbed another card. Places like that, once you're in, they think you should be in. Found Cantu's cell, gave him a nice drink filled with arsenic. Your 'team' came in, I left. Cantu died while they watched."

"Why kill him?" Was clear on why they'd use arsenic — Reyes had died from arsenic poisoning at our party and every person there with Mom had been at that party, too. They were going to be questioned, potentially for hours. Brilliant move, really. Therefore, I knew Clarence hadn't come up with it. "Uncles Victor and Peter, you said you thought Cantu was the Mastermind." They hadn't, and I hoped that would give them a clue.

"Him? He was never in charge. He wanted to be, but he got on the radar too fast. He was useful, but if the boss had wanted him out of lockup, he'd have been out a long time ago. He'd played his part, and his usefulness was done."

"By boss, you don't mean Ronaldo al Dejahl, do you?"

"No idea what happened to him. Don't care. He didn't cover my back when I needed it."

"Who did?"

Clarence grinned. "You get to die without knowing. I know the saying — curiosity killed the cat. You'll hate dying even more because you won't know who's in charge, and who's going to be raising your daughter."

"Always with you people it's the stealing of babies and little children. Pathetic."

"Raul will be coming soon," Doreen said. "He had to take care of some other business. Someone was looking for Clarence at Georgetown. I think his new partner will be with him, too."

Belayed worry about Reader and that team. Hopefully they were still all alive and unharmed. "So, you're waiting for Raul?"

"Yes," Clarence said. "He wants the confirmation of who actually killed his wife before we kill all of you."

So he didn't know for sure. Or he suspected and wanted proof. Or else that's what Raul told Clarence and there was something else going on. I voted for whatever was behind Door Number Three. "How does his new chick feel about his slavish devotion to a dead woman? And have you been the one killing all the various politicians?"

He shrugged. "She doesn't mind. And, no, that wasn't me. I have a different part to play." He was in love with this phrase. I'd never heard it from him before, so my bet was one of his new besties liked it and Clarence had picked it up.

"Yeah, trying to blow up the Embassy, and killing Cantu. Seems like they're not utilizing you a lot or giving you the lead parts."

"Oh, I cleaned up the mess with Brewer."

"I thought that was someone else's plan."

Clarence looked angry. "Someone else who screwed up. Took care of her, too."

"So, you killed Pia Ryan and then you set up the car bomb in Cliff Goodman's car and dumped her body off to blow up along with him?"

"Yeah. Too damn bad he had that remote starter thing. Would have been nice to get rid of you, the big king, and the know-it-all jerk at the same time."

"Doesn't that count as you screwing up?"

He shrugged. "It won't matter. They'll end up deciding Pia was the one who set the bomb and that cleans her part up nicely."

Presumably because the authorities would be thinking the wrong person had tried to kill Cliff and then could assume she'd killed anyone else that was convenient. "Have you seen your wife and children?"

"No. She chose her family over me, turned my children against me."

She had? Good for Sylvia. "So, who's been killing all the representatives? Pia did some, right? But not all. And Cantu's gone, too, at least according to you. So I'm not buying it—you and Raul must have killed the rest of the representatives."

"Pia did her share." Clarence shrugged again. "It's a game. Raul thinks it's funny. None of them are as important to the boss as he is. And as I am," he added with smug pride. "Pia's gone, yeah, but there are plenty who want to work with the boss. Raul's even given them a few pointers. From a distance. Some people understand how to utilize talents and some don't."

"So why did you guys allow Eugene Montgomery to try to kill Edmund Brewer at my party? I get why killing someone there would be bad for American Centaurion, but really, it just seemed stupid. Every other death looked natural or accidental."

Clarence's eyes narrowed and the smile left his face. "Some people insist on using the easy resource that's at hand. Though her plan worked. The boss might even be impressed, but then again, the others screwed up so badly, she might be ahead by not being as far behind."

She. And the she he was talking about sounded very much alive, so it was doubtful he meant Pia. "Who else besides Pia and Cantu screwed up?"

"Wouldn't you like to know? I'm not telling you anything."

Refrained from mentioning that he'd already told me a lot. "How did you hit Malcolm Buchanan with that drug?"

"It was easy."

Doubted that. In order to get Buchanan, Clarence would have had to slow down. And there wasn't a mark on Buchanan. There hadn't been a mark on Juvonic, either. "You used a blowgun."

Clarence looked surprised. "Yeah."

"Why did you dump him in the tunnels under the Gaultier Research facility?"

"For me to know—"

"And me to never find out, yeah, yeah. So let me guess. Someone from Gaultier is trying to get in good with your boss, and you don't like them." His mouth twitched. "Either that, or you have friends who are working there now, and you were showing off." His mouth twitched again, but he didn't respond. No worries, had a feeling both guesses were right. "So you did kill Representative Juvonic."

"No, that wasn't me." Interesting what made him talk.

"I saw someone up on the roof right before he was hit."

"Wasn't me. Wasn't Raul, either. Our jobs are to clean up their messes, not to help them." Them again. There were at least two still vying for the Apprentice job—Whitmore and our mystery woman. Mystery woman could be from Gaultier, but if she wasn't, then we had at least three vying for the job. Considering what was going on at Gaultier, we could have twenty vying for the job.

"And Raul's going to be here really soon," Doreen said. Got the impression she also wanted to say, "Hint, hint," but was smart enough to control herself. We probably didn't have any more time for me to plumb the rest of Clarence's information well.

"Uncles Peter and Victor, you know how you're the experts in your field?"

"Yes," the Dingo said tersely.

"Well, I'm the expert in mine. Please put your guns down."

"What?" Surly Vic sounded shocked.

"Guns. Down. Now. So Raul doesn't shoot you as soon as he arrives."

"Do it," Irving said, waving his gun at them. Really hoped he didn't pull the trigger by accident.

"Put yours down, too," Clarence said, as the assassins dropped their guns down.

"Maybe. Clarence, may I introduce you to Princesses Rahmi and Rhee? Girls, this is Clarence Valentino, Traitor at Large. Do you see him?"

"Yes," Rhee said.

"For the past few minutes," Rahmi added.

"Just making sure. Rahmi, Rhee—kill Clarence Valentino."

CHAPTER 92

THINGS HAPPENED VERY QUICKLY. Rahmi and Rhee leaped toward Clarence as Doreen and Irving flung themselves down and to the sides. White grabbed the assassin's guns at hyperspeed, and Raj shoved Gower down.

Clarence, however, was slow to react, presumably because this turn of events had really caught him by surprise. Which was fine with me, because the princesses caught him with their battle staffs.

I'd grown up with relatively easygoing cats and dogs. But occasionally a cat would come into our yard and attempt the feline form of Mob Protection. My cats never stood for that. So I'd seen more than a few catfights where the cats were boiling around each other, so busy fighting and flipping, clawing, screaming, and biting, that it was hard to tell where one cat started and another began.

This fight was like that.

Clarence had speed, size, and strength. But he'd never been Field trained, as Doreen had so nicely reminded me.

The princesses, on the other hand, weren't exactly tiny to begin with, and they were the top fighters on a planet that pretty much lived for fighting. Plus they had the battle staffs, and memory reminded me that those things hurt like hell when they connected with you. When activated, as they were now, they also glowed at one end, and that one end was more "lightsaber" than "piece of wood."

White shoved the guns at Raj and Paul, then ran and

grabbed Irving just before the fighters trampled him. Doreen, seeing that Irving was safe, got to us on her own.

"Doreen Coleman Weisman, *you*, my young lady, are an impressive liar."

She grinned. "Thanks. I've been working at it for years. I still don't think I can fool anyone for too long, but it's an important trait to have in the Embassy."

"You were obvious, and your husband was worse," the Dingo said. "Which is the only reason we dropped our weapons, because it was clear our 'niece' would not risk us shooting the two of you."

"Not obvious to Clarence, which was all that mattered."

Speaking of whom, he was still hanging in there. However, he wasn't fighting with any skill, and the same couldn't be said for Rahmi and Rhee. Clarence was doing a lot of flipping and jumping, while trying to grab the girls and slam them into things.

The operative word was "trying." The battle staffs gave the girls more reach and while he might have had a shot at running away from one of them, with there being two, any time he went away from one warrior princess, the other was right there, waiting for him.

Rhee gave a war cry and swept his legs while Rahmi gave an answering cry and slammed her staff against his chest. Clarence was down, flat on his back, each one of the girls with a foot on his chest, glowing ends of two battle staffs less than an inch from his head.

"Who has the right of the kill?" Rahmi shouted.

"Do you really want him dead?" Doreen asked. "He still has information."

"We'll have to torture him to get it, and we won't be able to trust it anyway. No, we got all we could, and you were awesome with that, I must say. It's time to end Clarence's personal family vendetta. Besides, I think Rahmi and Rhee's Earth Vacation would be considered a total downer if they didn't get to kill one bad guy. Though if it looks like Clarence is going to get away, I'm all for just shooting him, as long as the girls aren't hurt."

"Are you sure we got everything?" Doreen sounded doubtful.

"I agree with my 'niece,'" Surly Vic said. Wow, I'd moved up to official family for him, too. This Operation was just chock-full of surprises. "Anything he says now will be suspect, and he could waste much of your time or cause unrest."

"He needs to be dealt with," the Dingo added. "Permanently."

"Oh, I agree."

The princesses were arguing about who should kill Clarence. Which meant they weren't paying attention to him. Not good. Clarence used their distraction to flip and twist his lower body in such a way that he knocked them off his upper body as he flipped back to his feet.

Which was fine. I'd already aimed and I emptied the clip into him. Clarence fell back again, and this time he didn't get up. "Clarence, curiosity *did* kill the cat. But satisfaction brought her back." Dropped the clip, dug around in my purse, got out a new clip, put in it. Rahmi and Rhee stared at me, openmouthed.

"Princesses, that's how we do things across the galactic railroad tracks in the dirty downtown that is Earth. In the future, the 'honor' of the kill isn't nearly as important as ensuring that your very dangerous opponent is really most sincerely dead."

"I am so proud," the Dingo said. It was clear that he meant it.

"Is Raul truly on his way?" White asked as Raj gave the assassins back their guns.

"I hope not," Doreen said. "Lorraine texted me when they were rolling. I couldn't tell her I was with Clarence because that would have blown my cover. But I could warn her. She and I have a password thing where if one of us says one word, we're in trouble, and if we say the other word, it's the other person in trouble. I gave her the word."

"Good, so they were ready."

"Hope so. Clarence called Raul and told him what was going on. Raul said he'd handle it and meet us back here, in time to kill all of you himself."

"Who did Raul think he was going after at Georgetown?"

She shrugged. "A couple of uppity girls. I had to tell him Lorraine and Claudia both were going, Clarence knows us well enough to know that if one was there, the other would be, too. I didn't share that the 'we' Lorraine was talking about probably included Airborne, too."

"Actually, the 'we' includes Mossad as well. Let's hope Raul's toast."

"We don't want him dead," Gower said, patience clearly forced. "He's the only one with the answers."

"Well, our team knows that. Doreen, you weren't with Clarence when he hit the Pentagon, were you?"

"No. We were with him here, setting up the automatic guns, when he got that call from Raul. He told us he had to do something, took off, and was back in about fifteen minutes. Which, considering how fast he could move fit for what he just told you he did."

"He didn't tell us where he'd been until he was back," Irving added. "So we couldn't warn anyone until it was too late."

"Though I'd assume he wasn't thinking that, just making sure he didn't miss Mom's arrival."

"Yeah, I think so," Doreen agreed. "We waited for you quite a ways away. He set off the guns remotely."

"And we didn't have blanks," Irving said. "We would have switched the bullets otherwise, but neither one of us knew where to go to get blanks. I'm sorry."

"Is anyone on our side of things bleeding? No? Then no need to apologize. You did great."

Irving looked shyly proud. Considering he was a total math and science nerd, aka Dazzler Bait of the Highest Order, this kind of action wasn't his normal gig. Doreen looked proud, too. Like Lorraine and Claudia before her, though, I got the impression Doreen had just officially become an Adrenaline Junkie. Chalked another one up to my bad influence.

"Thanks, Kitty," Doreen said. "I didn't have time to tell you what we were planning. I'm glad you caught on."

"You did great. I'll even brag about you to Camilla the next time I see her. Okay, I don't want to leave Clarence's body here, there, or anywhere. Princesses, you need to carry him back to the Embassy, we'll dispose of him there. Doreen, you take Irving and get back, too." Received a look of relief and grateful thanks from Irving for this. "Tell them what you did, so no one there is surprised and so everyone there is ready in case Mom, Jeff, James, or Tim call for help of some kind."

"You sure you don't want the Poofs to eat him?" Doreen

asked. "It's a lot easier to explain and then we wouldn't have to leave you." Irving's expression went to resignation.

"No, not in this case. I'm cool with Tito and Dulce doing medical experiments on him, and they may want to." Doreen didn't look convinced, but she didn't argue. Besides, had no idea where my Poofs actually were. No sooner thought than Harlie and Poofikins appeared. On Doreen's shoulders. Her Poof and Irving's were on his shoulders. "Hey, have they been with you this whole time?"

"Yes, well, they showed up in the afternoon, when we met up with Clarence. I think they were protecting us and making sure we weren't being bad." She petted both Poofs, who purred at her. "And it's always nice to have the extra Poof backup."

My actual guess was that Harlie and Poofikins had followed Clarence after he'd killed Brewer, discovered he was with Doreen and Irving, and stuck around to ensure all was well. Which begged a question. "Poofies, did you all see Raul the Assassin?"

Much Poof mewling. Harlie and Poofikins rubbed up against Doreen and then bounded over to me. Doreen's Poof went back to her. "Huh. Um, okay."

"What did they say?" White asked.

"That Raul was for sure with Clarence when they killed Brewer. However, our Field agents were killed by those two prior to when we all went over for brunch, because the Poofs never saw it happen. And Raul is a scary person, but the Poofs felt that it was more vital to be sure that Doreen and Irving were being good than to follow the scary person." I didn't add that they hadn't felt the need because Bruno was on the case there. Why have the two assassins with us decide I was more insane than they probably thought I was by now?

"So, now what?" Irving asked.

"Now you all get back to the Embassy and stay there."

"You sure you're okay here?" Doreen asked.

"Have gun, A-Cs, and the two best assassins in the world, will travel." Surly Vic snorted a laugh. Everyone else gave me a "huh?" look. Oh, well, at least someone here found me amusing. "Yes, we'll be fine."

The four of them took off, Doreen looking uncertain about leaving us, Irving back to happy relief about going home, the princesses carrying the dead body like proud hunters returning from a very successful day out in the wild, and Clarence looking like the only part he'd be playing anymore was in the dinner theater revival of *Weekend at Bernie's*. Could only hope that he was going to stay dead this time.

"Now what?" Gower asked.

"If Raul is at the University, then we should go there," the Dingo said.

"Actually, no, you shouldn't. Because I wasn't joking—Mossad is there along with our people. And they want you two dead, too." My phone chose this moment to ring. Pulled it out. "Mom, are you guys okay?"

"Yes. Are you?"

"Yes. Clarence is dead but we got some intel from him. Is Cantu alive or dead?"

"Very dead, how did you know to ask?"

"Long story. Are you guys okay? My impression was that you were framed for Cantu's death."

"We were, and we're fine now, but only because Charles convinced the idiot on duty to call Cliff and Cliff called the President. Apparently my word wasn't enough for people here." Mom sounded furious.

"Cantu was poisoned, right?"

"Right. Arsenic. And yes, I understand why that looked suspect."

"Yeah. And someone there is in the Mastermind's pocket, or vying to be an Apprentice, because Clarence got in by piggybacking on you guys, and Raul knew to send him because he was advised the moment you made the call to clear your team to enter."

"Really? Interesting." Mom was quiet for a few seconds. "Variety of options. I'm going to need to investigate, right now."

"Okay, oh, and Mom? Be sure to announce to anyone and everyone that the killer was the Dingo. Do *not* give either Clarence or Raul the credit."

"Why?"

"Another long story. Just trust me on that. The Dingo and his partner did the deed, no one else. And please keep Kevin with you, and the other guys, too. I don't want anything to happen to you."

"Your husband is not willing to stay."

"Christopher probably isn't, either, is he?"

"Well, he's actually reading all the security video, so he's here for the duration. Which could make what you want me to say an issue."

"No, they can have an inside man. But they're the ones who did it. Promise me."

Mom heaved a sigh. "Oh, of course."

"It's for the greater good."

"Sure it is. Jeff wants to talk to you." The phone was handed off. "Baby, are you okay?"

"Yes, why aren't you staying to help Mom?"

"Because unless we strip search every single person here, I can't be sure that I'm reading them right. Cantu died in front of us and he never gave off a reading other than suspicious and smug."

"Crap. Okay, have you guys heard from James or Tim?"

"No. We just got our phones back and you were the first call."

"I'm touched. I think we're heading to Georgetown, then. Because Raul and, I'm betting, his new lady friend are there."

"You're not going without me."

"You're the target."

"So are you."

The Dingo took the phone from my hand. "You will return to your Embassy. So will your wife. You will stop giving Raul opportunities to achieve his purpose." Then he hung up and handed my phone back. "Either your team will have captured or killed Raul and his new partner, or they will have failed. His goal is to destroy you. It's time for you to go home."

"But—"

"You have a mystery to solve," Surly Vic said. "We have a colleague to kill, if he is not in custody."

"Mossad will not allow him to reach a police station," the Dingo said. He smiled at me. "But thank you for requesting that we get the credit for Cantu's death. I doubt your mother will comply, but the effort is appreciated. Now, get to safety."

Heaved a sigh. "Fine, fine. I have to figure out how to get Lillian Culver and Guy Gadoire to help us out with all the political crap anyway."

"What do you mean?" Gower asked.

"Per Senator McMillan, they're the two with the most influence. If we want the bills to die fast and without a lot of 'aliens are evil' conflict, we need their help, and we need it fast. Meaning I'm going to have to make nice with them in a big way. Meaning I'd rather go to a gunfight."

"They will help you," the Dingo said.

"I doubt it. Not without us having to do favors for them that will go against everything we believe in. Right now, we need their help desperately. They don't need ours nearly so much."

"It will work out, I'm sure." The Dingo looked at the men with me. "Get home, and ensure she goes home as well."

"We will," Gower said.

The assassins nodded to us, then they trotted off into the night.

"So, guys, what now?"

White took one hand, Gower took the other. "Now, we go home, as your 'uncles' suggested," White said. "And you allow Alpha and Airborne to do their jobs. Without you."

"Don't wanna."

"Your daughter's birthday is tomorrow," Raj said. "I believe it would be best if her mother and father were alive and there to celebrate it with her."

"Raj, make a note—I hate it when your logic doesn't support what I want to do."

He flashed the troubadour smile. "You can take it out of my pay."

"Do we pay you?"

"I'm earning important experience so necessary to career advancement."

"Wow. Raj, is the ability to lie a troubadour trait?"

He laughed. "All the world's a stage, Ambassador. Or so I've heard."

CHAPTER 93

WE ZIPPED HOME to find Jeff there, pacing in the foyer. "I wasn't sure you were really coming here," he said as he hugged me tightly.

"My 'uncles' wanted us both home and they impressed that upon everyone."

"In other words, we gave her no choice," Gower said.

"Why were you there at all, Paul?" Jeff asked.

Gower dodged the question by heading into the kitchen. The rest of us followed him. "Where's Chuck?" Naomi asked.

"Handling political things," Jeff said. "He's fine, so are all the others. I was ordered home by pretty much everyone."

"Has anyone heard from James or Tim or anyone with them?"

"Well, heard, no," Pierre said. "However, we've been manning the airwaves thanks to our brilliant computer geniuses, and there were reports of a massive paintball game on the Georgetown campus."

"Paintball?" Jeff sounded confused. He spoke for all of us.

Amy gave him the "duh" look. "Imageering altered footage and reports. We contacted Serene. The team is back in Dulce. They're all fine, other than some minor injuries. Lorraine was tipped off that there was going to be trouble, so they were ready." She winked at Doreen, who grinned.

"There's bad news, though," Len said. "They couldn't take Raul alive."

Kyle nodded. "From what we were told, Mossad took him out."

"That's because he was about to shoot me in the head," Reader said as he and Tim came in. "Under the circumstances, I felt okay with Jakob going for the kill shot."

"Kitty got plenty out of Clarence," Doreen said.

"Hopefully it'll help." Heaved a sigh. "I want to know what the home team found, and I'm sure the home team wants to know what everyone else did."

"Before that, I have something to return to you," Tim said. "Okay, stop playing around and unstealth yourself."

Bruno appeared at my feet. "Where have you been?" Picked him up and hugged him. He was heavy, but he appreciated the snuggle, because he wrapped his neck around mine and cooed.

"Why are you hugging that bird?" Jeff asked.

"Wow, I'm not gracing that with a response, Mister Parrot Lover. What was Bruno doing with you guys?" I asked as I put him down.

"As near as I can tell, he was following Raul," Tim said. "I say that because Bruno there stopped us from walking into an ambush."

"I thought you guys were warned by Lorraine and Doreen's Secret Word Club."

"Airborne was warned. James and I weren't warned."

"Well, good job, Bruno. As always." He'd gone after whoever shot Jeff. That had been pretty much confirmed to be Raul's new girl. "So, was Raul's girlfriend caught?"

"No," Reader said. "I'm not sure that she was with him."

Looked at Bruno. He shrugged his wings. She'd been there, but she was gone, and protecting the team had taken precedence. I could buy that and decided it wasn't vital enough to share.

"Let's tell you what we've found," Abigail said. "So that we can clean up the kitchen before Jamie's party tomorrow."

Right. The party. Memory shared that I had some work to do before then. "Okay, you know, everyone catch each other up. I have to make some calls." I didn't want to make them, but I was clear that I had no choice.

Stepped out of the room and went into Raj's office. He and Jeff came with me. "What are you doing?" Jeff asked.

"Something I have to do."

While Raj quietly explained the situation to Jeff, I contemplated my options. Chose to call Gadoire first, in part because it was less odious than calling Culver first. That I'd had these people's phone numbers stored was either a testament to my planning or just proof that the universe enjoyed a good joke. Bet on the latter.

"Hello, my dove. Do you need me?"

"Hi, Guy, and yes, in a way. We discovered that some of the invitations to our daughter's birthday party weren't mailed, and the one to you and Vance was in that group. So, I realize it's terribly short notice, and that tomorrow's Christmas, but was wondering if you'd be able to come."

"My dove, nothing would give me greater pleasure."

I could think of a lot of things that would give most adults greater pleasure than attending a one-year-old's party, but I kept that to myself. "Great! We'll see you tomorrow then. Three in the afternoon."

"I'll be there. Will it be alright if I bring dear Lydia with me? I don't believe it's safe for her to be alone right now."

I needed Gadoire's help. He could bring a Bengal tiger along and I'd have to smile and give it a party hat and a piece of cake. "Sure, that would be great."

We got off and I called Lillian Culver. She expressed great joy at the invitation along with the proper understanding of how people could forget to mail important letters, and guaranteed that she and Abner would be in attendance.

Politically required sucking-up done, all I wanted to do was go to sleep. Jeff picked it up. "Raj, can you cover whatever and fill us in tomorrow morning?" he asked as he picked me up.

"Absolutely. Get good rest."

"You too," I managed before I snuggled into Jeff's neck. Heard more voices as we went upstairs; sounded like some of the others were back. Good.

Jeff hypersped us upstairs and into our apartment. Dad and Jamie were both in their beds asleep, dogs with Dad, cats and Poofs with Jamie. Couldn't just lie down with my clothes on, though, because I was still wearing a bulletproof vest. Knew I was in dire need of sleep when Jeff undressing me didn't make me want to instantly have sex.

Oh, sure, I wanted to by the time I was in the standard-issue nightclothes and he was naked, but he got into his pajama bottoms and then into bed. "You need sleep," he said as he snuggled me up against him. "You had a big day and that fight with Naomi took a lot out of you."

"You knew about that?"

"Still not an emotion you have that isn't broadcast, baby. You were so angry you were an easy read, for more than emotions. I told Chuck about it, so he knows. He said you were right, by the way."

"Right about what?"

"That he doesn't want a big wedding. He just has no idea of how to get out of what they're being forced into."

Would have discussed this more but Jeff's body was warm, his heartbeats soothing, and I was asleep before I could say another word.

Slept like a rock and, happily, didn't wake up in the middle of the night. Having gone to bed after midnight might have helped. Knowing Raul and Clarence were both dead probably helped more.

The morning came bright and early with Jamie getting out of her crib by herself and jumping into bed with us. Chose to enjoy this as opposed to freak out about it, but we were clearly going to have our hands full by age two if this was what she was like at age one.

Half of her mountain of presents were for just us, and half were for later at her party. Mom had joined us somewhere in the night—had no idea how she'd gotten in without waking everyone up, but she'd managed it—and so the five of us had breakfast and then Jeff called for his parents to come over.

Alfred and Lucinda being with us made Jamie almost vibrate with happiness. She opened each present, showed it to each of us, and thanked the giver with huge hugs and kisses.

This took hours, which was fine with me. But soon enough it was lunchtime and then time to get ready for the party.

Jamie had insisted on being in an all-pink ensemble, including a sparkly pink tiara I was positive Pierre had found and suggested to her. Based on the fact that he was the one who'd arranged her outfit, it seemed a good bet.

I was back in a nice black-and-white dress with side slits. Oh those trendy Elves. Apparently they felt cocky about my wearing white, too. Chose not to complain and hoped their optimism wasn't misguided. Transferred the necessities from my purse to my handbag. My own home or not, wasn't going downstairs without my Glock, Jeff's adrenaline harpoon, or my iPod.

Contemplated asking Jeff to wear his fedora, but decided explaining why he was wearing a hat indoors to both his parents and mine would be the very definition of "totally embarrassing" so chose to live without his hat for today.

Walter advised that guests were starting to arrive, so we all headed down to the ballroom. Happily the first guests were all our friends and a lot of our family. The wisdom of holding the party in the ballroom wasn't lost on me anymore.

The fresh flowers—all pinks and whites—had already arrived by the time we got downstairs. Sadly, the press had already arrived, too. Saw a lot of familiar faces, most of them familiar because of Jeff's being sworn in and Cliff's car exploding. There were a couple blonde women in the group and I wondered if one of them had been the one who'd asked if we knew who the bomb was supposed to kill. None of them looked remarkably stupid, however, so I wasn't going to figure it out via those means.

Jeff had won the musical battle and there was some classical stuff on very low. It was a little too classy for a little girl's birthday party, but Jamie didn't seem to care and Jeff was happy with it, so I didn't whine.

As with our dinner party, we had a ton of Field agents in the Embassy, most on the second floor, but the rest of the facility wasn't being shirked. Hoped a superbeing didn't form anywhere right now, because it felt like every agent worldwide was here.

Politicians and other movers and shakers arrived and the party stopped being fun and started being work. Some, like Cliff, the Armstrongs, and the McMillans, I was happy to see. Some, like Whitmore, who we'd had to invite to this against everyone's better judgment, I wasn't.

Pierre was in charge of the festivities, of course, and he had Jamie and any kid under twelve in the middle portion of the ballroom, being entertained by a Little Theater troupe. The kids were loving it, which was nice. It also freed up me and Jeff to interact with the politicians. No rest for the wicked.

Jeff was cornered by a variety of senators, so I wandered, looking for Gadoire or Culver, neither of whom were here yet. Amy joined me. "You crashed last night."

"I totally did. What did I miss?"

"Not much. We did find some things. None of it's conclusive, of course, but there were fragments we were able to piece together. I think the L idea was sound, because it was just too consistently there in everyone's calendars, but Olga was right—it's going to take us a long time to narrow that down."

"That's it?"

"No. We found reference to Gaultier, as well as Somerall, Gardiner, and Cross."

"The Gaultier bigwigs you're fighting for control."

"Yeah. Like so much, not something we're going to figure out today. They could have been legitimate things—we couldn't find enough to be sure. There were other things like that—enough repetition to stand out, nothing concrete to take action against today."

"Oh, well, it is what it is."

Senator Armstrong extracted himself from Jeff's group and came over to me as Doreen came to get Amy for something. "Ah, Ambassador, wanted to let you know right away. The governor of California has asked, and Missus Brewer is going to fill her late husband's seat."

"Nathalie said yes to that?"

He nodded. "For the same reasons your husband did." Someone called him back over. "Have to go. Discussing how to handle the upcoming vote." He rejoined Jeff and the others.

Lillian Culver and Abner Schnekedy took this moment to arrive. She was in what I was coming to realize was her trademark all-red look, including the bright red lipstick. Tried not to think of her as Joker Jaws. Failed.

Took a big one for the team and hugged her while doing the air kiss. "Lillian, I'm so glad you could make it."

"Wouldn't miss it. I hear that Nathalie has some good news to help alleviate the pain of Edmund's suicide."

"Yes, I guess so. I mean if we count taking over for him

as good news." Resisted the impulse to say that Brewer hadn't been a suicide. There was a high probability the Master or the Apprentice were here, because pretty much the same people as had been at our dinner party were in attendance along with a lot of other guests and the press, who were busy taking tons of pictures.

Culver laughed. "Well, maybe it's better news for me."

Gadoire and Lydia were escorted inside. Did the greetings. "Great party," Lydia said. "I'm impressed with how well you've all bounced back from the tragedies of the past few days."

"I'd hardly say that. But a one-year-old shouldn't be punished for things that had nothing to do with her and that she couldn't possibly understand."

"Oh, I hear she's quite precocious," Lydia said.

"She's great, but again, people being killed isn't something I think is appropriate for any child to have to deal with or try to comprehend."

"I heard Edmund killed himself," Lydia replied. "Not that I'm suggesting that you think suicide is appropriate for children to know about, either."

There was something different about Lydia, and it wasn't mourning, because she didn't seem to be. She seemed more . . . aggressive than I was used to. She was a political animal, of course, but I'd only seen the "here with my husband" side of her. Found myself wondering if Eugene had actually acted as a restraint on her real personality.

I was preoccupied with thinking about the "new Lydia" so I didn't respond. She didn't seem to care. "But anyway, Guy, could we get something to drink, please?"

"Of course, my dear. Ambassador, dear Lillian, please excuse us." Gadoire ushered Lydia off. Wondered where Vance was and if he was aware that his husband seemed to be moving Lydia into their marriage. Or maybe Lydia was moving herself into Vance's marriage.

"Abner, be a love and fetch me something nice," Lillian said. "You know what I like." He smiled, kissed her cheek, and trailed after Gadoire. Lillian turned back to me. "You have a request, Ambassador. So let's save the time and you tell me what it is that I can do for you. I'll speak for Guy on this one, too. We've already chatted, right after your late night calls to both of us."

"Sorry about that, I'd lost track of the time. But, um, how did you know I have a request of any kind?"

She laughed softly. "You're very new at this. But I understand—it's awkward, the first time you need to reach out to your friends for help, the first time something seems beyond you." She took my hand in hers. Managed not to flinch, was relieved there really was no electrified joy buzzer in her palm. "We're here for you."

Focused on the goal, which was to prevent a lot of horrible things from happening. "I need you two to use your influence to help kill all the bills going through the House and Senate right now. Preferably before Congress officially starts the new session in January."

She laughed louder. "Is *that* all?"

"They don't have to die completely, but there are clear anti-alien lines in all of the bills that need to be removed, so the bills have to go back to committee or die."

"I see. And, just what can American Centaurion do for us in return?"

This was the part I was dreading. "I have no freaking idea. But I'll bet you do."

She smiled again and this time there was no mistaking it—Joker Jaws was in the house. "Oh, yes, I do. So does Guy. We'll think on it, and let you know. Somewhere before January third."

"Super. Thanks. I think."

She squeezed my hand, gently. "You'll get used to it. We do something for you, you do something for us, quid pro quo. After a while, you won't feel dirty about it." She looked around. "Is that Clifford? Haven't seen him in at least a week."

She sailed off toward Cliff, who spotted her coming and looked around for an escape route. He was too slow and she cornered him. Abner, Gadoire, and Lydia joined them. Nice to know I was dismissed until they'd determined what they could get out of us. Problem was, I knew they were going to get a lot.

Watched the four of them talk to Cliff. He definitely looked surrounded by barracuda. Looked around for where Nathalie was. Found her in the group Jeff was with. She looked like she was barely holding up. Jeff was on one side of her, Reader was on the other. Got the feeling they were protecting her, which I was more than fine with.

Chuckie joined Cliff and the Barracuda Brigade. Had to figure Cabal of Evil was no more, at least for now. Cliff looked relieved to have the support. Couldn't blame him.

Everything seemed calm, but we hadn't stopped anything or anyone. We had some information, we had some dead bad guys, we had more questions than answers. And we had people still missing. Most missing of all, of course, were the Master and Apprentice. With Raul and Clarence both dead, our chances of catching the Master were slim, at least right now. But one of the Apprentice Wannabes might be here.

Looked around. Lots of people, but one I'd gotten used to was missing. Supposedly Buchanan was going to be awake and with us. But I didn't see him anywhere. "Malcolm, I could really use someone to talk to," I said under my breath.

"Missus Chief, I thought you'd never ask."

CHAPTER 94

SPUN AROUND to see Buchanan there. Didn't think about it, just gave him a big hug. "You're okay!"

He laughed and hugged me back. "Yes, I am. And now the rumor mill has a great story, too. Can't wait for your husband's reaction to this."

"He's a little busy right now."

"And you're not enjoying Baby Chief's party. I know I've missed a lot." His eyes narrowed. "Doctor Hernandez explained that I've lost thirty minutes. He's briefed me somewhat, but I know there's more going on than I know about."

"Where's Colonel Hamlin?"

He shook his head. "I remember that I left the Embassy with him because he had proof of the whole Mastermind idea somewhere. If his intel was good, I was going to hide him. If it wasn't, I was going to arrest or kill him."

"And?"

"That's it. So I figure we got hit pretty close to when we left the Embassy. We were in my car. I don't know that it's been recovered."

"Yet another problem for another day." Considered what else we could do. Besides give up and just become like everyone else here and not even care when people dropped dead next to us if that meant we could make a political "in."

"What's wrong with this picture?" I asked aloud.

I'd meant my current situation, but Buchanan didn't take it that way. He scanned the room. "Nathalie Brewer—first impression would be that you should be worried that she's after your husband. Closer look says that she's emotionally upset and using him as a shield, and that he's aware of this and okay with it. Which I assume means you're okay with it."

"Yeah, that's pretty accurate. What else is wrong?"

He scanned some more. "The Secretary of Transportation isn't being gregarious. It's clear he hates being here, and he hates everyone who's associated with the A-Cs in any way. He's barely able to hide it, which is a change from a few months ago, when he didn't appear to know you all existed."

"Or that he was sleeping with an android. What else?"

Buchanan looked at the group around Cliff and Chuckie. "It's a Washington Wife class reunion here, isn't it?"

"Yeah, well, other than the ones who are dead. But I know what you mean." Couldn't wait to tell Buchanan that I was about to make a deal with Joker Jaws and Pepé Le Pew. That would be more pleasant than telling Jeff or my mother, though.

He cocked his head. "Is one of those women Lydia Montgomery?"

"Yes."

"Doctor Hernandez said Eugene killed someone and then was killed by an assassin. She's not acting like anyone near her has had so much as a hangnail."

"She's spent every night since his death with Gadoire, too. Supposedly because she couldn't be left alone." And Clarence said that "she" had used the easy resource at hand, and since it had worked the boss might be impressed, but only because the others had failed so badly.

The Dingo had told me to figure out who benefited from Eugene's being arrested for murder. But maybe the proper question was who benefited if Pia Ryan was out of the Apprentice Wannabe Race. Or perhaps, the answer to all my questions was going to boil down to the same person.

"Malcolm, are you really a hundred percent?"

"Other than those missing thirty minutes and all the time I was asleep, yes."

"Great. I need you to get a search warrant, as fast as possible. Call the K-9 guys, and take them with you."

"Where are we going?"

"To the murderer's house."

CHAPTER 95

BUCHANAN MADE HIS CALLS. Even on Christmas Day, the P.T.C.U. could score a warrant in under five minutes. Sent him off with four Field agents grabbed at random—didn't like the idea of losing Buchanan since we'd only just gotten him back. They were meeting up with the K-9 squad and heading to the house in question.

Had some time to kill, and I wanted some muscle with me. All I'd use normally were occupied. Found Rahmi and Rhee and gently dragged them away from the Little Theater troop's rendition of *The Princess and the Frog.* Gave them some instructions which they seemed clear on.

Still didn't see Vance anywhere. Sent him a text. Discovered he was sulking in his room because he and Gadoire had had a huge fight about Lydia. Told him the game was afoot and to get his butt down here and fight for his man. Refrained from asking him why he'd want to fight for Gadoire—people couldn't help who they loved.

The princesses and I joined the group with Chuckie and Cliff. "Hey, I'd like to introduce you to Princesses Rahmi and Rhee."

The princesses bowed. "We are honored," Rahmi said.

Did all the introductions, the princesses bowed to everyone again in turn. "They come from another planet. Different from Jeff's planet."

"Oh?" Culver said. "How interesting."

Cliff and Chuckie were giving me "WTF?" looks. I ignored them. "On their planet, they have strict rules about murder. So I've been trying to explain to them why we haven't punished anyone for Santiago's death. Or Edmund's. Or Eugene's."

"Eugene was punished for Santiago's death," Lydia said with a sniff that I was sure was supposed to sound like she was a second away from breaking down. Couldn't speak for anyone else, but I didn't buy it.

"Actually, I think he was punished for something else."

"What's that?" Gadoire asked, as Vance joined us.

"Eugene was a bad boy, wasn't he? I mean, he seemed like this nice, normal guy. But he was cheating on his wife with a former supermodel."

"That was over," Lydia snapped.

"Funny, three days ago you said you didn't know about his affair with Nathalie. So I'm betting you did, and while it was going on, too, not just after it was over. After all, you're not a stupid woman. So I'm also betting you knew that, once Nathalie had broken their affair off, Eugene took up with someone else in the group. Pia Ryan to be exact."

"We barely knew her and my personal business is none of yours."

"It is when you murder people in my home. Then it becomes all my business. There's a lot of murder going on right now—lots of representatives dead, and everyone's just acting like it's business as usual. But the way Santiago was killed, that was showy. In a really bad way."

"What does that have to do with me? Other than my husband being shot in your driveway?"

"Why the phony outrage, Lydia? That's exactly what you wanted to have happen."

"Kitty," Cliff said in a warning tone, "be careful with what you're saying."

"Why? See, I'm just a nosy person. Can't help it. Always been a failing. So when someone I care about gets murdered, I just sort of have to find out why. Pathological, really. Just had to dig into what the hell was going on. And while I dug, something kept bothering me, over and over again."

"What was that?" Abner asked. Was sure he thought I was going nuts and he was baiting me. Worked for what I wanted, so I was good with it.

"Well, all the things Eugene told me before he died." Lydia stiffened but didn't speak. I continued. "He'd been set

up by Pia Ryan to kill Edmund because Pia had convinced
Eugene that Edmund was a robot."

No one in this group snorted or even looked shocked.
Not a surprise, really. "That rumor's been around for a
while," Culver said. "Not about Edmund, just in general."

"I'll bet it has. I can buy Pia using Eugene to help her kill
off someone. But what I can't buy is that she'd do all the
work to get him primed and ready, and believing that there
were many more 'robots' out there, and then set him up to
be caught red-handed."

"This is truly farfetched," Lydia said, with a little laugh.
"But do go on."

"Someone quite wise in the ways of murder and killing
suggested I ask not just why Santiago, accidentally standing
in for Edmund, was killed in such a public and showy way,
but to find out who would benefit from Edmund's death, or
from Eugene's capture."

Lydia gasped. "Nathalie's benefiting. Do you think she's
the one who did this?"

"Not really. She isn't power-hungry, and she doesn't want
to be a politician. For her, this is all a loss. Because her husband forgave her for her affair and their marriage was
stronger now. No, I think the person benefiting from Edmund, Eugene, and Pia dying is the person who hasn't forgiven one affair, let alone two."

"What do you mean?" Abner asked. This time he
sounded interested.

"You mean you think it's Lydia," Vance said. "I mean,
she's power-hungry, her husband was cheating on her, and
she's vying for the job as Ap—ouch!"

Rhee stepped on his foot. "I am so terribly sorry," she
said politely. Cliff and Chuckie both had their phones out
and were texting like mad.

"There's a backroom power struggle going on." Well,
that was easier than doing the whole Sith Lord explanation,
and it was still accurate. "In order to curry favor with the big
boss, lower level lieutenants have to do things, including kill
off people the big boss wants out of the way. They're in
competition with each other for the right-hand man slot.
Pia and Lydia were two of these lieutenants.

"Lydia has no love for Eugene any more—he's not interested in her Washington career and cheated on her with a

woman far more attractive than she is. She's got no love for Nathalie Brewer, either, who she can conveniently blame Eugene's straying on. And then Eugene takes up with Pia Ryan, who is also prettier than Lydia and who is also Lydia's rival for a position she really wants."

"How dare you accuse me of anything?" Lydia snapped.

"It's pretty easy. You're not exactly acting like you're mourning. You're celebrating, and I don't think it's because my daughter just turned one. You saw a chance to turn the tables on everyone and have your cheating husband kill the husband of his first mistress, ensuring that his current mistress would fall out of favor with the big boss."

"You have no proof of these ridiculous claims. I'll sue you for defamation."

"The press is eyeing us," Cliff said in a low voice. "I'm going to get them out of here." He headed off.

"That only works if you're not found guilty." Looked at my watch. "And, I'm betting that in about fifteen minutes, you're going to be found guilty." I looked at Gadoire. "Or you are."

"Excuse me?" he sounded shocked out of his mind.

"I'm not sure if she's been staying with you all this time because the evidence is at her house, or if she's been staying with you because the evidence is being planted at your house. If I were a betting girl, which I am, I'd say your house. Which is why we got more than one warrant."

"It's Christmas Day," Lydia snapped. "There's no way you could get a warrant that fast."

Chuckie's phone beeped. "Gotten that fast and then some," he said. "Police in Silver Spring just finished searching Pia Ryan's house. They found no arsenic, but they did find botulism toxin, in packets identical to the one I found on Eugene after he poisoned Santiago."

His phone beeped again. "D.C. police just finished searching Gadoire's place. There's a small stash of arsenic and some other very suspicious things. Heading to the Montgomery house now. I wonder what they'll find?"

He pulled handcuffs out of his inner pocket. "Lydia Montgomery, I'm arresting you on suspicion of murder and conspiracy." He slammed the cuffs on her, then pulled out another set. Sometimes I wondered how he carried all the metal and still seemed to saunter everywhere.

"I want my lawyer," Lydia said.

Chuckie smiled. "I'm not taking you to the police. You're going somewhere much more special. But you won't be alone. Guy Gadoire, you're under arrest on suspicion of murder and conspiracy."

"Chuckie . . . one moment before you put those cuffs on." I looked at Gadoire. "Guy, will this arrest cause issues for you?"

"Hell, yes," Vance answered for him. "Being arrested for something cool or acceptable, that's one thing. Being arrested for murdering a bunch of people because you were sleeping with Lydia Montgomery? That's career death."

Guy looked panicked. "Please, Mister Reynolds, you have to believe me—"

I put up my hand. "Chuckie, I'd take it as a deep, *personal* favor if you'd wait to arrest Guy until we're a hundred percent *sure* that he was involved in any way. Nothing I found suggested it. And I'll take complete responsibility for him, too."

Chuckie and I had known each other since we were thirteen. He knew what I was trying to tell him when I stressed those two words. He nodded slowly and put the cuffs away. "Don't leave town," he said to Gadoire. "You're still a person of interest."

Gadoire sagged with relief. "Person of interest is cool," Vance said reassuringly.

"Oh, good. Guy, a private word, just for a moment?" He nodded and staggered a couple steps away with me. "Lillian said that you knew why I was calling last night."

"Yes, you need a favor."

"I need a huge favor, Guy. I need all the bills going through the House and Senate killed or sent back to committee, and I need that to continue to happen until every one of them has the anti-alien wording removed. And it has to happen before January third. I'll be happy to tell you exactly what needs to come out of each bill if necessary."

"Not necessary at all, my dove. I'm happy to do this favor for you." He glanced at Chuckie. "Especially since you have gone out of your way to defend and protect me." He turned back to me. "Did she really do all that?"

"And more. I'd like you to be checked out by our Embassy doctor, to make sure she didn't, ah, do something to you." Like turn him into an android. "But, first, Guy, can I count on you? As in, you're doing this for me out of the goodness of your heart, and not because you expect any kind of payback from me or anyone else connected with American Centaurion later?"

"Absolutely, my dove. Absolutely."

"Wonderful." Motioned for Rahmi and Rhee to come over. "Please escort our friend down to the Great Tito and ask him to ensure that all is right with Monsieur Gadoire."

They hustled Gadoire off and Vance went along. I went back to Chuckie, who was handing Lydia off to Kevin and a nice complement of Field agents. Cliff rejoined us, too. "Press is all gone," Cliff said. "Moved off for your sake, not hers."

"Police are on their way," Chuckie said. "We can get back to Jamie's party now. But, before we do, how'd you figure it out?"

"Someone helped me figure out what was wrong with the picture."

CHAPTER 96

THE REST OF THE PARTY WAS GREAT. Jamie had a fabulous time, and with the press gone and Lydia in custody, I felt pretty decent.

I hadn't avenged all the murders of all those people yet, but I'd avenged the ones I could. Reyes, Brewer, even Eugene and Pia. We'd caught all the people responsible for their deaths. Okay, not the Mastermind, but everyone else.

"You took a real chance with that accusation," Christopher said while we were munching on cake and Jamie was dancing with Jeff. I had a huge corner piece loaded with icing which I'd claimed as Mother of the Birthday Girl and I was enjoying it. "What if you'd been wrong?"

"Then I'd have tried again, but she was the only one who fit all the parameters. She was the one who stood to gain the most by Eugene's being arrested—sympathy, support, and her cheating husband dead, worth a lot. Chance to hurt both her rivals at the same time? Priceless."

"I got nothing out of the video tapes. If Clarence was there, even when he slowed down he was at hyperspeed."

"As long as he stays dead this time, I'm good with it." Saw Culver and Abner getting ready to go. "Guard my cake. I am not done with that, so don't let anyone throw it away and tell Jeff to get his own piece."

Trotted after Culver and caught them at the front door. "We were just slipping out," Culver said. "Abner, be a dear and fetch the car."

He sighed. "Of course. Nice seeing you again, Kitty." He

headed off down the street. Had no idea where they'd parked.

"It was a nice party," Culver said as she stepped outside. I followed her and shut the door behind me. "And congratulations on getting another friend of mine arrested."

Apparently the gloves were off now. Fine by me. "If your friends weren't a bunch of murderers that wouldn't be such a problem. I'd think you'd care more about the friends of yours who were killed."

She shrugged. "The dead can't help you any more, nor can they be helped." She smiled widely. It remained horrifying. "It was quite neat how you got Guy's support. You're far more savvy than you let on, or my husband could recognize."

"Backhanded flattery's nice. Knowing what you want from us for your help would be better."

She shrugged. "You'll do what I want, when I want it. I think that will be the easiest plan, don't you?"

"I do not believe that is how it will work," a familiar voice said from behind Culver. She froze, eyes wide. "You feel my gun in your back, yes?" She nodded. "Good. Look up on the roof across the street. What do you see?"

We both looked. "Nothing," Culver said.

I squinted. "I can just make out a guy with what I think is a sniper rifle." Or, as I thought of him now, Uncle Surly Vic.

"Yes, good. Now, you will listen to me. I understand you, Lillian Culver. I know all about you—who you work for, what you do, where you go, where you live, when you sleep. And I know all about your husband, too."

"Yes?" she asked. "What do you want? Money?"

He laughed softly. "No. I want you to be nice to my niece. She is a kind girl, and a brave girl, but she is not a ruthless girl." His voice hardened. "I, however, am a very ruthless man. You will help her because if you do not, your husband will die, and then you will die."

"My clients are powerful people," Culver said. Had to hand it to her, she wasn't panicking and while her voice was shaking a little, she didn't sound totally frightened.

The Dingo laughed, one of those low bad guy laughs. He was good at it. "Yes, they are. Your clients are ruthless men and women, like me. They understand that the price of the finest weapon is high. You are not the finest weapon, you are a mouthpiece. And they can always find another effective mouthpiece."

"You're bluffing."

"I thought you might say that."

Abner pulled up in their car. "Nice Bentley. No wonder you guys drove."

"You're going to threaten to kill my husband and then Kitty's going to tell you not to, and you think that will make me help them without payback? Nice try, but I say again, you're bluffing."

Abner got out of the car. Heard a muffled shot. Abner went down.

Told myself I was being an idiot, but I couldn't stop my feet from running to him. Abner was shot and bleeding like crazy, but he wasn't dead. Picked him up and ran him to the front door. There were no more bullets.

There was also no more Dingo. Culver was still there, however, and she was white. "He shot him." She sounded shocked and, for the first time, freaked out.

"He doesn't really bluff. He was being nice, and he still is. I think we need to get Abner to a hospital. Or I can take him to our infirmary. However, my uncle is wrong. I'm willing to be ruthless to protect my people, and what they believe in."

"What do you mean?"

"Abner's going to bleed out fast. I can have our staff help him, and probably save his life, or you can take your chances that the ambulance will get him to the Georgetown Medical Center in time. You pick. But know that if he enters the American Centaurion Embassy again, then you are agreeing to my terms, which is that you help me get those bills killed or sent back to committee, and you do it well before New Year's Eve."

She looked down at Abner. I truly had no guess as to what she was going to say. She touched his cheek. "Can I come with him?"

"Yes." Managed not to let the relief show in my voice. "But if he can't be saved, I'm still holding you to the deal. Because if I don't, then my uncle will kill you next."

She nodded. "I know who the Dingo is. I'd imagine how you've hidden that you're his relative would be an interesting story."

"One for another day. Let's get Abner down to the Great Tito."

The door opened. Jeff and Raj were there, along with Tito, Nurse Carter, and a gurney. I put Abner on the gurney, Tito and Nurse Carter took off with him. "Melanie and Emily are prepping the surgery," Jeff said.

Raj offered his arm to Culver. "I'll escort you down. I'm sure he'll be fine."

Culver took his arm, then looked at me. "I'll start making calls as soon as I collect myself."

"Sounds good. I'll put your car into our parking garage."

She smiled, a rather normal smile. Well, for her. "Thank you. I sense this is the beginning of a beautiful friendship." She and Raj went after Tito.

Jeff looked at the car in the street. "Is that their car?"

"Yeah."

"You're covered with blood." He pulled out his phone. "Yeah, kid, you and the other jock get down to the front door immediately."

"It's not my blood."

"I know." He looked up and around. "Are they still here?"

"My 'uncles'? No idea. Kind of betting on yes, but who knows."

"Your mother said she told the authorities everyone is convinced the Dingo killed Cantu while he was in lock-down."

"Good. They'll get a nice payday and their rep will go that much higher."

"So that's why they almost killed a man on our doorstep?"

"Yeah. Lillian and Guy are the only ones who can get those bills killed in such a way that we and the President won't be completely screwed."

"That was a pretty tough tradeoff, baby."

"This? This was nothing compared to what it could have been. This was the only solution that would work in our favor. And my 'uncles' knew it would be, too."

"I suppose. Reynolds asked me to tell you that they found a plethora of evidence at Lydia's house. He thinks some of it might have been planted."

"Not by me, or by my 'uncles.' Maybe by the Mastermind. Or Raul's chick. But no matter what, Lydia's out of the running to be the next Mastermind Celebrity Apprentice. So that's a job damn well done."

Len and Kyle appeared. "Kitty, are you okay?" Len sounded freaked out. Kyle looked freaked out. Looked down. Jeff hadn't been kidding—I was covered with blood. So much for the Optimism of the Elves.

"Yeah, this isn't my blood. Need you two to park that Bentley in our garage. While I go change clothes."

The boys nodded and went to the car. Jeff took my hand and we went inside and up to our apartment. "Can I put on jeans and a T-shirt now?" I asked as I stripped off the bloodied dress and jumped into the shower.

"No. I think I want you in something nice. But I'll take my hat and coat, if that'll make you happy."

"Definitely." Didn't have to wash my hair, so I was out of the shower fast. "Where are we going?"

"Surprise. Just waiting for the rest of the guests to leave. Take your real purse, though."

Dumped my handbag into my purse while Jeff handed me the dress he wanted me to wear. It was the green dress I'd had on for our dinner party or, more likely, a duplicate. Akiko had started making duplicates early in her relationship with our Embassy. "You sure this isn't courting bad luck?"

He grinned. "Nah, it's just a sexy dress and I'd like to see you in it again for a happy occasion."

"Okay. You're the boss."

Jeff snorted. "Since when? You're the boss of me, baby, and you always have been." Then he kissed me, and I decided to table that discussion for another time.

CHAPTER 97

ALL THE GUESTS who weren't our friends and family were gone. Jamie was asleep on Chuckie's shoulder while he and Naomi talked to his parents. "She fell asleep while we were dancing," Chuckie said. "Didn't have the heart to wake her up."

Gave his mom and dad a big hug. "When did you two get here?"

"Just a few minutes ago," Jeff answered for them. "We'll be back. Keep Jamie, will you, Chuck?" Chuckie nodded as Jeff walked me over to Christopher.

"What was that all about?"

"Tell you later."

"Fine. Is my cake still around anywhere?"

"No, it got cleared with everything else," Christopher said. "And before you whine to me about it, you know you can get more any time."

"It's not the same," I muttered.

"I'll get you more, baby. In a while." Jeff left me and went over to Pierre. They were instantly in deep discussion. Reader joined them.

Decided not to worry about it. Found Nathalie. She was leaning against the wall. "How're you doing?"

"Oh, alright, I suppose." She sighed and I put my arm around her. "Tomorrow I get sworn in, to do a job I never wanted to do, to replace the husband I never wanted to lose. Then there will be his funeral, and Santiago's. I must plan

Edmund's and I wish to attend Santiago's. I believe your
Embassy will be making the arrangements."

"I'm sure we will." Maybe that's what Jeff, Reader, and
Pierre were talking about.

"I just . . . I would like to have something happy, you
know? Christmas has no meaning for me, at least today. I
would like to celebrate life and honor the lives gone. Your
daughter's party was lovely, but all we did was talk about
political work that needs to be done."

"Yeah, I know what you mean."

Jeff looked around the room. "Great, everyone's here.
Gather up your belongings, folks. We're taking a little excursion."

Saw a floater gate appear, one of the big ones. "Haven't
seen a gate like that since your wedding, Kitty," Michael
said to me.

"The wedding I missed?" Caroline asked with a laugh.

"Everyone's a critic. Where does Jeff have us going? And
why?"

Others were asking this, but they were going through the
gate. Raj joined us. "I'll escort Missus Brewer," he said, as
he took Nathalie's arm. "We have eight Field teams in the
infirmary."

"Thanks, Raj." This way, Nathalie wouldn't be at risk
from my barfing on her and we wouldn't be at risk of anyone wandering our Embassy unattended. Tito and Nurse
Carter were missing out on the excursion, whatever it was.
Figured I'd find out soon if they'd be relieved or disappointed later.

Jeff had Chuckie keep Jamie for the gate transfer. Assumed this was because he knew he'd have to carry me.
Which he did. "Where are we going?"

"You'll find out." Jeff held me a little tighter and I buried
my face in his neck. Always the nicest part of a gate transfer.

This one was a few seconds, so I knew we were traveling
some distance. Felt us stop and, once my stomach settled,
opened my eyes. "This place looks familiar."

"It should." Jeff put me down. "Let's go, everyone, we're
on a schedule."

"What's going on?" Chuckie asked.

"I have no idea. Jeff won't tell me. If Jamie's too heavy I
can take her."

Chuckie shot me the "oh, please" look. "I think I can manage one little girl." He looked around. "We're in the Mandalay Bay."

"You're sure?" Looked around again. "I guess we are. The question is why?"

We walked into a room that had a lot of chairs set up in neat rows with a wide aisle between them. Elvis was in there. Well, someone dressed like him. As we got closer, realized it was Gower. Looking somewhat embarrassed. What was going on suddenly dawned on me and I started to laugh.

Jeff heard me and grinned. "Let's get this show on the road." He took Jamie from Chuckie now. "Hope you like the costume. It was the best we could find on short notice."

Chuckie gaped. "Ah, is what I think happening actually happening?"

"Yeah, it is." He looked at Raj. "You'll be able to do it more quietly."

Raj laughed. "Would everyone who is unaware of what's going on and why we're here please find a seat and sit down?" His voice carried to all parts of the room, without the walls shaking. Everyone moved as requested. Troubadours really had a lot more going for them than Christopher had led me to believe.

Erika and Stanley Gower were here. They sat with Chuckie's parents. Jeff kissed Jamie and got her to wake up. Pierre gave her a little pink basket with rose petals in it.

Jeff and Reader each took an arm and led Chuckie up to where Gower was standing. Pierre motioned to me, and I followed him and Jamie to find Michael, Abigail, and Naomi. "You sure you want me here?"

Naomi grinned. "Yeah, I'm sure. Are we doing what I think we're doing?"

"Yeah, we are. You're getting married by your brother, who is also an Elvis Impersonator. At least for this hour. It's a convenient thing that we were all dressed up for Jamie's party."

Music started. "Blue Christmas" by Johnny Mathis. Pierre coached Jamie down the aisle. I followed after her, then Abigail.

"We're breaking with traditions," Gower said. "Because the only traditions that truly matter are that we love one another, fight for one another, protect one another, and cherish our time together."

"Hear, hear," Tim called from the audience. The song changed to "It's Now Or Never" by the king himself.

"We're missing a few people we'd like to have with us," Gower went on. "But circumstances ensure that there are always a few people missing at any wedding. What shouldn't be at a wedding, however, are governments and political agendas. All there should be is love between two people and the people who love them."

The room applauded. Clearly all those in attendance agreed.

"Can't Help Falling In Love" by Elvis came on now, as Michael walked Naomi down the aisle. Saw Amy and Caroline start to cry.

"Who gives this woman to marry this man?" Gower asked.

"We all do," Michael replied. He kissed his sister's cheek, then joined Caroline and his parents.

Chuckie took Naomi's hand and brought her up to Gower. "I just want to tell you both that there are only a few people I'd dress up as Elvis for." This earned a good laugh, which meant that those of us tearing up got to have the fun of laughing through our tears.

"This ceremony can be quite long. It can also be sped up. I think you two have had a much longer engagement than either of you wanted. So let's see if we can make the wedding go a little faster. Do you, Charles Martin Reynolds, take this woman to be your wife, in sickness, health, good times, bad times, richer, poorer, until death alone parts you?"

Chuckie cleared his throat. "I do."

"Do you, Naomi Marie Gower, take this man to be your husband, in sickness, health, good times, bad times, richer, poorer, until death alone parts you?"

Naomi smiled. "I do."

"The rings, please?" Gower asked. Jeff stepped forward and gave them to him. Gower handed one to each of them. Chuckie slid the ring onto Naomi's finger. His hand shook a little. I started to really have to blink a lot to stop from crying. Naomi slid the ring on his finger, and her hand didn't shake at all.

"These rings are symbols of your love and your union—unbroken, never-ending, precious, never-tarnishing, enduring, and beautiful. And with the rings willingly given and happily received, as Sovereign Pontifex, I pronounce you married. What has been joined will never be broken, in this world or the next." Gower paused for a moment, then grinned. "Now, kiss your bride, and make it good."

Chuckie grinned and pulled Naomi to him as "Viva Las Vegas" from Elvis came on. He dipped her, and kissed her, while the crowd cheered.

Once they'd straightened up, Gower put his hands up, and everyone quieted. "Let me be the first to present Mister and Missus Charles and Naomi Reynolds."

More cheers, as they walked down the aisle. They reached the end and turned around. "Where to now?" Chuckie asked.

Jeff grinned. "Back home. The Embassy should be all set up for your reception by now."

Chuckie shrugged and picked Naomi up. "Guess I'll carry you through the gate versus over the threshold." He kissed her as they stepped through.

The rest of us followed them. Jeff picked Jamie up. "Can you make it through without me carrying you?"

Took Jamie from him. "Nope. You get to carry both of us."

He laughed and picked us up. "That will never be a problem. Holding my family in my arms is the best part of my life."

The transfer wasn't nearly as bad as normal, possibly because I kissed Jeff through the entire experience.

CHAPTER 98

THE RECEPTION WENT more slowly than the wedding had, but it was fun and comfortable, and Chuckie looked incredibly happy and more relaxed than I'd seen him in at least a year. Naomi looked like her old self, only with more confidence and a happy glow I'd never seen before.

The joy of seeing them both so happy and right together made all the horror from the past few days move into "the past." I still wanted to find and stop all the evil bad guy plans, but that's what tomorrow was for. Today was, as Nathalie had requested, happy.

Kyle and I were back in charge of the music, so "Beyond Beautiful" by Aerosmith was playing. Most of the guests were dancing, Jamie included. Cliff was her current partner and she was having a blast. Had a feeling she was going to expect a wedding and reception as her birthday cap-off every year.

Vance and Gadoire had joined us. Gadoire had a clean bill of health, and was confirmed as human. Reader was dancing with Nathalie, and she seemed okay. Not deliriously happy, but better than she'd been. She was tough, and we'd help her. She and Jeff could be the bonded newbies in the House and have each other's backs. It was more than a lot of people got.

Senators McMillan and Armstrong and their wives had joined us as well. They were sitting with Lillian Culver while she made phone calls. Abner was going to pull through, and our medical team and a team from Dulce were watching him. Tito was still with him, but Nurse Carter was up and dancing with White.

The music switched to "You and Me" by Lifehouse. Jeff and I took a break from the dance floor and sat down, me in his lap. "Think they liked it?" he asked me.

"I think you just proved to Chuckie, beyond a shadow of a doubt, that you're really his good, true friend, which is the best present he could ever get. Yes, he loved it and Naomi needed it. You're really the biggest romantic softie in the world, you know that, right?"

"As long as you like that, I'm good with it."

"I don't like it, Jeff. I love it, and everything else about you."

He hugged me. "Good to know." He was about to kiss me when the music stopped.

"Attention, please," Raj said. The room stopped and turned toward his voice. Made a mental note to ensure Raj always used his power for good. "We have an important announcement."

The guests moved to the sides of the room. Michael was standing next to Raj. He looked incredibly nervous. "The road to Chuck and Naomi's wedding was really long, and for a while I wasn't sure this day would ever come. The events of the past few days have pointed out to me that nothing in life is certain, including tomorrow."

He cleared his throat. "So, I've asked permission of the man who's very much like a father to you," he said as he walked over to Caroline and took her hand. Caroline looked like she didn't know whether this was a joke or not. "Senator McMillan told me that a real man is bold and takes chances for the important things."

Michael went down on one knee. Caroline's expression changed to shock. He pulled a ring box out of his pocket. "Caroline Chase, I'd like to know if you'd be willing to make an honest man out of me and marry me."

"Yes," Caroline managed, right before she burst into tears. Michael stood up and kissed her, among cheers and congratulations. "Everybody Loves a Happy Ending" by Tears for Fears came on our Embassy Airwaves.

Jeff sighed happily. "Nice to see them both settle down."

"Did you know this was coming?"

"Amazingly, yes, because neither one of them is sporting

an emotional blocker or overlay. Had to tell Michael to hold off until the reception—he was revved up and ready to propose at Jamie's party."

"This was better."

Jeff hugged me. "I agree. This is the best, though." Then he kissed me. And, as with so many things, he was right.

Coming in December 2013:
the eighth novel in the *Alien* series
from Gini Koch

ALIEN RESEARCH

Read on for a sneak preview

"AMBASSADOR, would you please tell the Committee your full name?"

"Katherine Sarah Katt Martini."

"Do you know the whereabouts of one Herbert Gaultier?"

"No." My bet was Hell, but the Committee probably didn't want to hear that.

"Do you know if he's alive or dead?"

I hesitated. I was under oath. "I think he's dead."

"Do you?" The senator in charge of the hearing leaned forward. "Is that because you killed him?"

"No. I didn't kill him." Christopher White had killed him. But he'd had to.

"What about Leventhal Reid?"

"Nope, didn't kill him, either." My husband, Jeff, had killed Reid. To save my life.

"LaRue Demorte Gaultier—did you kill her?"

"No. Esteban Cantu killed her." Accidentally, of course, but that one wasn't on me. "Then he was arrested. And I didn't kill him, either." Other bad guys had killed him, before we could get information from him.

"John Cooper?"

"Nope, didn't do him in, either." Charles Reynolds had killed Cooper. Again, in self-defense, defending me and himself.

"Ronaldo Al Dejahl, who killed him?"

"Um, everybody and nobody. Because my bet is that he's

still alive. But lots of us have tried to kill him, and you should be grateful." James Reader had used the first guy we thought was Ronaldo for a body shield, Jeff had beaten up the real one, but he'd escaped, and my bet was he'd survived the beat down he'd gotten during Operation Destruction, too, and was out there somewhere, waiting to strike.

The Committee didn't seem impressed. I didn't look around, but the room was huge and it seemed filled to capacity with a blur of official looking people in politically fashion-forward suits, all of whom were giving me the Frowny Face of Displeasure.

"The entire former American Centaurion Diplomatic Corps?" the senator in charge went on. "What about them? And Howard Taft? Antony Marling and Madeline Cartwright? Ronald Yates? And Beverly, that woman who had the most boring speaking voice in the world. Did you kill all of them and many others, including Gregory from Alpha Four, and Uma from Alpha Six, and the Mephistopheles in-control superbeing?"

Now, these were not so easy to not lie under oath about.

"Yes, sort of, well, yes, really in the case of Beverly and a bunch of the others. I didn't do Gregory in, though." Tito Hernandez had done that. "I took out Moira from Beta Twelve, though." Jeff had handled her mate, Kyrellis. Just barely, but he'd managed it. "They were all evil and trying to destroy everyone good and the Earth. By the way, how did you know Beverly was Miz Monotone?"

The Committee looked at me derisively. "We're in your dream," the senator in charge said. "And we agree that whoever thought it was a good idea for you to be in such a public position was an idiot."

"Can we sentence her yet?" one of the other Committee members asked. "Or at least ruin her husband's budding political career?" The rest of the Committee nodded eagerly. They were all over the idea of disgracing Representative Martini.

"Can I wake up now?"

"Do you want to?" the senator in charge asked.

"Am I hanging out with a Congressional Grand Jury when I wake up?"

"Not as far as any of us know. Today. Tomorrow? Who knows?"

"That's the story of my life. By the way, as far as dream men go, none of you are what I'd like to have the next time I have a horrible nightmare."

"Who would you prefer?" the senator in charge asked.

"Billy Zane would be a good option, he doesn't get nearly enough work. Hugh Jackman. Chris Evans, really, anyone who starred in *The Avengers* would be acceptable. Tom Cruise, Will Smith, Nathan Fillion, pick a hot leading man of choice."

"Sorry. You already live with the best looking people on Earth. You're stuck with us. See you next time, Ambassador."

"Can't wait."

The senator in charge nodded. "Tomorrow night will come soon enough."

"As near as I can tell, only if I keep on killing bad guys."

My eyes opened and I looked around. I wasn't in a big room with a lot of important people looking at me while I incriminated myself and everyone else I knew. I was lying in bed.

I'd had a version of this dream pretty much every night since Jeff had become the Appointed Representative for New Mexico's 2nd District, starting right after Operation Sherlock had concluded.

Sure, people being murdered left and right and my somehow becoming the "adopted niece" of the two best assassins in the business could give anyone nightmares. But those situations never came up in my dreams. No, I got the nightly reminder of what I was really stressed over—my husband was now in a very public position and we had a hell of a lot of skeletons in our big walk-in closet.

Rolled over. Sure enough, Jeff was in bed next to me. Mr. Clock said it was five in the morning. Heaved a sigh of relief and snuggled next to Jeff.

He made the low growl that sounded like a purr in his sleep and pulled me closer to him. Buried my face in between his awesome pecs, rubbed against the hair on his chest, and let his double heartbeats lull me back to sleep. Thankfully, this time, dreamless.

The smooth sounds of Robert Palmer's "Addicted to Love" woke me up. Jeff wasn't in bed with me. Not so unusual—he usually heard the alarm before I did.

Got up and trotted into the bathroom. No Jeff. Checked in the closet. No Jeff. Went to the nursery. No Jeff and no Jamie. No animals, either from Earth or Alpha Four, were in evidence, either. Wondered if I was, in fact, having another nightmare. Decided to check. "Com on!"

"Yes, Ambassador?" The voice wasn't Walter's. And Walter always called me Chief, because I was now the sole Chief of Mission. But the voice was familiar.

"Who is this?"

"It's William, Chief." Walter's older brother.

"What is one of our top Imageers doing handling Embassy Security? Or, to put it another way, what's the point of this weird dream?"

"Ahhh, you're not asleep, at least as far as I know, Ambassador."

"Well, if you were in my dream you'd say that."

"Are you feeling alright, Ambassador? Do I need to have Doctor Hernandez or Nurse Carter go up and check you out?"

Contemplated if I felt awake as the music changed to The Pretender's version of "I Got You Babe." One more song and I could confirm if this was the music mix Jeff had made for our anniversary or not. He'd put a lot of thought into it and I'd been using it as our wakeup music for the past two months.

"If I'm really awake, where are Jeff and Jamie?"

"Representative Martini took your daughter to daycare already, Ambassador. He asked me to tell you that she'd woken up early and he didn't want to wake you."

"Why not?"

"He said you've been sleeping poorly."

True enough. "Okay, so why are you here instead of Walter?"

"Walter's at a Security training session at Dulce."

"Why is he at the Science Center for training?"

"Because there's a big dust storm around Home Base and the training session needs to be held both indoors and outdoors."

"Gotcha. And you're here because . . . ?"

"Because someone needed to cover Embassy Security, and it was decided that I was the most trustworthy option."

"Cannot argue with that logic. Other than to mention that I wasn't informed of any training sessions or temporary personnel switches."

William cleared his throat. "Ah, you don't need to be informed, Ambassador. Gladys handles all of that, and if she says it's time for training, it's time for training, and if she says I'm covering during Walter's training session, then I'm covering."

"Gotcha." Couldn't argue. Gladys was the Head of Security for all A-C operations worldwide. She was considered scary formidable and I concurred on the scary. Three-plus years in and I'd never seen her in person, or seen a picture of her. I was okay with this, mostly because Gladys was one of the few people around who could intimidate me, and she had sarcasm down to an art form.

"Ambassador, do you need assistance in some way?"

"Why aren't you calling me Kitty?" The music changed to Tom Petty's "Yer So Bad." Yep, we were on Jeff's 2nd Anniversary Mix, ergo, I was hopefully really awake.

William laughed. "Because Walter left me very specific instructions, and it's vital to the running of this Embassy that whoever's on the com call you Ambassador or Chief. Per his very detailed page about titles and why they matter here."

"I love Walter. And you, too."

"Always good to know. Representative Martini is downstairs, having a breakfast meeting with several politicians who are, per your husband, all friends. He said that if you were up in time you should join them."

"How much time do I have?"

"They all just got here a few minutes ago, and I think this meeting will run long, so you should be good."

"Awesome, thanks." I took a shower and got dressed while ZZ Top's "Gimme All Your Lovin'," Wall Of Voodoo's "Hands Of Love," Pat Benatar's "Never Wanna Leave You," and Tina Turner's "Best" played.

In the good old days before my daughter was born, I'd have taken longer to get ready, and not because I was skimping on the lather, rinse, repeat portions or anything now. During Operation Drug Addict some of our enemies had slipped some seriously strong, power altering drugs into Jeff's system, which he'd then passed along to our child when I'd gotten pregnant, and she'd in turn passed along to me. We were all about the sharing around here.

So I was now kind of half A-C, though differently from how Jamie was truly half A-C. I had the super-strength, which wasn't quite as good as the regular A-Cs under most circumstances, but was still pretty darned good for any human who wasn't nicknamed The Rock. I also had faster healing and regeneration, which was excellent.

I also had hyperspeed. Jamie was eighteen months old, and I was just now sort of getting to a place where I could use hyperspeed for normal, mundane things and not crash through a wall or knock myself out.

Jeff's cousin, Christopher White, had also become enhanced—though he'd done it intentionally—and he and I worked on my skills all the time. This month, the focus was on completing my personal routine using hyperspeed. So far, showering and drying off had gone well, but I used regular human for hair care because I didn't want to look like I had mange and it was really easy to yank your hair out when you were super strong.

As "Looking Hot" from No Doubt hit my personal airwaves, I trotted to our huge walk-in closet to choose today's ensemble. A-Cs were in love with the colors black and white, and Armani, in a way that made casual obsessions—like mine for all things Aerosmith or Golum's for the Ring—seem to be merely pale imitations of fidelity.

Therefore, my closet had a lot of black slim skirts, white oxfords, and a variety of black or black and white high heels in it. Happily, because I was both human, well, mostly human, and the ambassador, I got to wear colors and other styles, at least occasionally. And because I was me, I also had a lot of jeans, several pairs of Converse, and an extremely large and eclectic set of concert T-shirts and hoodies.

Political breakfast or no, it was the start of July and I was going for casual. Got into jeans, my Converse, and my newest Aerosmith T-shirt, because having Steven, Joe, and the rest of my boys on my chest ensured I would prevail over all obstacles. In honor of "Looking Hot," I selected a cute No Doubt hoodie, because summer back East was still nothing like summer in Pueblo Caliente, Arizona, and I

could easily get chilled. Plus it looked hella cute with this particular Aerosmith shirt.

Thusly dressed, I grabbed my purse. Yes, I lived on half of the top floor of the Embassy, and I was going down only six floors to get to the kitchen area. However, I'd learned a lot during my tenure with Centaurion Division, and one of the main lessons was that I always needed my purse and its contents handy.

I had a lot of different purses and handbags available to me, but Old Trusty, my big, black, cheap leather purse was still my go-to option. It took a licking and kept on holding everything and not falling apart. Ensured my Glock, my iPod, speakers, and earbuds, Jeff's adrenaline harpoon, my wallet, a bottle of extra hold hairspray, my brush and a scrunchie, and anything else I could think of were in it. Shoved my phone into the back pocket of my jeans.

Turned off the alarm clock as "Honey, Honey" from ABBA came on. Took the stairs down in part because using hyperspeed meant it was faster than taking one of the elevators, and in other part because it was likely Christopher was with Jeff, and I didn't feel like getting the "you need to practice all the time" lecture.

Reached the first floor in record time and without issue. Congratulated myself as I slowed to a human-speed walk. So far it'd been a cheerful hyperspeed morning.

The American Centaurion Embassy went up seven floors, down two which were basement and parking garage levels, and then went down a lot more due to the hidden elevator that connected us to the Tunnels of Doom. It was a city block long and wide, and since Operation Destruction, was connected via a steel and bulletproof glass walkway on the second floors to the neighboring building we now owned, operated, and had personnel living in, which was nicknamed The Zoo.

The first floor, being the main entryway and therefore the place the most people who weren't part of American Centaurion in some way would come in, had the most normal stuff in it. Offices, dining room, kitchen, and some small parlors and salons. No one was in any of the rooms as I went by, meaning they were likely all in the kitchen. This meeting seemed a lot more important all of a sudden.

As I neared the kitchen I heard voices. ". . . been quiet

for the past few months." A voice I didn't recognize. Supposedly the politicians here were all friends, but I knew our friends' voices.

"That doesn't mean plans aren't forming, it just means we haven't spotted what they are." That was a voice I recognized without trying—Chuckie was here. Know a guy since the first day of 9th grade, know his voice at any time. "Sir, I don't want to sound negative, but you need to consider the ramifications of what you're suggesting."

Sir? Chuckie almost never called anyone "sir." Wondered if I had time to go up and change into the Female Armani Standard Issue.

Someone's head popped around the door. Jeff's head, to be exact. He smiled. "You look great as always, baby. Come on, you're just in time."

"Just in time for what?"

"Just in time to meet the head of the F.B.I.'s newly created Alien Activities Division."